'First time readers of Naipaul should start with his first books: *The Mystic Masseur* (1957), and *Miguel Street* (1959). Original comic capers, they pioneered the territory now taken for granted by writers from the old colonies. Naipaul wrote them before he was twenty-five, and more than forty years on writers are still trying to capture that delightful picaresque tone, and have seldom succeeded in doing so.'

Tarun J. Tejpal, (2001)

V. S. NAIPAUL was born, of Indian ancestry, in Trinidad in 1932. He came to England in 1950. He spent four years at University College, Oxford, and began to write, in London, in 1954. He has pursued no other profession.

His works of fiction comprise: *The Mystic Masseur* (1957; John Llewellyn Rhys Memorial Prize), *The Suffrage of Elvira* (1958), *Miguel Street* (1959; Somerset Maugham Award), *A House for Mr Biswas* (1961), *Mr Stone and the Knights Companion* (1963; Hawthornden Prize), *The Mimic Men* (1967; W. H. Smith Award), *A Flag on the Island* (1967), a collection of short stories. In 1971 he was awarded the Booker Prize for *In a Free State*; since then he has published five novels: *Guerrillas* (1975), *A Bend in the River* (1979), *The Enigma of Arrival* (1987), *A Way in the World* (1994) and *Half a Life* (2001).

In 1960 he began to travel. *The Middle Passage* (1962) records his impressions of colonial society in the West Indies and South America. *An Area of Darkness* (1964), *India: A Wounded Civilization* (1977) and *India: A Million Mutinies Now* (1990) form his acclaimed 'Indian Trilogy'. *The Loss of El Dorado*, a masterly study of New World history, was published in 1969, and a selection of his longer essays, *The Overcrowded Barracoon*, appeared in 1972. *The Return of Eva Perón* (with *The Killings in Trinidad*) (1980) derives from experiences of travel in Argentina, Trinidad and the Congo. *Finding the Centre* (1984) is distinguished by the author's narrative on his emergence as a writer, 'Prologue to an Autobiography'. *A Turn in the South* (1989) describes his journey through the Deep South of America.

Among the Believers: An Islamic Journey (1981), a large-scale work, is the result of seven months' travel in 1979 and 1980 in Iran, Pakistan, Malaysia and Indonesia. Its important sequel, *Beyond Belief* (1998), is on the theme of Islamic conversion in these countries.

Letters Between a Father and Son, the early correspondence between the author and his family, appeared in 1999.

In 1990, V. S. Naipaul received a knighthood for services to literature; in 1993, he was the first recipient of the David Cohen British Literature Prize in recognition of a 'lifetime's achievement of a living British writer'. He was awarded the Nobel Prize for Literature in 2001.

ALSO BY V. S. NAIPAUL

FICTION

The Suffrage of Elvira
A House for Mr Biswas
Mr Stone and the Knights Companion
The Mimic Men
A Flag on the Island
In a Free State
Guerrillas
A Bend in the River
The Enigma of Arrival
A Way in the World
Half a Life

NON-FICTION

The Middle Passage
An Area of Darkness
The Loss of El Dorado
The Overcrowded Barracoon
India: A Wounded Civilization
The Return of Eva Perón
Among the Believers: An Islamic Journey
Finding the Centre
A Turn in the South
India: A Million Mutinies Now
Beyond Belief
Letters Between a Father and Son

V. S. NAIPAUL

Miguel Street

PICADOR

The Mystic Masseur first published 1957 by André Deutsch
Miguel Street first published 1959 by André Deutsch

This omnibus edition published 2002 by Picador
an imprint of Pan Macmillan Ltd
Pan Macmillan, 20 New Wharf Road, London N1 9RR
Basingstoke and Oxford
Associated companies throughout the world
www.panmacmillan.com

ISBN 0 330 48712 4

1 3 5 7 9 8 6 4 2

A CIP catalogue record for this book is available from
the British Library.

Typeset by Intype London Ltd
Printed and bound in Great Britain by
Mackays of Chatham plc, Chatham, Kent

For my Mother and Kamla

Contents

1. Bogart

EVERY MORNING WHEN he got up Hat would sit on the banister of his back verandah and shout across, 'What happening there, Bogart?'

Bogart would turn in his bed and mumble softly, so that no one heard, 'What happening there, Hat?'

It was something of a mystery why he was called Bogart; but I suspect that it was Hat who gave him the name. I don't know if you remember the year the film *Casablanca* was made. That was the year when Bogart's fame spread like fire through Port of Spain and hundreds of young men began adopting the hard-boiled Bogartian attitude.

Before they called him Bogart they called him Patience, because he played that game from morn till night. Yet he never liked cards.

Whenever you went over to Bogart's little room you found him sitting on his bed with the cards in seven lines on a small table in front of him.

'What happening there, man?' he would ask quietly, and then he would say nothing for ten or fifteen minutes. And somehow you felt you couldn't really talk to Bogart, he looked so bored and superior. His eyes were small and sleepy. His face was fat and his hair was gleaming black. His arms were plump. Yet he was not a funny man. He did everything with a captivating languor. Even when he licked his thumb to deal out the cards there was grace in it.

He was the most bored man I ever knew.

He made a pretence of making a living by tailoring, and he had even paid me some money to write a sign for him:

TAILOR AND CUTTER
Suits made to Order
Popular and Competitive Prices

He bought a sewing-machine and some blue and white and brown chalks. But I never could imagine him competing with anyone; and I cannot remember him making a suit. He was a little bit like Popo, the carpenter next door, who never made a stick of furniture, and was always planing and chiselling and making what I think he called mortises. Whenever I asked him, 'Mr Popo, what you making?' he would reply, 'Ha, boy! That's the question. I making the thing without a name.' Bogart was never even making anything like this.

Being a child, I never wondered how Bogart came by any money. I assumed that grown-ups had money as a matter of course. Popo had a wife who worked at a variety of jobs; and ended up by becoming the friend of many men. I could never think of Bogart as having mother or father; and he never brought a woman to his little room. This little room of his was called the servant-room but no servant to the people in the main house ever lived there. It was just an architectural convention.

It is still something of a miracle to me that Bogart managed to make friends. Yet he did make many friends; he was at one time quite the most popular man in the street. I used to see him squatting on the pavement with all the big men of the street. And while Hat or Edward or Eddoes was talking, Bogart would just look down and draw rings with his fingers on the pavement. He never laughed audibly. He never told a story. Yet whenever there was a fête or something like that, everybody would say, 'We must have Bogart.

He smart like hell, that man.' In a way he gave them great solace and comfort, I suppose.

And so every morning, as I told you, Hat would shout, very loudly, 'What happening there, Bogart?'

And he would wait for the indeterminate grumble which was Bogart saying, 'What happening there, Hat?'

But one morning, when Hat shouted, there was no reply. Something which had appeared unalterable was missing.

Bogart had vanished; had left us without a word.

The men in the street were silent and sorrowful for two whole days. They assembled in Bogart's little room. Hat lifted up the deck of cards that lay on Bogart's table and dropped two or three cards at a time reflectively.

Hat said, 'You think he gone Venezuela?'

But no one knew. Bogart told them so little.

And the next morning Hat got up and lit a cigarette and went to his back verandah and was on the point of shouting, when he remembered. He milked the cows earlier than usual that morning, and the cows didn't like it.

A month passed; then another month. Bogart didn't return.

Hat and his friends began using Bogart's room as their club-house. They played *wappee* and drank rum and smoked, and sometimes brought the odd stray woman to the room. Hat was presently involved with the police for gambling and sponsoring cock-fighting; and he had to spend a lot of money to bribe his way out of trouble.

It was as if Bogart had never come to Miguel Street. And after all Bogart had been living in the street only for four years or so. He had come one day with a single suitcase, looking for a room, and he had spoken to Hat who was squatting outside his gate, smoking a cigarette and reading the cricket scores in the evening paper. Even then he hadn't said much. All he said – that was Hat's story – was, 'You know any rooms?' and Hat had led him to the next yard where there was this furnished servant-room going for eight dollars a month. He had installed himself there immediately, brought out a pack of cards, and begun playing patience.

This impressed Hat.

For the rest he had always remained a man of mystery. He became Patience.

When Hat and everybody else had forgotten or nearly forgotten Bogart, he returned. He turned up one morning just about seven and found Eddoes had a woman on his bed. The woman jumped up and screamed. Eddoes jumped up, not so much afraid as embarrassed.

Bogart said, 'Move over. I tired and I want to sleep.'

He slept until five that afternoon, and when he woke up he found his room full of the old gang. Eddoes was being very loud and noisy to cover up his embarrassment. Hat had brought a bottle of rum.

Hat said, 'What happening there, Bogart?'

And he rejoiced when he found his cue taken up. 'What happening there, Hat?'

Hat opened the bottle of rum, and shouted to Boyee to go buy a bottle of soda water.

Bogart asked, 'How the cows, Hat?'

'They all right.'

'And Boyee?'

'He all right too. Ain't you just hear me call him?'

'And Errol?'

'He all right too. But what happening, Bogart? *You* all right?'

Bogart nodded, and drank a long Madrassi shot of rum. Then another, and another; and they had presently finished the bottle.

'Don't worry,' Bogart said. 'I go buy another.'

They had never seen Bogart drink so much; they had never heard him talk so much; and they were alarmed. No one dared to ask Bogart where he had been.

Bogart said, 'You boys been keeping my room hot all the time.'

'It wasn't the same without you,' Hat replied.

But they were all worried. Bogart was hardly opening his lips when he spoke. His mouth was twisted a little, and his accent was getting slightly American.

'Sure, sure,' Bogart said, and he had got it right. He was just like an actor.

Hat wasn't sure that Bogart was drunk.

In appearance, you must know, Hat recalled Rex Harrison, and he had done his best to strengthen the resemblance. He combed his hair backwards, screwed up his eyes, and he spoke very nearly like Harrison.

'Damn it, Bogart,' Hat said, and he became very like Rex Harrison. 'You may as well tell us everything right away.'

Bogart showed his teeth and laughed in a twisted, cynical way.

'Sure I'll tell,' he said, and got up and stuck his thumbs inside his waistband. 'Sure, I'll tell everything.'

He lit a cigarette, leaned back in such a way that the smoke got into his eyes; and, squinting, he drawled out his story.

He had got a job on a ship and had gone to British Guiana. There he had deserted, and gone into the interior. He became a cowboy on the Rupununi, smuggled things (he didn't say what) into Brazil, and had gathered some girls from Brazil and taken them to Georgetown. He was running the best brothel in the town when the police treacherously took his bribes and arrested him.

'It was a high-class place,' he said, 'no bums. Judges and doctors and big shot civil servants.'

'What happen?' Eddoes asked. 'Jail?'

'How you so stupid?' Hat said. 'Jail, when the man here with we. But why you people so stupid? Why you don't let the man talk?'

But Bogart was offended, and refused to speak another word.

*

From then on the relationship between these men changed. Bogart became the Bogart of the films. Hat became Harrison. And the morning exchange became this:

'Bogart!'

'Shaddup, Hat!'

Bogart now became the most feared man in the street. Even Big Foot was said to be afraid of him. Bogart drank and swore and gambled with the best. He shouted rude remarks at girls walking by themselves in the street. He bought a hat, and pulled down the brim over his eyes. He became a regular sight, standing against the high concrete fence of his yard, hands in his pockets, one foot jammed against the wall, and an eternal cigarette in his mouth.

Then he disappeared again. He was playing cards with the gang in his room, and he got up and said, 'I'm going to the latrine.'

They didn't see him for four months.

When he returned, he had grown a little fatter but he had become a little more aggressive. His accent was now pure American. To complete the imitation, he began being expansive towards children. He called out to them in the streets, and gave them money to buy gum and chocolate. He loved stroking their heads, and giving them good advice.

The third time he went away and came back he gave a great party in his room for all the children or kids, as he called them. He bought cases of Solo and Coca-Cola and Pepsi-Cola and about a bushel of cakes.

Then Sergeant Charles, the policeman who lived up Miguel Street at number forty-five, came and arrested Bogart.

'Don't act tough, Bogart,' Sergeant Charles said.

But Bogart failed to take the cue.

'What happening, man? I ain't do anything.'

Sergeant Charles told him.

There was a little stir in the papers. The charge was bigamy;

but it was up to Hat to find out all the inside details that the newspapers never mention.

'You see,' Hat said on the pavement that evening, 'the man leave his first wife in Tunapuna and come to Port of Spain. They couldn't have children. He remain here feeling sad and small. He go away, find a girl in Caroni and he give she a baby. In Caroni they don't make joke about that sort of thing and Bogart had to get married to the girl.'

'But why he leave she?' Eddoes asked.

'To be a man, among we men.'

2. The Thing Without a Name

THE ONLY THING that Popo, who called himself a carpenter, ever built was the little galvanized-iron workshop under the mango tree at the back of his yard. And even that he didn't quite finish. He couldn't be bothered to nail on the sheets of galvanized-iron for the roof, and kept them weighted down with huge stones. Whenever there was a high wind the roof made a frightening banging noise and seemed ready to fly away.

And yet Popo was never idle. He was always busy hammering and sawing and planing. I liked watching him work. I liked the smell of the woods – cyp and cedar and crapaud. I liked the colour of the shavings, and I liked the way the sawdust powdered Popo's kinky hair.

'What you making, Mr Popo?' I asked.

Popo would always say, 'Ha, boy! That's the question. I making the thing without a name.'

I liked Popo for that. I thought he was a poetic man.

One day I said to Popo, 'Give me something to make.'

'What you want to make?' he said.

It was hard to think of something I really wanted.

'You see,' Popo said. 'You thinking about the thing without a name.'

Eventually I decided on an egg-stand.

'Who you making it for?' Popo asked.

'Ma.'

He laughed. 'Think she going use it?'

My mother was pleased with the egg-stand, and used it for about a week. Then she seemed to forget all about it; and began putting the eggs in bowls or plates, just as she did before.

And Popo laughed when I told him. He said, 'Boy, the only thing to make is the thing without a name.'

After I painted the tailoring sign for Bogart, Popo made me do one for him as well.

He took the little red stump of a pencil he had stuck over his ear and puzzled over the words. At first he wanted to announce himself as an architect; but I managed to dissuade him. He wasn't sure about the spelling. The finished sign said:

BUILDER AND CONTRACTOR
Carpenter
And Cabinet-Maker

And I signed my name, as sign-writer, in the bottom right-hand corner.

Popo liked standing up in front of the sign. But he had a little panic when people who didn't know about him came to inquire.

'The carpenter fellow?' Popo would say. 'He don't live here again.'

I thought Popo was a much nicer man than Bogart. Bogart said little to me; but Popo was always ready to talk. He talked about serious things, like life and death and work, and I felt he really liked talking to me.

Yet Popo was not a popular man in the street. They didn't think he was mad or stupid. Hat used to say, 'Popo too conceited, you hear.'

It was an unreasonable thing to say. Popo had the habit of taking a glass of rum to the pavement every morning. He never sipped the rum. But whenever he saw someone he knew he dipped his middle finger in the rum, licked it, and then waved to the man.

'We could buy rum too,' Hat used to say. 'But we don't show off like Popo.'

I myself never thought about it in that way, and one day I asked Popo about it.

Popo said, 'Boy, in the morning, when the sun shining and it still cool, and you just get up, it make you feel good to know that you could go out and stand up in the sun and have some rum.'

Popo never made any money. His wife used to go out and work, and this was easy, because they had no children. Popo said, 'Women and them like work. Man not make for work.'

Hat said, 'Popo is a man-woman. Not a proper man.'

Popo's wife had a job as a cook in a big house near my school. She used to wait for me in the afternoons and take me into the big kitchen and give me a lot of nice things to eat. The only thing I didn't like was the way she sat and watched me while I ate. It was as though I was eating for her. She asked me to call her Auntie.

She introduced me to the gardener of the big house. He was a good-looking brown man, and he loved his flowers. I liked the gardens he looked after. The flower-beds were always black and wet; and the grass green and damp and always cut. Sometimes he let me water the flower-beds. And he used to gather the cut grass into little bags which he gave me to take home to my mother. Grass was good for the hens.

One day I missed Popo's wife. She wasn't waiting for me.

Next morning I didn't see Popo dipping his finger in the glass of rum on the pavement.

And that evening I didn't see Popo's wife.

I found Popo sad in his workshop. He was sitting on a plank and twisting a bit of shaving around his fingers.

Popo said, 'Your auntie gone, boy.'

'Where, Mr Popo?'

'Ha, boy! That's the question,' and he pulled himself up there.

Popo found himself then a popular man. The news got around very quickly. And when Eddoes said one day, 'I wonder what happen to Popo. Like he got no more rum,' Hat jumped up and almost cuffed him. And then all the men began to gather in Popo's workshop, and they would talk about cricket and football and pictures – everything except women – just to try to cheer Popo up.

Popo's workshop no longer sounded with hammering and sawing. The sawdust no longer smelled fresh, and became black, almost like dirt. Popo began drinking a lot, and I didn't like him when he was drunk. He smelled of rum, and he used to cry and then grow angry and want to beat up everybody. That made him an accepted member of the gang.

Hat said, 'We was wrong about Popo. He is a man, like any of we.'

Popo liked the new companionship. He was at heart a loquacious man, and always wanted to be friendly with the men of the street and he was always surprised that he was not liked. So it looked as though he had got what he wanted. But Popo was not really happy. The friendship had come a little too late, and he found he didn't like it as much as he'd expected. Hat tried to get Popo interested in other women, but Popo wasn't interested.

Popo didn't think I was too young to be told anything.

'Boy, when you grow old as me,' he said once, 'you find that you don't care for the things you thought you woulda like if you coulda afford them.'

That was his way of talking, in riddles.

*

Then one day Popo left us.

Hat said, 'He don't have to tell me where he gone. He gone looking for he wife.'

Edward said, 'Think she going come back with he?'

Hat said, 'Let we wait and see.'

We didn't have to wait long. It came out in the papers. Hat said it was just what he expected. Popo had beaten up a man in Arima, the man had taken his wife away. It was the gardener who used to give me bags of grass.

Nothing much happened to Popo. He had to pay a fine, but they let him off otherwise. The magistrate said that Popo had better not molest his wife again.

They made a calypso about Popo that was the rage that year. It was the road-march for the Carnival, and the Andrews Sisters sang it for an American recording company:

> A certain carpenter feller went to Arima
> Looking for a mopsy called Emelda.

It was a great thing for the street.

At school, I used to say, 'The carpenter feller was a good, good friend of mine.'

And, at cricket matches, and at the races, Hat used to say, 'Know him? God, I used to drink with that man night and day. Boy, he could carry his liquor.'

*

Popo wasn't the same man when he came back to us. He growled at me when I tried to talk to him, and he drove out Hat and the others when they brought a bottle of rum to the workshop.

Hat said, 'Woman send that man mad, you hear.'

But the old noises began to be heard once more from Popo's workshop. He was working hard, and I wondered whether he was still making the thing without a name. But I was too afraid to ask.

He ran an electric light to the workshop and began working in the night-time. Vans stopped outside his house and were always depositing and taking away things. Then Popo began painting his house. He used a bright green, and he painted the roof a bright red. Hat said, 'The man really mad.'

And added, 'Like he getting married again.'

Hat wasn't too far wrong. One day, about two weeks later, Popo returned, and he brought a woman with him. It was his wife. My auntie.

'You see the sort of thing woman is,' Hat commented. 'You see the sort of thing they like. Not the man. But the new house paint up, and all the new furniture inside it. I bet you if the man in Arima had a new house and new furnitures, she wouldnta come back with Popo.'

But I didn't mind. I was glad. It was good to see Popo standing outside with his glass of rum in the mornings and dipping his finger into the rum and waving at his friends; and it was good to ask him again, 'What you making, Mr Popo?' and to get the old answer, 'Ha, boy! That's the question. I making the thing without a name.'

Popo returned very quickly to his old way of living, and he was still devoting his time to making the thing without a name. He had stopped working, and his wife got her job with the same people near my school.

People in the street were almost angry with Popo when his wife came back. They felt that all their sympathy had been mocked and wasted. And again Hat was saying, 'That blasted Popo too conceited, you hear.'

But this time Popo didn't mind.

He used to tell me, 'Boy, go home and pray tonight that you get happy like me.'

*

What happened afterwards happened so suddenly that we didn't even know it had happened. Even Hat didn't know about it until he read it in the papers. Hat always read the papers. He read them from about ten in the morning until about six in the evening.

Hat shouted out, 'But what is this I seeing?' and he showed us the headlines: CALYPSO CARPENTER JAILED

It was a fantastic story. Popo had been stealing things left and right. All the new furnitures, as Hat called them, hadn't been made by Popo. He had stolen things and simply remodelled them. He had stolen too much as a matter of fact, and had had to sell the things he didn't want. That was how he had been caught. And we understood now why the vans were always outside Popo's house. Even the paint and the brushes with which he had redecorated the house had been stolen.

Hat spoke for all of us when he said, 'That man too foolish. Why he had to sell what he thief? Just tell me that. Why?'

We agreed it was a stupid thing to do. But we felt deep inside ourselves that Popo was really a man, perhaps a bigger man than any of us.

And as for my auntie . . .

Hat said, 'How much jail he get? A year? With three months off for good behaviour, that's nine months in all. And I give she three months good behaviour too. And after that, it ain't going to have no more Emelda in Miguel Street, you hear.'

But Emelda never left Miguel Street. She not only kept her job as cook, but she started taking in washing and ironing as well. No one in the street felt sorry that Popo had gone to jail because of the shame; after all that was a thing that could happen to any of us. They felt sorry only that Emelda was going to be left alone for so long.

He came back as a hero. He was one of the boys. He was a better man than either Hat or Bogart.

But for me, he had changed. And the change made me sad.

For Popo began working.

He began making morris chairs and tables and wardrobes for people.

And when I asked him, 'Mr Popo, when you going start making the thing without a name again?' he growled at me.

'You too troublesome,' he said. 'Go away quick, before I lay my hand on you.'

3. George and The Pink House

I WAS MUCH more afraid of George than I was of Big Foot, although Big Foot was the biggest and the strongest man in the street. George was short and fat. He had a grey moustache and a big belly. He looked harmless enough but he was always muttering to himself and cursing and I never tried to become friendly with him.

He was like the donkey he had tied in the front of his yard, grey and old and silent except when it brayed loudly. You felt that George was never really in touch with what was going on around him all the time, and I found it strange that no one should have said that George was mad, while everybody said that Man-man, whom I liked, was mad.

George's house also made me feel afraid. It was a broken-down wooden building, painted pink on the outside, and the galvanized-iron roof was brown from rust. One door, the one to the right, was always left open. The inside walls had never been painted, and were grey and black with age. There was a dirty bed in one corner and in another there was a table and a stool. That was all. No curtains, no pictures on the wall. Even Bogart had a picture of Lauren Bacall in his room.

I found it hard to believe that George had a wife and a son and a daughter.

Like Popo, George was happy to let his wife do all the work in the house and the yard. They kept cows, and again I hated

George for that. Because the water from his pens made the gutters stink, and when we were playing cricket on the pavement the ball often got wet in the gutter. Boyee and Errol used to wet the ball deliberately in the stinking gutter. They wanted to make it shoot.

George's wife was never a proper person. I always thought of her just as George's wife, and that was all. And I always thought, too, that George's wife was nearly always in the cow-pen.

And while George sat on the front concrete step outside the open door of his house, his wife was busy.

George never became one of the gang in Miguel Street. He didn't seem to mind. He had his wife and his daughter and his son. He beat them all. And when the boy Elias grew too big, George beat his daughter and his wife more than ever. The blows didn't appear to do the mother any good. She just grew thinner and thinner; but the daughter, Dolly, thrived on it. She grew fatter and fatter, and giggled more and more every year. Elias, the son, grew more and more stern, but he never spoke a hard word to his father.

Hat said, 'That boy Elias have too much good mind.'

One day Bogart, of all people, said, 'Ha! I mad to break old George tail up, you hear.'

And the few times when Elias joined the crowd, Hat would say, 'Boy, I too sorry for you. Why you don't fix the old man up good?'

Elias would say, 'It is all God work.'

Elias was only fourteen or so at the time. But that was the sort of boy he was. He was serious and he had big ambitions.

I began to be terrified of George, particularly when he bought two great Alsatian dogs and tied them to pickets at the foot of the concrete steps.

Every morning and afternoon when I passed his house, he would say to the dogs, 'Shook him!'

And the dogs would bound and leap and bark; and I could see their ropes stretched tight and I always felt that the ropes would break at the next leap. Now, when Hat had an Alsatian, he made it like me. And Hat had said to me then, 'Never fraid dog. Go brave. Don't run.'

And so I used to walk slowly past George's house, lengthening out my torture.

I don't know whether George disliked me personally, or whether he simply had no use for people in general. I never discussed it with the other boys in the street, because I was too ashamed to say I was afraid of barking dogs.

Presently, though, I grew used to the dogs. And even George's laughter when I passed the house didn't worry me very much.

One day George was on the pavement as I was passing; I heard him mumbling. I heard him mumble again that afternoon and again the following day. He was saying, 'Horse-face!'

Sometimes he said, 'Like it only have horse-face people living in this place.'

Sometimes he said, 'Short-arse!'

And, 'But how it have people so short-arse in the world?'

I pretended not to hear, of course, but after a week or so I was almost in tears whenever George mumbled these things.

One evening, when we had stopped playing cricket on the pavement because Boyee had hit the ball into Miss Hilton's yard, and that was a lost ball (it counted six and out) – that evening, I asked Elias, 'but what your father have with me so? Why he does keep on calling me names?'

Hat laughed, and Elias looked a little solemn.

Hat said, 'What sort of names?'

I said, 'The fat old man does call me horse-face.' I couldn't bring myself to say the other name.

Hat began laughing.

Elias said, 'Boy, my father is a funny man. But you must forgive him. What he say don't matter. He old. He have life hard. He not educated like we here. He have a soul just like any of we, too besides.'

And he was so serious that Hat didn't laugh and whenever I walked past George's house, I kept on saying to myself, 'I must forgive him. He ain't know what he doing.'

And then Elias's mother died, and had the shabbiest and the saddest and the loneliest funeral Miguel Street had ever seen.

That empty front room became sadder and more frightening for me.

The strange thing was that I felt a little sorry for George. The Miguel Street men held a post-mortem outside Hat's house. Hat said, 'He did beat she too bad.'

Bogart nodded and drew a circle on the pavement with his right index finger.

Edward said, 'I think he kill she, you know. Boyee tell me that the evening before she dead he hear George giving the woman licks like fire.'

Hat said, 'What you think they have doctors and magistrates in this place for? For fun?'

'But I telling you,' Edward said. 'It really true. Boyee wouldn't lie about a thing like that. The woman dead from blows. I telling you. London can take it; but not George wife.'

Not one of the men said a word for George.

Boyee said something I didn't expect him to say. He said, 'The person I really feel sorry for is Dolly. You suppose he going to beat she still?'

Hat said wisely, 'Let we wait and see.'

*

Elias dropped out of our circle.

*

George was very sad for the first few days after the funeral. He drank a lot of rum and went about crying in the streets, beating his chest and asking everybody to forgive him, and to take pity on him, a poor widower.

He kept up the drinking into the following weeks, and he was still running up and down the street, making everyone feel foolish when he asked for forgiveness. 'My son Elias,' George used to say, 'my son Elias forgive me, and he is a educated boy.'

When he came to Hat, Hat said, 'What happening to your cows? You milking them? You feeding them? You want to kill your cows now too?'

George sold all his cows to Hat.

'God will say is robbery,' Hat laughed. 'I say is a bargain.'

Edward said, 'It good for George. He beginning to pay for his sins.'

'Well, I look at it this way,' Hat said. 'I give him enough money to remain drunk for two whole months.'

*

George was away from Miguel Street for a week. During that time we saw more of Dolly. She swept out the front room and begged flowers of the neighbours and put them in the room. She giggled more than ever.

Someone in the street (not me) poisoned the two Alsatians.

We hoped that George had gone away for good.

He did come back, however, still drunk, but no longer crying or helpless, and he had a woman with him. She was a very Indian woman, a little old, but she looked strong enough to handle George.

'She look like a drinker sheself,' Hat said.

This woman took control of George's house, and once more Dolly retreated into the back, where the empty cow-pens were.

We heard stories of beatings and everybody said he was sorry for Dolly and the new woman.

My heart went out to the woman and Dolly. I couldn't understand how anybody in the world would want to live with George, and I wasn't surprised when one day, about two weeks later, Popo told me, 'George new wife leave him, you ain't hear?'

Hat said, 'I wonder what he going do when the money I give him finish.'

*

We soon saw.

The pink house, almost overnight, became a full and noisy place. There were many women about, talking loudly and not paying too much attention to the way they dressed. And whenever I passed the pink house, these women shouted abusive remarks at me; and some of them did things with their mouths, inviting me to 'come to mooma'. And there were not only these new women. Many American soldiers drove up in jeeps, and Miguel Street became full of laughter and shrieks.

Hat said, 'That man George giving the street a bad name, you know.'

It was as though Miguel Street belonged to these new people. Hat and the rest of the boys were no longer assured of privacy when they sat down to talk things over on the pavement.

But Bogart became friendly with the new people and spent two or three evenings a week with them. He pretended he was disgusted at what he saw, but I didn't believe him because he was always going back.

'What happening to Dolly?' Hat asked him one day.

'She dey,' Bogart said, meaning that she was all right.

'Ah know she dey,' Hat said. 'But how she dey?'

'Well, she cleaning and cooking.'

'For everybody?'

'Everybody.'

Elias had a room of his own which he never left whenever he

came home. He ate his meals outside. He was trying to study for some important exam. He had lost interest in his family, Bogart said, or rather, implied.

George was still drinking a lot; but he was prospering. He was wearing a suit now, and a tie.

Hat said, 'He must be making a lot of money, if he have to bribe all the policemen and them.'

What I couldn't understand at all, though, was the way these new women behaved to George. They all appeared to like him as well as respect him. And George wasn't attempting to be nice in return either. He remained himself.

*

One day he said to everyone, 'Dolly ain't have no mooma now. I have to be father and mother to the child. And I say is high time Dolly get married.'

His choice fell on a man called Razor. It was hard to think of a more suitable name for this man. He was small. He was thin. He had a neat, sharp moustache above neat, tiny lips. The creases on his trousers were always sharp and clean and straight. And he was supposed to carry a knife.

Hat didn't like Dolly marrying Razor. 'He too sharp for we,' he said. 'He is the sort of man who wouldn't think anything about forgetting a knife in your back, you know.'

But Dolly still giggled.

Razor and Dolly were married at church, and they came back to a reception in the pink house. The women were all dressed up, and there were lots of American soldiers and sailors drinking and laughing and congratulating George. The women and the Americans made Dolly and Razor kiss and kiss, and they cheered. Dolly giggled.

Hat said, 'She ain't giggling, you know. She crying really.'

Elias wasn't at home that day.

The women and the Americans sang *Sweet Sixteen* and *As Time Goes By*. Then they made Dolly and Razor kiss again. Someone shouted, 'Speech!' and everybody laughed and shouted, 'Speech! Speech!'

Razor left Dolly standing by herself giggling.

'Speech! Speech!' the wedding guests called.

Dolly only giggled more.

Then George spoke out. 'Dolly, you married, it true. But don't think you too big for me to put you across my lap and cut your tail.' He said it in a jocular manner, and the guests laughed.

Then Dolly stopped giggling and looked stupidly at the people.

For a moment so brief you could scarcely measure it there was absolute silence; then an American sailor waved his hands drunkenly and shouted, 'You could put this girl to better work, George.' And everybody laughed.

Dolly picked up a handful of gravel from the yard and was making as if to throw it at the sailor. But she stopped suddenly, and burst into tears.

There was much laughing and cheering and shouting.

I never knew what happened to Dolly. Edward said one day that she was living in Sangre Grande. Hat said he saw her selling in the George Street Market. But she had left the street, left it for good. As the months went by, the women began to disappear and the numbers of jeeps that stopped outside George's house grew smaller.

'You gotta be organized,' Hat said.

Bogart nodded.

Hat added, 'And they have lots of nice places all over the place in Port of Spain these days. The trouble with George is that he too stupid for a big man.'

Hat was a prophet. Within six months, George was living alone in his pink house. I used to see him then, sitting on the steps, but he never looked at me any more. He looked old and weary and very sad.

He died soon afterwards. Hat and the boys got some money together and we buried him at Lapeyrouse Cemetery. Elias turned up for the funeral.

4. His Chosen Calling

AFTER MIDNIGHT there were two regular noises in the street. At about two o'clock you heard the sweepers; and then, just before dawn, the scavenging-carts came and you heard the men scraping off the rubbish the sweepers had gathered into heaps.

No boy in the street particularly wished to be a sweeper. But if you asked any boy what he would like to be, he would say, 'I going be a cart-driver.'

There was certainly a glamour to driving the blue carts. The men were aristocrats. They worked early in the morning, and had the rest of the day free. And then they were always going on strike. They didn't strike for much. They struck for things like a cent more a day; they struck if someone was laid off. They struck when the war began; they struck when the war ended. They struck when India got independence. They struck when Gandhi died.

Eddoes, who was a driver, was admired by most of the boys. He said his father was the best cart-driver of his day, and he told us great stories of the old man's skill. Eddoes came from a low Hindu caste, and there was a lot of truth in what he said. His skill was a sort of family skill, passing from father to son.

One day I was sweeping the pavement in front of the house where I lived, and Eddoes came and wanted to take away the broom from me. I liked sweeping and didn't want to give him the broom.

'Boy, what you know about sweeping?' Eddoes asked, laughing.

I said, 'What, it have so much to know?'

Eddoes said, 'This is my job, boy. I have experience. Wait until you big like me.'

I gave him the broom.

I was sad for a long time afterwards. It seemed that I would never never grow as big as Eddoes, never have that thing he called experience. I began to admire Eddoes more than ever; and more than ever I wanted to be a cart-driver.

But Elias was not that sort of boy.

When we who formed the Junior Miguel Street Club squatted on the pavement, talking, like Hat and Bogart and the others, about things like life and cricket and football, I said to Elias, 'So you don't want to be a cart-driver? What you want to be then? A sweeper?'

Elias spat neatly into the gutter and looked down. He said very earnestly, 'I think I going be a doctor, you hear.'

If Boyee or Errol had said something like that, we would all have laughed. But we recognized that Elias was different, that Elias had brains.

We all felt sorry for Elias. His father George brutalized the boy with blows, but Elias never cried, never spoke a word against his father.

One day I was going to Chin's shop to buy three cents' worth of butter, and I asked Elias to come with me. I didn't see George about, and I thought it was safe.

We were just about two houses away when we saw George. Elias grew scared. George came up and said sharply, 'Where you going?' And at the same time he landed a powerful cuff on Elias's jaw.

George liked beating Elias. He used to tie him with rope, and then beat him with rope he had soaked in the gutters of his cow-pen. Elias didn't cry even then. And shortly after, I would see

George laughing with Elias, and George used to say to me, 'I know what you thinking. You wondering how me and he get so friendly so quick.'

The more I disliked George, the more I liked Elias.

I was prepared to believe that he would become a doctor some day.

Errol said, 'I bet you when he come doctor and thing he go forget the rest of we. Eh, Elias?'

A small smile appeared on Elias's lips.

'Nah,' he said. 'I wouldn't be like that. I go give a lot of money and thing to you and Boyee and the rest of you fellows.' And Elias waved his small hands, and we thought we could see the Cadillac and the black bag and the tube-thing that Elias was going to have when he became a doctor.

Elias began going to the school at the other end of Miguel Street. It didn't really look like a school at all. It looked just like any house to me, but there was a sign outside that said:

TITUS HOYT, I.A. (London, External)
Passes in the Cambridge
School Certificate Guaranteed

The odd thing was that although George beat Elias at the slightest opportunity, he was very proud that his son was getting an education. 'The boy learning a hell of a lot, you know. He reading Spanish, French and Latin, and he writing Spanish, French and Latin.'

The year before his mother died, Elias sat for the Cambridge Senior School Certificate.

Titus Hoyt came down to our end of the street.

'That boy going pass with honours,' Titus Hoyt said. 'With honours.'

We saw Elias dressed in neat khaki trousers and white shirt, going to the examination room, and we looked at him with awe.

Errol said, 'Everything Elias write not remaining here, you know. Every word that boy write going to England.'

It didn't sound true.

'What you think it is at all?' Errol said. 'Elias have brains, you know.'

Elias's mother died in January, and the results came out in March.

Elias hadn't passed.

Hat looked through the list in the *Guardian* over and over again, looking for Elias's name, saying, 'You never know. People always making mistake, especially when it have so much names.'

Elias's name wasn't in the paper.

Boyee said, 'What else you expect? Who correct the papers? English man, not so? You expect them to give Elias a pass?'

Elias was with us, looking sad and not saying a word.

Hat said, 'Is a damn shame. If they know what hell the boy have to put up with, they woulda pass him quick quick.'

Titus Hoyt said, 'Don't worry. Rome wasn't built in a day. This year! This year, things going be much much better. We go show those Englishmen and them.'

Elias left us and he began living with Titus Hoyt. We saw next to nothing of him. He was working night and day.

One day in the following March, Titus Hoyt rode up to us and said, 'You hear what happen?'

'What happen?' Hat asked.

'The boy is a genius,' Titus Hoyt said.

'Which boy?' Errol asked.

'Elias.'

'What Elias do?'

'The boy gone and pass the Cambridge Senior School Certificate.'

Hat whistled. 'The Cambridge Senior School Certificate?'

Titus Hoyt smiled. 'That self. He get a third grade. His name going to be in the papers tomorrow. I always say it, and I saying it again now, this boy Elias have too much brains.'

Hat said later, 'Is too bad that Elias father dead. He was a good-for-nothing, but he wanted to see his son a educated man.'

Elias came that evening, and everybody, boys and men, gathered around him. They talked about everything but books, and Elias, too, was talking about things like pictures and girls and cricket. He was looking very solemn, too.

There was a pause once, and Hat said, 'What you going to do now, Elias? Look for work?'

Elias spat. 'Nah, I think I will write the exam again.'

I said, 'But why?'

'I want a second grade.'

We understood. He wanted to be a doctor.

Elias sat down on the pavement, and said, 'Yes, boy. I think I going to take that exam again, and this year I going to be so good that this Mr Cambridge go bawl when he read what I write for him.'

We were silent, in wonder.

'Is the English and litritcher that does beat me.'

In Elias's mouth litritcher was the most beautiful word I heard. It sounded like something to eat, something rich like chocolate.

Hat said, 'You mean you have to read a lot of poultry and thing?'

Elias nodded. We felt it wasn't fair, making a boy like Elias do litritcher and poultry.

*

Elias moved back into the pink house which had been empty since his father died. He was studying and working. He went back to

Titus Hoyt's school, not as pupil, but as a teacher, and Titus Hoyt said he was giving him forty dollars a month.

Titus Hoyt added, 'He worth it, too. He is one of the brightest boys in Port of Spain.'

Now that Elias was back with us, we noticed him better. He was the cleanest boy in the street. He bathed twice a day and scrubbed his teeth twice a day. He did all this standing up at the tap in front of the house. He swept the house every morning before going to school. He was the opposite of his father. His father was short and fat and dirty. He was tall and thin and clean. His father drank and swore. He never drank and no one ever heard him use a bad word.

My mother used to say to me, 'Why you don't take after Elias? I really don't know what sort of son God give me, you hear.'

And whenever Hat or Edward beat Boyee and Errol, they always said, 'Why you beating we for? Not everybody could be like Elias, you know.'

Hat used to say, 'And it ain't only that he got brains. The boy Elias have nice *ways* too.'

So I think I was a little glad when Elias sat the examination for the third time, and failed.

Hat said, 'You see how we catch these Englishmen and them. Nobody here can tell me that the boy didn't pass the exam, but you think they go want to give him a better grade? Ha!'

And everybody said, 'Is a real shame.'

And when Hat asked Elias, 'What you going to do now, boy?' Elias said, 'You know, I think I go take up a job. I think I go be a sanitary inspector.'

We saw him in khaki uniform and khaki topee, going from house to house with a little note-book.

'Yes,' Elias said. 'Sanitary inspector, that's what I going to be.'

Hat said, 'It have a lot of money in that, I think. I hear your father George uses to pay the sanitary inspector five dollars a month to keep his mouth shut. Let we say you get about ten or even eight people like that. That's – let me see . . . ten fives is fifty, eight fives is forty. There, fifty, forty dollars straight. And mark you, that ain't counting your salary.'

Elias said, 'Is not the money I thinking about. I really like the work.'

It was easy to understand that.

Elias said, 'But it have a exam, you know.'

Hat said, 'But they don't send the papers to England for that?'

Elias said, 'Nah, but still, I fraid exams and things, you know. I ain't have any luck with them.'

Boyee said, 'But I thought you was thinking of taking up doctoring.'

Hat said, 'Boyee, I going to cut your little tail if you don't shut up.'

But Boyee didn't mean anything bad.

Elias said, 'I change my mind. I think I want to be a sanitary inspector. I really like the work.'

*

For three years Elias sat the sanitary inspectors' examination, and he failed every time.

Elias began saying, 'But what the hell you expect in Trinidad? You got to bribe everybody if you want to get your toenail cut.'

Hat said, 'I meet a man from a boat the other day, and he tell me that the sanitary inspector exams in British Guiana much easier. You could go to B.G. and take the exams there and come back and work here.'

Elias flew to B.G., wrote the exam, failed it, and flew back.

Hat said, 'I meet a man from Barbados. He tell me that the exams easier in Barbados. It easy, easy, he say.'

Elias flew to Barbados, wrote the exam, failed it, and flew back.

Hat said, 'I meet a man from Grenada the other day – '

Elias said, 'Shut your arse up, before it have trouble between we in this street.'

*

A few years later I sat the Cambridge Senior School Certificate Examination myself, and Mr Cambridge gave me a second grade. I applied for a job in the Customs, and it didn't cost me much to get it. I got a khaki uniform with brass buttons, and a cap. Very much like the sanitary inspector's uniform.

Elias wanted to beat me up the first day I wore the uniform.

'What your mother do to get you that?' he shouted, and I was going for him, when Eddoes put a stop to it.

Eddoes said, 'He just sad and jealous. He don't mean anything.'

For Elias had become one of the street aristocrats. He was driving the scavenging-carts.

'No theory here,' Elias used to say. 'This is the practical. I really like the work.'

5. Man-man

EVERYBODY IN Miguel Street said that Man-man was mad, and so they left him alone. But I am not so sure now that he was mad, and I can think of many people much madder than Man-man ever was.

He didn't look mad. He was a man of medium height, thin; and he wasn't bad-looking either. He never stared at you the way I expected a mad man to do; and when you spoke to him you were sure of getting a very reasonable reply.

But he did have some curious habits.

He went up for every election, city council or legislative council, and then he stuck posters everywhere in the district. These posters were well printed. They just had the word 'Vote' and below that, Man-man's picture.

At every election he got exactly three votes. That I couldn't understand. Man-man voted for himself, but who were the other two?

I asked Hat.

Hat said, 'I really can't say, boy. Is a real mystery. Perhaps is two jokers. But they is funny sort of jokers if they do the same thing so many times. They must be mad just like he.'

And for a long time the thought of these two mad men who voted for Man-man haunted me. Every time I saw someone doing anything just a little bit odd, I wondered, 'Is he who vote for Man-man?'

At large in the city were these two men of mystery.

Man-man never worked. But he was never idle. He was hypnotized by the word, particularly the written word, and he would spend a whole day writing a single word.

One day I met Man-man at the corner of Miguel Street.

'Boy, where you going?' Man-man asked.

'I going to school,' I said.

And Man-man, looking at me solemnly, said in a mocking way, 'So you goes to school, eh?'

I said automatically, 'Yes, I goes to school.' And I found that without intending it I had imitated Man-man's correct and very English accent.

That again was another mystery about Man-man. His accent. If you shut your eyes while he spoke, you would believe an Englishman – a good-class Englishman who wasn't particular about grammar – was talking to you.

Man-man said, as though speaking to himself, 'So the little man is going to school.'

Then he forgot me, and took out a long stick of chalk from his pocket and began writing on the pavement. He drew a very big S in outline and then filled it in, and then the C and the H and the O. But then he started making several O's, each smaller than the last, until he was writing in cursive, O after flowing O.

When I came home for lunch, he had got to French Street, and he was still writing O's, rubbing off mistakes with a rag.

In the afternoon he had gone round the block and was practically back in Miguel Street.

I went home, changed from my school-clothes into my home-clothes and went out to the street.

He was now half-way up Miguel Street.

He said, 'So the little man gone to school today?'

I said, 'Yes.'

He stood up and straightened his back.

Then he squatted again and drew the outline of a Massive L and filled that in slowly and lovingly.

When it was finished, he stood up and said, 'You finish your work. I finish mine.'

Or it was like this. If you told Man-man you were going to the cricket, he would write CRICK and then concentrate on the E's until he saw you again.

One day Man-man went to the big café at the top of Miguel Street and began barking and growling at the customers on the stools as though he were a dog. The owner, a big Portuguese man with hairy hands, said, 'Man-man, get out of this shop before I tangle with you.'

Man-man just laughed.

They threw Man-man out.

Next day, the owner found that someone had entered his café during the night, and had left all the doors open. But nothing was missing.

Hat said, 'One thing you must never do is trouble Man-man. He remember everything.'

That night the café was entered again and the doors again left open.

The following night the café was entered and this time little blobs of excrement were left on the centre of every stool and on top of every table and at regular intervals along the counter.

The owner of the café was the laughing-stock of the street for several weeks, and it was only after a long time that people began going to the café again.

Hat said, 'Is just like I say. Boy, I don't like meddling with that man. These people really bad-mind, you know. God make them that way.'

It was things like this that made people leave Man-man alone. The only friend he had was a little mongrel dog, white with black spots on the ears. The dog was like Man-man in a way, too. It was a curious dog. It never barked, never looked at you, and if you looked at it, it looked away. It never made friends with any other dog, and if some dog tried either to get friendly or aggressive, Man-man's dog gave it a brief look of disdain and ambled away, without looking back.

Man-man loved his dog, and the dog loved Man-man. They were made for each other, and Man-man couldn't have made a living without his dog.

Man-man appeared to exercise a great control over the movements of his dog's bowels.

Hat said, 'That does really beat me. I can't make that one out.'

It all began in Miguel Street.

One morning, several women got up to find that the clothes they had left to bleach overnight had been sullied by the droppings of a dog. No one wanted to use the sheets and the shirts after that, and when Man-man called, everyone was willing to give him the dirty clothes.

Man-man used to sell these clothes.

Hat said, 'Is things like this that make me wonder whether the man really mad.'

From Miguel Street Man-man's activities spread, and all the people who had suffered from Man-man's dog were anxious to get other people to suffer the same thing.

We in Miguel Street became a little proud of him.

*

I don't know what it was that caused Man-man to turn good. Perhaps the death of his dog had something to do with it. The dog was run over by a car, and it gave, Hat said, just one short squeak, and then it was silent.

Man-man wandered about for days, looking dazed and lost.

He no longer wrote words on the pavement; no longer spoke

to me or to any of the other boys in the street. He began talking to himself, clasping his hands and shaking as though he had ague.

Then one day he said he had seen God after having a bath.

This didn't surprise many of us. Seeing God was quite common in Port of Spain, and, indeed, in Trinidad at that time. Ganesh Pundit, the mystic masseur from Fuente Grove, had started it. He had seen God, too, and had published a little booklet called *What God Told Me*. Many rival mystics and not a few masseurs had announced the same thing, and I suppose it was natural that since God was in the area Man-man should see Him.

Man-man began preaching at the corner of Miguel Street, under the awning of Mary's shop. He did this every Saturday night. He let his beard grow and he dressed in a long white robe. He got a Bible and other holy things and stood in the white light of an acetylene lamp and preached. He was an impressive preacher, and he preached in an odd way. He made women cry, and he made people like Hat really worried.

He used to hold the Bible in his right hand and slap it with his left and say in his perfect English accent, 'I have been talking to God these few days, and what he tell me about you people wasn't really nice to hear. These days you hear all the politicians and them talking about making the island self-sufficient. You know what God tell me last night? Last night self, just after I finish eating? God say, "Man-man, come and have a look at these people." He show me husband eating wife and wife eating husband. He show me father eating son and mother eating daughter. He show me brother eating sister and sister eating brother. That is what these politicians and them mean by saying that the island going to become self-sufficient. But, brethren, it not too late now to turn to God.'

*

I used to get nightmares every Saturday night after hearing Man-man preach. But the odd thing was that the more he frightened people the more they came to hear him preach. And when the collection was made they gave him more than ever.

In the week-days he just walked about, in his white robe, and he begged for food. He said he had done what Jesus ordered and he had given away all his goods. With his long black beard and his bright deep eyes, you couldn't refuse him anything. He noticed me no longer, and never asked me, 'So you goes to school?'

The people in Miguel Street didn't know what to make of the change. They tried to comfort themselves by saying that Man-man was really mad, but, like me, I think they weren't sure that Man-man wasn't really right.

What happened afterwards wasn't really unexpected.

Man-man announced that he was a new Messiah.

Hat said one day, 'You ain't hear the latest?'

We said, 'What?'

'Is about Man-man. He say he going to be crucified one of these days.'

'Nobody go touch him,' Edward said. 'Everybody fraid of him now.'

Hat explained. 'Not, it ain't that. He going to crucify hisself. One of these Fridays he going to Blue Basin and tie hisself to a cross and let people stone him.'

Somebody – Errol, I think – laughed, but finding that no one laughed with him, fell silent again.

But on top of our wonder and worry, we had this great pride in knowing that Man-man came from Miguel Street.

Little hand-written notices began appearing in the shops and cafés and on the gates of some houses, announcing Man-man's forthcoming crucifixion.

'They going to have a big crowd in Blue Basin,' Hat announced, and added with pride, 'and I hear they sending some police too.'

That day, early in the morning, before the shops opened and the trolley-buses began running in Ariapita Avenue, the big crowd assembled at the corner of Miguel Street. There were lots of men dressed in black and even more women dressed in white. They were singing hymns. There were also about twenty policemen, but they were not singing hymns.

When Man-man appeared, looking very thin and very holy, women cried and rushed to touch his gown. The police stood by, prepared to handle anything.

A van came with a great wooden cross.

Hat, looking unhappy in his serge suit, said, 'They tell me it make from match-wood. It ain't heavy. It light light.'

Edward said, in a snapping sort of way, 'That matter? Is the heart and the spirit that matter.'

Hat said, 'I ain't saying nothing.'

Some men began taking the cross from the van to give it to Man-man, but he stopped them. His English accent sounded impressive in the early morning. 'Not here. Leave it for Blue Basin.'

Hat was disappointed.

We walked to Blue Basin, the waterfall in the mountains to the north-west of Port of Spain, and we got there in two hours. Man-man began carrying the cross from the road, up the rocky path and then down to the Basin.

Some men put up the cross, and tied Man-man to it.

Man-man said, 'Stone me, brethren.'

The women wept and flung bits of sand and gravel at his feet.

Man-man groaned and said, 'Father, forgive them. They ain't know what they doing.' Then he screamed out, 'Stone me, brethren!'

A pebble the size of an egg struck him on the chest.

Man-man cried, 'Stone, stone, STONE me, brethren! I forgive you.'

Edward said, 'The man really brave.'

People began flinging really big stones at Man-man, aiming at his face and chest.

Man-man looked hurt and surprised. He shouted, 'What the hell is this? What the hell you people think you doing? Look, get me down from this thing quick, let me down quick, and I go settle with that son of a bitch who pelt a stone at me.'

From where Edward and Hat and the rest of us stood, it sounded like a cry of agony.

A bigger stone struck Man-man; the women flung the sand and gravel at him.

We heard Man-man's shout, clear and loud, 'Cut this stupidness out. Cut it out, I tell you. I finish with this arseness, you hear.' And then he began cursing so loudly and coarsely that the people stopped in surprise.

The police took away Man-man.

The authorities kept him for observation. Then for good.

6. B. Wordsworth

THREE BEGGARS CALLED punctually every day at the hospitable houses in Miguel Street. At about ten an Indian came in his dhoti and white jacket, and we poured a tin of rice into the sack he carried on his back. At twelve an old woman smoking a clay pipe came and she got a cent. At two a blind man led by a boy called for his penny.

Sometimes we had a rogue. One day a man called and said he was hungry. We gave him a meal. He asked for a cigarette and wouldn't go until we had lit it for him. That man never came again.

The strangest caller came one afternoon at about four o'clock. I had come back from school and was in my home-clothes. The man said to me, 'Sonny, may I come inside your yard?'

He was a small man and he was tidily dressed. He wore a hat, a white shirt and black trousers.

I asked, 'What you want?'

He said, 'I want to watch your bees.'

We had four small gru-gru palm trees and they were full of uninvited bees.

I ran up the steps and shouted, 'Ma, it have a man outside here. He say he want to watch the bees.'

My mother came out, looked at the man and asked in an unfriendly way, 'What you want?'

The man said, 'I want to watch your bees.'

His English was so good, it didn't sound natural, and I could see my mother was worried.

She said to me, 'Stay here and watch him while he watch the bees.'

The man said, 'Thank you, Madam. You have done a good deed today.'

He spoke very slowly and very correctly as though every word was costing him money.

We watched the bees, this man and I, for about an hour, squatting near the palm trees.

The man said, 'I like watching bees. Sonny, do you like watching bees?'

I said, 'I ain't have the time.'

He shook his head sadly. He said, 'That's what I do, I just watch. I can watch ants for days. Have you ever watched ants? And scorpions, and centipedes, and *congorees* – have you watched those?'

I shook my head.

I said, 'What you does do, mister?'

He got up and said, 'I am a poet.'

I said, 'A good poet?'

He said, 'The greatest in the world.'

'What your name, mister?'

'B. Wordsworth.'

'B for Bill?'

'Black. Black Wordsworth. White Wordsworth was my brother. We share one heart. I can watch a small flower like the morning glory and cry.'

I said, 'Why you does cry?'

'Why, boy? Why? You will know when you grow up. You're a poet, too, you know. And when you're a poet you can cry for everything.'

I couldn't laugh.

He said, 'You like your mother?'

'When she not beating me.'

He pulled out a printed sheet from his hip-pocket and said, 'On this paper is the greatest poem about mothers and I'm going to sell it to you at a bargain price. For four cents.'

I went inside and I said, 'Ma, you want to buy a poetry for four cents?'

My mother said, 'Tell that blasted man to haul his tail away from my yard, you hear.'

I said to B. Wordsworth, 'My mother say she ain't have four cents.'

B. Wordsworth said, 'It is the poet's tragedy.'

And he put the paper back in his pocket. He didn't seem to mind.

I said, 'Is a funny way to go round selling poetry like that. Only calypsonians do that sort of thing. A lot of people does buy?'

He said, 'No one has yet bought a single copy.'

'But why you does keep on going round, then?'

He said, 'In this way I watch many things, and I always hope to meet poets.'

I said, 'You really think I is a poet?'

'You're as good as me,' he said.

And when B. Wordsworth left, I prayed I would see him again.

*

About a week later, coming back from school one afternoon, I met him at the corner of Miguel Street.

He said, 'I have been waiting for you for a long time.'

I said, 'You sell any poetry yet?'

He shook his head.

He said, 'In my yard I have the best mango tree in Port of Spain. And now the mangoes are ripe and red and very sweet and juicy. I have waited here for you to tell you this and to invite you to come and eat some of my mangoes.'

He lived in Alberto Street in a one-roomed hut placed right in the centre of the lot. The yard seemed all green. There was the big mango tree. There was a coconut tree and there was a plum tree. The place looked wild, as though it wasn't in the city at all. You couldn't see all the big concrete houses in the street.

He was right. The mangoes were sweet and juicy. I ate about six, and the yellow mango juice ran down my arms to my elbows and down my mouth to my chin and my shirt was stained.

My mother said when I got home, 'Where you was? You think you is a man now and could go all over the place? Go cut a whip for me.'

She beat me rather badly, and I ran out of the house swearing that I would never come back. I went to B. Wordsworth's house. I was so angry, my nose was bleeding.

B. Wordsworth said, 'Stop crying, and we will go for a walk.'

I stopped crying, but I was breathing short. We went for a walk. We walked down St Clair Avenue to the Savannah and we walked to the race-course.

B. Wordsworth said, 'Now, let us lie on the grass and look up at the sky, and I want you to think how far those stars are from us.'

*

I did as he told me, and I saw what he meant. I felt like nothing, and at the same time I had never felt so big and great in all my life. I forgot all my anger and all my tears and all the blows.

When I said I was better, he began telling me the names of the stars, and I particularly remembered the constellation of Orion the Hunter, though I don't really know why. I can spot Orion even today, but I have forgotten the rest.

Then a light was flashed into our faces, and we saw a policeman. We got up from the grass.

The policeman said, 'What you doing here?'

B. Wordsworth said, 'I have been asking myself the same question for forty years.'

We became friends, B. Wordsworth and I. He told me, 'You must never tell anybody about me and about the mango tree and the coconut tree and the plum tree. You must keep that a secret. If you tell anybody, I will know, because I am a poet.'

I gave him my word and I kept it.

I liked his little room. It had no more furniture than George's front room, but it looked cleaner and healthier. But it also looked lonely.

One day I asked him, 'Mister Wordsworth, why you does keep all this bush in your yard? Ain't it does make the place damp?'

He said, 'Listen, and I will tell you a story. Once upon a time a boy and girl met each other and they fell in love. They loved each other so much they got married. They were both poets. He loved words. She loved grass and flowers and trees. They lived happily in a single room, and then one day, the girl poet said to the boy poet, "We are going to have another poet in the family." But this poet was never born, because the girl died, and the young poet died with her, inside her. And the girl's husband was very sad, and he said he would never touch a thing in the girl's garden. And so the garden remained, and grew high and wild.'

I looked at B. Wordsworth, and as he told me this lovely story, he seemed to grow older. I understood his story.

We went for long walks together. We went to the Botanical Gardens and the Rock Gardens. We climbed Chancellor Hill in the late afternoon and watched the darkness fall on Port of Spain, and watched the lights go on in the city and on the ships in the harbour.

He did everything as though he were doing it for the first time in his life. He did everything as though he were doing some church rite.

He would say to me, 'Now, how about having some ice-cream?'

And when I said, yes, he would grow very serious and say, 'Now, which café shall we patronize?' As though it were a very important thing. He would think for some time about it, and finally say, 'I think I will go and negotiate the purchase with that shop.'

The world became a most exciting place.

*

One day, when I was in his yard, he said to me, 'I have a great secret which I am now going to tell you.'

I said, 'It really secret?'

'At the moment, yes.'

I looked at him, and he looked at me. He said, 'This is just between you and me, remember. I am writing a poem.'

'Oh.' I was disappointed.

He said, 'But this is a different sort of poem. This is the greatest poem in the world.'

I whistled.

He said, 'I have been working on it for more than five years now. I will finish it in about twenty-two years from now, that is, if I keep on writing at the present rate.'

'You does write a lot, then?'

He said, 'Not any more. I just write one line a month. But I make sure it is a good line.'

I asked, 'What was last month's good line?'

He looked up at the sky, and said, '*The past is deep.*'

I said, 'It is a beautiful line.'

B. Wordsworth said, 'I hope to distil the experiences of a whole month into that single line of poetry. So, in twenty-two years, I shall have written a poem that will sing to all humanity.'

I was filled with wonder.

*

Our walks continued. We walked along the sea-wall at Docksite one day, and I said, 'Mr Wordsworth, if I drop this pin in the water, you think it will float?'

He said, 'This is a strange world. Drop your pin, and let us see what will happen.'

The pin sank.

I said, 'How is the poem this month?'

But he never told me any other line. He merely said, 'Oh, it comes, you know. It comes.'

Or we would sit on the sea-wall and watch the liners come into the harbour.

But of the greatest poem in the world I heard no more.

*

I felt he was growing older.

*

'How you does live, Mr Wordsworth?' I asked him one day.

He said, 'You mean how I get money?'

When I nodded, he laughed in a crooked way.

He said, 'I sing calypsoes in the calypso season.'

'And that last you the rest of the year?'

'It is enough.'

'But you will be the richest man in the world when you write the greatest poem?'

He didn't reply.

*

One day when I went to see him in his little house, I found him lying on his little bed. He looked so old and so weak, that I found myself wanting to cry.

He said, 'The poem is not going well.'

He wasn't looking at me. He was looking through the window at the coconut tree, and he was speaking as though I wasn't there. He said, 'When I was twenty I felt the power within myself.' Then, almost in front of my eyes, I could see his face growing older and more tired. He said, 'But that – that was a long time ago.'

And then – I felt it so keenly, it was as though I had been slapped by my mother. I could see it clearly on his face. It was there for everyone to see. Death on the shrinking face.

He looked at me, and saw my tears and sat up.

He said, 'Come.' I went and sat on his knees.

He looked into my eyes, and he said, 'Oh, you can see it, too. I always knew you had the poet's eye.'

He didn't even look sad, and that made me burst out crying loudly.

He pulled me to his thin chest, and said, 'Do you want me to tell you a funny story?' and he smiled encouragingly at me.

But I couldn't reply.

He said, 'When I have finished this story, I want you to promise that you will go away and never come back to see me. Do you promise?'

I nodded.

He said, 'Good. Well, listen. That story I told you about the boy poet and the girl poet, do you remember that? That wasn't true. It was something I just made up. All this talk about poetry and the greatest poem in the world, that wasn't true, either. Isn't that the funniest thing you have heard?'

But his voice broke.

I left the house, and ran home crying, like a poet, for everything I saw.

*

I walked along Alberto Street a year later, but I could find no sign of the poet's house. It hadn't vanished, just like that. It had been pulled down, and a big, two-storeyed building had taken its place. The mango tree and the plum tree and the coconut tree had all been cut down, and there was brick and concrete everywhere.

It was just as though B. Wordsworth had never existed.

7. The Coward

BIG FOOT WAS really big and really black, and everybody in Miguel Street was afraid of him. It wasn't his bigness or his blackness that people feared, for there were blacker and bigger people about. People were afraid of him because he was so silent and sulky; he *looked* dangerous, like those terrible dogs that never bark but just look at you from the corner of their eyes.

Hat used to say, 'Is only a form of showing off, you know, all this quietness he does give us. He quiet just because he ain't have anything to say, that's all.'

Yet you could hear Hat telling all sorts of people at the races and cricket, 'Big Foot and me? We is bosom pals, man. We grow up together.'

And at school I myself used to say, 'Big Foot does live in my street, you hear. I know him good good, and if any one of all you touch me, I go tell Big Foot.'

At that time I had never spoken a single word to Big Foot.

We in Miguel Street were proud to claim him because he was something of a character in Port of Spain, and had quite a reputation. It was Big Foot who flung the stone at Radio Trinidad building one day and broke a window. When the magistrate asked why he did it, Big Foot just said, 'To wake them up.'

A well-wisher paid the fine for him.

Then there was the time he got a job driving one of the diesel-buses. He drove the bus out of the city to Carenage, five miles away, and told the passengers to get out and bathe. He stood by to see that they did.

After that he got a job as a postman, and he had a great time misplacing people's letters. They found him at Docksite, with the bag half full of letters, soaking his big feet in the Gulf of Paria.

He said, 'Is hard work, walking all over the place, delivering people letters. You come like a postage stamp, man.'

All Trinidad thought of him as a comedian, but we who knew him thought otherwise.

It was people like Big Foot who gave the steel-bands a bad name. Big Foot was always ready to start a fight with another band, but he looked so big and dangerous that he himself was never involved in any fight, and he never went to jail for more than three months or so at a time.

Hat, especially, was afraid of Big Foot. Hat often said, 'I don't know why they don't lose Big Foot in jail, you know.'

You would have thought that when he was beating his pans and dancing in the street at Carnival, Big Foot would at least smile and look happy. But no. It was on occasions like this that he prepared his sulkiest and grimmest face; and when you saw him beating a pan, you felt, to judge by his earnestness, that he was doing some sacred act.

One day a big crowd of us – Hat, Edward, Eddoes, Boyee, Errol and myself – went to the cinema. We were sitting in a row, laughing and talking all during the film, having a good time.

A voice from behind said, very quietly, 'Shut up.'

We turned and saw Big Foot.

He lazily pulled out a knife from his trouser pocket, flicked the blade open, and stuck it in the back of my chair.

He looked up at the screen and said in a frightening friendly way, 'Talk.'

We didn't say a word for the rest of the film.

Afterwards Hat said, 'You does only get policeman son behaving in that way. Policeman son and priest son.'

Boyee said, 'You mean Big Foot is priest son?'

Hat said, 'You too stupid. Priests and them does have children?'

We heard a lot about Big Foot's father from Hat. It seemed he was as much a terror as Big Foot. Sometimes when Boyee and Errol and I were comparing notes about beatings, Boyee said, 'The blows we get is nothing to what Big Foot uses to get from his father. That is how he get so big, you know. I meet a boy from Belmont the other day in the Savannah, and this boy tell me that blows does make you grow.'

Errol said, 'You is a blasted fool, man. How you does let people give you stupidness like that?'

Once Hat said, 'Every day Big Foot father, the policeman, giving Big Foot blows. Like medicine. Three times a day after meals. And hear Big Foot talk afterwards. He used to say, "When I get big and have children, I go beat them, beat them."'

I didn't say it then, because I was ashamed; but I had often felt the same way when my mother beat me.

I asked Hat, 'And Big Foot mother? She used to beat him too?'

Hat said, 'Oh, God! That woulda kill him. Big Foot didn't have any mother. His father didn't married, thank God.'

*

The Americans were crawling all over Port of Spain in those days, making the city really hot. Children didn't take long to find out that they were easy people, always ready to give with both hands. Hat began working a small racket. He had five of us going all over the district begging for chewing gum and chocolate. For every packet of chewing gum we gave him we got a cent. Sometimes I made as much as twelve cents in a day. Some boy told me later that Hat was selling the chewing gum for six cents a packet, but I didn't believe it.

One afternoon, standing on the pavement outside my house, I saw an American soldier down the street, coming towards me. It was about two o'clock in the afternoon, very hot, and the street was practically empty.

The American behaved in a very surprising way when I sprinted down to ask, 'Got any gum, Joe?'

He mumbled something about begging kids and I think he was going to slap me or cuff me. He wasn't very big, but I was afraid. I think he was drunk.

He set his mouth.

A gruff voice said, 'Look, leave the boy alone, you hear.'

It was Big Foot.

Not another word was said. The American, suddenly humble, walked away, making a great pretence of not being in a hurry.

Big Foot didn't even look at me.

I never said again, 'Got any gum, Joe?'

*

Yet this did not make me like Big Foot. I was, I believe, a little more afraid of him.

I told Hat about the American and Big Foot.

Hat said, 'All the Americans not like that. You can't throw away twelve cents a day like that.'

But I refused to beg any more.

I said, 'If it wasn't for Big Foot, the man woulda kill me.'

Hat said, 'You know, is a good thing Big Foot father dead before Big Foot really get big.'

I said, 'What happen to Big Foot father, then?'

Hat said, 'You ain't hear? It was a famous thing. A crowd of black people beat him up and kill him in 1937 when they was having the riots in the oilfields. Big Foot father was playing hero, just like Big Foot playing hero now.'

I said, 'Hat, why you don't like Big Foot?'

Hat said, 'I ain't have anything against him.'

I said, 'Why you fraid him so, then?'

Hat said, 'Ain't you fraid him too?'

I nodded. 'But I feel you do him something and you worried.'

Hat said, 'Nothing really. It just funny. The rest of we use to give Big Foot hell too. He was thin thin when he was small, you know, and we use to have a helluva time chasing him all over the place. He couldn't run at all.'

I felt sorry for Big Foot.

I said, 'How that funny?'

Hat said, 'You go hear. You know the upshot? Big Foot come the best runner out of all of we. In the school sports he run the hundred yards in ten point four seconds. That is what they say, but you know how Trinidad people can't count time. Anyway, then we all want to come friendly with him. But he don't want we at all at all.'

And I wondered then why Big Foot held himself back from beating Hat and the rest of the people who had bullied him when he was a boy.

But still I didn't like him.

*

Big Foot became a carpenter for a while, and actually built two or three enormous wardrobes, rough, ugly things. But he sold them. And then he became a mason. There is no stupid pride among Trinidad craftsmen. No one is a specialist.

He came to our yard one day to do a job.

I stood by and watched him. I didn't speak to him, and he didn't speak to me. I noticed that he used his feet as a trowel. He mumbled, 'Is hard work, bending down all the time.'

He did the job well enough. His feet were not big for nothing.

About four o'clock he knocked off, and spoke to me.

He said, 'Boy, let we go for a walk. I hot and I want to cool off.'

I didn't want to go, but I felt I had to.

We went to the sea-wall at Docksite and watched the sea. Soon it began to grow dark. The lights came on in the harbour. The world seemed very big, dark, and silent. We stood up without speaking a word.

Then a sudden sharp yap very near us tore the silence.

The suddenness and strangeness of the noise paralysed me for a moment.

It was only a dog; a small white and black dog with large flapping ears. It was dripping wet, and was wagging its tail out of pure friendliness.

I said, 'Come, boy,' and the dog shook off the water from its coat on me and then jumped all over me, yapping and squirming.

I had forgotten Big Foot, and when I looked for him I saw him about twenty yards away running for all he was worth.

I shouted, 'Is all right, Big Foot.'

But he stopped before he heard my shout.

He cried out loudly, 'Oh God, I dead, I dead. A big big bottle cut up my foot.'

I and the dog ran to him.

But when the dog came to him he seemed to forget his foot which was bleeding badly. He began hugging and stroking the wet dog, and laughing in a crazy way.

*

He had cut his foot very badly, and next day I saw it wrapped up. He couldn't come to finish the work he had begun in our yard.

I felt I knew more about Big Foot than any man in Miguel Street, and I was afraid that I knew so much. I felt like one of those small men in gangster films who know too much and get killed.

And thereafter I was always conscious that Big Foot knew what I was thinking. I felt his fear that I would tell.

But although I was bursting with Big Foot's secret I told no one. I would have liked to reassure him but there was no means.

His presence in the street became something that haunted me. And it was all I could do to stop myself telling Hat, 'I not fraid of Big Foot. I don't know why you fraid him so.'

*

Errol, Boyee, and myself sat on the pavement discussing the war.

Errol said, 'If they just make Lord Anthony Eden Prime Minister, we go beat up the Germans and them bad bad.'

Boyee said, 'What Lord Eden go do so?'

Errol just haaed, in a very knowing way.

I said, 'Yes, I always think that if they make Lord Anthony Eden Prime Minister, the war go end quick quick.'

Boyee said, 'You people just don't know the Germans. The Germans strong like hell, you know. A boy was telling me that these Germans and them could eat a nail with their teeth alone.'

Errol said, 'But we have Americans on we side now.'

Boyee said, 'But they not big like the Germans. All the Germans and them big big and strong like Big Foot, you know, and they braver than Big Foot.'

Errol, said, 'Shh! Look, he coming.'

Big Foot was very near, and I felt he could hear the conversation. He was looking at me, and there was a curious look in his eyes.

Boyee said, 'Why you shhhing me so for? I ain't saying anything bad. I just saying that the Germans brave as Big Foot.'

Just for a moment, I saw the begging look in Big Foot's eyes. I looked away.

When Big Foot had passed, Errol said to me, 'Like Big Foot have something with you, boy.'

*

One afternoon Hat was reading the morning paper. He shouted to us, 'But look at what I reading here, man.'

We asked, 'What happening now?'

Hat said, 'Is about Big Foot.'

Boyee said, 'What, they throw him in jail again?'

Hat said, 'Big Foot taking up boxing.'

I understood more than I could say.

Hat said, 'He go get his tail mash up. If he think that boxing is just throwing yourself around, he go find out his mistake.'

The newspapers made a big thing out of it. The most popular headline was *Prankster Turns Pugilist*.

And when I next saw Big Foot, I felt I could look him in the eyes.

And now I wasn't afraid of him, I was afraid for him.

But I had no need. Big Foot had what the sports-writers all called a 'phenomenal success'. He knocked out fighter after fighter, and Miguel Street grew more afraid of him and more proud of him.

Hat said, 'Is only because he only fighting stupid little people. He ain't meet anybody yet that have real class.'

Big Foot seemed to have forgotten me. His eyes no longer sought mine whenever we met, and he no longer stopped to talk to me.

He was the terror of the street. I, like everybody else, was frightened of him. As before, I preferred it that way.

He even began showing off more.

We used to see him running up and down Miguel Street in stupid-looking maroon shorts and he resolutely refused to notice anybody.

Hat was terrified.

He said, 'They shouldn't let a man who go to jail box.'

*

An Englishman came to Trinidad one day and the papers ran to interview him. The man said he was a boxer and a champion of the Royal Air Force. Next morning his picture appeared.

Two days later another picture of him appeared. This time he was dressed only in black shorts, and he had squared up towards the cameraman with his boxing gloves on.

The headline said, *'Who will fight this man?'*

And Trinidad answered, 'Big Foot will fight this man.'

The excitement was intense when Big Foot agreed. Miguel Street was in the news, and even Hat was pleased.

Hat said, 'I know is stupid to say, but I hope Big Foot beat him.' And he went around the district placing bets with everyone who had money to throw away.

We turned up in strength at the stadium on the night.

Hat rushed madly here and there, waving a twenty-dollar bill, shouting, 'Twenty to five, Big Foot beat him.'

I bet Boyee six cents that Big Foot would lose.

And, in truth, when Big Foot came out to the ring, dancing disdainfully in the ring, without looking at anybody in the crowd, we felt pleased.

Hat shouted, 'That is man!'

I couldn't bear to look at the fight. I looked all the time at the only woman in the crowd. She was an American or a Canadian woman and she was nibbling at peanuts. She was so blonde, her hair looked like straw. Whenever a blow was landed, the crowd roared, and the woman pulled in her lips as though she had given the blow, and then she nibbled furiously at her peanuts. She never shouted or got up or waved her hands. I hated that woman.

The roars grew louder and more frequent.

I could hear Hat shouting, 'Come on, Big Foot. Beat him up.

Beat him up, man.' Then, with panic in his voice, 'Remember your father.'

But Hat's shouts died away.

Big Foot had lost the fight, on points.

Hat paid out about a hundred dollars in five minutes.

He said, 'I go have to sell the brown and white cow, the one I buy from George.'

Edward said, 'Is God work.'

Boyee said to me, 'I go give you your six cents tomorrow.'

I said, 'Six cents *tomorrow*? But what you think I is? A millionaire? Look, man, give me money now now, you hear.'

He paid up.

But the crowd was laughing, laughing.

I looked at the ring.

Big Foot was in tears. He was like a boy, and the more he cried, the louder he cried, and the more painful it sounded.

The secret I had held for Big Foot was now shown to everybody.

Hat said, 'What, he crying?' And Hat laughed.

He seemed to forget all about the cow. He said, 'Well, well, look at man, eh!'

And all of us from Miguel Street laughed at Big Foot.

All except me. For I knew how he felt although he was a big man and I was a boy. I wished I had never betted that six cents with Boyee.

The papers next morning said, 'PUGILIST SOBS IN RING.'

Trinidad thought it was Big Foot, the comedian, doing something funny again.

But we knew otherwise.

Big Foot left Miguel Street, and the last I heard of him was that he was a labourer in a quarry in Laventille.

*

About six months later a little scandal was rippling through Trinidad, making everybody feel silly.

The R.A.F. champion, it turned out, had never been in the R.A.F., and as a boxer he was completely unknown.

Hat said, 'Well, what you expect in a place like this?'

8. The Pyrotechnicist

A STRANGER could drive through Miguel Street and just say 'Slum!' because he could see no more. But we, who lived there, saw our street as a world, where everybody was quite different from everybody else. Man-man was mad; George was stupid; Big Foot was a bully; Hat was an adventurer; Popo was a philosopher; and Morgan was our comedian.

Or that was how we looked upon him. But looking back now after so many years, I think he deserved a lot more respect than we gave him. It was his own fault, of course. He was one of those men who deliberately set out to clown and wasn't happy unless people were laughing at him, and he was always thinking of new crazinesses which he hoped would amuse us. He was the sort of man who, having once created a laugh by sticking the match in his mouth and trying to light it with his cigarette, having once done that, does it over and over again.

Hat used to say, 'Is a damn nuisance, having that man trying to be funny all the time, when all of we well know that he not so happy at all.'

I felt that sometimes Morgan knew his jokes were not coming off, and that made him so miserable that we all felt unkind and nasty.

Morgan was the first artist I ever met in my life. He spent nearly all his time, even when he was playing the fool, thinking about beauty. Morgan made fireworks. He loved fireworks, and he was full of theories about fireworks. Something about the Cosmic Dance or the Dance of Life. But this was the sort of talk that went clean over our heads in Miguel Street. And when Morgan saw this, he would begin using even bigger words. Just for the joke. One of the big words I learnt from Morgan is the title of this sketch.

But very few people in Trinidad used Morgan's fireworks. All the big fêtes in the island passed – Races, Carnival, Discovery Day, the Indian Centenary – and while the rest of the island was going crazy with rum and music and pretty women by the sea, Morgan was just going crazy with rage.

Morgan used to go to the Savannah and watch the fireworks of his rivals, and hear the cheers of the crowd as the fireworks spattered and spangled the sky. He would come in a great temper and beat all his children. He had ten of them. His wife was too big for him to beat.

Hat would say, 'We better send for the fire-brigade.'

And for the next two or three hours Morgan would prowl in a stupid sort of way around his back-yard, letting off fireworks so crazily that we used to hear his wife shouting, 'Morgan, stop playing the ass. You make ten children and you have a wife, and you can't afford to go and dead now.'

Morgan would roar like a bull and beat on the galvanized-iron fence.

He would shout, 'Everybody want to beat me. Everybody.'

Hat said, 'You know we hearing the real Morgan now.'

These fits of craziness made Morgan a real terror. When the fits were on him, he had the idea that Bhakcu, the mechanical genius who was my uncle, was always ready to beat him, and at about eleven o'clock in the evenings, the idea just seemed to explode in his head.

He would beat on the fence and shout, 'Bhakcu, you fat-belly good-for-nothing son-of-a-bitch, come out and fight like a man.'

Bhakcu would keep on reading the *Ramayana*, in his doleful singing voice; lying flat on his belly on his bed.

Bhakcu was a big man, and Morgan was a very small man, with the smallest hands and the thinnest wrists in Miguel Street.

Mrs Bhakcu would say, 'Morgan, why you don't shut up and go to sleep?'

Mrs Morgan would reply, 'Hey, you thin-foot woman! You better leave my husband alone, you hear. Why you don't look after your own?'

Mrs Bhakcu would say, 'You better mind your mouth. Otherwise I come up and turn your face with one slap, you hear.'

Mrs Bhakcu was four feet high, three feet wide, and three feet deep. Mrs Morgan was a little over six feet tall and built like a weight-lifter.

Mrs Morgan said, 'Why you don't get your big-belly husband to go and fix some more motor-car, and stop reading that damn stupid sing-song he always sing-songing?'

By this time Morgan would be on the pavement with us, laughing in a funny sort of way, saying, 'Hear them women and them!' He would drink some rum from a hip-flask and say, 'Just watch and see. You know the calypso?

> The more they try to do me bad
> Is the better I live in Trinidad.

Is the same thing with me, you know. This time so next year, I go have the King of England and the King of America paying me millions to make fireworks for them. The most beautiful fireworks anybody ever see.'

And Hat or somebody else would ask, 'You go make the fireworks for them?'

Morgan would say, 'Make *what*? Make nothing. By this time so next year, I go have the King of England and the King of America paying me millions to make fireworks for them. The most beautiful fireworks anybody ever see.'

And, in the meantime, in the back of the yard, Mrs Bhakcu was saying, '*He* have big belly. But what yours have? I don't know what yours going to sit on next year this time, you hear.'

And next morning Morgan was as straight and sober as ever, talking about his experiments.

This Morgan was more like a bird than a man. It was not only that he was as thin as a match-stick. He had a long neck that could swivel like a bird's. His eyes were bright and restless. And when he spoke it was in a pecking sort of way, as though he was not throwing out words, but picking up corn. He walked with a quick, tripping step, looking back over his shoulder at somebody following who wasn't there.

Hat said, 'You know how he get so? Is his wife, you know. He fraid she too bad. Spanish woman, you know. Full of blood and fire.'

Boyee said, 'You suppose that is why he want to make fireworks so?'

Hat said, 'People funny like hell. You never know with them.'

But Morgan used to make a joke of even his appearance, flinging out his arms and feet when he knew people were looking at him.

Morgan also made fun of his wife and his ten children. 'Is a miracle to me,' he said, 'that a man like me have ten children. I don't know how I manage it.'

Edward said, 'How you sure is your children?'

Morgan laughed, and said, 'I have my doubts.'

*

Hat didn't like Morgan. He said, 'Is hard to say. But it have something about him I can't really take. I always feel he overdoing everything. I always feel the man lying about everything. I feel that he even lying to hisself.'

I don't think any of us understood what Hat meant. Morgan was becoming a little too troublesome, and it was hard for all of us to begin smiling as soon as we saw him, which was what he wanted.

Still his firework experiments continued and every now and then we heard an explosion from Morgan's house, and we saw the puffs of coloured smoke. This was one of the standing amusements of the street.

But as time went by and Morgan found that no one was willing to buy his fireworks, he began to make fun even of his fireworks. He was not content with the laughter of the street when there was an explosion in his house.

Hat said, 'When a man start laughing at something he fight for all the time, you don't know whether to laugh or cry.' And Hat decided that Morgan was just a fool.

I suppose it was because of Hat that we decided not to laugh at Morgan any more.

Hat said, 'It go make him stop playing the fool.'

But it didn't.

Morgan grew wilder than ever, and began challenging Bhakcu to fight about two or three times a week. He began beating his children more than ever.

And he made one last attempt to make us laugh.

I heard about it from Chris, Morgan's fourth son. We were in the café at the corner of Miguel Street.

Chris said, 'Is a crime to talk to you now, you know.'

I said, 'Don't tell me. Is the old man again?'

Chris nodded and he showed me a sheet of paper, headed CRIME AND PUNISHMENT.

Chris said with pride, 'Look at it.'

It was a long list, with entries like this:

For fighting	i) at home	Five strokes
	ii) in the street	Seven strokes
	iii) at school	Eight strokes

Chris looked at me and said in a very worried way, 'It funny like hell, eh? This sort of thing make blows a joke.'

I said yes, and asked, 'But you say is a crime to talk to me. Where it is?'

Chris showed me:

For talking to street rabs	Four strokes
For playing with street rabs	Eight strokes

I said, 'But your father don't mind talking to us. What wrong if you talk to us?'

Chris said, 'But this ain't nothing at all. You must come on Sunday and see what happen.'

I could see that Chris was pleased as anything.

About six of us went that Sunday. Morgan was there to meet us and he took us into his drawing-room. Then he disappeared. There were many chairs and benches as though there was going to be a concert. Morgan's eldest son was standing at a little table in the corner.

Suddenly this boy said, 'Stand!'

We all stood up, and Morgan appeared, smiling all round.

I asked Hat, 'Why he smiling so?'

Hat said, 'That is how the magistrates and them does smile when they come in court.'

Morgan's eldest son shouted, 'Andrew Morgan!'

Andrew Morgan came and stood before his father.

The eldest boy read very loudly, 'Andrew Morgan, you are charged with stoning the tamarind tree in Miss Dorothy's yard; you are charged with ripping off three buttons for the purpose of purchasing some marbles; you are charged with fighting Dorothy Morgan; you are charged with stealing two *tolums* and three sugar-cakes. Do you plead guilty or not guilty?'

Andrew said, 'Guilty.'

Morgan, scribbling on a sheet of paper, looked up.

'Have you anything to say?'

Andrew said, 'I sorry, sir.'

Morgan said, 'We will let the sentences run concurrently. Twelve strokes.'

One by one, the Morgan children were judged and sentenced. Even the eldest boy had to receive some punishment.

Morgan then rose and said, 'These sentences will be carried out this afternoon.'

He smiled all round, and left the room.

*

The joke misfired completely.

Hat said, 'Nah, nah, man, you can't make fun of your own self and your own children that way, and invite all the street to see. Nah, it ain't right.'

I felt the joke was somehow terrible and frightening.

And when Morgan came out on the pavement that evening, his face fixed in a smile, he got none of the laughter he had expected. Nobody ran up to him and clapped him on the back, saying, 'But this man Morgan really mad, you hear. You hear how he beating his children these days . . .?' No one said anything like that. No one said anything to him.

It was easy to see he was shattered.

Morgan got really drunk that night and challenged everybody to fight. He even challenged me.

Mrs Morgan had padlocked the front gate, so Morgan could only run about in his yard. He was as mad as a mad bull, bellowing and butting at the fence. He kept saying over and over again, 'You people think I not a man, eh? My father had eight children. I is his son. I have ten. I better than all of you put together.'

Hat said, 'He soon go start crying and then he go sleep.'

But I spent a lot of time that night before going to sleep thinking about Morgan, feeling sorry for him because of that little devil he had inside him. For that was what I thought was wrong with him. I fancied that inside him was a red, grinning devil pricking Morgan with his fork.

*

Mrs Morgan and the children went to the country.

Morgan no longer came out to the pavement, seeking our company. He was busy with his experiments. There were a series of minor explosions and lots of smoke.

Apart from that, peace reigned in our end of Miguel Street.

I wondered what Morgan was doing and thinking in all that solitude.

The following Sunday it rained heavily, and everyone was forced to go to bed early. The street was wet and glistening, and by eleven there was no noise save for the patter of the rain on the corrugated-iron roofs.

A short, sharp shout cracked through the street, and got us up.

I could hear windows being flung open, and I heard people saying, 'What happen? What happen?'

'Is Morgan. Is Morgan. Something happening by Morgan.'

I was already out in the street and in front of Morgan's house. I never slept in pyjamas. I wasn't in that class.

The first thing I saw in the darkness of Morgan's yard was the figure of a woman hurrying away from the house to the back gate that opened on to the sewage trace between Miguel Street and Alfonso Street.

It was drizzling now, not very hard, and in no time at all quite a crowd had joined me.

It was all a bit mysterious – the shout, the woman disappearing, the dark house.

Then we heard Mrs Morgan shouting, 'Teresa Blake, Teresa Blake, what you doing with my man?' It was a cry of great pain.

Mrs Bhakcu was at my side. 'I always know about this Teresa, but I keep my mouth shut.'

Bhakcu said, 'Yes, you know everything, like your mother.'

A light came on in the house.

Then it went off again.

We heard Mrs Morgan saying, 'Why you fraid the light so for? Ain't you is man? Put the light on, let we see the great big man you is.'

The light went on; then off again.

We heard Morgan's voice, but it was so low we couldn't make out what he was saying.

Mrs Morgan said, 'Yes, hero.' And the light came on again.

We heard Morgan mumbling again.

Mrs Morgan said, 'No, hero.'

The light went off; then it went on.

Mrs Morgan was saying, 'Leave the light on. Come, let we show the big big hero to the people in the street. Come, let we show them what man really make like. You is not a antiman, you is real man. You ain't only make ten children with me, you going to make more with somebody else.'

We heard Morgan's voice, a fluting unhappy thing.

Mrs Morgan said, 'But what you fraid now for? Ain't you is the funny man? The clown? Come, let them see see the clown and the big man you is. Let them see what man really make like.'

Morgan was wailing by this time, and trying to talk.

Mrs Morgan was saying, 'If you try to put that light off, I break up your little thin tail like a match-stick here, you hear.'

Then the front door was flung open, and we saw.

Mrs Morgan was holding up Morgan by his waist. He was

practically naked, and he looked so thin, he was like a boy with an old man's face. He wasn't looking at us, but at Mrs Morgan's face, and he was squirming in her grasp, trying to get away. But Mrs Morgan was a strong woman.

Mrs Morgan was looking not at us, but at the man in her arm.

She was saying, 'But this is the big man I have, eh? So this is the man I married and slaving all my life for?' And then she began laughing, in a croaking, nasty way.

She looked at us for a moment, and said, 'Well, laugh now. He don't mind. He always want people to laugh at him.'

And the sight was so comic, the thin man held up so easily by the fat woman, that we did laugh. It was the sort of laugh that begins gently and then builds up into a bellowing belly laugh.

For the first time since he came to Miguel Street, Morgan was really being laughed at by the people.

*

And it broke him completely.

All the next day we waited for him to come out to the pavement, to congratulate him with our laughter. But we didn't see him.

Hat said, 'When I was little, my mother used to tell me, "Boy, you laughing all day. I bet you, you go cry tonight."'

*

That night my sleep was again disturbed. By shouts and sirens.

I looked through the window and saw a red sky and red smoke.

Morgan's house was on fire.

And what a fire! Photographers from the papers were climbing up into other people's houses to get their pictures, and people were looking at them and not at the fire. Next morning there was a first-class picture with me part of the crowd in the top right-hand corner.

But what a fire it was! It was the most beautiful fire in Port of

Spain since 1933 when the Treasury (of all places) burnt down, and the calypsonian sang:

> It was a glorious and a beautiful scenery
> Was the burning of the Treasury.

What really made the fire beautiful was Morgan's fireworks going off. Then for the first time everybody saw the astonishing splendour of Morgan's fireworks. People who used to scoff at Morgan felt a little silly. I have travelled in many countries since, but I have seen nothing to beat the fireworks show in Morgan's house that night.

But Morgan made no more fireworks.

Hat said, 'When I was a little boy, my mother used to say, "If a man want something, and he want it really bad, he does get it, but when he get it he don't like it."'

Both of Morgan's ambitions were fulfilled. People laughed at him, and they still do. And he made the most beautiful fireworks in the world. But as Hat said, when a man gets something he wants badly, he doesn't like it.

*

As we expected, the thing came out in court. Morgan was charged with arson. The newspaper people had a lot of fun with Morgan, within the libel laws. One headline I remember: *Pyrotechnist Alleged Pyromaniac*.

But I was glad, though, that Morgan got off.

They said Morgan went to Venezuela. They said he went mad. They said he became a jockey in Colombia. They said all sorts of things, but the people of Miguel Street were always romancers.

9. Titus Hoyt, I.A.

THIS MAN WAS born to be an active and important member of a local road board in the country. An unkind fate had placed him in the city. He was a natural guide, philosopher and friend to anyone who stopped to listen.

Titus Hoyt was the first man I met when I came to Port of Spain, a year or two before the war.

My mother had fetched me from Chaguanas after my father died. We travelled up by train and took a bus to Miguel Street. It was the first time I had travelled in a city bus.

I said to my mother, 'Ma, look, they forget to ring the bell here.'

My mother said, 'If you ring the bell you damn well going to get off and walk home by yourself, you hear.'

And then a little later I said, 'Ma, look, the sea.'

People in the bus began to laugh.

My mother was really furious.

Early next morning my mother said, 'Look now, I giving you four cents. Go to the shop on the corner of this road, Miguel Street, and buy two hops bread for a cent apiece, and buy a penny butter. And come back quick.'

I found the shop and I bought the bread and butter – the red, salty type of butter.

Then I couldn't find my way back.

I found about six Miguel Streets, but none seemed to have my house. After a long time walking up and down I began to cry. I sat down on the pavement, and got my shoes wet in the gutter.

Some little white girls were playing in a yard behind me. I looked at them, still crying. A girl wearing a pink frock came out and said, 'Why you crying?'

I said, 'I lost.'

She put her hands on my shoulder and said, 'Don't cry. You know where you live?'

I pulled out a piece of paper from my shirt pocket and showed her. Then a man came up. He was wearing white shorts and a white shirt, and he looked funny.

The man said, 'Why he crying?' In a gruff, but interested way.

The girl told him.

The man said, 'I will take him home.'

I asked the girl to come too.

The man said, 'Yes, you better come to explain to his mother.'

The girl said, 'All right, Mr Titus Hoyt.'

That was one of the first things about Titus Hoyt that I found interesting. The girl calling him 'Mr Titus Hoyt'. Not Titus, or Mr Hoyt, but Mr Titus Hoyt. I later realized that everyone who knew him called him that.

When we got home the girl explained to my mother what had happened, and my mother was ashamed of me.

Then the girl left.

Mr Titus Hoyt looked at me and said, 'He look like a intelligent little boy.'

My mother said in a sarcastic way, 'Like his father.'

Titus Hoyt said, 'Now, young man, if a herring and a half cost a penny and a half, what's the cost of three herrings?'

Even in the country, in Chaguanas, we had heard about that.

Without waiting, I said, 'Three pennies.'

Titus Hoyt regarded me with wonder.

He told my mother, 'This boy bright like anything, ma'am.

You must take care of him and send him to a good school and feed him good food so he could study well.'

My mother didn't say anything.

When Titus Hoyt left, he said, 'Cheerio!'

That was the second interesting thing about him.

My mother beat me for getting my shoes wet in the gutter but she said she wouldn't beat me for getting lost.

For the rest of that day I ran about the yard saying, 'Cheerio! Cheerio!' to a tune of my own.

That evening Titus Hoyt came again.

My mother didn't seem to mind.

To me Titus Hoyt said, 'You can read?'

I said yes.

'And write?'

I said yes.

'Well, look,' he said, 'get some paper and a pencil and write what I tell you.'

I said, 'Paper and pencil?'

He nodded.

I ran to the kitchen and said, 'Ma, you got any paper and pencil?'

My mother said, 'What you think I is? A shopkeeper?'

Titus Hoyt shouted, 'Is for me, ma'am.'

My mother said, 'Oh.' In a disappointed way.

She said, 'In the bottom drawer of the bureau you go find my purse. It have a pencil in it.'

And she gave me a copy-book from the kitchen shelf.

Mr Titus Hoyt said, 'Now, young man, write. Write the address of this house in the top right-hand corner, and below that, the date.' Then he asked, 'You know who we writing this letter to, boy?'

I shook my head.

He said, 'Ha, boy! Ha! We writing to the *Guardian*, boy.'

I said, 'The *Trinidad Guardian*? The paper? What, *me* writing to the *Guardian*! But only big big man does write to the *Guardian*.'

Titus Hoyt smiled. 'That's *why* you writing. It go surprise them.'

I said, 'What I go write to them about?'

He said, 'You go write it now. Write. To the Editor, *Trinidad Guardian*. Dear Sir, I am but a child of eight (How old you is? Well, it don't matter anyway) and yesterday my mother sent me to make a purchase in the city. This, dear Mr Editor, was my first peregrination p-e-r-e-g-r-i-n-a-t-i-o-n in this metropolis, and I had the misfortune to wander from the path my mother had indicated – '

I said, 'Oh God, Mr Titus Hoyt, where you learn all these big words and them? You sure you spelling them right?'

Titus Hoyt smiled. 'I spend all afternoon making up this letter,' he said.

I wrote: ' . . . and in this state of despair I was rescued by a Mr Titus Hoyt, of Miguel Street. This only goes to show, dear Mr Editor, that human kindness is a quality not yet extinct in this world.'

The *Guardian* never printed the letter.

When I next saw Titus Hoyt, he said, 'Well, never mind. One day, boy, one day, I go make them sit up and take notice of every word I say. Just wait and see.'

And before he left, he said, 'Drinking your milk?'

He had persuaded my mother to give me half a pint of milk every day. Milk was good for the brains.

It is one of the sadnesses of my life that I never fulfilled Titus Hoyt's hopes for my academic success.

I still remember with tenderness the interest he took in me. Sometimes his views clashed with my mother's. There was the business of the cobwebs, for instance.

Boyee, with whom I had become friendly very quickly, was

teaching me to ride. I had fallen and cut myself nastily on the shin.

My mother was attempting to cure this with sooty cobwebs soaked in rum.

Titus Hoyt was horrified. 'You ain't know what you doing,' he shouted.

My mother said, 'Mr Titus Hoyt, I will kindly ask you to mind your own business. The day you make a baby yourself I go listen to what you have to say.'

Titus Hoyt refused to be ridiculed. He said, 'Take the boy to the doctor, man.'

I was watching them argue, not caring greatly either way.

In the end I went to the doctor.

Titus Hoyt reappeared in a new role.

He told my mother, 'For the last two three months I been taking the first-aid course with the Red Cross. I go dress the boy foot for you.'

That really terrified me.

For about a month or so afterwards, people in Miguel Street could tell when it was nine o'clock in the morning. By my shrieks. Titus Hoyt loved his work.

All this gives some clue to the real nature of the man.

The next step followed naturally.

Titus Hoyt began to teach.

It began in a small way, after the fashion of all great enterprises.

He had decided to sit for the external arts degree of London University. He began to learn Latin, teaching himself, and as fast as he learned, he taught us.

He rounded up three or four of us and taught us in the verandah of his house. He kept chickens in his yard and the place stank.

That Latin stage didn't last very long. We got as far as the fourth declension, and then Boyee and Errol and myself began asking questions. They were not the sort of questions Titus Hoyt liked.

Boyee said, 'Mr Titus Hoyt, I think you making up all this, you know, making it up as you go on.'

Titus Hoyt said, 'But I telling you, I not making it up. Look, here it is in black and white.'

Errol said, 'I feel, Mr Titus Hoyt, that one man sit down one day and make all this up and have everybody else learning it.'

Titus Hoyt asked me, 'What is the accusative singular of *bellum*?'

Feeling wicked, because I was betraying him, I said to Titus Hoyt, 'Mr Titus Hoyt, when you was my age, how you woulda feel if somebody did ask you that question?'

And then Boyee asked, 'Mr Titus Hoyt, what is the meaning of the ablative case?'

So the Latin lessons ended.

*

But however much we laughed at him, we couldn't deny that Titus Hoyt was a deep man.

Hat used to say, 'He is a thinker, that man.'

Titus Hoyt thought about all sorts of things, and he thought dangerous things sometimes.

Hat said, 'I don't think Titus Hoyt like God, you know.'

Titus Hoyt would say, 'The thing that really matter is faith. Look, I believe that if I pull out this bicycle-lamp from my pocket here, and set it up somewhere, and really really believe in it and pray to it, what I pray for go come. That is what I believe.'

And so saying he would rise and leave, not forgetting to say, 'Cheerio!'

He had the habit of rushing up to us and saying, 'Silence, everybody. I just been thinking. Listen to what I just been thinking.'

One day he rushed up and said, 'I been thinking how this war could end. If Europe could just sink for five minutes all the Germans go drown – '

Eddoes said, 'But England go drown too.'

Titus Hoyt agreed and looked sad. 'I lose my head, man,' he said. 'I lose my head.'

And he wandered away, muttering to himself, and shaking his head.

One day he cycled right up to us when we were talking about the Barbados-Trinidad cricket match. Things were not going well for Trinidad and we were worried.

Titus Hoyt rushed up and said, 'Silence. I just been thinking. Look, boys, it ever strike you that the world not real at all? It ever strike you that we have the only mind in the world and you just thinking up everything else? Like me here, having the only mind in the world, and thinking up you people here, thinking up the war and all the houses and the ships and them in the harbour. That ever cross your mind?'

*

His interest in teaching didn't die.

We often saw him going about with big books. These books were about teaching.

Titus Hoyt used to say, 'Is a science, man. The trouble with Trinidad is that the teachers don't have this science of teaching.'

And, 'Is the biggest thing in the world, man. Having the minds of the young to train. Think of that. Think.'

It soon became clear that whatever we thought about it Titus Hoyt was bent on training our minds.

He formed the Miguel Street Literary and Social Youth Club, and had it affiliated to the Trinidad and Tobago Youth Association.

We used to meet in his house which was well supplied with things to eat and drink. The walls of his house were now hung with improving quotations, some typed, some cut out of magazines and pasted on bits of cardboard.

I also noticed a big thing called 'Time-table'.

From this I gathered that Titus Hoyt was to rise at five-thirty, read Something from Greek philosophers until six, spend fifteen minutes bathing and exercising, another five reading the morning paper, and ten on breakfast. It was a formidable thing altogether.

Titus Hoyt said, 'If I follow the time-table I will be a educated man in about three four years.'

The Miguel Street Club didn't last very long.

It was Titus Hoyt's fault.

No man in his proper senses would have made Boyee secretary. Most of Boyee's minutes consisted of the names of people present.

And then we all had to write and read something.

The Miguel Street Literary and Social Club became nothing more than a gathering of film critics.

Titus Hoyt said, 'No, man. We just can't have all you boys talking about pictures all the time. I will have to get some propaganda for you boys.'

Boyee said, 'Mr Titus Hoyt, what we want with propaganda? Is a German thing.'

Titus Hoyt smiled. 'That is not the proper meaning of the word, boy. I am using the word in it proper meaning. Is education, boy, that makes me know things like that.'

Boyee was sent as our delegate to the Youth Association annual conference.

When he came back Boyee said, 'Is a helluva thing at that youth conference. Is only a pack of old, old people it have there.'

The attraction of the Coca-Cola and the cakes and the ice-cream began to fade. Some of us began staying away from meetings.

Titus Hoyt made one last effort to keep the club together.

One day he said, 'Next Sunday the club will go on a visit to Fort George.'

There were cries of disapproval.

Titus Hoyt said, 'You see, you people don't care about your country. How many of you know about Fort George? Not one of you here know about the place. But is history, man, your history, and you must learn about things like that. You must remember that the boys and girls of today are the men and women of tomorrow. The old Romans had a saying, you know. *Mens sana in corpore sano.* I think we will make the walk to Fort George.'

Still no one wanted to go.

Titus Hoyt said, 'At the top of Fort George it have a stream, and it cool cool and the water crystal clear. You could bathe there when we get to the top.'

We couldn't resist that.

The next Sunday a whole group of us took the trolley-bus to Mucurapo.

When the conductor came round to collect the fares, Titus Hoyt said, 'Come back a little later.' And he paid the conductor only when we got off the bus. The fare for everybody came up to about two shillings. But Titus Hoyt gave the conductor a shilling, saying, 'We don't want any ticket, man!' The conductor and Titus Hoyt laughed.

It was a long walk up the hill, red and dusty, and hot.

Titus Hoyt told us, 'This fort was built at a time when the French and them was planning to invade Trinidad.'

We gasped.

We had never realized that anyone considered us so important.

Titus Hoyt said, 'That was in 1803, when we was fighting Napoleon.'

We saw a few old rusty guns at the side of the path and heaps of rusty cannon-balls.

I asked, 'The French invade Trinidad, Mr Titus Hoyt?'

Titus Hoyt shook his head in a disappointed way. 'No, they didn't attack. But we was ready, man. Ready for them.'

Boyee said, 'You sure it have this stream up there you tell us about, Mr Titus Hoyt?'

Titus Hoyt said, 'What you think I is? A liar?'

Boyee said, 'I ain't saying nothing.'

We walked and sweated. Boyee took off his shoes.

Errol said, 'If it ain't have that stream up there, somebody going to catch hell.'

We got to the top, had a quick look at the graveyard where there were a few tombstones of British soldiers dead long ago; and we looked through the telescope at the city of Port of Spain large and sprawling beneath us. We could see the people walking in the streets as large as life.

Then we went looking for the stream.

We couldn't find it.

Titus Hoyt said, 'It must be here somewhere. When I was a boy I use to bathe in it.'

Boyee said, 'And what happen now? It dry up?'

Titus Hoyt said, 'It look so.'

Boyee got really mad, and you couldn't blame him. It was hard work coming up that hill, and we were all hot and thirsty.

He insulted Titus Hoyt in a very crude way.

Titus Hoyt said, 'Remember, Boyee, you are the secretary of the Miguel Street Literary and Social Club. Remember that you have just attended a meeting of the Youth Association as our delegate. Remember these things.'

Boyee said, 'Go to hell, Hoyt.'

We were aghast.

So the Literary Club broke up.

*

It wasn't long after that Titus Hoyt got his Inter Arts degree and set up a school of his own. He had a big sign placed in his garden:

Titus Hoyt, I.A. (London, External) *Passes in the Cambridge School Certificate Guaranteed*

One year the *Guardian* had a brilliant idea. They started the Needy Cases Fund to help needy cases at Christmas. It was popular and after a few years was called The Neediest Cases Fund. At the beginning of November the *Guardian* announced the target for the fund and it was a daily excitement until Christmas Eve to see how the fund rose. It was always front page news and everybody who gave got his name in the papers.

In the middle of December one year, when the excitement was high, Miguel Street was in the news.

Hat showed us the paper and we read:

FOLLOW THE EXAMPLE OF THIS TINYMITE!

The smallest and most touching response to our appeal to bring Yuletide cheer to the unfortunate has come in a letter from Mr Titus Hoyt, I.A., a headmaster of Miguel Street, Port of Spain. The letter was sent to Mr Hoyt by one of his pupils who wishes to remain anonymous. We have Mr Hoyt's permission to print the letter in full.

'Dear Mr Hoyt, I am only eight and, as you doubtless know, I am a member of the GUARDIAN Tinymites League. I read Aunt Juanita every Sunday. You, dear Mr Hoyt, have always extolled the virtue of charity and you have spoken repeatedly of the fine work the GUARDIAN Neediest Cases Fund is doing to bring Yuletide cheer to the unfortunate. I have decided to yield to your earnest entreaty. I have very little money to offer – a mere six cents, in fact, but take it, Mr Hoyt, and send it to the GUARDIAN Neediest Cases Fund. May it bring Yuletide cheer to some poor unfortunate! I know it is not much. But, like the widow, I give my mite. I remain, dear Mr Hoyt, One of Your Pupils.'

And there was a large photograph of Titus Hoyt, smiling and pop-eyed in the flash of the camera.

10. The Maternal Instinct

I SUPPOSE LAURA holds a world record.

Laura had eight children.

There is nothing surprising in that.

These eight children had seven fathers.

Beat that!

It was Laura who gave me my first lesson in biology. She lived just next door to us, and I found myself observing her closely.

I would notice her belly rising for months.

Then I would miss her for a short time.

And the next time I saw her she would be quite flat.

And the leavening process would begin again in a few months.

To me this was one of the wonders of the world in which I lived, and I always observed Laura. She herself was quite gay about what was happening to her. She used to point to it, and say, 'This thing happening again, but you get use to it after the first three four times. Is a damn nuisance, though.'

She used to blame God, and speak about the wickedness of men.

For her first six children she tried six different men.

Hat used to say, 'Some people hard to please.'

But I don't want to give you the impression that Laura spent all her time having babies and decrying men, and generally feeling sorry for herself. If Bogart was the most bored person in the street,

Laura was the most vivacious. She was always gay, and she liked me.

She would give me plums and mangoes when she had them; and whenever she made sugar-cakes she would give me some.

Even my mother, who had a great dislike of laughter, especially in me, even my mother used to laugh at Laura.

She often said to me, 'I don't know why Laura muching you up so for. Like she ain't have enough children to mind.'

I think my mother was right. I don't think a woman like Laura could have ever had too many children. She loved all her children, though you wouldn't have believed it from the language she used when she spoke to them. Some of Laura's shouts and curses were the richest things I have ever heard, and I shall never forget them.

Hat said once, 'Man, she like Shakespeare when it come to using words.'

Laura used to shout, 'Alwyn, you broad-mouth brute, come here.'

And, 'Gavin, if you don't come here this minute, I make you fart fire, you hear.'

And, 'Lorna, you black bow-leg bitch, why you can't look what you doing?'

*

Now, to compare Laura, the mother of eight, with Mary the Chinese, also mother of eight, doesn't seem fair. Because Mary took really good care of her children and never spoke harshly to them. But Mary, mark you, had a husband who owned a shop, and Mary could afford to be polite and nice to her children, after stuffing them full of chop-suey and chow-min, and chow-fan, and things with names like that. But who could Laura look to for money to keep her children?

The men who cycled slowly past Laura's house in the evening, whistling for Laura, were not going to give any of their money to Laura's children. They just wanted Laura.

I asked my mother, 'How Laura does live?'

My mother slapped me, saying, 'You know, you too fast for a little boy.'

I suspected the worst.

But I wouldn't have liked that to be true.

So I asked Hat. Hat said, 'She have a lot of friends who does sell in the market. They does give she things free, and sometimes one or two or three of she husbands does give she something too, but that not much.'

The oddest part of the whole business was Laura herself. Laura was no beauty. As Boyee said one day, 'She have a face like the top of a motor-car battery.' And she was a little more than plump.

I am talking now of the time when she had had only six children.

*

One day Hat said, 'Laura have a new man.'

Everybody laughed, 'Stale news. If Laura have she way, she go try every man once.'

But Hat said, 'No, is serious. He come to live with she for good now. I see him this morning when I was taking out the cows.'

We watched and waited for this man.

We later learned that he was watching and waiting for us.

In no time at all this man, Nathaniel, had become one of the gang in Miguel Street. But it was clear that he was not really one of us. He came from the east end of Port of Spain, which we considered dirtier; and his language was really coarse.

He made out that he was a kind of terror in the east end around Piccadilly Street. He told many stories about gang-fights, and he let it be known that he had disfigured two or three people.

Hat said, 'I think he lying like hell, you know.'

I distrusted him myself. He was a small man, and I always felt that small men were more likely to be wicked and violent.

But what really sickened us was his attitude to women. We were none of us chivalrous, but Nathaniel had a contempt for women which we wouldn't like. He would make rude remarks when women passed.

Nathaniel would say, 'Women just like cows. Cow and they is the same thing.'

And when Miss Ricaud, the welfare woman, passed, Nathaniel would say, 'Look at that big cow.'

Which wasn't in good taste, for we all thought that Miss Ricaud was too fat to be laughed at, and ought instead to be pitied.

Nathaniel, in the early stages, tried to make us believe that he knew how to keep Laura in her place. He hinted that he used to beat her. He used to say, 'Woman and them like a good dose of blows, you know. You know the calypso:

> Every now and then just knock them down.
> Every now and then just throw them down.
> Black up their eye and bruise up their knee
> And then they love you eternally.

Is gospel truth about woman.'

Hat said, 'Woman is a funny thing, for truth, though. I don't know what a woman like Laura see in Nathaniel.'

Eddoes said, 'I know a helluva lot about woman. I think Nathaniel lying like hell. I think when he with Laura he got his tail between his legs all the time.'

We used to hear fights and hear the children screaming all over the place, and when we saw Nathaniel, he would just say, 'Just been beating some sense into that woman.'

Hat said, 'Is a funny thing. Laura don't look any sadder.'

Nathaniel said, 'Is only blows she really want to keep she happy.'

Nathaniel was lying of course. It wasn't he who was giving the blows, it was Laura. That came out the day when Nathaniel tried to wear a hat to cover up a beaten eye.

Eddoes said, 'It look like they make up that calypso about men, not women.'

Nathaniel tried to get at Eddoes, who was small and thin. But Hat said, 'Go try that on Laura. I know Laura. Laura just trying not to beat you up too bad just to keep you with she, but the day she start getting tired of you, you better run, boy.'

We prayed for something to happen to make Nathaniel leave Miguel Street.

Hat said, 'We ain't have to wait long. Laura making baby eight months now. Another month, and Nathaniel gone.'

Eddoes said, 'That would be a real record. Seven children with seven different man.'

The baby came.

It was on a Saturday. Just the evening before I had seen Laura standing in her yard leaning on the fence.

The baby came at eight o'clock in the morning. And, like a miracle, just two hours later, Laura was calling across to my mother.

I hid and looked.

Laura was leaning on her window-sill. She was eating a mango, and the yellow juice was smeared all over her face.

She was saying to my mother, 'The baby come this morning.'

And my mother only said, 'Boy or girl?'

Laura said, 'What sort of luck you think I have? It looks like I really blight. Is another girl. I just thought I would let you know, that's all. Well, I got to go now. I have to do some sewing.'

And that very evening it looked as though what Hat said was going to come true. For that evening Laura came out to the pavement and shouted to Nathaniel, 'Hey, Nathaniel, come here.'

Hat said, 'But what the hell is this? Ain't is this morning she make baby?'

Nathaniel tried to show off to us. He said to Laura, 'I busy. I ain't coming.'

Laura advanced, and I could see fight in her manner. She said, 'You ain't coming? Ain't coming? But what is this I hearing?'

Nathaniel was worried. He tried to talk to us, but he wasn't talking in a sensible way.

Laura said, 'You think you is a man. But don't try playing man with me, you hear. Yes, Nathaniel, is you I talking to, you with your bottom like two stale bread in you pants.'

This was one of Laura's best, and we all began laughing. When she saw us laughing, Laura burst out too.

Hat said, 'This woman is a real case.'

*

But even after the birth of his baby Nathaniel didn't leave Miguel Street. We were a little worried.

Hat said, 'If she don't look out she go have another baby with the same man, you know.'

It wasn't Laura's fault that Nathaniel didn't go. She knocked him about a lot, and did so quite openly now. Sometimes she locked him out, and then we would hear Nathaniel crying and coaxing from the pavement, 'Laura, darling, Laura, *doux-doux*, just let me come in tonight. Laura, *doux-doux*, let me come in.'

He had dropped all pretence now of keeping Laura in her place. He no longer sought our company, and we were glad of that.

Hat used to say, 'I don't know why he don't go back to the Dry River where he come from. They ain't have any culture there, and he would be happier.'

I couldn't understand why he stayed.

Hat said, 'It have some man like that. They like woman to kick them around.'

And Laura was getting angrier with Nathaniel.

One day we heard her tell him, 'You think because you give me one baby, you own me. That baby only come by accident, you hear.'

She threatened to get the police.

Nathaniel said, 'But who go mind your children?'

Laura said, 'That is my worry. I don't want you here. You is only another mouth to feed. And if you don't leave me right right now I go go and call Sergeant Charles for you.'

It was this threat of the police that made Nathaniel leave.

He was in tears.

But Laura was swelling out again.

Hat said, 'Oh, God! Two babies by the same man!'

*

One of the miracles of life in Miguel Street was that no one starved. If you sit down at a table with pencil and paper and try to work it out, you will find it impossible. But I lived in Miguel Street, and can assure you that no one starved. Perhaps they did go hungry, but you never heard about it.

Laura's children grew.

The eldest daughter, Lorna, began working as a servant in a house in St Clair and took typing lessons from a man in Sackville Street.

Laura used to say, 'It have nothing like education in the world. I don't want my children to grow like me.'

In time, Laura delivered her eighth baby, as effortlessly as usual.

That baby was her last.

It wasn't that she was tired or that she had lost her love of the human race or lost her passion for adding to it. As a matter of fact, Laura never seemed to grow any older or less cheerful. I always felt that, given the opportunity, she could just go on and on having babies.

*

The eldest daughter, Lorna, came home from her typing lessons late one night and said, 'Ma, I going to make a baby.'

I heard the shriek that Laura gave.

And for the first time I heard Laura crying. It wasn't ordinary crying. She seemed to be crying all the cry she had saved up since she was born; all the cry she had tried to cover up with her laughter. I have heard people cry at funerals, but there is a lot of showing-off in their crying. Laura's crying that night was the most terrible thing I had heard. It made me feel that the world was a stupid, sad place, and I almost began crying with Laura.

All the street heard Laura crying.

Next day Boyee said, 'I don't see why she so mad about that. She does do the same.'

Hat got so annoyed that he took off his leather belt and beat Boyee.

I didn't know who I felt sorrier for – Laura or her daughter.

I felt that Laura was ashamed now to show herself in the street. When I did see her I found it hard to believe that she was the same woman who used to laugh with me and give me sugar-cakes.

She was an old woman now.

She no longer shouted at her children, no longer beat them. I don't know whether she was taking especial care of them or whether she had lost interest in them.

But we never heard Laura say a word of reproach to Lorna.

That was terrible.

Lorna brought her baby home. There were no jokes about it in the street.

Laura's house was a dead, silent house.

Hat said, 'Life is helluva thing. You can see trouble coming and you can't do a damn thing to prevent it coming. You just got to sit and watch and wait.'

*

According to the papers, it was just another week-end tragedy, one of many.

Lorna was drowned at Carenage.

Hat said, 'Is what they always do, swim out and out until they tired and can't swim no more.'

And when the police came to tell Laura about it, she had said very little.

Laura said, 'It good. It good. It better that way.'

11. The Blue Cart

THERE WERE MANY reasons why I wanted to be like Eddoes when I grew up.

He was one of the aristocrats of the street. He drove a scavenging-cart and so worked only in the mornings.

Then, as everybody said, Eddoes was a real 'saga-boy'. This didn't mean that he wrote epic poetry. It meant that he was a 'sweet-man', a man of leisure, well-dressed, and keen on women.

Hat used to say, 'For a man who does drive a scavenging-cart, this Eddoes too clean, you hear.'

Eddoes was crazy about cleanliness.

He used to brush his teeth for hours.

In fact, if you were telling a stranger about Eddoes you would say, 'You know – the little fellow with a tooth-brush always in his mouth.'

This was one thing in Eddoes I really admired. Once I stuck a tooth-brush in my mouth and walked about our yard in the middle of the day.

My mother said, 'You playing man? But why you don't wait until your pee make froth?'

That made me miserable for days.

But it didn't prevent me taking the tooth-brush to school and wearing it there. It caused quite a stir. But I quickly realized that only a man like Eddoes could have worn a tooth-brush and carried it off.

Eddoes was always well-dressed. His khaki trousers were always creased and his shoes always shone. He wore his shirts with three buttons undone so you could see his hairy chest. His shirt cuffs were turned up just above the wrist and you could see his gold wrist-watch.

Even when Eddoes wore a coat you saw the watch. From the way he wore the coat you thought that Eddoes hadn't realized that the end of the coat-sleeve had been caught in the watch-strap.

It was only when I grew up I realized how small and how thin Eddoes really was.

I asked Hat, 'You think is true all this talk Eddoes giving us about how woman running after him?'

Hat said, 'Well, boy, woman these days funny like hell. They go run after a dwarf if he got money.'

I said, 'I don't believe you.'

I was very young at the time.

But I always thought, 'If it have one man in this world woman bound to like, that man is Eddoes.'

He sat on his blue cart with so much grace. And how smart that tooth-brush was in his mouth!

But you couldn't talk to him when he was on his cart. Then he was quite different from the Eddoes we knew on the ground, then he never laughed, but was always serious. And if we tried to ride on the back of his cart, as we used to on the back of the ice-cart, Eddoes would crack his whip at us in a nasty way, and shout, 'What sort of cart you think this is? Your father can't buy cart like this, you hear?'

Every year Eddoes won the City Council's award for the cleanest scavenging-cart.

And to hear Eddoes talk about his job was to make yourself feel sad and inferior.

He said he knew everybody important in Port of Spain, from the Governor down.

He would say, 'Collected two three tins of rubbish from the Director of Medical Services yesterday. I know him good, you know. Been collecting his rubbish for years, ever since he was a little doctor in Woodbrook, catching hell. So I see him yesterday and he say, "Eddoes (that is how he does always call me, you know) Eddoes," he say, "come and have a drink." Well, when I working I don't like drinking because it does keep you back. But he nearly drag me off the cart, man. In the end I had to drink with him. He tell me all his troubles.'

There were also stories of rich women waiting for him behind rubbish tins, women begging Eddoes to take away their rubbish.

But you should have seen Eddoes on those days when the scavengers struck. As I have told you already, these scavengers were proud people and stood for no nonsense from anybody.

They knew they had power. They could make Port of Spain stink in twenty-four hours if they struck.

On these important days Eddoes would walk slowly and thoughtfully up and down Miguel Street. He looked grim then, and fierce, and he wouldn't speak to a soul.

He wore a red scarf and a tooth-brush with a red handle on these days.

Sometimes we went to Woodford Square to the strike meeting, to gaze at these exciting people.

It amazed me to see Eddoes singing. The songs were violent, but Eddoes looked so sad.

Hat told me, 'It have detectives here, you know. They taking down every word Eddoes and them saying.'

It was easy to recognize the detectives. They were wearing a sort of plain clothes uniform – brown hats, white shirts, and brown trousers. They were writing in big note-books with red pencils.

And Eddoes didn't look scared!

We all knew that Eddoes wasn't a man to be played with.

*

You couldn't blame Eddoes then for being proud.

One day Eddoes brought home a pair of shoes and showed it to us in a quiet way, as though he wasn't really interested whether we looked at the shoes or not.

He said, brushing his teeth, and looking away from us, 'Got these shoes today from the *labasse*, the dump, you know. They was just lying there and I pick them up.'

We whistled. The shoes were practically new.

'The things people does throw away,' Eddoes said.

And he added, 'This is a helluva sort of job, you know. You could get anything if you really look. I know a man who get a whole bed the other day. And when I was picking up some rubbish from St Clair the other day this stupid woman rush out, begging me to come inside. She say she was going to give me a radio.'

Boyee said, 'You mean these rich people does just throw away things like that?'

Eddoes laughed and looked away, pitying our simplicity.

The news about Eddoes and the shoes travelled round the street pretty quickly. My mother was annoyed. She said, 'You see what sort of thing life is. Here I is, working my finger to the bone. Nobody flinging me a pair of shoes just like that, you know. And there you got that thin-arse little man, doing next to nothing, and look at all the things he does get.'

Eddoes presently began getting more things. He brought home a bedstead, he brought home dozens of cups and saucers only slightly cracked, lengths and lengths of wood, all sorts of bolts and screws, and sometimes even money.

Eddoes said, 'I was talking to one of the old boys today. He tell me the thing is to never throw away shoes. Always look in shoes people throw away, and you go find all sort of thing.'

The time came when we couldn't say if Eddoes was prouder of his job or of his collection of junk.

He spent half an hour a day unloading the junk from his cart.

And if anybody wanted a few nails, or a little piece of corrugated iron, the first person they asked was Eddoes.

He made a tremendous fuss when people asked him, though I feel he was pleased.

He would say, 'I working hard all day, getting all these materials and them, and people think they could just come running over and say, "Give me this, give me that."'

In time, the street referred to Eddoes's collection of junk as Eddoes's 'materials'.

One day, after he opened his school, Titus Hoyt was telling us that he had to spend a lot of money to buy books.

He said, 'It go cost me at least sixty dollars.'

Eddoes asked, 'How much book you getting for that?'

Titus Hoyt said, 'Oh, about seven or eight.'

Eddoes laughed in a scornful way.

Eddoes said, 'I could get a whole handful for you for about twelve cents. Why you want to go and spend so much money on eight books for?'

Eddoes sold a lot of books.

Hat bought twenty cents' worth of book.

It just shows how Titus Hoyt was making everybody educated.

And there was this business about pictures.

Eddoes said one day, 'Today, I pick up two nice pictures, two nice nice sceneries, done frame and everything.'

I went home and I said, 'Ma, Eddoes say he go sell us some sceneries for twelve cents.'

My mother behaved in an unexpected way.

She wiped her hand on her dress and came outside.

Eddoes brought the sceneries over. He said, 'The glass a little dirty, but you could always clean that. But they is nice sceneries.'

They were engravings of ships in stormy seas. I could see my mother almost ready to cry from joy. She repeated, 'I always always want to have some nice sceneries.' Then, pointing at me, she said to Eddoes, 'This boy father was always painting sceneries, you know.'

Eddoes looked properly impressed.

He asked, 'Sceneries nice as this?'

My mother didn't reply.

After a little talk my mother paid Eddoes ten cents.

And if Eddoes had something that nobody wanted to buy, he always went to my uncle Bhakcu, who was ready to buy anything.

He used to say, 'You never know when these things could come in handy.'

Hat began saying, 'I think all this materials getting on Eddoes' mind, you know. It have some men like that.'

I wasn't worried until Eddoes came to me one day and said, 'You ever think of collecting old bus-ticket?'

The idea had never crossed my mind.

Eddoes said, 'Look, there's something for a little boy like you to start with. For every thousand you collect I go give you a penny.'

I said, 'Why you want bus-ticket?' He laughed as though I were a fool.

I didn't collect any bus-tickets, but I noticed a lot of other boys doing so. Eddoes had told them that for every hundred they collected they got a free ride.

Hat said, 'Is to start getting worried when he begin collecting pins.'

*

But something happened that made Eddoes sober as a judge again.

He said one day, 'I in trouble!'

Hat said, 'Don't tell us that is thief you been thiefing all this materials and them?'

Eddoes shook his head.

He said, 'A girl making baby for me.'

Hat said, 'You sure is for you?'

Eddoes said, 'She say so.'

It was hard to see why this should get Eddoes so worried.

Hat said, 'But don't be stupid, man. Is the sort of thing that does happen to anybody.'

But Eddoes refused to be consoled.

He collected junk in a listless way.

Then he stopped altogether.

Hat said, 'Eddoes behaving as though he invent the idea of making baby.'

*

Hat asked again, 'You sure this baby is for you, and not for nobody else? It have some woman making a living this way, you know.'

Eddoes said, 'Is true she have other baby, but I in trouble.'

Hat said, 'She is like Laura?'

Eddoes said, 'Nah, Laura does only have one baby for one man. This girl does have two three.'

Hat said, 'Look, you mustn't worry. You don't know is your baby. Wait and see. Wait and see.'

Eddoes said sadly, 'She say if I don't take the baby she go make me lose my job.'

We gasped.

Eddoes said, 'She know lots of people. She say she go make them take me away from St Clair and put me in Dry River, where the people so damn poor they don't throw away nothing.'

I said, 'You mean you not going to find any materials there?'

Eddoes nodded, and we understood.

Hat said, 'The calypsonian was right, you hear.

Man centipede bad.
Woman centipede more than bad.

I know the sort of woman. She have a lot of baby, take the baby by the fathers, and get the fathers to pay money. By the time she thirty thirty-five, she getting so much money from so much man, and she ain't got no baby to look after and no responsibility. I know the thing.'

Boyee said, 'Don't worry, Eddoes. Wait and see if it is your baby. Wait and see.'

Hat said, 'Boyee, ain't you too damn small to be meddling with talk like this?'

*

The months dragged by.

One day Eddoes announced, 'She drop the baby yesterday.'

Hat said, 'Boy or girl?'

'Girl.'

We felt very sorry for Eddoes.

Hat asked, 'You think is yours?'

'Yes.'

'You bringing it home?'

'In about a year or so.'

'Then you ain't got nothing now to worry about. If is your child, bring she home, man. And you still going round St Clair, getting your materials.'

Eddoes agreed, but he didn't look any happier.

*

Hat gave the baby a nickname long before she arrived in Miguel Street. He called her Pleasure, and that was how she was called until she became a big girl.

The baby's mother brought Pleasure one night, but she didn't stay long. And Eddoes's stock rose when we saw how beautiful the mother was. She was a wild, Spanish-looking woman.

But one glance at Pleasure made us know that she couldn't be Eddoes's baby.

Boyee began whistling the calypso:

> Chinese children calling me Daddy!
> I black like jet,
> My wife like tar-baby,
> And still –
> Chinese children calling me Daddy!
> Oh God, somebody putting milk in my coffee.

Hat gave Boyee a pinch, and Hat said to Eddoes, 'She is a good-looking child, Eddoes. Like you.'

Eddoes said, 'You think so, Hat?'

Hat said, 'Yes, man. I think she go grow up to be a sweet girl just as how she father is a sweet-man.'

I said, 'You have a nice daughter, Eddoes.'

The baby was asleep and pink and beautiful.

Errol said, 'I could wait sixteen years until she come big enough.'

Eddoes by this time was smiling and for no reason at all was bursting out into laughter.

Hat said, 'Shut up, Eddoes. You go wake the baby up.'

And Eddoes asked, 'You really think she take after me, Hat?'

Hat said, 'Yes, man. I think you do right, you know, Eddoes. If I wasn't so careful myself and if I did have children outside I woulda bring them all home and put them down. Bring them all home and put them down, man. Nothing to shame about.'

Eddoes said, 'Hat, it have a bird-cage I pick up long time now. Tomorrow I go bring it for you.'

Hat said, 'Is a long long time now I want a good bird-cage.'

*

And in no time at all Eddoes became the old Eddoes we knew, proud of his job, his junk; and now proud, too, of Pleasure.

She became the street baby and all the women, Mrs Morgan, Mrs Bhakcu, Laura, and my mother, helped to look after her.

And if there was anyone in Miguel Street who wanted to laugh, he kept his mouth shut when Pleasure got the first prize in the Cow and Gate Baby competition, and her picture came out in the papers.

12. Love, Love, Love, Alone

ABOUT NINE O'CLOCK one morning a hearse and a motor-car stopped outside Miss Hilton's house. A man and a woman got out of the car. They were both middle-aged and dressed in black. While the man whispered to the two men in the hearse, the woman was crying in a controlled and respectable way.

So I suppose Miss Hilton got the swiftest and most private funeral in Miguel Street. It was nothing like the funeral we had for the other old widow, Miss Ricaud, the M.B.E. and social worker, who lived in a nicer part of the street. At that funeral I counted seventy-nine cars and a bicycle.

The man and the woman returned at midday and there was a bonfire in the yard. Mattresses and pillows and sheets and blankets were burned.

Then all the windows of the grey wooden house were thrown open, a thing I had never seen before.

At the end of the week a sign was nailed on the mango tree: FOR SALE.

Nobody in the street knew Miss Hilton. While she lived, her front gate was always padlocked and no one ever saw her leave or saw anybody go in. So even if you wanted to, you couldn't feel sorry and say that you missed Miss Hilton.

When I think of her house I see just two colours. Grey and green. The green of the mango tree, the grey of the house and the grey of the high galvanized-iron fence that prevented you from getting at the mangoes.

If your cricket ball fell in Miss Hilton's yard you never got it back.

It wasn't the mango season when Miss Hilton died. But we got back about ten or twelve of our cricket balls.

*

We were prepared to dislike the new people even before they came. I think we were a little worried. Already we had one man who kept on complaining about us to the police. He complained that we played cricket on the pavement; and if we weren't playing cricket he complained that we were making too much noise anyway.

Sergeant Charles would come and say, 'Boys, the Super send me. That blasted man ring up again. Take it a little easier.'

*

One afternoon when I came back from school Hat said, 'Is a man and a woman. She pretty pretty, but he ugly like hell, man. Portuguese, they look like.'

I didn't see much. The front gate was open, but the windows were shut again.

I heard a dog barking in an angry way.

One thing was settled pretty quickly. Whoever these people were they would never be the sort to ring up the police and say we were making noise and disturbing their sleep.

A lot of noise came from the house that night. The radio was going full blast until midnight when Trinidad Radio closed down. The dog was barking and the man was shouting. I didn't hear the woman.

There was a great peace next morning.

I waited until I saw the woman before going to school.

Boyee said, 'You know, Hat, I think I see that woman somewhere else. I see she when I was delivering milk up Mucurapo way.'

This lady didn't fit in with the rest of us in Miguel Street. She was too well-dressed. She was a little too pretty and a little too refined, and it was funny to see how she tried to jostle with the other women at Mary's shop trying to get scarce things like flour and rice.

I thought Boyee was right. It was easier to see this woman hopping about in shorts in the garden of one of the nice Mucurapo houses, with a uniformed servant fussing around in the background.

After the first few days I began to see more of the man. He was tall and thin. His face was ugly and had pink blotches.

Hat said, 'God, he is a first-class drinking-man, you hear.'

It took me some time to realize that the tall man was drunk practically all the time. He gave off a sickening smell of bad rum, and I was afraid of him. Whenever I saw him I crossed the road.

If his wife, or whoever she was, dressed better than any woman in the street, he dressed worse than any of us. He was even dirtier than George.

He never appeared to do any work.

I asked Hat, 'How a pretty nice woman like that come to get mix up with a man like that?'

Hat said, 'Boy, you wouldn't understand. If I tell you you wouldn't believe me.'

Then I saw the dog.

It looked as big as a ram-goat and as vicious as a bull. It had the same sort of thin face its master had. I used to see them together.

Hat said, 'If that dog ever get away it go have big trouble here in this street.'

A few days later Hat said, 'You know, it just strike me. I ain't see those people bring in any furnitures at all. It look like all they have is that radio.'

Eddoes said, 'It have a lot of things I could sell them.'

I used to think of the man and the dog and the woman in that house, and I felt sorry and afraid for the woman. I liked her too for the way she went about trying to make out that everything was all right for her, trying to make out that she was just another woman in the street, with nothing odd for people to notice.

Then the beatings began.

The woman used to run out screaming. We would hear the terrible dog barking and we would hear the man shouting and cursing and using language so coarse that we were all shocked.

Hat said to the bigger men, 'Is easy to put two and two and see what happening there.'

And Edward and Eddoes laughed.

I said, 'What happening, Hat?'

Hat laughed.

He said, 'You too small to know, boy. Wait until you in long pants.'

So I thought the worst.

The woman behaved as though she had suddenly lost all shame. She ran crying to anybody in the street, saying, 'Help me! Help me! He will kill me if he catches me.'

One day she rushed to our house.

She didn't make any apology for coming unexpectedly or anything like that. She was too wild and frightened even to cry.

I never saw my mother so anxious to help anyone. She gave the woman tea and biscuits. The woman said, 'I can't understand what has come over Toni these days. But it is only in the nights he is like this, you know. He is so kind in the mornings. But about midday something happens and he just goes mad.'

At first my mother was being excessively refined with the woman, bringing out all her fancy words and fancy pronunciations, pronouncing comfortable as cum-foughtable, and making war rhyme with bar, and promising that everything was deffy-nightly going to be all right. Normally my mother referred to males as man, but with this woman she began speaking about the ways of mens and them, citing my dead father as a typical example.

My mother said, 'The onliest thing with this boy father was that it was the other way round. Whenever I uses to go to the room where he was he uses to jump out of bed and run away bawling – run away screaming.'

But after the woman had come to us about three or four times my mother relapsed into her normal self, and began treating the woman as though she were like Laura or like Mrs Bhakcu.

My mother would say, 'Now, tell me, Mrs Hereira, why you don't leave this good-for-nothing man?'

Mrs Hereira said, 'It is a stupid thing to say to you or anybody else, but I like Toni. I love him.'

My mother said, 'Is a damn funny sort of love.'

Mrs Hereira began to speak about Toni as though he were a little boy she liked.

She said, 'He has many good qualities, you know. His heart is in the right place, really.'

My mother said, 'I wouldn't know about heart, but what I know is that he want a good clout on his backside to make him see sense. How you could let a man like that disgrace you so?'

Mrs Hereira said, 'No, I know Toni. I looked after him when he was sick. It is the war, you know. He was a sailor and they torpedoed him twice.'

My mother said, 'They shoulda try again.'

'You mustn't talk like this,' Mrs Hereira said.

My mother said, 'Look, I just talking my mind, you hear. You come here asking me advice.'

'I didn't ask for advice.'

'You come here asking me for help, and I just trying to help you. That's all.'

'I don't want your help or advice,' Mrs Hereira said.

My mother remained calm. She said, 'All right, then. Go back to the great man. Is my own fault, you hear. Meddling in white people business. You know what the calypso say:

> Is love, love, love, alone
> That cause King Edward to leave the throne.

Well, let me tell you. You not King Edward, you hear. Go back to your great love.'

Mrs Hereira would be out of the door, saying, 'I hope I never come back here again.'

But next evening she would be back.

One day my mother said, 'Mrs Hereira, everybody fraid that dog you have there. That thing too wild to be in a place like this.'

Mrs Hereira said, 'It isn't my dog. It's Toni's, and not even I can touch it.'

*

We despised Toni.

Hat said, 'Is a good thing for a man to beat his woman every now and then, but this man does do it like exercise, man.'

And he was also despised because he couldn't carry his liquor.

People used to find him sleeping in all sorts of places, dead drunk.

He made a few attempts to get friendly with us, making us feel uncomfortable more than anything else.

He used to say, 'Hello there, boys.'

And that appeared to be all the conversation he could make. And when Hat and the other big men tried to talk to him, as a kindness, I felt that Toni wasn't really listening.

He would get up and walk away from us suddenly, without a word, when somebody was in the middle of a sentence.

Hat said, 'Is a good thing too. I feel that if I look at him long enough I go vomit. You see what a dirty thing a white skin does be sometimes?'

And, in truth, he had a nasty skin. It was yellow and pink and white, with brown and black spots. The skin above his left eye had the raw pink look of scalded flesh.

But the strange thing I noticed was that if you just looked at Toni's hands and saw how thin and wrinkled they were, you felt sorry for him, not disgusted.

But I looked at his hands only when I was with Hat and the rest.

I suppose Mrs Hereira saw only his hands.

Hat said, 'I wonder how long this thing go last.'

*

Mrs Hereira obviously intended it to last a long time.

She and my mother became good friends after all, and I used to hear Mrs Heriera talking about her plans. She said one day she wanted some furniture, and I think she did get some in.

But most of the time she talked about Toni, and from the way she talked, anybody would believe that Toni was just an ordinary man.

She said, 'Toni is thinking about leaving Trinidad. We could start a hotel in Barbados.'

Or, 'As soon as Toni gets well again, we will go for a long cruise.'

And again, 'Toni is really a disciplined man, you know. Great will-power, really. We'll be all right when he gets his strength back.'

*

Toni still behaved as though he didn't know about all these plans for himself. He refused to settle down. He got wilder and more unpleasant.

Hat said, 'He behaving like some of those uncultured people from John-John. Like he forget that latrines make for some purpose.'

And that wasn't all. He appeared to develop an extraordinary dislike for the human race. One look at a perfect stranger was enough to start Toni cursing.

Hat said, 'We have to do something about Toni.'

I was there the evening they beat him up.

For a long time afterwards the beating-up was on Hat's mind.

It was a terrible thing, really. Hat and the rest of them were not angry. And Toni himself wasn't angry. He wasn't anything. He made no effort to return the blows. And the blows he got made no impression on him. He didn't look frightened. He didn't cry. He didn't plead. He just stood up and took it.

He wasn't being brave.

Hat said, 'He just too damn drunk.'

In the end Hat was angry with himself. He said, 'I taking advantage. We shouldnta do it. The man ain't have feelings, that's all.'

And from the way Mrs Hereira talked, it was clear that she didn't know what had happened.

Hat said, 'That's a relief, anyway.'

*

And through all these weeks, one question was always uppermost in our minds. How did a woman like Mrs Hereira get mixed up with Toni?'

Hat said he knew. But he wanted to know who Mrs Hereira was, and so did we all. Even my mother wondered aloud about this.

Boyee had an idea.

He said, 'Hat, you know the advertisements people does put out when their wife or their husband leave them?'

Hat said, 'Boyee, you know you getting too damn big too damn fast. How the hell a little boy like you know about a thing like that?'

Boyee took this as a compliment.

Hat said, 'How you know anyway that Mrs Hereira leave she husband? How you know that she ain't married to Toni?

Boyee said, 'I telling you, Hat. I used to see that woman up Mucurapo way when I was delivering milk. I telling you so, man.'

Hat said, 'White people don't do that sort of thing, putting advertisement in the paper and thing like that.'

Eddoes said, 'You ain't know what you talking about, Hat. How much white people you know?'

In the end Hat promised to read the paper more carefully.

*

Then big trouble started.

Mrs Hereira ran out of her house screaming one day, 'He's going mad! He's going mad, I tell you. He will kill me this time sure.'

She told my mother, 'He grabbed a knife and began chasing me. He was saying, "I will kill you, I will kill you." Talking in a very quiet way.'

'You do him something?' my mother asked.

Mrs Hereira shook her head.

She said, 'It is the first time he threatened to kill me. And he was serious, I tell you.'

Up till then Mrs Hereira hadn't been crying, but now she broke down and cried like a girl.

She was saying, 'Toni has forgotten all I did for him. He has forgotten how I took care of him when he was sick. Tell me, you think that's right? I did everything for him. Everything. I gave up everything. Money and family. All for him. Tell me, is it right for him to treat me like this? Oh, God! What did I do to deserve all this?'

And so she wept and talked and wept.

We left her to herself for some time.

Then my mother said, 'Toni look like the sort of man who could kill easy, easy, without feeling that he really murdering. You want to sleep here tonight? You could sleep on the boy bed. He could sleep on the floor.'

Mrs Hereira wasn't listening.

My mother shook her and repeated her offer.

Mrs Hereira said, 'I am all right now, really. I will go back and talk to Toni. I think I did something to offend him. I must go back and find out what it is.'

'Well, I really give up,' my mother said. 'I think you taking this love business a little too far, you hear.'

So Mrs Hereira went back to her house. My mother and I waited for a long time, waiting for a scream.

But we heard nothing.

And the next morning Mrs Hereira was composed and refined as ever.

*

But day by day you could see her losing her freshness and saddening her beauty. Her face was getting lined. Her eyes were red and swollen, and the dark patches under them were ugly to look at.

*

Hat jumped up and said, 'I know it! I know it! I know it a long time now.'

He showed us the Personal column in the classified advertisements. Seven people had decided to leave their spouses. We followed Hat's finger and read:

> I, Henry Hubert Christiani, declare that my wife, Angela Mary Christiani, is no longer under my care and protection, and I am not responsible for any debt or debts contracted by her.

Boyee said, 'Is the selfsame woman.'

Eddoes said, 'Yes, Christiani. Doctor fellow. Know him good good. Used to pick rubbish for him.'

Hat said, 'Now I ask you, why, why a woman want to leave a man like that for this Toni?'

Eddoes said, 'Yes, know Christiani good good. Good house, nice car. Full of money, you know. It have a long time now I see him. Know him from the days when I used to work Mucurapo way.'

And in about half an hour the news had spread through Miguel Street.

*

My mother said to Mrs Hereira, 'You better call the police.'

Mrs Hereira said, 'No, no. Not the police.'

My mother said, 'Like you fraid police more than you fraid Toni.'

Mrs Hereira said, 'The scandal – '

'Scandal hell!' my mother said. 'You life in trouble and you thinking about scandal. Like if this man ain't disgrace you enough already.'

My mother said, 'Why you don't go back to your husband?'

She said it as though she expected Mrs Hereira to jump up in surprise.

But Mrs Hereira remained very calm.

She said, 'I don't feel anything about him. And I just can't stand that clean doctor's smell he has. It chokes me.'

I understood her perfectly, and tried to get my mother's eye.

Toni was growing really wild.

He used to sit on his front steps with a half-bottle of rum in his hand. The dog was with him.

He appeared to have lost touch with the world completely. He seemed to be without feeling. It was hard enough to imagine Mrs Hereira, or Mrs Christiani, in love with him. But it was impossible to imagine him being in love with anybody.

I thought he was like an animal, like his dog.

*

One morning, Mrs Hereira came over and said, very calmly, 'I have decided to leave Toni.'

She was so calm I could see my mother getting worried.

My mother said, 'What happen now?'

Mrs Hereira said, 'Nothing. Last night he made the dog jump at me. He didn't look as if he knew what he was doing. He didn't laugh or anything. I think he is going mad, and if I don't get out I think he will kill me.'

My mother said, 'Who you going back to?'

'My husband.'

'Even after what he print in the papers?'

Mrs Hereira said, 'Henry is like a boy, you know, and he thinks he can frighten me. If I go back today, he will be glad to have me back.'

And saying that, she looked different, and hard.

My mother said, 'Don't be so sure. He know Toni?'

Mrs Hereira laughed, in a crazy sort of way. 'Toni was Henry's friend, not mine. Henry brought him home one day. Toni was sick like anything. Henry was like that, you know. I never met a man who liked doing good works so much as Henry. He was all for good works and sanitation.'

My mother said, 'You know, Mrs Hereira, I really wish you was like me. If somebody did marry you off when you was fifteen, we wouldnta been hearing all this nonsense, you hear. Making all this damn fuss about your heart and love and all that rubbish.'

Mrs Hereira began to cry.

My mother said, 'Look, I didn't want to make you cry like this. I sorry.'

Mrs Hereira sobbed, 'No, it isn't you, it isn't you.'

My mother looked disappointed.

We watched Mrs Hereira cry.

Mrs Hereira said, 'I have left about a week's food with Toni.'

My mother said, 'Toni is a big man. You mustn't worry about him.'

*

He made terrible noises when he discovered that she had left him. He bayed like a dog and bawled like a baby.

Then he got drunk. Not drunk in the ordinary fashion; it got to the stage where the rum was keeping him going.

He forgot all about the dog, and it starved for days.

He stumbled drunk and crying from house to house, looking for Mrs Hereira.

And when he got back he took it out on the dog. We used to hear the dog yelping and growling.

In the end even the dog turned on him.

Somehow it managed to get itself free and it rushed at Toni.

Toni was shocked into sense.

The dog ran out of the house, and Toni ran after it. Toni squatted and whistled. The dog stopped, pricked up its ears, and turned round to look. It was funny seeing this drunk crazy man smiling and whistling at his dog, trying to get him back.

The dog stood still, staring at Toni.

Its tail wagged twice, then fell.

Toni got up and began walking towards the dog. The dog turned and ran.

*

We saw him sprawling on a mattress in one of the rooms. The room was perfectly empty. Nothing but the mattress and the empty rum bottles and the cigarette ends.

He was drunk and sleeping, and his face was strangely reposed.

The thin and wrinkled hands looked so frail and sad.

*

Another FOR SALE sign was nailed to the mango tree. A man with about five little children bought the house.

From time to time Toni came around to terrify the new people.

He would ask for money, for rum, and he had the habit of asking for the radio. He would say, 'You have Angela's radio there. I charging rent for that, you know. Two dollars a month. Give me two dollars now.'

The new owner was a small man, and he was afraid of Toni. He never answered.

Toni would look at us and laugh and say, 'You know about Angela's radio, eh, boys? You know about the radio? Now, what this man playing at?'

Hat said, 'Who will tell me why they ever have people like Toni in this world!'

After two or three months he stopped coming to Miguel Street.

*

I saw Toni many years later.

I was travelling to Arima, and just near the quarry at Laventille I saw him driving a lorry.

He was smoking a cigarette.

That and his thin arms are all I remember.

And riding to Carenage one Sunday morning, I passed the Christiani's house, which I had avoided for a long time.

Mrs Christiani, or Mrs Hereira, was in shorts. She was reading the paper in an easy chair in the garden. Through the open doors of the house I saw a uniformed servant laying the table for lunch.

There was a black car, a new, big car, in the garage.

13. The Mechanical Genius

My Uncle Bhakcu was very nearly a mechanical genius. I cannot remember a time when he was not the owner of a motor-vehicle of some sort. I don't think he always approved of the manufacturers' designs, however, for he was always pulling engines to bits. Titus Hoyt said that this was also a habit of the Eskimos. It was something he had got out of a geography book.

If I try to think of Bhakcu I never see his face. I can see only the soles of his feet as he worms his way under a car. I was worried when Bhakcu was under a car because it looked so easy for the car to slip off the jack and fall on him.

One day it did.

He gave a faint groan that reached the ears of only his wife.

She bawled, 'Oh God!' and burst into tears right away. 'I know something wrong. Something happen to *he*.'

Mrs Bhakcu always used this pronoun when she spoke of her husband.

She hurried to the side of the yard and heard Bhakcu groaning.

'Man,' she whispered, 'you all right?'

He groaned a little more loudly.

He said, 'How the hell I all right? You mean you so blind you ain't see the whole motor-car break up my arse?'

Mrs Bhakcu, dutiful wife, began to cry afresh.

She beat on the galvanized-iron fence.

'Hat,' Mrs Bhakcu called, 'Hat, come quick. A whole motor-car fall on *he*.'

Hat was cleaning out the cow-pen. When he heard Mrs Bhakcu he laughed. 'You know what I always does say,' Hat said. 'When you play the ass you bound to catch hell. The blasted car brand-new. What the hell he was tinkering with so?'

'*He* say the crank-shaft wasn't working nice.'

'And is there he looking for the crank-shaft?'

'Hat,' Bhakcu shouted from under the car, 'the moment you get this car from off me, I going to break up your tail.'

'Man,' Mrs Bhakcu said to her husband, 'how you so advantageous? The man come round with his good good mind to help you and now you want to beat him up?'

Hat began to look hurt and misunderstood.

Hat said, 'It ain't nothing new. Is just what I expect. Is just what I does always get for interfering in other people business. You know I mad to leave you and your husband here and go back to the cow-pen.'

'No, Hat. You mustn't mind *he*. Think what you would say if a whole big new motor-car fall on you.'

Hat said, 'All right, all right. I have to go and get some of the boys.'

We heard Hat shouting in the street. 'Boyee and Errol!'

No answer.

'Bo-yee and Ehhroll!'

'C-ming, Hat.'

'Where the hell you boys been, eh? You think you is man now and you could just stick your hands in your pocket and walk out like man? You was smoking, eh?'

'Smoking, Hat?'

'But what happen now? You turn deaf all of a sudden?'

'Was Boyee was smoking, Hat.'

'Is a lie, Hat. Was Errol really. I just stand up watching him.'

'Somebody make you policeman now, eh? Is cut-arse for both of you. Errol, go cut a whip for Boyee. Boyee, go cut a whip for Errol.'

We heard the boys whimpering.

From under the car Bhakcu called, 'Hat, why you don't leave the boys alone? You go bless them bad one of these days, you know, and then they go lose you in jail. Why you don't leave the boys alone? They big now.'

Hat shouted back, 'You mind your own business, you hear. Otherwise I leave you under that car until you rotten, you hear.'

Mrs Bhakcu said to her husband, 'Take it easy, man.'

But it was nothing serious after all. The jack had slipped but the axle rested on a pile of wooden blocks, pinning Bhakcu to the ground without injuring him.

When Bhakcu came out he looked at his clothes. These were a pair of khaki trousers and a sleeveless vest, both black and stiff with engine grease.

Bhakcu said to his wife, 'They really dirty now, eh?'

She regarded her husband with pride. 'Yes, man,' she said. 'They really dirty.'

Bhakcu smiled.

Hat said, 'Look, I just sick of lifting up motor-car from off you, you hear. If you want my advice, you better send for a proper mechanic.'

Bhakcu wasn't listening.

He said to his wife, 'The crank-shaft was all right. Is something else.'

Mrs Bhakcu said, 'Well, you must eat first.'

She looked at Hat and said, '*He* don't eat when *he* working on the car unless I remind *he*.'

Hat said, 'What you want me do with that? Write it down with a pencil on a piece of paper and send it to the papers?'

I wanted to watch Bhakcu working on the car that evening,

so I said to him, 'Uncle Bhakcu, your clothes looking really dirty and greasy. I wonder how you could bear to wear them.'

He turned and smiled at me. 'What you expect, boy?' he said. 'Mechanic people like me ain't have time for clean clothes.'

'What happen to the car, Uncle Bhakcu?' I asked.

He didn't reply.

'The tappet knocking?' I suggested.

One thing Bhakcu had taught me about cars was that tappets were always knocking. Give Bhakcu any car in the world, and the first thing he would tell you about it was, 'The tappet knocking, you know. Hear. Hear it?'

'The tappet knocking?' I asked.

He came right up to me and asked eagerly, 'What, you hear it knocking?'

And before I had time to say, 'Well, something did knocking,' Mrs Bhakcu pulled him away, saying, 'Come and eat now, man. God, you get your clothes really dirty today.'

*

The car that fell on Bhakcu wasn't really a new car, although Bhakcu boasted that it very nearly was.

'It only do two hundred miles,' he used to say.

Hat said, 'Well, I know Trinidad small, but I didn't know it was so small.'

I remember the day it was bought. It was a Saturday. And that morning Mrs Bhakcu came to my mother and they talked about the cost of rice and flour and the black market. As she was leaving, Mrs Bhakcu said, '*He* gone to town today. He *say* he got to buy a new car.'

*

So we waited for the new car.

Midday came, but Bhakcu didn't.

Hat said, 'Two to one, that man taking down the engine right this minute.'

About four o'clock we heard a banging and a clattering, and looking down Miguel Street towards Docksite we saw the car. It was a blue Chevrolet, one of the 1939 models. It looked rich and new. We began to wave and cheer, and I saw Bhakcu waving his left hand.

We danced into the road in front of Bhakcu's house, waving and cheering.

The car came nearer and Hat said, 'Jump, boys! Run for your life. Like he get mad.'

It was a near thing. The car just raced past the house and we stopped cheering.

Hat said, 'The car out of control. It go have a accident, if something don't happen quick.'

Mrs Bhakcu laughed. 'What you think it is at all?' she said.

But we raced after the car, crying after Bhakcu.

He wasn't waving with his left hand. He was trying to warn people off.

By a miracle, it stopped just before Ariapita Avenue.

Bhakcu said, 'I did mashing down the brakes since I turn Miguel Street, but the brakes ain't working. Is a funny thing. I overhaul the brakes just this morning.'

Hat said, 'It have two things for you to do. Overhaul your head or haul your arse away before you get people in trouble.'

Bhakcu said, 'You boys go have to give me a hand to push the car back home.'

As we were pushing it past the house of Morgan, the pyrotechnicist, Mrs Morgan shouted, 'Ah, Mrs Bhakcu, I see you buy a new car today, man.'

Mrs Bhakcu didn't reply.

Mrs Morgan said, 'Ah, Mrs Bhakcu, you think your husband go give me a ride in his new car?'

Mrs Bhakcu said, 'Yes, *he* go give you a ride, but first *your* husband must give *me* a ride on his donkey-cart when he buy it.'

Bhakcu said to Mrs Bhakcu, 'Why you don't shut your mouth up?'

Mrs Bhakcu said, 'But how you want me to shut my mouth up? You is my husband, and I have to stand up for you.'

Bhakcu said very sternly, 'You only stand up for me when I tell you, you hear.'

We left the car in front of Bhakcu's house, and we left Mr and Mrs Bhakcu to their quarrel. It wasn't a very interesting one. Mrs Bhakcu kept on claiming her right to stand up for her husband, and Mr Bhakcu kept on rejecting the claim. In the end Bhakcu had to beat his wife.

This wasn't as easy as it sounds. If you want to get a proper picture of Mrs Bhakcu you must consider a pear as a scale-model. Mrs Bhakcu had so much flesh, in fact, that when she held her arms at her sides, they looked like marks of parenthesis.

And as for her quarrelling voice . . .

Hat used to say, 'It sound as though it coming from a gramophone record turning fast fast backwards.'

For a long time I think Bhakcu experimented with rods for beating his wife, and I wouldn't swear that it wasn't Hat who suggested a cricket bat. But whoever suggested it, a second-hand cricket bat was bought from one of the groundsmen at the Queen's Park Oval, and oiled, and used on Mrs Bhakcu.

Hat said, 'Is the only thing she really could feel, I think.'

The strangest thing about this was that Mrs Bhakcu herself kept the bat clean and well-oiled. Boyee tried many times to borrow the bat, but Mrs Bhakcu never lent it.

*

So on the evening of the day when the car fell on Bhakcu I went to see him at work.

'What you did saying about the tappet knocking?' he said.

'I didn't say nothing,' I said. 'I was asking you.'

'Oh.'

Bhakcu worked late into the night, taking down the engine. He worked all the next day, Sunday, and all Sunday night. On Monday morning the mechanic came.

Mrs Bhakcu told my mother, 'The company send the mechanic man. The trouble with these Trinidad mechanics is that they is just piss-in-tail little boys who don't know the first thing about cars and things.'

I went round to Bhakcu's house and saw the mechanic with his head inside the bonnet. Bhakcu was sitting on the running-board, rubbing grease over everything the mechanic handed him. He looked so happy dipping his finger in the grease that I asked, 'Let me rub some grease, Uncle Bhakcu.'

'Go away, boy. You too small.'

I sat and watched him.

He said, 'The tappet was knocking, but I fix it.'

I said, 'Good.'

The mechanic was cursing.

I asked Bhakcu, 'How the points?'

He said, 'I have to check them up.'

I got up and walked around the car and sat on the running-board next to Bhakcu.

I looked at him and I said, 'You know something?'

'What?'

'When I did hear the engine on Saturday, I didn't think it was beating nice.'

Bhakcu said, 'You getting to be a real smart man, you know. You learning fast.'

I said, 'Is what you teach me.'

It was, as a matter of fact, pretty nearly the limit of my

knowledge. The knocking tappet, the points, the beat of the engine and – yes, I had forgotten one thing.

'You know, Uncle Bhakcu,' I said.

'What, boy?'

'Uncle Bhakcu, I think is the carburettor.'

'You really think so, boy?'

'I sure, Uncle Bhakcu.'

'Well, I go tell you, boy. Is the first thing I ask the mechanic. He don't think so.'

The mechanic lifted a dirty and angry face from the engine and said, 'When you have all sort of ignorant people messing about with a engine the white people build with their own hands, what the hell else you expect?'

Bhakcu winked at me.

He said, '*I* think is the carburettor.'

*

Of all the drills, I liked the carburettor drill the best. Sometimes Bhakcu raced the engine while I put my palm over the carburettor and off again. Bhakcu never told me why we did this and I never asked. Sometimes we had to siphon petrol from the tank, and I would pour this petrol into the carburettor while Bhakcu raced the engine. I often asked him to let me race the engine, but he wouldn't agree.

One day the engine caught fire, but I jumped away in time. The fire didn't last.

Bhakcu came out of the car and looked at the engine in a puzzled way. I thought he was annoyed with it, and I was prepared to see him dismantle it there and then.

That was the last time we did that drill with the carburettor.

*

At last the mechanic tested the engine and the brakes, and said, 'Look, the car good good now, you hear. It cost me more work than if I was to build over a new car. Leave the damn thing alone.'

After the mechanic left, Bhakcu and I walked very thoughtfully two or three times around the car. Bhakcu was stroking his chin, not talking to me.

Suddenly he jumped into the driver's seat, and pressed the horn-button a few times.

He said, 'What you think about the horn, boy?'

I said, 'Blow it again, let me hear.'

He pressed the button again.

Hat pushed his head through a window and shouted, 'Bhakcu, keept the damn car quiet, you hear, man. You making the place sound as though it have a wedding going on.'

We ignored Hat.

I said, 'Uncle Bhakcu, I don't think the horn blowing nice.'

He said, 'You really don't think so?'

I made a face and spat.

So we began to work on the horn.

When we were finished there was a bit of flex wound round the steering-column.

Bhakcu looked at me and said, 'You see, you could just take this wire now and touch it on any part of the metal-work, and the horn blow.'

It looked unlikely, but it did work.

I said, 'Uncle Bhakcu, how you know about all these things?'

He said, 'You just keep on learning all the time.'

*

The men in the street didn't like Bhakcu because they considered him a nuisance. But I liked him for the same reason that I liked Popo, the carpenter. For, thinking about it now, Bhakcu was also an artist. He interfered with motor-cars for the joy of the thing, and he never seemed worried about money.

But his wife was worried. She, like my mother, thought that she was born to be a clever handler of money, born to make money sprout from nothing at all.

She talked over the matter with my mother one day.

My mother said, 'Taxi making a lot of money these days, taking Americans and their girl friends all over the place.'

So Mrs Bhakcu made her husband buy a lorry.

This lorry was really the pride of Miguel Street. It was a big new Bedford and we all turned out to welcome it when Bhakcu brought it home for the first time.

Even Hat was impressed. 'If is one thing the English people could build,' he said, 'is a lorry. This is not like your Ford and your Dodge, you know.'

Bhakcu began working on it that very afternoon, and Mrs Bhakcu went around telling people, 'Why not come and see how *he* working on the Bedford?'

From time to time Bhakcu would crawl out from under the lorry and polish the wings and the bonnet. Then he would crawl under the lorry again. But he didn't look happy.

The next day the people who had lent the money to buy the Bedford formed a deputation and came to Bhakcu's house, begging him to desist.

Bhakcu remained under the lorry all the time, refusing to reply. The money-lenders grew angry, and some of the women among them began to cry. Even that failed to move Bhakcu, and in the end the deputation just had to go away.

When the deputation left, Bhakcu began to take it out on his wife. He beat her and he said, 'Is you who want me to buy lorry. Is you. Is *you*. All you thinking about is money, money. Just like your mother.'

But the real reason for his temper was that he couldn't put

back the engine as he had found it. Two or three pieces remained outside and they puzzled him.

The agents sent a mechanic.

He looked at the lorry and asked Bhakcu, very calmly, 'Why you buy a Bedford?'

Bhakcu said, 'I like the Bedford.'

The mechanic shouted, 'Why the arse you didn't buy a Rolls-Royce? They does sell those with the engine sealed down.'

Then he went to work, saying sadly, 'Is enough to make you want to cry. A nice, new new lorry like this.'

The starter never worked again. And Bhakcu always had to use the crank.

Hat said, 'Is a blasted shame. Lorry looking new, smelling new, everything still shining, all sort of chalk-mark still on the chassis, and this man cranking it up like some old Ford pram.'

But Mrs Bhakcu boasted, 'Fust crank, the engine does start.'

One morning – it was a Saturday, market day – Mrs Bhakcu came crying to my mother. She said, '*He* in hospital.'

My mother said, 'Accident?'

Mrs Bhakcu said, '*He* was cranking up the lorry just outside the Market. Fust crank, the engine start. But it was in gear and it roll *he* up against another lorry.'

Bhakcu spent a week in hospital.

All the time he had the lorry, he hated his wife, and he beat her regularly with the cricket bat. But she was beating him too, with her tongue, and I think Bhakcu was really the loser in these quarrels.

It was hard to back the lorry into the yard and it was Mrs Bhakcu's duty and joy to direct her husband.

One day she said, 'All right, man, back back, turn a little to the right, all right, all clear. Oh God! No, no, no, man! Stop! You go knock the fence down.'

Bhakcu suddenly went mad. He reversed so fiercely he cracked the concrete fence. Then he shot forward again, ignoring Mrs Bhakcu's screams, and reversed again, knocking down the fence altogether.

He was in a great temper, and while his wife remained outside crying he went to his little room, stripped to his pants, flung himself belly down on the bed, and began reading the *Ramayana*.

The lorry wasn't making money. But to make any at all, Bhakcu had to have loaders. He got two of those big black Grenadian small-islanders who were just beginning to pour into Port of Spain. They called Bhakcu 'Boss' and Mrs Bhakcu 'Madam', and this was nice. But when I looked at these men sprawling happily in the back of the lorry in their ragged dusty clothes and their squashed-up felt hats, I used to wonder whether they knew how much worry they caused, and how uncertain their own position was.

Mrs Bhakcu's talk was now all about these two men.

She would tell my mother mournfully, 'Day after tomorrow we have to pay the loaders.' Two days later she would say, as though the world had come to an end, 'Today we pay the loaders.' And in no time at all she would be coming around to my mother in distress again, saying, 'Day after tomorrow we have to pay the loaders.'

Paying the loaders – for months I seemed to hear about nothing else. The words were well known in the street, and became an idiom.

Boyee would say to Errol on a Saturday, 'Come, let we go to the one-thirty show at Roxy.'

And Errol would turn out his pockets and say, 'I can't go, man. I pay the loaders.'

Hat said, 'It looks as though Bhakcu buy the lorry just to pay the loaders.'

The lorry went in the end. And the loaders too. I don't know what happened to them. Mrs Bhakcu had the lorry sold just at a time when lorries began making money. They bought a taxi. By now the competition was fierce and taxis were running eight miles for twelve cents, just enough to pay for oil and petrol.

Mrs Bhakcu told my mother, 'The taxi ain't making money.'

So she bought another taxi, and hired a man to drive it. She said, 'Two better than one.'

Bhakcu was reading the *Ramayana* more and more.

And even that began to annoy the people in the street.

Hat said, 'Hear the two of them now. She with that voice she got, and he singing that damn sing-song Hindu song.'

Picture then the following scene. Mrs Bhakcu, very short, very fat, standing at the pipe in her yard, and shrilling at her husband. He is in his pants, lying on his belly, dolefully intoning the *Ramayana*. Suddenly he springs up and snatches the cricket bat in the corner of the room. He runs outside and begins to beat Mrs Bhakcu with the bat.

The silence that follows lasts a few minutes.

And then only Bhakcu's voice is heard, as he does a solo from the *Ramayana*.

*

But don't think that Mrs Bhakcu lost any pride in her husband. Whenever you listened to the rows between Mrs Bhakcu and Mrs Morgan, you realized that Bhakcu was still his wife's lord and master.

Mrs Morgan would say, 'I hear your husband talking in his sleep last night, loud loud.'

'He wasn't talking,' Mrs Bhakcu said, 'he was singing.'

'Singing? Hahahahaaah! You know something, Mrs Bhakcu?'

'What, Mrs Morgan?'

'If your husband sing for his supper, both of all you starve like hell.'

'*He* know a damn lot more than any of the ignorant man it have in this street, you hear. *He* could read and write, you know.

English *and* Hindi. How you so ignorant you don't know that the *Ramayana* is a holy book? If you coulda understand all the good thing *he* singing, you wouldn't be talking all this nonsense you talking now, you hear.'

'How your husband this morning, anyway? He fix any new cars lately?'

'I not going to dirty my mouth arguing with you here, you hear. *He* know how to fix his car. Is a wonder nobody ain't tell your husband where he can fix all his so-call fireworks.'

*

Mrs Bhakcu used to boast that Bhakcu read the *Ramayana* two or three times a month. 'It have some parts he know by heart,' she said.

But that was little consolation, for money wasn't coming in. The man she had hired to drive the second taxi was playing the fool. She said, 'He robbing me like hell. He say that the taxi making so little money I owe him now.' She sacked the driver and sold the car.

She used all her financial flair. She began rearing hens. That failed because a lot of the hens were stolen, the rest attacked by street dogs, and Bhakcu hated the smell anyway. She began selling bananas and oranges, but she did that more for her own enjoyment than for the little money it brought in.

My mother said, 'Why Bhakcu don't go out and get a work?'

Mrs Bhakcu said, 'But how you want that?'

My mother said, '*I* don't want it. I was thinking about you.'

Mrs Bhakcu said, 'You could see he working with all the rude and crude people it have here in Port of Spain?'

My mother said, 'Well, he have to do something. People don't pay to see a man crawling under a motor-car or singing *Ramayana*.'

Mrs Bhakcu nodded and looked sad.

My mother said, 'But what I saying at all? You sure Bhakcu know the *Ramayana*?'

'I sure sure.'

My mother said, 'Well, it easy easy. He is a Brahmin, he know the *Ramayana*, and he have a car. Is easy for him to become a pundit, a real proper pundit.'

Mrs Bhakcu clapped her hands. 'Is a first-class idea. Hindu pundits making a lot of money these days.'

So Bhakcu became a pundit.

*

He still tinkered with his car. He had to stop beating Mrs Bhakcu with the cricket bat, but he was happy.

I was haunted by thoughts of the *dhoti*-clad Pundit Bhakcu, crawling under a car, attending to a crank-shaft, while poor Hindus waited for him to attend to their souls.

14. Caution

IT WAS NOT UNTIL 1947 that Bolo believed that the war was over. Up till then he used to say, 'Is only a lot of propaganda. Just lies for black people.'

In 1947 the Americans began pulling down their camp in the George V Park and many people were getting sad.

I went to see Bolo one Sunday and while he was cutting my hair he said, 'I hear the war over.'

I said, 'So I hear too. But I still have my doubts.'

Bolo said, 'I know what you mean. These people is master of propaganda, but the way I look at it is this. If they was still fighting they woulda want to keep the camp.'

'But they not keeping the camp,' I said.

Bolo said, 'Exactly. Put two and two together and what you get? Tell me, what you get?'

I said, 'Four.'

He clipped my hair thoughtfully for a few moments.

He said, 'Well, I glad the war over.'

When I paid for my trim I said, 'What you think we should do now, Mr Bolo? You think we should celebrate?'

He said, 'Gimme time, man. Gimme time. This is a big thing. I have to think it over.'

And there the matter rested.

*

I remember the night when the news of peace reached Port of Spain. People just went wild and there was a carnival in the streets. A new calypso sprang out of nothing and everybody was dancing in the streets to the tune of:

> All day and all night Miss Mary Ann
> Down by the river-side she taking man.

Bolo looked at the dancers and said, 'Stupidness! Stupidness! How black people so stupid?'

I said, 'But you ain't hear, Mr Bolo? The war over.'

He spat. 'How you know? You was fighting it?'

'But it come over on the radio and I read it in the papers.'

Bolo laughed. He said, 'Anybody would think you was still a little boy. You mean you come so big and you still does believe anything you read in the papers?'

I had heard this often before. Bolo was sixty and the only truth he had discovered seemed to be, 'You mustn't believe anything you read in the papers.'

It was his whole philosophy, and it didn't make him happy. He was the saddest man in the street.

I think Bolo was born sad. Certainly I never saw him laugh except in a sarcastic way, and I saw him at least once a week for eleven years. He was a tall man, not thin, with a face that was a caricature of sadness, the mouth curling downwards, the eyebrows curving downwards, the eyes big and empty of expression.

It was an amazement to me that Bolo made a living at all after he had stopped barbering. I suppose he would be described in a census as a carrier. His cart was the smallest thing of its kind I knew.

It was a little box on two wheels and he pushed it himself, pushed with his long body in such an attitude of resignation and futility you wondered why he pushed it at all. On this cart he could take just about two or three sacks of flour or sugar.

On Sundays Bolo became a barber again, and if he was proud of anything he was proud of his barbering.

Often Bolo said to me, 'You know Samuel?'

Samuel was the most successful barber in the district. He was so rich he took a week's holiday every year, and he liked everybody to know it.

I said, 'Yes, I know Samuel. But I don't like him to touch my hair at all. He can't cut hair. He does zog up my head.'

Bolo said, 'You know who teach Samuel all he know about cutting hair? You know?'

I shook my head.

'I. I teach Samuel. He couldn't even shave hisself when he start barbering. He come crying and begging, "Mr Bolo, Mr Bolo, teach me how to cut people hair, I beg you." Well, I teach him, and look what happen, eh. Samuel rich rich, and I still living in one room in this break-down old house. Samuel have a room where he does cut hair, I have to cut hair in the open under this mango tree.'

I said, 'But it nice outside, it better than sitting down in a hot room. But why you stop cutting hair regular, Mr Bolo?'

'Ha, boy, that is asking a big big question. The fact is, I just can't trust myself.'

'Is not true. You does cut hair good good, better than Samuel.'

'It ain't that I mean. Boy, when it have a man sitting down in front of you in a chair, and you don't like this man, and you have a razor in your hand, a lot of funny things could happen. I does only cut people hair these days when I like them. I can't cut any-and-everybody hair.'

*

Although in 1945 Bolo didn't believe that the war was over, in 1939 he was one of the great alarmists. In those days he bought all three Port of Spain newspapers, the *Trinidad Guardian*, the *Port of Spain Gazette*, and the *Evening News*. When the war broke out and the *Evening News* began issuing special bulletins, Bolo bought those too.

Those were the days when Bolo said, 'It have a lot of people who think they could kick people around. They think because we poor we don't know anything. But I ain't in that, you hear. Every day I sit down and read my papers regular regular.'

More particularly, Bolo was interested in the *Trinidad Guardian*. At one stage Bolo bought about twenty copies of that paper every day.

The *Guardian* was running a Missing Ball Competition. They printed a photograph of a football match in progress, but they had rubbed the ball out. All you had to do to win a lot of money was to mark the position of the ball with an X.

Spotting the missing ball became one of Bolo's passions.

In the early stages Bolo was happy enough to send in one X a week to the *Guardian*.

It was a weekly excitement for all of us.

Hat used to say, 'Bolo, I bet you forget all of us when you win the money. You leaving Miguel Street, man, and buying a big house in St Clair, eh?'

Bolo said, 'No, I don't want to stay in Trinidad. I think I go go to the States.'

Bolo began marking two X's. Then three, four, six. He never won a penny. He was getting almost constantly angry.

He would say, 'Is just a big bacchanal, you hear. The paper people done make up their mind long long time now who going to win the week prize. They only want to get all the black people money.'

Hat said, 'You mustn't get discouraged. You got try really hard again.'

Bolo bought sheets of squared paper and fitted them over the Missing Ball photograph. Wherever the lines crossed he marked an X. To do this properly Bolo had to buy something like a hundred to a hundred and fifty *Guardians* every week.

Sometimes Bolo would call Boyee and Errol and me and say, 'Now, boys, where you think this missing ball is? Look, I want you to shut your eyes and mark a spot with this pencil.'

And sometimes again Bolo would ask us, 'What sort of things you been dreaming this week?'

If you said you didn't dream at all, Bolo looked disappointed. I used to make up dreams and Bolo would work them out in relation to the missing ball.

People began calling Bolo 'Missing Ball'.

Hat used to say, 'Look the man with the missing ball.'

One day Bolo went up to the offices of the *Guardian* and beat up a sub-editor before the police could be called.

In court Bolo said, 'The ball not missing, you hear. It wasn't there in the first place.'

Bolo was fined twenty-five dollars.

The *Gazette* ran a story:

THE CASE OF THE MISSING BALL
Penalty for a foul

Altogether Bolo spent about three hundred dollars trying to spot the missing ball, and he didn't even get a consolation prize.

It was shortly after the court case that Bolo stopped barbering regularly and also stopped reading the *Guardian*.

I can't remember now why Bolo stopped reading the *Evening News*, but I know why he stopped reading the *Gazette*.

A great housing shortage arose in Port of Spain during the war, and in 1942 a philanthropist came to the rescue of the unhoused. He said he was starting a co-operative housing scheme. People who wished to take part in this venture had to deposit some two hundred dollars, and after a year or so they would get brand-new houses for next to nothing. Several important men blessed the new scheme, and lots of dinners were eaten to give the project a good start.

The project was heavily advertised and about five or six houses were built and handed over to some of the people who had eaten the dinners. The papers carried photographs of people putting keys into locks and stepping over thresholds.

Bolo saw the photographs and the advertisements in the *Gazette*, and he paid in his two hundred dollars.

In 1943 the Director of the Co-operative Housing Society disappeared and with him disappeared two or three thousand dream houses.

Bolo stopped reading the *Gazette*.

It was on a Sunday in November that year that Bolo made his announcement to those of us who were sitting under the mango tree, waiting for Bolo to cut our hair.

He said, 'I saying something now. And so help me God, if I ever break my word, it go be better if I lose my two eyes. Listen. I stop reading papers. If even I learn Chinese I ain't go read Chinese papers, you hearing. You mustn't believe anything you read in the papers.'

Bolo was cutting Hat's hair at the moment, and Hat hurriedly got up and left.

Later Hat said, 'You know what I think. We will have to stop getting trim from Bolo. The man get me really frighten now, you hear.'

We didn't have to think a lot about Hat's decision because a few days later Bolo came to us and said, 'I coming round to see you people one by one because is the last time you go see me.'

He looked so sad I thought he was going to cry.

Hat said, 'What you thinking of doing now?'

Bolo said, 'I leaving this island for good. Is only a lot of damn crooks here.'

Eddoes said, 'Bolo, you taking your box-cart with you?'

Bolo said, 'No. Why, you like it?'

Eddoes said, 'I was thinking. It look like good materials to me.'

Bolo said, 'Eddoes, take my box-cart.'

Hat said, 'Where you going, Bolo?'

Bolo said, 'You go hear.'

And so he left us that evening.

Eddoes said, 'You think Bolo going mad?'

Hat said, 'No. He going Venezuela. That is why he keeping so secret. The Venezuelan police don't like Trinidad people going over.'

Eddoes said, 'Bolo is a nice man and I sorry he leaving. You know, it have some people I know who go be glad to have that box-cart Bolo leave behind.'

We went to Bolo's little room that very evening and we cleaned it of all the useful stuff he had left behind. There wasn't much. A bit of oil-cloth, two or three old combs, a cutlass, and a bench. We were all sad.

Hat said, 'People really treat poor Bolo bad in this country. I don't blame him for leaving.'

Eddoes was looking over the room in a practical way. He said, 'But Bolo take away everything, man.'

Next afternoon Eddoes announced, 'You know how much I pick up for that box-cart? Two dollars!'

Hat said, 'You does work damn fast, you know, Eddoes.'

Then we saw Bolo himself walking down Miguel Street.

Hat said, 'Eddoes, you in trouble.'

Eddoes said, 'But he give it to me. I didn't thief it.'

Bolo looked tired and sadder than ever.

Hat said, 'What happen, Bolo? You make a record, man. Don't tell me you go to Venezuela and you come back already.'

Bolo said, 'Trinidad people! Trinidad people! I don't know why

Hitler don't come here and bomb all the sons of bitches it have in this island. He bombing the wrong people, you know.'

Hat said, 'Sit down, Bolo, and tell we what happen.'

Bolo said, 'Not yet. It have something I have to settle first. Eddoes, where my box-cart?'

Hat laughed.

Bolo said, 'You laughing, but I don't see the joke. Where my box-cart, Eddoes? You think you could make box-cart like that?'

Eddoes said, 'Your box-cart, Bolo? But you give it to me.'

Bolo said, 'I asking you to give it back to me.'

Eddoes said, 'I sell it, Bolo. Look the two dollars I get for it.'

Bolo said, 'But you quick, man.'

Eddoes was getting up.

Bolo said, 'Eddoes, it have one thing I begging you not to do. I begging you, Eddoes, not to come for trim by me again, you hear. I can't trust myself. And go and buy back my box-cart.'

Eddoes went away, muttering, 'Is a funny sort of world where people think their little box-cart so good. It like my big blue cart?'

Bolo said, 'When I get my hand on the good-for-nothing thief who take my money and say he taking me Venezuela, I go let him know something. You know what the man do? He drive around all night in the motor-launch and then put we down in a swamp, saying we reach Venezuela. I see some people. I begin talking to them in Spanish, they shake their head and laugh. You know is what? He put me down in Trinidad self, three four miles from La Brea.'

Hat said, 'Bolo, you don't know how lucky you is. Some of these people woulda kill you and throw you overboard, man. They say they don't like getting into trouble with the Venezuelan police. Is illegal going over to Venezuela, you know.'

We saw very little of Bolo after this. Eddoes managed to get the box-cart back, and he asked me to take it to Bolo.

Eddoes said, 'You see why black people can't get on in this

world. You was there when he give it to me with his own two hands, and now he want it back. Take it back to him and tell him Eddoes say he could go to hell.'

I told Bolo, 'Eddoes say he sorry and he send back the box-cart.'

Bolo said, 'You see how black people is. They only quick to take, take. They don't want to give. That is why black people never get on.'

I said, 'Mr Bolo, it have something I take too, but I bring it back. Is the oil-cloth. I did take it and give it to my mother, but she ask me to bring it back.'

Bolo said, 'Is all right. But, boy, who trimming you these days? You head look as though fowl sitting on it.'

I said, 'Is Samuel trim me, Mr Bolo. But I tell you he can't trim. You see how he zog up my head.'

Bolo said, 'Come Sunday, I go trim you.'

I hesitated.

Bolo said, 'You fraid? Don't be stupid. I like you.'

So I went on Sunday.

Bolo said, 'How you getting on with your lessons?'

I didn't want to boast.

Bolo said, 'It have something I want you to do for me. But I not sure whether I should ask you.'

I said, 'But ask me, Mr Bolo. I go do anything for you.'

He said, 'No, don't worry. I go tell you next time you come.'

A month later, I went again and Bolo said, 'You could read?'

I reassured him.

He said, 'Well, is a secret thing I doing. I don't want nobody to know. You could keep a secret?'

I said, 'Yes, I could keep a secret.'

'A old man like me ain't have much to live for,' Bolo said. 'A old man like me living by hisself have to have something to live for. Is why I doing this thing I tell you about.'

'What is this thing, Mr Bolo?'

He stopped clipping my hair and pulled out a printed sheet from his trouser pocket.

He said, 'You know what this is?'

I said, 'Is a sweepstake ticket.'

'Right. You smart, man. Is really a sweepstake ticket.'

I said, 'But what you want me do, Mr Bolo?'

He said, 'First you must promise not to tell anybody.'

I gave my word.

He said, 'I want you to find out if the number draw.'

The draw was made about six weeks later and I looked for Bolo's number. I told him, 'You number ain't draw, Mr Bolo.'

He said, 'Not even a proxime accessit?'

I shook my head.

But Bolo didn't look disappointed. 'Is just what I expect,' he said.

For nearly three years this was our secret. And all during those years Bolo bought sweepstake tickets, and never won. Nobody knew and even when Hat or somebody else said to him, 'Bolo, I know a thing you could try. Why you don't try sweepstake?' Bolo would say, 'I done with that sort of thing, man.'

At the Christmas meeting of 1948 Bolo's number was drawn. It wasn't much, just about three hundred dollars.

I ran to Bolo's room and said, 'Mr Bolo, the number draw.'

Bolo's reaction wasn't what I expected. He said, 'Look, boy, you in long pants now. But don't get me mad, or I go have to beat you bad.'

I said, 'But it really draw, Mr Bolo.'

He said, 'How the hell you know it draw?'

I said, 'I see it in the papers.'

At this Bolo got really angry and he seized me by the collar. He screamed, 'How often I have to tell you, you little good-for-nothing son of a bitch, that you mustn't believe all that you read in the papers?'

So I checked up with the Trinidad Turf Club.

I said to Bolo, 'Is really true.' Bolo refused to believe.

He said, 'These Trinidad people does only lie, lie. Lie is all they know. They could fool you, boy, but they can't fool me.'

I told the men of the street, 'Bolo mad like hell. The man win three hundred dollars and he don't want to believe.'

One day Boyee said to Bolo, 'Ay, Bolo, you win a sweepstake then.'

Bolo chased Boyee, shouting, 'You playing the ass, eh. You making joke with a man old enough to be your grandfather.'

And when Bolo saw me, he said, 'Is so you does keep secret? Is so you does keep secret? But why all you Trinidad people so, eh?'

And he pushed his box-cart down to Eddoes' house, saying, 'Eddoes, you want box-cart, eh? Here, take the box-cart.'

And he began hacking the cart to bits with his cutlass.

To me he shouted, 'People think they could fool me.'

And he took out the sweepstake ticket and tore it. He rushed up to me and forced the pieces into my shirt pocket.

*

Afterwards he lived to himself in his little room, seldom came out to the street, never spoke to anybody. Once a month he went to draw his old-age pension.

15. Until the Soldiers Came

EDWARD, HAT'S BROTHER, was a man of many parts, and I always thought it a sad thing that he drifted away from us. He used to help Hat with the cows when I first knew him and, like Hat, he looked settled and happy enough. He said he had given up women for good, and he concentrated on cricket, football, boxing, horse-racing, and cockfighting. In this way he was never bored, and he had no big ambition to make him unhappy.

Like Hat, Edward had a high regard for beauty. But Edward didn't collect birds of beautiful plumage, as Hat did. Edward painted.

His favourite subject was a brown hand clasping a black one. And when Edward painted a brown hand, it was a brown hand. No nonsense about light and shades. And the sea was a blue sea, and mountains were green.

Edward mounted his pictures himself and framed them in red passe-partout. The big department stores, Salvatori's, Fogarty's, and Johnson's, distributed Edward's work on commission.

To the street, however, Edward was something of a menace.

He would see Mrs Morgan wearing a new dress and say, 'Ah, Mrs Morgan, is a nice nice dress you wearing there, but I think it could do with some sort of decoration.'

Or he would see Eddoes wearing a new shirt and say, 'Eh, eh, Eddoes, you wearing a new shirt, man. You write your name in it, you know, otherwise somebody pick it up brisk brisk one of these days. Tell you what, I go write it for you.'

He ruined many garments in this way.

He also had the habit of giving away ties he had decorated himself. He would say, 'I have something for you. Take it and wear it. I giving it to you because I like you.'

And if the tie wasn't worn, Edward would get angry and begin shouting, 'But you see how ungrateful black people is. Listen to this. I see this man not wearing tie. I take a bus and I go to town. I walk to Johnson's and I look for the gents' department. I meet a girl and I buy a tie. I take a bus back home. I go inside my room and take up my brush and unscrew my paint. I dip my brush in paint and I put the brush on the tie. I spend two three hours doing that, and after all this, the man ain't wearing my tie.'

But Edward did a lot more than just paint.

One day, not many months after I had come to the street, Edward said, 'Coming back on the bus from Cocorite last night I only hearing the bus wheel cracking over crab back. You know the place by the coconut trees and the swamp? There it just crawling with crab. People say they even climbing up the coconut trees.'

Hat said, 'They does come out a lot at full moon. Let we go tonight and catch some of the crabs that Edward see.'

Edward said, 'Is just what I was going to say. We will have to take the boys because it have so much crab even they could pick up a lot.'

So we boys were invited.

Edward said, 'Hat, I was thinking. It go be a lot easier to catch the crab if we take a shovel. It have so much you could just shovel them up.'

Hat said, 'All right. We go take the cow-pen shovel.'

Edward said, 'That settle. But look, all-you have strong shoes? You better get strong shoes, you know, because these crab and them ain't playing big and if you don't look out they start walking away with your big toe before you know what is what.'

Hat said, 'I go use the leggings I does wear when I cleaning out the cow-pen.'

Edward said, 'And we better wear gloves. I know a man was catching crab one day and suddenly he see his right hand walking away from him. He look again and see four five crab carrying it away. This man jump up and begin one bawling. So we have to be careful. If you boys ain't have gloves just wrap some cloth over your hands. That go be all right.'

So late that night we all climbed into the Cocorite bus, Hat in his leggings, Edward in his, and the rest of us carrying cutlasses and big brown sacks.

The shovel Hat carried still stank from the cow-pen and people began squinging up their noses.

Hat said, 'Let them smell it. They does all want milk when the cow give it.'

People looked at the leggings and the cutlasses and the shovel and the sacks and looked away quickly. They stopped talking. The conductor didn't ask for our fares. The bus was silent until Edward began to talk.

Edward said, 'We must try and not use the cutlass. It ain't nice to kill. Try and get them live and put them in the bag.'

Many people got off at the next stop. By the time the bus got to Mucurapo Road it was carrying only us. The conductor stood right at the front talking to the driver.

Just before we got to the Cocorite terminus Edward said, 'Oh God, I know I was forgetting something. We can't bring back all the crab in a bus. I go have to go and telephone for a van.'

He got off one stop before the terminus.

We walked a little way in the bright moonlight, left the road and climbed down into the swamp. A tired wind blew from the sea, and the smell of stale sea-water was everywhere. Under the coconut trees it was dark. We walked a bit further in. A cloud covered the moon and the wind fell.

Hat called out, 'You boys all right? Be careful with your foot. I don't want any of you going home with only three toes.'

Boyee said, 'But I ain't seeing any crab.'

Ten minutes later Edward joined us.

He said, 'How many bags you full?'

Hat said, 'It look like a lot of people had the same idea and come and take away all the crab.'

Edward said, 'Rubbish. You don't see the moon ain't showing. We got to wait until the moon come out before the crab come out. Sit down, boys, let we wait.'

The moon remained clouded for half an hour.

Boyee said, 'It making cold and I want to go home. I don't think it have any crab.'

Errol said, 'Don't mind Boyee. I know him. He just frighten of the dark and he fraid the crab bite him.'

At this point we heard a rumbling in the distance.

Hat said, 'It look like the van come.'

Edward said, 'It ain't a van really. I order a big truck from Sam.'

We sat in silence waiting for the moon to clear. Then about a dozen torch-lights flashed all around us. Someone shouted, 'We ain't want any trouble. But if any one of you play the fool you going to get beat up bad.'

We saw what looked like a squad of policemen surrounding us.

Boyee began to cry.

Edward said, 'It have man beating their wife. It have people breaking into other people house. Why you policeman don't go and spend your time doing something with sense, eh? Just for a change.'

A policeman said, 'Why you don't shut up? You want me to spit in your mouth?'

Another policeman said, 'What you have in those bags?'

Edward said, 'Only crab. But take care. They is big crab and they go bite off your hand.'

Nobody looked inside the bags and then a man with a lot of stripes said, 'Everybody playing bad-man these days. Everybody getting full of smart answers, like the Americans and them.'

A policeman said, 'They have bag, they have cutlass, they have shovel, they have glove.'

Hat said, 'We was catching crab.'

The policeman said, 'With shovel? Eh, eh, what happen that you suddenly is God and make a new sort of crab you could catch with shovel?'

It took a lot of talk to make the policemen believe our story.

The officer in charge said, 'I go like to lay my hands on the son of a bitch who telephoned and say you was going to kill somebody.'

Then the policemen left.

It was late and we had missed the last bus.

Hat said, 'We had better wait for the truck Edward order.'

Edward said, 'Something tell me that truck ain't coming now.'

Hat said very slowly, half laughing and half serious, 'Edward, you is my own brother, but you know you really is a son of a bitch.'

Edward sat down and just laughed and laughed.

*

Then the war came. Hitler invaded France and the Americans invaded Trinidad. Lord Invader made a hit with his calypso:

I was living with my decent and contented wife
Until the soldiers came and broke up my life.

For the first time in Trinidad there was work for everybody, and the Americans paid well. Invader sang:

Father, mother, and daughter
Working for the Yankee dollar!
Money in the land!
The Yankee dollar, oh!

Edward stopped working in the cow-pen and got a job with the Americans at Chaguaramas.

Hat said, 'Edward, I think you foolish to do that. The Americans ain't here forever and ever. It ain't have no sense in going off and working for big money and then not having nothing to eat after three four years.'

Edward said, 'This war look as though it go last a long long time. And the Americans not like the British, you know. They does make you work hard, but they does pay for it.'

Edward sold his share of the cows to Hat, and that marked the beginning of his drift away from us.

Edward surrendered completely to the Americans. He began wearing clothes in the American style, he began chewing gum, and he tried to talk with an American accent. We didn't see much of him except on Sundays, and then he made us feel small and inferior. He grew fussy about his dress, and he began wearing a gold chain around his neck. He began wearing straps around his wrists, after the fashion of tennis-players. These straps were just becoming fashionable among smart young men in Port of Spain.

Edward didn't give up painting, but he no longer offered to paint things for us, and I think most people were relieved. He entered some poster competition, and when his design didn't win even a consolation prize, he grew really angry with Trinidad.

One Sunday he said, 'I was stupid to send in anything I paint with my own two hands for Trinidad people to judge. What they know about anything? Now, if I was in America, it woulda be different. The Americans is people. They know about things.'

To hear Edward talk, you felt that America was a gigantic

country inhabited by giants. They lived in enormous houses and they drove in the biggest cars of the world.

Edward used to say, 'Look at Miguel Street. In America you think they have streets so narrow? In America this street could pass for a sidewalk.'

One night I walked down with Edward to Docksite, the American army camp. Through the barbed wire you could see the huge screen of an open-air cinema.

Edward said, 'You see the sort of theatre they come and build in a stupid little place like Trinidad. Imagine the sort of thing they have in the States.'

And we walked down a little further until we came to a sentry in his box.

Edward used his best American accent and said, 'What's cooking, Joe?'

To my surprise the sentry, looking fierce under his helmet, replied, and in no time at all Edward and the sentry were talking away, each trying to use more swear-words than the other.

When Edward came back to Miguel Street he began swaggering along and he said to me, 'Tell them. Tell them how good I does get on with the Americans.'

And when he was with Hat he said, 'Was talking the other night with a American – damn good friend – and he was telling me that as soon as the Americans enter the war the war go end.'

Errol said, 'It ain't *that* we want to win the war. As soon as they make Lord Anthony Eden Prime Minister the war go end quick quick.'

Edward said, 'Shut up, kid.'

But the biggest change of all was the way Edward began talking of women. Up till then he used to say that he was finished with them for good. He made out that his heart had been broken a long time ago and he had made a vow. It was a vague and tragic story.

But now on Sundays Edward said, 'You should see the sort of

craft they have at the base. Nothing like these stupid Trinidad girls, you know. No, partner. Girls with style, girls with real class.'

I think it was Eddoes who said, 'I shouldn't let it worry you. They wouldn't tangle with you, those girls. They want big big American men. You safe.'

Edward called Eddoes a shrimp and walked away in a huff.

He began lifting weights, and in this, too, Edward was running right at the head of fashion. I don't know what happened in Trinidad about that time, but every young man became suddenly obsessed with the Body Beautiful idea, and there were physique competitions practically every month. Hat used to console himself by saying, 'Don't worry. Is just a lot of old flash, you hear. They say they building muscle muscle. Just let them cool off and see what happen. All that thing they call muscle turn fat, you know.'

Eddoes said, 'Is the funniest sight you could see. At the Dairies in Philip Street all you seeing these days is a long line of black black men sitting at the counter and drinking quart bottles of white milk. All of them wearing sleeveless jersey to show off their big arm.'

In about three months Edward made his appearance among us in a sleeveless jersey. He had become a really big man.

Presently he began talking about the women at the base who were chasing him.

He said, 'I don't know what they see in me.'

*

Somebody had the idea of organizing a Local Talent on Parade show and Edward said, 'Don't make me laugh. What sort of talent they think Trinidad have?'

The first show was broadcast and we all listened to it in Eddoes' house, Edward kept on laughing all the time.

Hat said, 'Why you don't try singing yourself, then?'

Edward said, 'Sing for who? Trinidad people?'

Hat said, 'Do them a favour.'

To everybody's surprise Edward began singing, and the time came when Hat had to say, 'I just can't live in the same house with Edward. I think he go have to move.'

Edward moved, but he didn't move very far. He remained on our side of Miguel Street.

He said, 'Is a good thing. I was getting tired of the cow smell.'

Edward went up for one of the Local Talent shows and in spite of everything we all hoped that he would win a prize of some sort. The show was sponsored by a biscuit company and I think the winner got some money.

'They does give the others a thirty-one-cent pack of biscuits,' Hat said.

Edward got a package of biscuits.

He didn't bring it home, though. He threw it away.

He said, 'Throw it away. Why I shouldn't throw it away? You see, is just what I does tell you. Trinidad people don't know good thing. They just born stupid. Down at the base it have Americans *begging* me to sing. They know what is what. The other day, working and singing at the base, the colonel come up and tell me I had a nice voice. He was begging me to go to the States.'

Hat said, 'Why you don't go then?'

Edward said fiercely, 'Gimme time. Wait and see if I don't go.'

Eddoes said, 'What about all those woman and them who was chasing you? They catch up with you yet or they pass you?'

Edward said, 'Listen, Joe, I don't want to start getting tough with you. Do me a favour and shut up.'

When Edward brought any American friends to his house he pretended that he didn't know us, and it was funny to see him walking with them, holding his arms in the American way, hanging loosely, like a gorilla's.

Hat said, 'All the money he making he spending it on rum and ginger, curryfavouring with them Americans.'

In a way, I suppose, we were all jealous of him.

Hat began saying, 'It ain't hard to get a work with the Americans. I just don't want to have boss, that's all. I like being my own boss.'

Edward didn't mix much with us now.

*

One day he came to us with a sad face and said, 'Hat, it look like if I have to get married.'

He spoke with his Trinidad accent.

Hat looked worried. He said, 'Why? Why? Why you have to get married?'

'She making baby.'

'Is a damn funny thing to say. If everybody married because woman making baby for them it go be a hell of a thing. What happen that you want to be different now from everybody else in Trinidad? You come so American?'

Edward hitched up his tight American-style trousers and made a face like an American film actor. He said, 'You know all the answers, don't you? This girl is different. Sure I fall in love maybe once maybe twice before, but this kid's different.'

Hat said, 'She's got what it takes?'

Edward said, 'Yes.'

Hat said, 'Edward, you is a big man. It clear that you make up your mind to married this girl. Why you come round trying to make me force you to married her? You is a big man. You ain't have to come to me to get permission to do this to do that.'

When Edward left, Hat said, 'Whenever Edward come to me with a lie, he like a little boy. He can't lie to me. But if he married this girl, although I ain't see she, I feel he go live to regret it.'

*

Edward's wife was a tall and thin white-skinned woman. She looked very pale and perpetually unwell. She moved as though every step cost her effort. Edward made a great fuss about her and never introduced us.

The women of the street lost no time in passing judgement.

Mrs Morgan said, 'She is a born trouble-maker, that woman. I feel sorry for Edward. He got hisself in one mess.'

Mrs Bhakcu said, 'She is one of these modern girls. They want their husband to work all day and come home and cook and wash and clean up. All they know is to put powder and rouge on their face and walk out swinging their backside.'

And Hat said, 'But how she making baby? I can't see anything.'

Edward dropped out of our circle completely.

Hat said, 'She giving him good hell.'

And one day, Hat shouted across the road to Edward, 'Joe, come across here for a moment.'

Edward looked very surly. He asked in Trinidadian, 'What you want?'

Hat smiled and said, 'What about the baby? When it coming?'

Edward said, 'What the hell you want to know for?'

Hat said, 'I go be a funny sort of uncle if I wasn't interested in my nephew.'

Edward said, 'She ain't making no more baby.'

Eddoes said, 'So it was just a line she was shooting then?'

Hat said, 'Edward, you lying. You make up all that in the first place. She wasn't making no baby, and you know that. She didn't tell you she was making baby, and you know that too. If you want to married the woman why you making all this thing about it?'

Edward looked very sad. 'If you want to know the truth, I don't think she could make baby.'

And when this news filtered through to the women of the street, they all said what my mother said.

She said, 'How you could see pink and pale people ever making baby?'

And although we had no evidence, and although Edward's house was still noisy with Americans, we felt that all was not well with Edward and his wife.

*

One Friday, just as it was getting dark, Edward ran up to me and said, 'Put down that stupidness you reading and go and get a policeman.'

I said, 'Policeman? But how I go go and get policeman just like that.'

Edward said, 'You could ride?'

I said, 'Yes.'

Edward said, 'You have a bicycle lamp?'

I said, 'No.'

Edward said, 'Take the bike and ride without lamp. You bound to get policeman.'

I said, 'And when I get this policeman, what I go tell him?'

Edward said, 'She try to kill sheself again.'

Before I had cycled to Ariapita Avenue I had met not one but two policemen. One of them was a sergeant. He said, 'You thinking of going far, eh?'

I said, 'Is you I was coming to find.'

The other policeman laughed.

The sergeant said to him, 'He smart, eh? I feel the magistrate go like that excuse. Is a new one and even me like it.'

I said, 'Come quick, Edward wife try to kill sheself again.'

The sergeant said, 'Oh, Edward wife always killing sheself, eh?' And he laughed. He added, 'And where this Edward wife try to kill sheself again, eh?'

I said, 'Just a little bit down Miguel Street.'

The constable said, 'He really smart, you know.'

The sergeant said, 'Yes. We leave him here and go and find somebody who try to kill sheself. Cut out this nonsense, boy. Where your bicycle licence?'

I said, 'Is true what I telling you. I go come back with you and show you the house.'

Edward was waiting for us. He said, 'You take a damn long time getting just two policemen.'

The policemen went inside the house with Edward and a little crowd gathered on the pavement.

Mrs Bhakcu said, 'Is just what I expect. I know from the first it was going to end up like this.'

Mrs Morgan said, 'Life is a funny thing. I wish I was like she and couldn't make baby. And it have a woman now trying to kill sheself because she can't make baby.'

Eddoes said, 'How you know is that she want to kill sheself for?'

Mrs Morgan shook a fat shoulder. 'What else?'

From then on I began to feel sorry for Edward because the men in the street and the women didn't give him a chance. And no matter how many big parties Edward gave at his house for Americans, I could see that he was affected when Eddoes shouted, 'Why you don't take your wife to America, boy? Those American doctors smart like hell, you know. They could do anything.' Or when Mrs Bhakcu suggested that she should have a blood test at the Caribbean Medical Commission at the end of Ariapita Avenue.

The parties at Edward's house grew wilder and more extravagant. Hat said, 'Every party does have an end and have to go home. Edward only making hisself more miserable.'

The parties certainly were not making Edward's wife any happier. She still looked frail and cantankerous, and now we sometimes heard Edward's voice raised in argument with her. It was not the usual sort of man-and-wife argument we had in the street. Edward sounded exasperated, but anxious to please.

Eddoes said, 'I wish any woman I married try behaving like that. Man, I give she one good beating and I make she straight straight like bamboo.'

Hat said, 'Edward ask for what he get. And the stupid thing is that I believe Edward really love the woman.'

Edward would talk to Hat and Eddoes and the other big men when they spoke to him, but when we boys tried talking to him, he had no patience. He would threaten to beat us and so we left him alone.

But whenever Edward passed, Boyee, brave and stupid as ever, would say in an American accent, 'What's up, Joe?'

Edward would stop and look angrily at Boyee and then lunge at him, shouting and swearing. He used to say, 'You see the sort of way Trinidad children does behave? What else this boy want but a good cut-arse?'

One day Edward caught Boyee and began flogging him.

At every stroke Boyee shouted, 'No, Edward.'

And Edward got madder and madder.

Then Hat ran up and said, 'Edward, put down that boy this minute or else it have big big trouble in this street. Put him down, I tell you. I ain't fraid of your big arms, you know.'

The men in the street had to break up the fight.

And when Boyee was freed, he shouted to Edward, 'Why you don't make child yourself and then beat it?'

Hat said, 'Boyee, I going to cut your tail this minute. Errol, go break a good whip for me.'

*

It was Edward himself who broke the news.

He said, 'She leave me.' He spoke in a very casual way.

Eddoes said, 'I sorry too bad, Edward.'

Hat said, 'Edward, boy, the things that not to be don't be.'

Edward didn't seem to be paying too much attention.

So Eddoes went on, 'I didn't like she from the first and I don't think a man should married a woman who can't make baby – '

Edward said, 'Eddoes, shut your thin little mouth up. And you, too, Hat, giving me all this make-up sympathy. I know how sad all-you is, all-you so sad all-you laughing.'

Hat said, 'But who laughing? Look, Edward, go and give anybody else all this temper, you hear, but leave me out. After all, it ain't nothing strange for a man wife to run away. Is like the calypso Invader sing:

> I was living with my decent and contented wife
> Until the soldiers came and broke up my life.

It ain't your fault, is the Americans' fault.'

Eddoes said, 'You know who she run away with?'

Edward said, 'You hear me say she run away with anybody?'

Eddoes said, 'No, you didn't say that, but is what I feel.'

Edward said sadly, 'Yes, she run away. With a American soldier. And I give the man so much of my rum to drink.'

But after a few days Edward was running around telling people what had happened and saying, 'Is a damn good thing. I don't want a wife that can't make baby.'

And now nobody made fun of Edward's Americanism, and I think we were all ready to welcome him back to us. But he wasn't really interested. We hardly saw him in the street. When he wasn't working he was out on some excursion.

Hat said, 'Is love he really love she. He looking for she.'

In the calypso by Lord Invader the singer loses his wife to the Americans and when he begs her to come back to him, she says:

> 'Invader, I change my mind,
> I living with my Yankee soldier.'

This was exactly what happened to Edward.

He came back in a great temper. He was miserable. He said, 'I leaving Trinidad.'

Eddoes said, 'Where you going? America?'

Edward almost cuffed Eddoes.

Hat said, 'But how you want to let one woman break up your life so? You behaving as if you is the first man this thing happen to.'

But Edward didn't listen.

At the end of the month he sold his house and left Trinidad. I think he went to Aruba or Curaçao, working with the big Dutch oil company.

*

And some months later Hat said, 'You know what I hear? Edward wife have a baby for she American.'

16. Hat

HAT LOVED TO make a mystery of the smallest things. His relationship to Boyee and Errol, for instance. He told strangers they were illegitimate children of his. Sometimes he said he wasn't sure whether they were his at all, and he would spin a fantastic story about some woman both he and Edward lived with at the same time. Sometimes again, he would make out that they were his sons by an early marriage, and you felt you could cry when you heard Hat tell how the boys' mother had gathered them around her death-bed and made them promise to be good.

It took me some time to find out that Boyee and Errol were really Hat's nephews. Their mother, who lived up in the bush near Sangre Grande, died soon after her husband died, and the boys came to live with Hat.

The boys showed Hat little respect. They never called him Uncle, only Hat; and for their part they didn't mind when Hat said they were illegitimate. They were, in fact, willing to support any story Hat told about their birth.

I first got to know Hat when he offered to take me to the cricket at the Oval. I soon found out that he had picked up eleven other boys from four or five streets around, and was taking them as well.

We lined up at the ticket-office and Hat counted us loudly. He said, 'One and twelve half.'

Many people stopped minding their business and looked up.

The man selling tickets said, 'Twelve half?'

Hat looked down at his shoes and said, 'Twelve half.'

We created a lot of excitement when all thirteen of us, Hat at the head, filed around the ground, looking for a place to sit.

People shouted, 'They is all yours, mister?'

Hat smiled, weakly, and made people believe it was so. When we sat down he made a point of counting us loudly again. He said, 'I don't want your mother raising hell when I get home, saying one missing.'

It was the last day of the last match between Trinidad and Jamaica. Gerry Gomez and Len Harbin were making a great stand for Trinidad, and when Gomez reached his 150 Hat went crazy and danced up and down, shouting, 'White people is God, you hear!'

A woman selling soft drinks passed in front of us.

Hat said, 'How you selling this thing you have in the glass and them?'

The woman said, 'Six cents a glass.'

Hat said, 'I want the wholesale price. I want thirteen.'

The woman said, 'These children is all yours?'

Hat said, 'What wrong with that?'

The woman sold the drinks at five cents a glass.

When Len Harbin was 89, he was out lbw, and Trinidad declared.

Hat was angry. 'Lbw? Lbw? How he lbw? Is only a lot of robbery. And is a Trinidad umpire too. God, even umpires taking bribe now.'

Hat taught me many things that afternoon. From the way he pronounced them, I learned about the beauty of cricketers' names, and he gave me all his own excitement at watching a cricket match.

I asked him to explain the scoreboard.

He said, 'On the left-hand side they have the names of the batsman who finish batting.'

I remember that because I thought it such a nice way of saying that a batsman was out: to say that he had finished batting.

All during the tea interval Hat was as excited as ever. He tried to get all sorts of people to take all sorts of crazy bets. He ran about waving a dollar-note and shouting, 'A dollar to a shilling, Headley don't reach double figures.' Or, 'A dollar, Stollmeyer field the first ball.'

The umpires were walking out when one of the boys began crying.

Hat said, 'What you crying for?'

The boy cried and mumbled.

Hat said, 'But what you crying for?'

A man shouted, 'He want a bottle.'

Hat turned to the man and said, 'Two dollars, five Jamaican wickets fall this afternoon.'

The man said, 'Is all right by me, if is hurry you is to lose your money.'

A third man held the stakes.

The boy was still crying.

Hat said, 'But you see how you shaming me in front of all these people? Tell me quick what you want.'

The boy only cried. Another boy came up to Hat and whispered in his ear.

Hat said, 'Oh, God! How? Just when they coming out.'

He made us all stand. He marched us away from the grounds and made us line up against the galvanized-iron paling of the Oval.

He said, 'All right, now, pee. Pee quick, all of all-you.'

The cricket that afternoon was fantastic. The Jamaican team, which included the great Headley, lost six wickets for thirty-one runs. In the fading light the Trinidad fast bowler, Tyrell Johnson, was unplayable, and his success seemed to increase his speed.

A fat old woman on our left began screaming at Tyrell Johnson, and whenever she stopped screaming she turned to us and said very quietly, 'I know Tyrell since he was a boy so high. We use to pitch marble together.' Then she turned away and began screaming again.

Hat collected his bet.

This, I discovered presently, was one of Hat's weaknesses – his passion for impossible bets. At the races particularly, he lost a lot of money, but sometimes he won, and then he made so much he could afford to treat all of us in Miguel Street.

I never knew a man who enjoyed life as much as Hat did. He did nothing new or spectacular – in fact, he did practically the same things every day – but he always enjoyed what he did. And every now and then he managed to give a fantastic twist to some very ordinary thing.

He was a bit like his dog. This was the tamest Alsatian I have ever known. One of the things I noticed in Miguel Street was the way dogs resembled their owners. George had a surly, mean mongrel. Tom's dog was a terrible savage. Hat's dog was the only Alsatian I knew with a sense of humour.

In the first place it behaved oddly, for an Alsatian. You could make it the happiest dog on earth if you flung things for it to retrieve. One day, in the Savannah, I flung a guava, into some thick bushes. He couldn't get at the guava, and he whined and complained. He suddenly turned and ran back past me, barking loudly. While I turned to see what was wrong, he ran back to the bushes. I saw nothing strange, and when I looked back I was just in time to see him taking another guava behind the bushes.

I called him and he rushed up whining and barking.

I said, 'Go on, boy. Go on and get the guava.'

He ran back to the bushes and poked and sniffed a bit and then dashed behind the bushes to get the guava he had himself placed there.

I only wish the beautiful birds Hat collected were as tame as the Alsatian. The macaws and the parrots looked like angry and quarrelsome old women and they attacked anybody. Sometimes Hat's house became a dangerous place with all these birds around. You would be talking quietly when you would suddenly feel a prick and a tug on your calf. The macaw or the parrot. Hat tried to make us believe they didn't bite him, but I know that they did.

Strange that both Hat and Edward became dangerous when they tried meddling with beauty. There was Edward with his painting, and Hat with his sharp-beaked macaws.

Hat was always getting into trouble with the police. Nothing serious, though. A little cockfighting here, some gambling there, a little drinking somewhere else, and so on.

But it never soured him against the law. In fact, every Christmas Sergeant Charles, with the postman and the sanitary inspector, came to Hat's place for a drink.

Sergeant Charles would say, 'Is only a living I have to make, you know, Hat. Nobody ain't have to tell me. I know I ain't going to get any more promotion, but still.'

Hat would say, 'Is all right, Sergeant. None of we don't mind. How your children these days? How Elijah?'

Elijah was a bright boy.

'Elijah? Oh, I think he go get a exhibition this year. Is all we could do, eh, Hat? All we could do is try. We can't do no more.'

And they always separated as good friends.

But once Hat got into serious trouble for watering his milk.

He said, 'The police and them come round asking me how the water get in the milk. As if I know. I ain't know how the water get there. You know I does put the pan in water to keep the milk cool, and prevent it from turning. I suppose the pan did have a hole, that's all. A tiny little hole.'

Edward said, 'It better to be frank and tell the magistrate that.'

Hat said, 'Edward, you talking as if Trinidad is England. You ever hear that people tell the truth in Trinidad and get away? In Trinidad the more you innocent, the more they throw you in jail, and the more bribe you got to hand out. You got to bribe the magistrate. You got to give them fowl, big Leghorn hen, and you got to give them money. You got to bribe the inspectors. By the time you finish bribing it would be better if you did take your jail quiet quiet.'

Edward said, 'It is the truth. But you can't plead guilty. You have to make up some new story.'

Hat was fined two hundred dollars and the magistrate preached a long sermon at him.

He was in a real temper when he came back from court. He tore off his tie and coat and said, 'Is a damn funny world. You bathe, you put on a clean shirt, you put on tie and you put on jacket, you shine up your shoe. And all for what? Is only to go in front of some stupid magistrate for him to abuse you.'

It rankled for days.

Hat said, 'Hitler was right, man. Burn all the law books. Burn all of them up. Make a big pile and set fire to the whole damn thing. Burn them up and watch them burn. Hitler was right, man. I don't know why we fighting him for.'

Eddoes said, 'You talking a lot of nonsense, you know, Hat.'

Hat said, 'I don't want to talk about it. Don't want to talk about it. Hitler was right. Burn the law books. Burn all of them up. Don't want to talk about it.'

For three months Hat and Sergeant Charles were not on speaking terms. Sergeant Charles was hurt, and he was always sending messages of goodwill to Hat.

One day he called me and said, 'You go be seeing Hat this evening?'

I said, 'Yes.'

'You did see him yesterday?'

'Yes.'

'How he is?'

'How?'

'Well, I mean, how he looking? He looking well? Happy?'

I said, 'He looking damn vex.'

Sergeant Charles said, 'Oh.'

I said, 'All right.'

'Look, before you go away – '

'What?'

'Nothing. No, no. Wait before you go. Tell Hat how for me, you hear.'

I told Hat, 'Sergeant Charles call me to his house today and begin one crying and begging. He keep on asking me to tell you that he not vex with you, that it wasn't he who tell the police about the milk and the water.'

Hat said, '*Which* water in *which* milk?'

I didn't know what to say.

Hat said, 'You see the sort of place Trinidad coming now. Somebody say it had water in my milk. Nobody see me put water in the milk, but everybody talking now as if they see me. Everybody talking about *the* water in *the* milk.'

Hat, I saw, was enjoying even this.

*

I always looked upon Hat as a man of settled habits, and it was hard to think of him looking otherwise than he did. I suppose he was thirty-five when he took me to that cricket-match, and forty-three when he went to jail. Yet he always looked the same to me.

In appearance, as I have said, he was like Rex Harrison. He was dark-brown in complexion, of medium height medium build. He had a slightly bow-legged walk and he had flat feet.

I was prepared to see him do the same things for the rest of his life. Cricket, football, horse-racing; read the paper in the mornings and afternoons; sit on the pavement and talk; get noisily drunk on Christmas Eve and New Year's Eve.

He didn't appear to need anything else. He was self-sufficient, and I didn't believe he even needed women. I knew, of course, that he visited certain places in the city from time to time, but I thought he did this more for the vicious thrill than for the women.

And then this thing happened. It broke up the Miguel Street Club, and Hat himself was never the same afterwards.

In a way, I suppose, it was Edward's fault. I don't think any of us realized how much Hat loved Edward and how heartbroken he was when Edward got married. He couldn't hide his delight when Edward's wife ran away with the American soldier, and he was greatly disappointed when Edward went to Aruba.

Once he said, 'Everybody growing up or they leaving.'

Another time he said, 'I think I was a damn fool not to go and work with the Americans, like Edward and so much other people.'

Eddoes said, 'Hat going to town a lot these nights.'

Boyee said, 'Well, he is a big man. Why he shouldn't do what he want to do?'

Eddoes said, 'It have some men like that. As a matter of fact, it does happen to all man. They getting old and they get frighten and they want to remain young.'

I got angry with Eddoes because I didn't want to think of Hat in that way and the worst thing was that I was ashamed because I felt Eddoes was right.

I said, 'Eddoes, why you don't take your dirty mind somewhere else, eh? Why you don't leave all your dirtiness in the rubbish-dump?'

And then one day Hat brought home a woman.

I felt a little uneasy now in Hat's company. He had become a man with responsibility and obligations, and he could no longer give us all his time and attention. To make matters worse, everybody pretended that the woman wasn't there. Even Hat. He never spoke about her and he behaved as though he wanted us to believe that everything was just the same.

She was a pale-brown woman, about thirty, somewhat plump,

and her favourite colour was blue. She called herself Dolly. We used to see her looking blankly out of the windows of Hat's house. She never spoke to any of us. In fact, I hardly heard her speak at all, except to call Hat inside.

But Boyee and Edward were pleased with the changes she brought.

Boyee said, 'Is the first time I remember living with a woman in the house, and it make a lot of difference. Is hard to explain, but I find it nicer.'

My mother said, 'You see how man stupid. Hat see what happen to Edward and you mean to say that Hat still get hisself mix up with this woman?'

Mrs Morgan and Mrs Bhakcu saw so little of Dolly they had little to dislike in her, but they agreed that she was a lazy good-for-nothing.

Mrs Morgan said, 'This Dolly look like a old *madame* to me, you hear.'

It was easy enough for us to forget that Dolly was there, because Hat continued living as before. We still went to all the sports and we still sat on the pavement and talked.

Whenever Dolly piped, 'Hat, you coming?' Hat wouldn't reply.

About half an hour later Dolly would say, 'Hat, you coming or you ain't coming?'

And Hat would say then, 'I coming.'

I wondered what life was like for Dolly. She was nearly always inside the house and Hat was nearly always outside. She seemed to spend a great deal of her time at the front window looking out.

They were really the queerest couple in the street. They never went out together. We never heard them laughing. They never even quarrelled.

Eddoes said, 'They like two strangers.'

Errol said, 'Don't mind that, you hear. All you seeing Hat sitting quiet quiet here, but is different when he get inside. He ain't the same man when he talking with Dolly. He buy she a lot of joolry, you know.'

Eddoes said, 'I have a feeling she a little bit like Matilda. You know, the woman in the calypso:

> Matilda, Matilda,
> Matilda, you thief my money
> And gone Venezuela.

Buying joolry! But what happening to Hat? He behaving as though he is a old man. Woman don't want joolry from a man like Hat, they want something else.'

Looking on from the outside, though, one could see only two changes in Hat's household. All the birds were caged, and the Alsatian was chained and miserable.

But no one spoke about Dolly to Hat. I suppose the whole business had come as too much of a surprise.

What followed was an even bigger surprise, and it was some time before we could get all the details. At first I noticed Hat was missing, and then I heard rumours.

This was the story, as it later came out in court. Dolly had run away from Hat, taking all his gifts of course. Hat had chased her and found her with another man. There was a great quarrel, the man had fled, and Hat had taken it out on Dolly. Afterwards, the police statement said, he had gone, in tears, to the police station to give himself up. He said, 'I kill a woman.'

But Dolly wasn't dead.

We received the news as though it was news of a death. We couldn't believe it for a day or two.

And then a great hush fell on Miguel Street. No boys and men gathered under the lamp-post outside Hat's house, talking about this and that and the other. No one played cricket and disturbed people taking afternoon naps. The Club was dead.

Cruelly, we forgot all about Dolly and thought only about Hat.

We couldn't find it in our hearts to find fault with him. We suffered with him.

We saw a changed man in court. He had grown older, and when he smiled at us he smiled only with his mouth. Still, he put on a show for us and even while we laughed we were ready to cry.

The prosecutor asked Hat, 'Was it a dark night?'

Hat said, 'All night dark.'

Hat's lawyer was a short fat man called Chittaranjan who wore a smelly brown suit.

Chittaranjan began reeling off Portia's speech about mercy, and he would have gone on to the end if the judge hadn't said, 'All this is interesting and some of it even true but, Mr Chittaranjan, you are wasting the court's time.'

Chittaranjan made a great deal of fuss about the wild passion of love. He said Antony had thrown away an empire for the sake of love, just as Hat had thrown away his self-respect. He said that Hat's crime was really a *crime passionel*. In France, he said – and he knew what he was talking about, because he had been to Paris – in France, Hat would have been a hero. Women would have garlanded him.

Eddoes said, 'Is this sort of lawyer who does get man hang, you know.'

Hat was sentenced to four years.

We went to Frederick Street jail to see him. It was a disappointing jail. The walls were light cream, and not very high, and I was surprised to see that most of the visitors were very gay. Only a few women wept, but the whole thing was like a party, with people laughing and chatting.

Eddoes, who had put on his best suit for the occasion, held his hat in his hand and looked around. He said to Hat, 'It don't look too bad here.'

Hat said, 'They taking me to Carrera next week.'

Carrera was the small prison-island a few miles from Port of Spain.

Hat said, 'Don't worry about me. You know me. In two three weeks I go make them give me something easy to do.'

*

Whenever I went to Carenage or Point Cumana for a bathe, I looked across the green water to the island of Carrera, rising high out of the sea, with its neat pink buildings. I tried to picture what went on inside those buildings, but my imagination refused to work. I used to think, 'Hat there, I here. He know I here, thinking about him?'

But as the months passed I became more and more concerned with myself, and I wouldn't think about Hat for weeks on end. It was useless trying to feel ashamed. I had to face the fact that I was no longer missing Hat. From time to time when my mind was empty, I would stop and think how long it would be before he came out, but I was not really concerned.

I was fifteen when Hat went to jail and eighteen when he came out. A lot happened in those three years. I left school and I began working in the customs. I was no longer a boy. I was a man, earning money.

*

Hat's homecoming fell a little flat. It wasn't only that we boys had grown older. Hat too had changed. Some of the brightness had left him, and conversation was hard to make.

He visited all the houses he knew and he spoke about his experiences with great zest.

My mother gave him tea.

Hat said, 'Is just what I expect. I get friendly with some of the turnkey and them, and you know what happen? I pull two three strings and – bam! – they make me librarian. They have a big library there, you know. All sort of big book. Is the sort of place Titus Hoyt would like. So much book with nobody to read them.'

I offered Hat a cigarette and he took it mechanically.

Then he shouted, 'But, eh-eh, what is this? You come a big man now! When I leave you wasn't smoking. Was a long time now, though.'

I said, 'Yes. Was a long time.'

A long time. But it was just three years, three years in which I had grown up and looked critically at the people around me. I no longer wanted to be like Eddoes. He was so weak and thin, and I hadn't realized he was so small. Titus Hoyt was stupid and boring, and not funny at all. Everything had changed.

When Hat went to jail, part of me had died.

17. How I Left Miguel Street

MY MOTHER SAID, 'You getting too wild in this place. I think is high time you leave.'

'And go where? Venezuela?' I said.

'No, not Venezuela. Somewhere else, because the moment you land in Venezuela they go throw you in jail. I know you and I know Venezuela. No, somewhere else.'

I said, 'All right. You think about it and decide.'

My mother said, 'I go go and talk to Ganesh Pundit about it. He was a friend of your father. But you must go from here. You getting too wild.'

I suppose my mother was right. Without really knowing it, I had become a little wild. I was drinking like a fish, and doing a lot besides. The drinking started in the customs, where we confiscated liquor on the slightest pretext. At first the smell of the spirits upset me, but I used to say to myself, 'You must get over this. Drink it like medicine. Hold your nose and close your eyes.' In time I had become a first-class drinker, and I began suffering from drinker's pride.

Then there were the sights of the town Boyee and Errol introduced me to. One night, not long after I began working, they took me to a place near Marine Square. We climbed to the first floor and found ourselves in a small crowded room lit by green bulbs. The green light seemed as thick as jelly. There were many women all about the room, just waiting and looking. A big sign said: *Obscene Language Forbidden.*

We had a drink at the bar, a thick sweet drink.

Errol asked me, 'Which one of the women you like?'

I understood immediately, and I felt disgusted. I ran out of the room and went home, a little sick, a little frightened. I said to myself, 'You must get over this.'

Next night I went to the club again. And again.

We made wild parties and took rum and women to Maracas Bay for all-night sessions.

'You getting too wild,' my mother said.

I paid her no attention until the time I drank so much in one evening that I remained drunk for two whole days afterwards. When I sobered up, I made a vow neither to smoke nor drink again.

I said to my mother, 'Is not my fault really. Is just Trinidad. What else anybody can do here except drink?'

About two months later my mother said, 'You must come with me next week. We going to see Ganesh Pundit.'

Ganesh Pundit had given up mysticism for a long time. He had taken to politics and was doing very nicely. He was a minister of something or the other in the Government, and I heard people saying that he was in the running for the M.B.E.

We went to his big house in St Clair and we found the great man, not dressed in *dhoti* and *koortah*, as in the mystic days, but in an expensive-looking lounge suit.

He received my mother with a good deal of warmth.

He said, 'I do what I could do.'

My mother began to cry.

To me Ganesh said, 'What you want to go abroad to study?'

I said, 'I don't want to study anything really. I just want to go away, that's all.'

Ganesh smiled and said, 'The Government not giving away

that sort of scholarship yet. Only ministers could do what you say. No, you have to study something.'

I said, 'I never think about it really. Just let me think a little bit.'

Ganesh said, 'All right. You think a little bit.'

My mother was crying her thanks to Ganesh.

I said, 'I know what I want to study. Engineering.' I was thinking about my uncle Bhakcu.

Ganesh laughed and said, 'What *you* know about engineering?'

I said, 'Right now, nothing. But I could put my mind to it.'

My mother said, 'Why don't you want to take up law?'

I thought of Chittaranjan and his brown suit and I said, 'No, not law.'

Ganesh said, 'It have only one scholarship remaining. For drugs.'

I said, 'But I don't want to be a druggist. I don't want to put on a white jacket and sell lipstick to woman.'

Ganesh smiled.

My mother said, 'You mustn't mind the boy. Pundit. He will study drugs.' And to me, 'You could study anything if you put your mind to it.'

Ganesh said, 'Think. It mean going to London. It mean seeing snow and seeing the Thames and seeing the big Parliament.'

I said, 'All right. I go study drugs.'

My mother said, 'I don't know what I could do to thank you, Pundit.'

And, crying, she counted out two hundred dollars and gave it to Ganesh. She said, 'I know it ain't much, Pundit. But is all I have. Is a long time I did saving it up.'

Ganesh took the money sadly and he said, 'You mustn't let that worry you. You must give only what you can afford.'

My mother kept on crying and in the end even Ganesh broke down.

When my mother saw this, she dried her tears and said, 'If you only know, Pundit, how worried I is. I have to find so much money for so much thing these days, and I don't really know how I going to make out.'

Ganesh now stopped crying. My mother began to cry afresh.

This went on for a bit until Ganesh gave back a hundred dollars to my mother. He was sobbing and shaking and he said, 'Take this and buy some good clothes for the boy.'

I said, 'Pundit, you is a good man.'

This affected him strongly. He said, 'Is when you come back from England, with all sort of certificate and paper, a big man and a big druggist, is then I go come round and ask you for what you owe me.'

I told Hat I was going away.

He said, 'What for? Labouring?'

I said, 'The Government give me a scholarship to study drugs.'

He said, 'Is you who wangle that?'

I said, 'Not me. My mother.'

Eddoes said, 'Is a good thing. A druggist fellow I know – picking up rubbish for him for years now – this fellow rich like anything. Man, the man just rolling in money.'

The news got to Elias and he took it badly. He came to the gate one evening and shouted, 'Bribe, bribe. Is all you could do. Bribe.'

My mother shouted back. 'The only people who does complain about bribe is those who too damn poor to have anything to bribe with.'

In about a month everything was fixed for my departure. The Trinidad Government wrote to the British Consul in New York about me. The British Council got to know about me. The Americans gave me a visa after making me swear that I wouldn't overthrow their government by armed force.

The night before I left, my mother gave a little party. It was something like a wake. People came in looking sad and telling me how much they were going to miss me, and then they forgot about me and attended to the serious business of eating and drinking.

Laura kissed me on the cheek and gave me a medallion of St Christopher. She asked me to wear it around my neck. I promised that I would and put the medallion in my pocket. I don't know what happened to it. Mrs Bhakcu gave me a sixpenny piece which she said she had had specially consecrated. It didn't look different from other sixpenny pieces and I suppose I spent it. Titus Hoyt forgave me everything and brought me Volume Two of the Everyman edition of Tennyson. Eddoes gave me a wallet which he swore was practically new. Boyee and Errol gave me nothing. Hat gave me a carton of cigarettes. He said, 'I know you say you ain't smoking again. But take this, just in case you change your mind.' The result was that I began smoking again.

Uncle Bhakcu spent the night fixing the van which was to take me to the airport next morning. From time to time I ran out and begged him to take it easy. He said he thought the carburettor was playing the fool.

Next morning Bhakcu got up early and was at it again. We had planned to leave at eight, but at ten to, Bhakcu was still tinkering. My mother was in a panic and Mrs Bhakcu was growing impatient.

Bhakcu was underneath the car, whistling a couplet from the *Ramayana*. He came out, laughed, and said, 'You getting frighten, eh?'

Presently we were all ready. Bhakcu had done little damage to the engine and it still worked. My bags were taken to the van and I was ready to leave the house for the last time.

My mother said, 'Wait.'

She placed a brass jar of milk in the middle of the gateway.

I cannot understand, even now, how it happened. The gateway was wide, big enough for a car, and the jar, about four inches wide, was in the middle. I thought I was walking at the edge of the gateway, far away from the jar. And yet I kicked the jar over.

My mother's face fell.

I said, 'Is a bad sign?'

She didn't answer.

Bhakcu was blowing the horn.

We got into the van and Bhakcu drove away, down Miguel Street and up Wrightson Road to South Quay. I didn't look out of the windows.

My mother was crying. She said, 'I know I not going to ever see you in Miguel Street again.'

I said, 'Why? Because I knock the milk down?'

She didn't reply, still crying for the spilt milk.

Only when we had left Port of Spain and the suburbs I looked outside. It was a clear, hot day. Men and women were working in rice-fields. Some children were bathing under a stand-pipe at the side of the road.

We got to Piarco in good time, and at this stage I began wishing I had never got the scholarship. The airport lounge frightened me. Fat Americans were drinking strange drinks at the bar. American women, wearing haughty sun-glasses, raised their voices whenever they spoke. They all looked too rich, too comfortable.

Then the news came, in Spanish and English. Flight 206 had been delayed for six hours.

I said to my mother, 'Let we go back to Port of Spain.'

I had to be with those people in the lounge soon anyway, and I wanted to put off the moment.

And back in Miguel Street the first person I saw was Hat. He was strolling flat-footedly back from the café, with a paper under his arm. I waved and shouted at him.

All he said was, 'I thought you was in the air by this time.'

I was disappointed. Not only by Hat's cool reception. Disappointed because although I had been away, destined to be gone for good, everything was going on just as before, with nothing to indicate my absence.

I looked at the overturned brass jar in the gateway and I said to my mother, 'So this mean I was never going to come back here, eh?'

She laughed and looked happy.

So I had my last lunch at home, with my mother and Uncle Bhakcu and his wife. Then back along the hot road to Piarco where the plane was waiting. I recognized one of the customs' officers, and he didn't check my baggage.

The announcement came, a cold, casual thing.

I embraced my mother.

I said to Bhakcu, 'Uncle Bhak, I didn't want to tell you before, but I think I hear your tappet knocking.'

His eyes shone.

I left them all and walked briskly towards the aeroplane, not looking back, looking only at my shadow before me, a dancing dwarf on the tarmac.

V. S. NAIPAUL was born, of Indian ancestry, in Trinidad in 1932. He came to England in 1950. He spent four years at University College, Oxford, and began to write, in London, in 1954. He has pursued no other profession.

His works of fiction comprise: *The Mystic Masseur* (1957; John Llewellyn Rhys Memorial Prize), *The Suffrage of Elvira* (1958), *Miguel Street* (1959; Somerset Maugham Award), *A House for Mr Biswas* (1961), *Mr Stone and the Knights Companion* (1963; Hawthornden Prize), *The Mimic Men* (1967; W. H. Smith Award) and *A Flag on the Island* (1967), a collection of short stories. In 1971 he was awarded the Booker Prize for *In a Free State*; since then he has published five novels: *Guerrillas* (1975), *A Bend in the River* (1979), *The Enigma of Arrival* (1987), *A Way in the World* (1994) and *Half a Life* (2001).

In 1960 he began to travel. *The Middle Passage* (1962) records his impressions of colonial society in the West Indies and South America. *An Area of Darkness* (1964), *India: A Wounded Civilization* (1977) and *India: A Million Mutinies Now* (1990) form his acclaimed 'Indian Trilogy'. *The Loss of El Dorado*, a masterly study of New World history, was published in 1969, and a selection of his longer essays, *The Overcrowded Barracoon*, appeared in 1972. *The Return of Eva Perón* (with *The Killings in Trinidad*) (1980) derives from experiences of travel in Argentina, Trinidad and the Congo. *Finding the Centre* (1984) is distinguished by the author's narrative on his emergence as a writer, 'Prologue to an Autobiography'. *A Turn in the South* (1989) describes his journey through the Deep South of America.

Among the Believers: An Islamic Journey (1981), a large-scale work, is the result of seven months' travel in 1979 and 1980 in Iran, Pakistan, Malaysia and Indonesia. Its important sequel, *Beyond Belief* (1998), is on the theme of Islamic conversion in these countries.

Letters Between a Father and Son, the early correspondence between the author and his family, appeared in 1999.

In 1990, V. S. Naipaul received a knighthood for services to literature; in 1993, he was the first recipient of the David Cohen British Literature Prize in recognition of a 'lifetime's achievement of a living British writer'. He was awarded the Nobel Prize for Literature in 2001.

Also by V. S. Naipaul

FICTION

The Suffrage of Elvira
A House for Mr Biswas
Mr Stone and the Knights Companion
The Mimic Men
A Flag on the Island
In a Free State
Guerrillas
A Bend in the River
The Enigma of Arrival
A Way in the World
Half a Life

NON-FICTION

The Middle Passage
An Area of Darkness
The Loss of El Dorado
The Overcrowded Barracoon
India: A Wounded Civilization
The Return of Eva Perón
Among the Believers: An Islamic Journey
Finding the Centre
A Turn in the South
India: A Million Mutinies Now
Beyond Belief
Letters Between a Father and Son

V. S. NAIPAUL

The Mystic Masseur

PICADOR

The Mystic Masseur first published 1957 by André Deutsch
Miguel Street first published 1959 by André Deutsch

This omnibus edition published 2002 by Picador
an imprint of Pan Macmillan Ltd
Pan Macmillan, 20 New Wharf Road, London N1 9RR
Basingstoke and Oxford
Associated companies throughout the world
www.panmacmillan.com

ISBN 0 330 48712 4

1 3 5 7 9 8 6 4 2

A CIP catalogue record for this book is available from the British Library.

Typeset by Intype London Ltd
Printed and bound in Great Britain by
Mackays of Chatham plc, Chatham, Kent

To the Memory of my Father

and for Gordon Woolford

Contents

All characters, organizations, and incidents in this novel are fictitious. This is a necessary assurance because, although its politicians have taken to calling it a country, Trinidad is a small island, no bigger than Lancashire, with a population somewhat smaller than Nottingham's. In this novel the geography of the island is distorted. Dates are, unavoidably, mentioned; but no actual holder of any office is portrayed. The strike mentioned in Chapter Twelve has no basis in fact.

1. The Struggling Masseur

LATER HE WAS TO BE famous and honoured throughout the South Caribbean; he was to be a hero of the people and, after that, a British representative at Lake Success. But when I first met him he was still a struggling masseur, at a time when masseurs were ten a penny in Trinidad.

This was just at the beginning of the war, when I was still at school. I had been bullied into playing football, and in my first game I had been kicked hard on the shin and laid up for weeks afterwards.

My mother distrusted doctors and never took me to one. I am not blaming her for this because in those days people went by preference to the unqualified masseur or the quack dentist.

'I know the sort of doctors it have in Trinidad,' my mother used to say. 'They think nothing of killing two three people before breakfast.'

This wasn't as bad as it sounds: in Trinidad the midday meal is called breakfast.

My foot was hot and swollen, and getting more and more painful. 'So what we going to do?' I asked.

'Do?' my mother said. 'Do? Give the foot a little more time. You never know what could happen.'

I said, '*I* know what going to happen. I going lose the whole damn foot, and you know how these Trinidad doctors like cutting off black people foot.'

My mother grew a little worried and she made a large mud-plaster for the foot that evening.

Two days later she said, 'It looking a little serious. Is only Ganesh now for you, boy.'

'Who the hell is this Ganesh?'

This was a question many people were going to ask later on.

'Who is *this* Ganesh?' my mother mocked. '*This* Ganesh? You see the sort of education they giving you children these days. Your foot break up and hurting, and still you talking about this man as though you is his father when the man old enough to be your father.'

I said, 'What he does do?'

'Oh, he does cure people.'

She spoke in a guarded way and I felt that she didn't want to talk too much about Ganesh because his gift of healing was a holy thing.

It was a long drive to Ganesh's, more than two hours. He lived in a place called Fuente Grove, not far from Princes Town. Fuente Grove – Fountain Grove – seemed a curious name. There was no hint of a fountain anywhere, no hint even of water. For miles around the land was flat, treeless, and hot. You drove through miles and miles of sugar-cane; then the sugar-cane stopped abruptly to make room for Fuente Grove. It was a sad little village, just a dozen or so thatched huts strung out on the edge of the narrow lumpy road. Beharry's shop was the one sign of a social life and we stopped outside it. It was a wooden building, dingy distemper flaking off the walls and the corrugated-iron roof warped and rusted. A little notice said that Beharry was licensed to sell spirituous liquors, and I could see the man so privileged – as I thought – sitting on a stool in front of the counter. Spectacles rested on the tip of his nose and he was reading the *Trinidad Sentinel* at arm's length.

Our taxi-driver shouted, 'Ai!'

The paper was lowered. 'Oi! *I* is Beharry.' He slid off the stool and began rubbing the palms of his hands over his little belly. 'Is the pundit you looking for, not so?'

The taxi-driver said, 'Nah. We come all the way from Port of Spain just for the scenery.'

Beharry was not prepared for this incivility. He stopped rubbing his belly and started to tuck his vest into his khaki trousers. A big woman appeared behind the counter and when she saw us she pulled her veil over her head.

'These people want to find out something,' Beharry told her, and went behind the counter.

The woman shouted, 'Who you looking for?'

My mother replied, 'The pundit we looking for.'

'Just go down the road a little bit,' the woman said. 'You can't miss the house. It have a mango tree in the yard.'

The woman was right. We couldn't miss Ganesh's house. It had the only tree in the village and it looked a little better than most of the huts.

The driver honked the horn and a woman appeared from behind the house. She was a young woman, big-boned but thin, and she was trying to give us some attention and shoo away some fowls with a *cocoye* broom at the same time. She examined us for a while and then began shouting, 'Man! Eh, manwa!'

Then she looked hard at us again and pulled her veil over her head.

She shouted again, 'Eh, eh, you ain't hear me calling you? Man! Eh, manwa!'

A high voice came fluting out of the house. 'Yes, man.'

The driver turned off the engine and we heard sounds of shuffling inside the house.

Presently a young man came out on the small verandah. He was dressed in the ordinary way, trousers and vest, and I didn't think he looked particularly holy. He wasn't wearing the dhoti and

koortah and turban I had expected. I was a little reassured when I saw that he was holding a big book. To look at us he had to shelter his eyes from the glare with his free hand, and as soon as he saw us he ran down the wooden steps and across the yard and said to my mother, 'Is nice to see you. How is everything these days?'

The taxi-driver, now curiously correct, was staring at the heat waves jigging up from the black road, and chewing on a match-stick.

Ganesh saw me and said, 'Ooh, ooh, something happen to the boy.' And he made a few sad noises.

My mother got out of the car, straightened her dress, and said, 'You know, Baba, how children getting out of hand these days. Look at this boy.'

All three of them, Ganesh, my mother, and the taxi-driver, looked at me.

I said, 'But what happen that all you people looking at me so for? I kill priest?'

'Look at this boy,' my mother said. 'You think he make for any rough game?'

Ganesh and the taxi-driver shook their heads.

'Eh, eh,' my mother continued, 'look at my crosses one day. I see the boy coming home limping. I say, "What happen that you limping, boy?" He answer me back brave brave like a man, "I was playing football." I say, "Playing the fool, you mean." '

Ganesh said to the taxi-driver, 'Help me take the boy inside the house.'

As they carried me in I noticed that someone had tried to scratch a little garden into the hard and dusty front yard, but nothing remained now except the bottle-borders and a few tough stumps of hibiscus.

Ganesh looked the only cool thing in the village. His eyes were deep black, his skin was yellowish, and he was just a little flabby.

But nothing had prepared me for what I was to see inside Ganesh's hut. As soon as we entered my mother winked at me, and I could see that even the taxi-driver was fighting to control his astonishment. There were books, books, here, there, and everywhere; books piled crazily on the table, books rising in mounds in the corners, books covering the floor. I had never before seen so many books in one place.

'How much books it have here, pundit?' I asked.

'I never really count them,' Ganesh said, and called, 'Leela!'

The woman with the *cocoye* broom came so quickly I fancied she was waiting to be called.

'Leela,' Ganesh said, 'the boy want to know how much book it have here.'

'Let me see,' Leela said, and hitched up the broom to her waistband. She started to count off the fingers of her left hand. 'Four hundred Everyman, two hundred Penguin – six hundred. Six hundred, and one hundred Reader's Library, make seven hundred. I think with all the other book it have about fifteen hundred good book here.'

The taxi-driver whistled, and Ganesh smiled.

'They is all yours, pundit?' I asked.

'Is my only vice,' Ganesh said. 'Only vice. I don't smoke. I don't drink. But I must have my books. And, mark you, every week I going to San Fernando to buy more, you know. How much book I buy last week, Leela?'

'Only three, man,' she said. 'But they was big books, big big books. Six to seven inches altogether.'

'Seven inches,' Ganesh said.

'Yes, seven inches,' Leela said.

I supposed Leela was Ganesh's wife because she went on to say, with mock irritation, 'That is all he good for. You know how much I does tell him not to read all the time. But you can't stop him from reading. Night and day he reading.'

Ganesh gave a short laugh and signalled to Leela and the taxi-driver to leave the room. He made me lie down on a blanket on the floor and began feeling my leg all over. My mother remained in a corner, watching. From time to time Ganesh thumped my foot and I gave a great yelp of pain and he said, 'Ummh,' very thoughtfully.

I tried to forget Ganesh thumping my leg about and concentrated on the walls. They were covered with religious quotations, in Hindi and English, and with Hindu religious pictures. My gaze settled on a beautiful four-armed god standing in an open lotus.

When Ganesh had done examining me, he rose and said, 'Nothing wrong with the boy at all, *maharajin*. Nothing at all. Is the trouble with so much people who does come to me. Nothing really wrong with them. The only thing I could say about the boy is that he have a little bad blood. That is all. It have nothing I could do.'

And he began mumbling a Hindi couplet over me while I lay on the floor. If I had been sharper I would have paid more attention to that, for it showed, I am convinced, the incipient mystical leanings of the man.

My mother came and looked down at me and asked Ganesh in a barely querulous way, 'You sure *nothing* wrong with the boy? The foot look very bad to me.'

Ganesh said, 'Don't worry. I giving you something here that will get the boy foot better in two two's. Is a little mixture I make up myself. Give it to the boy three times a day.'

'Before or after meals?' my mother asked.

'*Never* after!' Ganesh warned.

My mother was satisfied.

'And,' Ganesh added, 'you can mix a little bit with the boy food. You never know what good could come of that.'

After seeing all those books in Ganesh's hut I was ready to believe in him and quite prepared to take his mixture. And I

respected him even more when he gave my mother a little booklet, saying, 'Take it. I giving it to you free although it cost me a lot to write it and print it.'

I said, 'Is really you who write this book, pundit?'

He smiled and nodded.

As we drove away I said, 'You know, Ma, I really wish I did read all those books Ganesh Pundit have in his house.'

It was hurtful and surprising, therefore, when two weeks later my mother said, 'You know, I have a good mind to leave you alone and let you get better by yourself. If you did only go with a good mind to see Ganesh, you woulda be better and walking about by now.'

In the end I went to a doctor in St Vincent Street who took one look at my foot, said, 'Abscess. Will have to cut it.' And charged ten dollars.

*

I never read Ganesh's booklet, *101 Questions and Answers on the Hindu Religion*; and although I had to take his terrible mixture three times a day (I refused to have it in my food), I held no ill-will towards him. On the contrary, I often thought with a good deal of puzzled interest about the little man locked away with all those fifteen hundred books in the hot and dull village of Fuente Grove.

'Trinidad full of crazy people,' I said.

'Say that if it make you happy,' my mother snapped back. 'But Ganesh ain't the fool you think he is. He is the sorta man who woulda be a *rishi* in India. The day go come when you go be proud to tell people that you did know Ganesh. Now shut your mouth up so that I could dress the foot for you.'

*

Less than a year later Trinidad woke up to find page three of the *Trinidad Sentinel* carrying a column advertisement with a photograph of Ganesh and the caption:

> Interested people were urged to reply to Fuente Grove for a free, illustrated folder giving full particulars.

I don't imagine many people wrote in for further information about Ganesh. We were used to advertisements like that, and Ganesh's caused little comment. None of us foresaw that advertisement's astounding consequences. It was only later on, when Ganesh had won the fame and fortune he deserved so well, that people remembered it. Just as I have.

*

Nineteen forty-six was the turning-point of Ganesh's career; and, as if to underline the fact, in that year he published his autobiography, *The Years of Guilt* (Ganesh Publishing Co. Ltd, Port of Spain. $2.40). The book, variously described as a spiritual thriller and a metaphysical whodunit, had a considerable success of esteem in Central America and the Caribbean. Ganesh, however, confessed that the autobiography was a mistake. So, in the very year of publication it was suppressed and the Ganesh Publishing Company itself wound up. The wider world has not learnt of Ganesh's early struggles, and Trinidad resents this. I myself believe that the history of Ganesh is, in a way, the history of our times; and there may be people who will welcome this imperfect account of the man Ganesh Ramsumair, masseur, mystic, and, since 1953, M.B.E.

2. Pupil and Teacher

GANESH WAS NEVER really happy during the four years he spent at the Queen's Royal College. He went there when he was nearly fifteen and he was not as advanced as the other boys of his own age. He was always the oldest boy in his class, with some boys three or even four years younger than himself. But he was lucky to go to the college at all. It was by the purest chance that his father got the money to send him there. For years the old man had held on to five acres of waste land near Fourways in the hope that the oil companies would sink a well in it, but he could not afford to bribe the drillers and in the end he had to be content with a boundary well. It was disappointing and unfair, but opportune; and the royalties were enough to keep Ganesh in Port of Spain.

Mr Ramsumair made a lot of noise about sending his son to the 'town college', and the week before the term began he took Ganesh all over the district, showing him off to friends and acquaintances. He had Ganesh dressed in a khaki suit and a khaki toupee and many people said the boy looked like a little sahib. The women cried a little and begged Ganesh to remember his dead mother and be good to his father. The men begged him to study hard and help other people with his learning.

Father and son left Fourways that Sunday and took the bus to Princes Town. The old man wore his visiting outfit: dhoti, *koortah*, white cap, and an unfurled umbrella on the crook of his left arm.

They knew they looked important when they got into the train at Princes Town.

'Careful with your suit now,' the old man said loudly, and his neighbours heard. 'Remember you are going to the town college.'

When they got to St Joseph, Ganesh began to feel shy. Their dress and manner were no longer drawing looks of respect. People were smiling, and when they got off at the railway terminus in Port of Spain, a woman laughed.

'I did tell you not to dress me up like this,' Ganesh lied, and was near to sobbing.

'Let them laugh,' the old man replied in Hindi, and passed the palm of his hand over his thick grey moustache. 'Jackasses bray at anything.'

'Jackass' was his favourite word of abuse, perhaps because the Hindi word was so rich and expressive: *gaddaha*.

They hurried to the house in Dundonald Street where Ganesh was to board, and Mrs Cooper, the tall and plump Negro landlady, laughed when she saw them but said, 'The boy look like a real smart man, man.'

'She is a good lady,' the old man told Ganesh in Hindi. 'You don't have to worry about the food or anything here. She will look after you.'

Ganesh preferred not to remember what happened the next day when he was taken to school. The old boys laughed, and although he had not worn the khaki toupee, he felt uncomfortable in his khaki suit. Then there was the scene in the principal's office: his father gesticulating with his white cap and umbrella; the English principal patient, then firm, and finally exasperated; the old man enraged, muttering, '*Gaddaha! Gaddaha!*'

*

Ganesh never lost his awkwardness. He was so ashamed of his Indian name that for a while he spread a story that he was really

called Gareth. This did him little good. He continued to dress badly, he didn't play games, and his accent remained too clearly that of the Indian from the country. He never stopped being a country boy. He still believed that reading by any light other than daylight was bad for the eyes, and as soon as his classes were over he ran home to Dundonald Street and sat on the back steps reading. He went to sleep with the hens and woke before the cocks. 'That Ramsumair boy is a real crammer,' boys laughed; but Ganesh never became more than a mediocre student.

A fresh mortification awaited him. When he went home for his first holidays and had been shown off again, his father said, 'It is time for the boy to become a real brahmin.'

The initiation ceremony was held that very week. They shaved his head, gave him a little saffron bundle, and said, 'All right, off you go now. Go to Benares and study.'

He took his staff and began walking away briskly from Fourways.

As arranged, Dookhie the shopkeeper ran after him, crying a little and begging in English, 'No, boy. No. Don't go away to Benares to study.'

Ganesh kept on walking.

'But what happen to the boy?' people asked. 'He taking this thing really serious.'

Dookhie caught Ganesh by the shoulder and said, 'Cut out this nonsense, man. Stop behaving stupid. You think I have all day to run after you? You think you really going to Benares? That is in India, you know, and this is Trinidad.'

They brought him back home. But the episode is significant.

His head was still practically bald when he went back to school, and the boys laughed so much that the principal called him and said, 'Ramsumair, you are creating a disturbance in the school. Wear something on your head.'

So Ganesh wore his khaki toupee in the classroom until his hair grew again.

There was another Indian boy, called Indarsingh, living in the house at Dundonald Street. He was also at the Queen's Royal College, and although he was six months younger than Ganesh he was three forms ahead. He was a brilliant boy and everybody who knew him said he was going to be a great man. At sixteen Indarsingh was making long speeches in the Literary Society Debates, reciting verses of his own at Recitation Contests, and he always won the Impromptu Speech Contests. Indarsingh also played all games, not very well, but he had the sportsman's instincts and it was this that caused him to be held up to the boys as an ideal. Indarsingh once persuaded Ganesh to play fooball. When Ganesh bared his pale, jaundiced legs, a boy spat in disgust and said, 'Eh, eh, your foot don't see sun at all at all!' Ganesh played no more football, but he remained friendly with Indarsingh. Indarsingh, for his part, found Ganesh useful. 'Come for a little walk in the Botanical Gardens,' he would say to Ganesh, and during the whole of the walk Indarsingh would talk non-stop, rehearsing his speech for the next debate. At the end he would say, 'Good eh? Demn good.' This Indarsingh was a short, square boy, and his walk, like his talk, had the short man's jauntiness.

Indarsingh was Ganesh's only friend, but the friendship was not to last. At the end of Ganesh's second year Indarsingh won a scholarship and went to England. To Ganesh, Indarsingh had achieved a greatness beyond ambition.

In due course Ganesh wrote the Cambridge School Certificate and surprised everybody by passing in the second grade. Mr Ramsumair sent his congratulations to Ganesh, offered an annual prize to the college, and told Ganesh that he had found a nice girl for him to marry.

'The old man really rushing you,' Mrs Cooper said.

Ganesh wrote back that he had no intention of getting married,

and when his father replied that if Ganesh didn't want to get married he must consider himself an orphan, Ganesh decided to consider himself an orphan.

'You have to get a work now,' Mrs Cooper said. 'Mind you, I not thinking about what you have to pay me, but still you must get a work. Why you don't go and see your headmaster?'

So he did. The headmaster looked a little puzzled and asked, 'What do you want to do?'

'Teach,' Ganesh said, because he felt he ought to flatter his headmaster.

'Teach? Strange. Primary schools?'

'What you mean, sir?'

'You're not thinking of teaching in *this* school?'

'Nah, sir. You making joke.'

In the end, with the headmaster's help, Ganesh was enrolled in the Government Training College for teachers in Port of Spain, where there were many more Indians, and he felt less ill at ease. He was taught many important subjects and from time to time he practised on little classes from schools near by. He learned to write on a blackboard and overcame his dislike of the sound of scraping chalk. Then they turned him out to teach.

They sent him to a school in a rowdy district in the east end of Port of Spain. The headmaster's office was also a classroom choked up with young boys. The headmaster sat under a picture of King George V and gave Ganesh an interview.

'You don't know how lucky you is,' he began, and jumped up immediately, saying, 'Gimme a chance. It have a boy here I must give a good cut-arse to. Just gimme a chance.'

He squeezed his way between desks to a boy in the back row. The class was instantly silent and it was possible to hear the noise from the other classrooms. Then Ganesh heard the boy squealing behind the blackboard.

The headmaster was sweating when he came back to Ganesh.

He wiped his big face with a mauve handkerchief and said, 'Yes, I was telling you that you is a lucky man. Most of the times they just lose a new man like you somewhere in the country, all up by Cunaripo and all sorta outa the way places.'

The headmaster laughed and Ganesh felt he had to laugh too; but as soon as he did so the headmaster became stern and said, 'Mr Ramsumair, I don't know what views you have about educating the young, but I want to let you know right away, before we even start, that the purpose of this school is to form, not to inform. Everything is planned.' He pointed to a framed time-table, done in inks of three colours, hanging next to the picture of King George V. 'Miller, the man you replacing, paint that. He sick,' the headmaster said.

'It look good and I sorry Miller sick,' Ganesh said.

The headmaster leaned back in his chair and beat a ruler on the green blotter in front of him. 'What is the purpose of the school?' he asked suddenly.

'Form – ' Ganesh began.

'Not – ' the headmaster encouraged.

'Inform.'

'You quick, Mr Ramsumair. You is a man after my own heart. You and me going to get on good good.'

Ganesh was given Miller's class, the Remove. It was a sort of rest-station for the mentally maimed. Boys remained there uninformed for years and years, and some didn't even want to leave. Ganesh tried all the things he had been taught at the Training College, but the boys didn't play fair.

'I can't teach them nothing at all,' he complained to the headmaster. 'You teach them Theorem One this week and next week they forget it.'

'Look, Mr Ramsumair. I like you, but I must be firm. Quick, what is the purpose of the school?'

'Form not inform.'

Ganesh gave up trying to teach the boys anything, and was happy enough to note a week-to-week improvement in his Record Book. According to that book, the Remove advanced from Theorem One to Theorem Two in successive weeks, and then moved on unexhausted to Theorem Three.

Having much time on his hands, Ganesh was able to observe Leep next door. Leep had been at the Training College with him, and Leep was still keen. He was nearly always at the blackboard, writing, erasing, constantly informing, except for the frequent occasions when he rushed off to flog some boy and disappeared behind the celotex screen which separated his class from Ganesh's.

On the Friday before Miller was due back at the school (he had had a fractured pelvis), the headmaster called Ganesh and said, 'Leep sick.'

'What happen?'

'He just say he sick and he can't come on Monday.'

Ganesh leaned forward.

'Now don't quote me,' the headmaster said. 'Don't quote me at all. But this is how I look at it. If you leave the boys alone, they leave you alone. They is good boys, but the parents – God! So when Miller come back, you have to take Leep class.'

Ganesh agreed; but he took Leep's class for only one morning.

Miller was very angry with Ganesh when he returned, and at the recess on Monday morning went to complain to the headmaster. Ganesh was summoned.

'I leave a good good class,' Miller said. 'The boys was going on all right. Eh, eh, I turn my back for a week – well, two three months – and when I turn round again, what I see? The boys and them ain't learn nothing new and they even forget what I spend so much time trying to teach them. This teaching is a art, but it have all sort of people who think they could come up from the cane-field and start teaching in Port of Spain.'

Ganesh, suddenly angry for the first time in his life, said, 'Man, go to hell, man!'

And left the school for good.

*

He went for a walk along the wharves. It was early afternoon and the gulls mewed amid the masts of sloops and schooners. Far out, he saw the ocean liners at anchor. He allowed the idea of travel to enter his mind and just as easily allowed it to go out again. He spent the rest of the afternoon in a cinema, but this was torture. He especially resented the credit titles. He thought, 'All these people with their name in big print on the screen have their bread butter, you hear. Even those in little little print. They not like me.'

He needed all Mrs Cooper's solace when he went back to Dundonald Street.

'I can't take rudeness like that,' he told her.

'You a little bit like your father, you know. But you mustn't worry, boy. I can feel your aura. You have a powerhouse for a aura, man. But still, you was wrong throwing up a good work like that. It wasn't as if they was working you hard.'

At dinner she said, 'You can't go and ask your headmaster again.'

'No,' he agreed quickly.

'I been thinking. I have a cousin working in the Licensing Office. He could get you a job there, I think. You could drive motor car?'

'I can't even drive donkey-cart, Mrs Cooper.'

'It don't matter. He could always get a licence for you, and then you ain't have to do much driving. You just have to test other drivers, and if you anything like my cousin, you could make a lot of money giving out licence to all sort of fool with money.'

She thought again. 'And, yes. It have a man I know does work

at Cable and Wireless. Eh, but my brain coming like a sieve these days. It have a telegram here for you, come this afternoon.'

She went to the sideboard and pulled an envelope from under a vase stuffed with artificial flowers.

Ganesh read the telegram and passed it to her.

'What damn fool send this?' she said. 'It enough to make anybody dead of heart failure. *Bad news come home now.* Who is this Ramlogan who sign it?'

'Never hear about him,' Ganesh said.

'What you think it is?'

'Oh, you know . . .'

'But ain't that strange?' Mrs Cooper interrupted. 'Just last night I was dreaming about a dead. Yes, it really strange.'

3. Leela

ALTHOUGH IT WAS nearly half past eleven when his taxi got to Fourways that night, the village was alive and Ganesh knew that Mrs Cooper was right. Someone had died. He sensed the excitement and recognized all the signs. Lights were on in most of the houses and huts, there was much activity on the road, and his ears caught the faint hum, as of distant revelry. It wasn't long before he realized that it was his father who had died. Fourways seemed to be waiting for the taxi and the moment people saw Ganesh sitting in the back they began to wail.

The house itself was chaos. He had hardly opened the taxi doors when scores of people he didn't know scrambled towards him with outstretched arms, bawling; and led, almost carried, him into the house which was full of even more mourners he didn't know or remember.

He could hear the taxi-driver saying over and over, 'Man, I guess long time what the case was. We stepping on the gas all the way from Port of Spain, driving like madness all in the dark. And the boy so mash up inside he not even crying.'

A fat, sobbing man embraced Ganesh and said, 'You get my telegram? Fust telegram I send. I is Ramlogan. You don't know me but I know your father. Just yesterday, just yesterday' – Ramlogan broke down and wept afresh – 'just yesterday I meet him and I say, "Baba" – I does always call him that – "Baba," I say, "come inside and have something to eat." I take over Dookhie

shop now, you know. Yes, Dookhie dead nearly seven months now and I take over the shop.'

Ramlogan's eyes were red and small with weeping. ' "Baba," I say, "come inside and have something to eat." And you know what he say?'

A woman put her arms around Ganesh and asked, 'What he say?'

'You want to know what he say?' Ramlogan embraced the woman. 'He say, "No, Ramlogan. I don't want to eat today." '

He could hardly finish the sentence.

The woman removed her hands from Ganesh and put them on her head. She shrieked, twice, then dropped into a wail: ' "No, Ramlogan, I don't want to eat today." '

Ramlogan wiped his eyes with a thick hairy finger. 'Today,' he sobbed, holding out both hands towards the bedroom, 'today he can't eat at all.'

The woman shrieked again. 'Today he can't eat at all.'

In her distress she tore the veil off her face and Ganesh recognized an aunt. He put his hand on her shoulder.

'You think I could see Pa?' he asked.

'Go and see your Pa, before he go for good,' Ramlogan said, the tears running down his fat cheeks to his unshaved chin. 'We wash the body and dress it and everything already.'

'Don't come with me,' Ganesh said. 'I want to be alone.'

When he had closed the door behind him the wailing sounded far away. The coffin rested on a table in the centre of the room and he couldn't see the body from where he was. To his left a small oil lamp burned low and threw monstrous shadows on the walls and the galvanized-iron ceiling. When he walked nearer the table his footsteps resounded on the floor-planks and the oil lamp shivered. The old man's moustache still bristled fiercely but the face had fallen and looked weak and tired. The air around the table felt cool and he saw that it came from the casing of

ice around the coffin. It was a room of the dead, strange with the smell of camphor balls, and there was nothing alive in it except himself and the squat yellow flame of the oil lamp, and they were both silent. Only, from time to time, the water from the melting ice plopped into the four pans at the feet of the table and punctured the silence.

He didn't know what he thought or felt but he didn't want to cry and left the room. They were waiting for him to come out and quickly encircled him. He heard Ramlogan saying, 'Come on, man, give the boy air. Is his father dead, you know. His only father.' And the wailing began again.

No one asked him about plans for the cremation. Everything seemed arranged already and Ganesh was content that it should be so. He allowed Ramlogan to take him away from the house, with its sobs and shrieks and lamentations, its gas lamps, oil lamps, bottle flambeaux, bright lights everywhere except in the small bedroom.

'No cooking here tonight,' Ramlogan said. 'Come and eat at the shop.'

Ganesh didn't sleep that night and everything he did seemed unreal. Afterwards he remembered the solicitude of Ramlogan – and his daughter; remembered returning to the house where no fire could be lit, remembered the sad songs of the women lengthening out the night; then, in the early morning, the preparations for the cremation. He had to do many things, and he did without thought or question everything the pundit, his aunt, and Ramlogan asked him. He remembered having to walk round the body of his father, remembered applying the last caste-marks to the old man's forehead, and doing many more things until it seemed that ritual had replaced grief.

*

When it was all over – his father burnt, the ashes scattered, and everybody, including his aunt, gone away – Ramlogan said, 'Well, Ganesh, you is a man now.'

Ganesh took stock of his position. First he considered money. He owed Mrs Cooper eleven dollars for two weeks board and lodging, and he found that of his own money he had no more than sixteen dollars and thirty-seven cents. He had about twenty dollars to collect from the school, but he had made up his mind not to ask for it and to return it if it were sent him. He had not stopped at the time to think who had paid for the cremation; it was only later, just before his marriage, he found that his aunt had paid for it. Money was not an immediate problem, now that he had the oil royalties – nearly sixty dollars a month – which made him practically a rich man in a place like Fourways. Still, the royalties could dry up at any moment; and although he was twenty-one, and educated, he had no means of earning a living.

One thing gave him hope. As he wrote afterwards in *The Years of Guilt*: 'In conversation with Shri Ramlogan I learnt a curious fact. My father had died that Monday morning between five minutes past ten and a quarter past ten – just about the time, in short, when I had the dispute with Miller, and was deciding to give up my teaching job. I was much struck by the coincidence, and it was only then, for the first time, I felt I had something big ahead of me. For it was indeed a singular conspiracy of events that pulled me away from the emptiness of urban life back into the stimulating peace and quiet of the country.'

Ganesh was happy to get away from Port of Spain. He had spent five years there but he had never become used to it or felt part of it. It was too big, too noisy, too alien. It was better to be back in Fourways, where he was known and respected and had the double glamour of a college education and a father recently dead. They called him 'sahib', and some parents encouraged their children

to call him 'Teacher Ganesh', but this brought back unhappy memories and Ganesh made them stop it.

'It wrong to call me that,' he said, adding cryptically, 'I feel I was teaching the wrong things to the wrong people.'

*

For more than two months he loafed. He didn't know what he wanted to do or what he could do, and he was beginning to doubt the value of doing anything at all. He ate at the houses of people he knew and, for the rest, merely wandered around. He bought a second-hand bicycle and went for long rides in the hilly lanes near Fourways.

People said, 'He doing a lot of thinking, that boy Ganesh. He full with worries, but still he thinking thinking all the time.'

Ganesh would have liked his thoughts to be deep and it disturbed him that they were simple things, concerned with passing trifles. He began to feel a little strange and feared he was going mad. He knew the Fourways people, and they knew him and liked him, but now he sometimes felt cut off from them.

*

But he couldn't escape Ramlogan. Ramlogan had a sixteen-year-old daughter he wanted married, and wanted married to Ganesh. It was an open secret in the village. Ganesh was always getting little gifts from Ramlogan – a special avocado pear, a tin of Canadian salmon or Australian butter – and whenever he passed the shop Ramlogan was sure to call him in.

'Eh, eh, sahib. What happening that you passing without saying a word? People go think we vex.'

Ganesh could not find it in his heart to refuse Ramlogan's invitation, though he knew that whenever he looked at the doorway leading to the room at the back of the shop he was going to see Ramlogan's daughter peering through the grimy lace curtains. He

had seen her on the night of his father's death, but he hadn't paid much attention to her then. Now he saw that the girl behind the curtains was tall; sometimes, when she peered too closely, he could see her eyes wide with mischief, simplicity, and awe, all at once.

He couldn't link the girl with her father. She was thin and fair, Ramlogan fat and almost black. He seemed to have only one shirt, a dirty striped blue thing which he wore collarless and open down his hairy chest to just where his round and big belly began. He looked of a piece with his shop. Ganesh got the impression that every morning someone went over everything in it – scales, Ramlogan, and all – with a greased rag.

'It ain't dirty,' Ramlogan said. 'It just *look* dirty. Sit down, sahib, sit down. You ain't have to blow any dust or anything away. You just sit down on that bench against the wall and let we have a good chat. I is not a educated man, but I like to hear educated people talk.'

Ganesh, reluctantly seated, did not at once respond.

'It have nothing like a good chat,' Ramlogan began, slipping off his stool and dusting the counter with his fat hands. 'I like hearing educated people giving off ideas.'

Meeting with further silence, Ramlogan remounted his stool and spoke about the death. 'Your father, sahib, was a good man.' His voice was heavy with grief. 'Still, we give him a good funeral. Fust funeral I attend in Fourways, you know, sahib. I see a lot of funeral in my time, but I go say now and I don't care who hear me say it, that your father funeral was the best I see. Smatterer fact, Leela – my daughter, you know, second and best – Leela say is the best funeral *she* see. She say she count more than five hundred people from all over Trinidad at the funeral, and it had a lot of cars following the body. People did like your father, sahib.'

Then they both fell silent, Ramlogan out of respect for the dead, Ganesh because he didn't know what he was expected to say; and the conversation ended.

'I like these little chats we does have, sahib,' Ramlogan would say, walking to the door with Ganesh. 'I ain't educated meself but I like to hear educated people giving off ideas. Well, sahib, why you don't drop in again? Let we say, tomorrow?'

Ramlogan later solved the conversation problem by pretending that he couldn't read and getting Ganesh to read the newspapers for him; and he listened, elbows on the counter, his hands holding his greasy head, his eyes filling with tears.

'This reading, sahib, is a great great thing,' Ramlogan once said. 'Just think. You take up this paper that to me just look like a dirty sheet with all sort of black mark and scrawl all over the place' – he gave a little self-deprecating laugh – 'you take this up and – eh! eh! – before I have time to even scratch my back, man, I hear you reading from it and making a lot of sense with it. A great thing, sahib.'

Another day he said, 'You does read real sweet, sahib. I could just shut my eye and listen. You know what Leela tell me last night, after I close up the shop? Leela ask me, "Pa, who was the man talking in the shop this morning? He sound just like a radio I hear in San Fernando." I tell she, "Girl, that wasn't a radio you was hearing. That was Ganesh Ramsumair. Pundit Ganesh Ramsumair," I tell she.'

'You making joke.'

'Ah, sahib. Why I should make joke with you, eh? You want me call Leela here self, and you could ask she?'

Ganesh heard a titter behind the lace curtain. He looked down quickly at the floor and saw it littered with empty cigarette boxes and discarded paper bags. 'Nah, nah. Don't bother the girl.'

A week after that Ramlogan told Ganesh, 'Something happen to Leela foot, sahib. I wonder if you would mind having a look at it.'

'I ain't a doctor, man. I ain't know anything about people foot.'

Ramlogan laughed and almost slapped Ganesh on the back. 'Man, how you could say a thing like that, sahib? Ain't you was

learning learning all all the time at the town college? And too besides, don't think I forgetting that your father was the best massager we had.'

For years old Mr Ramsumair had this reputation until, his luck running out, he massaged a young girl and killed her. The Princes Town doctor diagnosed appendicitis and Mr Ramsumair had to spend a lot of money to keep out of trouble. He never massaged afterwards.

'Wasn't his fault,' Ramlogan said, leading Ganesh behind the counter to the curtained doorway. 'He was still the best massager we ever had, and I too too proud that I know his one and only son.'

Leela was sitting in a hammock made from a sugar sack. She was wearing a clean cotton frock and her long black hair looked washed and combed.

'Why you don't have a look at Leela foot, sahib?'

Ganesh looked at Leela's foot, and a curious thing happened. 'I just seemed to touch it,' he wrote, 'and it was all right.'

Ramlogan did not hide his admiration. 'Like I tell you, sahib. You is your father son. Is only special people who could do that sort of thing. I wonder why you don't take up massaging.'

Ganesh remembered the queer feeling he had of being separated from the village people, and he felt that there was something in what Ramlogan said.

He didn't know what Leela thought because as soon as he had fixed her foot she giggled and ran away.

Thereafter Ganesh was a more willing visitor at Ramlogan's, and with every visit he noted improvements in the shop. The most spectacular of these was the introduction of a new glass case. It was given pride of place in the middle of the counter; it was so bright and clean it looked out of place.

'Is really Leela idea,' Ramlogan said. 'It does keep out the flies from the cakes and it more modern.'

The flies now congregated inside the case. Presently a pane was broken and patched up again with brown paper. The glass case now belonged.

Ramlogan said, 'I doing my best to make this Fourways a modern place – as you see – but is hard, man, sahib.'

*

Ganesh still went out cycling, his thoughts maundering between himself, his future, and life itself; and it was during one of his afternoon wanderings that he met the man who was to have a decisive influence on his life.

The first meeting was not happy. It happened on the dusty road that begins at Princes Town and wriggles like a black snake through the green of sugar-cane to Debe. He was not expecting to see anyone on the road at that dead time of day when the sun was almost directly overhead and the wind had ceased to rustle the sugar-cane. He had passed the level-crossing and was free-wheeling down the incline just before the small village of Parrot Trace when a man ran into the middle of the road at the bottom of the incline and waved to him to stop. He was a tall man and looked altogether odd, even for Parrot Trace. He was covered here and there in a yellow cotton robe like a Buddhist monk and he had a staff and a bundle.

'My brother!' the man shouted in Hindi.

Ganesh stopped because he couldn't do anything else; and, because he was afraid of the man, he was rude. 'Who you is, eh?'

'Indian,' the man said in English, with an accent Ganesh had never heard before. His long thin face was fairer than any Indian's and his teeth were bad.

'You only lying,' Ganesh said. 'Go away and let me go.'

The man tightened his face into a smile. 'I am Indian. Kashmiri. Hindu too.'

'So why for you wearing this yellow thing, then?'

The man fidgeted with his staff and looked down at his robe. 'It isn't the right thing, you mean?'

'Perhaps in Kashmir. Not here.'

'But the pictures – they look like this. I would very much like to talk with you,' he added, with sudden warmth.

'All right, all right,' Ganesh said soothingly, and before the man could say anything he was on his bicycle saddle and pedalling away.

When Ramlogan heard about the encounter he said, 'That was Mr Stewart.'

'He just did look crazy crazy to me. He had funny cateyes that frighten me, and you shoulda see the way the sweat was running down his red face. Like he not used to the heat.'

'I did meet him in Penal,' Ramlogan said. 'Just before I move here. Eight nine months back. Everybody say he mad.'

Ganesh learnt that Mr Stewart had recently appeared in South Trinidad dressed as a Hindu mendicant. He claimed that he was Kashmiri. Nobody knew where he came from or how he lived, but it was generally assumed that he was English, a millionaire, and a little mad.

'He a little bit like you, you know, sahib. He does think a lot. But I say, when you have so much money you could damn well afford to do a lot of thinking. Sahib, my people make me shame the way they does rob the man just because he have a lot of money and like to give it away. He does stay in one village, give away money, and then he does move somewhere else and start giving there.'

When Ganesh next saw Mr Stewart, in the village of Swampland, Mr Stewart was in distress, the object of a scrimmage of little boys who were doing their best to unwind his yellow robe. Mr Stewart was not resisting or protesting. He was simply looking about him in a bemused way. Ganesh quickly got off his cycle and picked up a handful of blue-metal stone from a pile left on the

verge by the Public Works Department and no doubt given up for lost.

'Don't hurt them,' Mr Stewart shouted, as Ganesh pursued the boys. 'They are only children. Put down the stones.'

The boys routed, Ganesh came up to Mr Stewart. 'You all right?'

'My dress *is* a little dusty,' Mr Stewart admitted, 'but I am still sound in wind and limb.' He brightened. 'I knew I was going to meet you again. Do you remember our first meeting?'

'I really sorry about that.'

'Oh, I understand. But we must have a talk soon. I feel I can talk to you. The vibrations are right. No, don't deny it. The vibrations are there all right.'

Ganesh smiled at the compliment and in the end accepted an invitation to tea. He did so only out of politeness and had no intention of going, but a talk with Ramlogan made him change his mind.

'He is a lonely man, sahib,' Ramlogan said. 'It have nobody here who really like him and, believe me, I don't think he half as mad as people say. I would go if I was you. You go get on all right with him, seeing that both of you is educated people.'

So Ganesh went to the thatched hut outside Parrot Trace where Mr Stewart now lived. From the outside it looked like any other hut, grass roof and mud walls, but inside it was all order and simplicity. There was a small bed, a small table, and a small chair.

'A man needs no more,' Mr Stewart said.

Ganesh was about to sit in the chair without being asked when Mr Stewart said, 'Nooh! Not that one.' He lifted up the chair and showed it. 'Something I made myself, but I fear it is a trifle unreliable. Made from local materials, you know.'

Ganesh was more interested in Mr Stewart's clothes. He was dressed conventionally, khaki trousers and white shirt, and there was no sign anywhere of the yellow robe.

Mr Stewart divined Ganesh's interest. 'It doesn't matter what you wear. No spiritual significance, I've decided.'

Mr Stewart showed Ganesh some day statuettes he had made of Hindu gods and goddesses and Ganesh was astonished, not by the artistry, but by the fact that Mr Stewart had made them at all.

Mr Stewart pointed to a water-colour on the wall. 'I've been working on that picture for years. Once or twice a year I get a new idea for it and it has to be drawn all over again.'

The water-colour, done in blues and yellows and browns, depicted a number of brown hands reaching out for a yellow light in the top left-hand corner.

'This, I think, is rather interesting.' Ganesh followed Mr Stewart's finger and saw a blue shrunk hand curling backwards from the yellow light. 'Some see Illumination,' Mr Stewart explained. 'But they do sometimes get burnt and withdraw.'

'Why all the hands brown?'

'Hindu hands. Only people really striving after the indefinite today. You look worried.'

'Yes, I worried.'

'About life?'

'I think so,' Ganesh said. 'Yes, I think I worried about life.'

'Doubts?' Mr Stewart probed.

Ganesh only smiled because he didn't know what Mr Stewart meant.

Mr Stewart sat down on the bed next to him and said, 'What do you do?'

Ganesh laughed. 'Nothing at all. I guess I just doing a lot of thinking.'

'Meditating?'

'Yes, meditating.'

Mr Stewart jumped up and clasped his hands before the water-colour. 'Typical!' he said, and closed his eyes as if in ecstasy. 'Typical!'

Then he opened his eyes and said, 'But now – tea.'

He had taken a lot of trouble to prepare tea. There were sandwiches of three sorts, biscuits, and cakes. And although Ganesh was beginning to like Mr Stewart and wanted to eat his food, all his Hindu instincts rose high and he was nauseated to bite into a cold egg-and-cress sandwich.

Mr Stewart saw. 'It doesn't matter,' he said. 'It's too hot, anyway.'

'Oh, I like it. But I more thirsty than hungry, that's all.'

They talked, and talked. Mr Stewart was anxious to learn all of Ganesh's problems.

'Don't think you are wasting your time meditating,' he said. 'I know the things that are worrying you, and I think one day you may find the answer. One day you may even bring it all out in a book. If I weren't so terribly afraid of getting involved I might have written a book myself. But you must find your own spiritual rhythm before you start doing anything. You must stop being *worried* about life.'

'All right,' Ganesh said.

Mr Stewart talked like a man who had saved up conversation for years. He told Ganesh all about his life, his experiences in the First World War, his disillusionment, his rejection of Christianity. Ganesh was entranced. Apart from the insistence that he was a Kashmiri Hindu, Mr Stewart was as sane as any of the masters at the Queen's Royal College; and as the afternoon wore on, his blue eyes ceased to be frightening and looked sad.

'Why you don't go to India then?' Ganesh asked.

'Politics. Don't want to get involved in any way. You can't imagine how soothing it is here. One day you may go to London – I pray not – and you will see how sick you can get gazing from your taxi at the stupid, cruel faces of the mob on the pavements. You can't help being involved there. Here there is no such need.'

The tropical night fell suddenly and Mr Stewart lit an oil lamp. The hut felt very small and very sad, and Ganesh was sorry that soon he had to go and leave Mr Stewart to his loneliness.

'You must write your thoughts,' Mr Stewart said. 'They may help other people. You know, I felt all along that I was going to meet someone like you.'

Before Ganesh left, Mr Stewart presented him with twenty copies of *The Science of Thought Review.*

'They have given me a great deal of comfort,' he said. 'And you may find them useful.'

Ganesh said in surprise, 'But is not an Indian magazine, Mr Stewart. It say here that it print in England.'

'Yes, in England,' Mr Stewart said sadly. 'But in one of the prettier parts. In Chichester, in Sussex.'

That was the end of their conversation and Ganesh saw no more of Mr Stewart. When he called at the hut some three weeks later, he found it occupied by a young labourer and his wife. Many years afterwards Ganesh learnt what had happened to Mr Stewart. About six months after their conversation he had returned to England and joined the army. He died in Italy.

This was the man whose memory Ganesh so handsomely honoured in the dedication of his autobiography:

TO LORD STEWART OF CHICHESTER
Friend and Counsellor
of Many Years

*

Ganesh had become more than a regular visitor at Ramlogan's. He was eating there every day now; and when he called, Ramlogan no longer allowed him to remain in the shop, but invited him in immediately to the room at the back. This caused Leela to retreat to the bedroom or the kitchen.

And even the back room began to undergo improvements. The table got an oilcloth cover; the unpainted, mildewed partitions became gay with huge Chinese calendars; the hammock made from a sugar sack was replaced by one made from a flour sack. A vase appeared one day on the oilcloth on the table; and less than a week later paper roses bloomed in the vase. Ganesh himself was treated with increasing honour. At first they fed him out of enamel dishes. Now they gave him earthenware ones. They knew no higher honour.

The table itself was to offer a further surprise. One day a whole series of booklets on The Art of Salesmanship appeared on it.

Ramlogan said, ‘I bet you does miss all the big books and thing you did have in Port of Spain, eh, sahib?’

Ganesh said he didn’t.

Ramlogan strove to be casual. ‘I have a few books myself. Leela put them out on the table.’

‘They look pretty and nice.’

‘Education, sahib, is one hell of a thing. Nobody did bother to send me to school, you know. When I was five they send me out to cut grass instead. But look at Leela and she sister. Both of them does read *and* write, you know, sahib. Although I don’t know what happening to Soomintra since she married that damn fool in San Fernando.’

Ganesh flipped through the pages of one of the booklets. ‘Yes, they look as really nice books.’

‘Is really for Leela I buy the book, sahib. I say, if the girl can read, we must give she something to read. Ain’t true, sahib?’

‘Is not true, Pa,’ a girl’s voice said, and they turned to see Leela at the kitchen door.

Ramlogan turned back quickly to Ganesh. ‘Is the sort of girl she is, sahib. She don’t like people to boast about she. She shy. And if it have one thing she hate, is to hear lies. I was just testing she, to show you.’

Leela, not looking at Ganesh, said to Ramlogan, 'You buy those books from Bissoon. When he went away you get so vex you say that if you see him again you go do for him.'

Ramlogan laughed and slapped his thigh. 'This Bissoon, sahib, is a real smart seller. He does talk just as a professor, not so good as you, but still good. But what really make me buy the books is that we did know one another when we was small and in the same grass-cutting gang. We was ambitious boys, sahib.'

Ganesh said again, 'I think they is good books.'

'Take them home, man. What book make for if not to read? Take them home and read them up, sahib.'

It was not long after that Ganesh saw a big new notice in the shop, painted on cardboard.

'Is Leela self who write that,' Ramlogan said. 'I didn't ask she to write it, mind you. She just sit down quiet quiet one morning after tea and write it off.'

It read:

NOTICE

NOTICE, IS. HEREBY; PROVIDED: THAT, SEATS!
ARE, PROVIDED. FOR; FEMALE: SHOP, ASSISTANTS!

Ganesh said, 'Leela know a lot of punctuation marks.'

That is it, sahib. All day the girl just sitting down and talking about these puncturation marks. She is like that, sahib.'

'But who is your shop assistants?'

'Leela say is the law to have the sign up, sahib. But, smatterer fact, I don't like the idea of having a girl in the shop.'

Ganesh had taken away the booklets on salesmanship and read them. The very covers, shining yellow and black, interested him; and what he read enthralled him. The writer had a strong feeling for colour and beauty and order. He spoke with relish about new paint, dazzling displays, and gleaming shelves.

'These is first-class books,' Ganesh told Ramlogan.

'You must tell Leela so, sahib. Look, I go call she and you you go tell she and then perhaps she go want to read the books sheself.'

It was an important occasion and Leela acted as though she felt its full importance. When she came in she didn't look up and when her father spoke she only lowered her head a bit more and sometimes she giggled, coyly.

Ramlogan said, 'Leela, you hear what the sahib tell me. He like the books.'

Leela giggled, but decorously.

Ganesh asked, 'Is you who write the sign?'

'Yes, is me who write the sign.'

Ramlogan slapped his thigh and said, 'What I did tell you, sahib? The girl can really read and really write.' He laughed.

Then Leela did a thing so unexpected it killed Ramlogan's laughter.

Leela spoke to Ganesh. She asked *him* a question!

'You could write too, sahib?'

It took him off his guard. To cover up his surprise he began rearranging the booklets on the table.

'Yes,' he said. 'I could write.' And then, stupidly, almost without knowing what he was saying, 'And one day I go write books like these. Just like these.'

Ramlogan's mouth fell open.

'You only joking, sahib.'

Ganesh slapped his hand down on the booklets, and heard himself saying, 'Yes, just like these. *Just* like these.'

Leela's wide eyes grew wider and Ramlogan shook his head in amazement and wonder.

4. The Quarrel with Ramlogan

'I SUPPOSE,' Ganesh wrote in *The Years of Guilt*, 'I had always, from the first day I stepped into Shri Ramlogan's shop, considered it as settled that I was going to marry his daughter. I never questioned it. It all seemed preordained.'

What happened was this.

One day when Ganesh called Ramlogan was wearing a clean shirt. Also, he looked freshly washed, his hair looked freshly oiled; and his movements were silent and deliberate, as though he were doing a *puja*. He dragged up the small bench from the corner and placed it near the table; then sat on it and watched Ganesh eat, all without saying a word. First he looked at Ganesh's face, then at Ganesh's plate, and there his gaze rested until Ganesh had eaten the last handful of rice.

'Your belly full, sahib?'

'Yes, my belly full.' Ganesh wiped his plate clean with an extended index finger.

'It must be hard for you, sahib, now that your father dead.'

Ganesh licked his finger. 'I don't really miss him, you know.'

'No, sahib, don't tell me. I *know* is hard for you. Supposing, just supposing – I just putting this up to you as a superstition, sahib – but just supposing you did want to get married, it have nobody at all to fix up things for you.'

'I don't even know if I want to get married.' Ganesh rose from

the table, rubbing his belly until he belched his appreciation of Ramlogan's food.

Ramlogan rearranged the roses in the vase. 'Still, you is a educated man, and you could take care of yourself. Not like me, sahib. Since I was five I been working, with nobody looking after me. Still, all that do something for me. Guess what it do for me, sahib.'

'Can't guess. Tell me what it do.'

'It give me cha'acter and sensa values, sahib. That's what it give me. Cha'acter and sensa values.'

Ganesh took the brass jar of water from the table and went to the Demerara window to wash his hands and gargle.

Ramlogan was smoothing out the oilcloth with both hands and dusting away some crumbs, mere specks. 'I know,' he said apologetically, 'that for a man like you, educated and reading books night and day, shopkeeping is a low thing. But I don't care what people think. You, sahib, answer me this as a educated man: you does let other people worry you?'

Ganesh, gargling, thought at once of Miller and the row at the school in Port of Spain, but when he spat out the water into the yard he said, 'Nah. I don't care what people say.'

Ramlogan pounded across the floor and took the brass jar from Ganesh. 'I go put this away, sahib. You sit down in the hammock. Ooops! Let me dust it for you first.'

When he had seated Ganesh, Ramlogan started to walk up and down in front of the hammock.

'People can't harm me,' he said, holding his hands at his back. 'All right, people don't like me. All right, they stop coming to my shop. That harm me? That change my cha'acter? I just go to San Fernando and open a little stall in the market. No, don't stop me, sahib. Is exactly what I would do. Take a stall in the market. And what happen? Tell me, what happen?'

Ganesh belched again, softly.

'What happen?' Ramlogan gave a short crooked laugh. 'Bam! In five years I have a whole chain of grocery shop. Who laughing then? Then you go see them coming round and begging, "Mr Ramlogan" – that's what it go be then, you know: *Mister* Ramlogan – "Mr Ramlogan, gimme this, gimme that, Mr Ramlogan." Begging me to go up for elections and a hundred and one stupid things.'

Ganesh said, 'You ain't have to start opening stall in San Fernando market now, thank God.'

'That is it, sahib. Just just as you say. Is all God work. Count my property now. Is true I is illiterate, but you just sit down in that hammock and count my property.'

Ramlogan was walking and talking with such unusual energy that the sweat broke and shone on his forehead. Suddenly he halted and stood directly in front of Ganesh. He took away his hands from behind his back and started to count off his fingers. 'Two acres near Chaguanas. Good land, too. Ten acres in Penal. You never know when I could scrape together enough to make the drillers put a oil-well there. A house in Fuente Grove. Not much, but is something. Two three houses in Siparia. Add up all that and you find you looking at a man worth about twelve thousand dollars, cool cool.'

Ramlogan passed his hand over his forehead and behind his neck. 'I know is hard to believe, sahib. But is the gospel truth. I think is a good idea, sahib, for you to married Leela.'

'All right,' Ganesh said.

*

He never saw Leela again until the night of their wedding, and both he and Ramlogan pretended he had never seen her at all, because they were both good Hindus and knew it was wrong for a man to see his wife before marriage.

He still had to go to Ramlogan's, to make arrangements for the

wedding, but he remained in the shop itself and never went to the back room.

'You is not like Soomintra damn fool of a husband,' Ramlogan told him. 'You is a modern man and you must have a modern wedding.'

So he didn't send the messenger around to give the saffron-dyed rice to friends and relations and announce the wedding. 'That old-fashion,' he said. He wanted printed invitations on scalloped and gilt-edged cards. 'And we must have nice wordings, sahib.'

'But you can't have nice wordings on a thing like a invitation.'

'You is the educated man, sahib. You could think of some.'

'*R.S.V.P.?*'

'What that mean?'

'It don't mean nothing, but it nice to have it.'

'Let we have it then, man, sahib! You is a modern man, and too besides, it sound as pretty wordings.'

Ganesh himself went to San Fernando to get the cards printed. The printer's shop was, at first sight, a little disappointing. It looked black and bleak and seemed to be manned only by a thin youth in ragged khaki shorts who whistled as he operated the hand-press. But when Ganesh saw the cards go in blank and come out with his prose miraculously transformed into all the authority of type, he was struck with something like awe. He stayed to watch the boy set up a cinema hand-bill. The boy, whistling without intermission, ignored Ganesh altogether.

'Is on this sort of machine they does print books?' Ganesh asked.

'What else you think it make for?'

'You print any good books lately?'

The boy dabbed some ink on the roller. 'You ever hear of Trinidad people writing books?'

'*I* writing a book.'

The boy spat into a bin full of ink-stained paper. 'This must

be a funny sort of shop, you know. The number of people who come in here and ask me to print the books they writing in invisible ink, man!'

'What you name?'

'Basdeo.'

'All right, Basdeo, boy. The day go come when I go send you a book to print.'

'Sure, man. Sure. You write it and I print it.'

Ganesh didn't think he liked Basdeo's Hollywood manner, and he instantly regretted what he had said. But so far as this business of writing books was concerned, he seemed to have no will: it was the second time he had committed himself. It all seemed pre-ordained.

*

'Yes, they is pretty invitation cards,' Ramlogan said, but there was no joy in his voice.

'But what happen now to make your face long long as mango?'

'Education, sahib, is one hell of a thing. When you is a poor illiterate man like me, all sort of people does want to take advantage on you.'

Ramlogan began to cry. 'Right now, right right now, as you sitting down on that bench there and I sitting down on this stool behind my shop counter, looking at these pretty pretty cards, you wouldn't believe what people trying to do to me. Right now it have a man in Siparia trying to rob my two house there, all because I can't read, and the people in Penal behaving in a funny way.'

'What they doing so?'

'Ah, sahib. That is just like you. I know you want to help me, but is too late now. All sort of paper with fine fine writing they did make me sign and everything, and now – now everything lost.'

Ganesh had not seen Ramlogan cry so much since the funeral.

He said, 'Well, look. If is the dowry you worried about, you could stop. I don't want a big dowry.'

'Is the shame, sahib, that eating me up. You know how with these Hindu weddings everybody does know how much the boy get from the girl father. When, the morning after the wedding the boy sit down and they give him a plate of kedgeree, with the girl father having to give money and keep on giving until the boy eat the kedgeree, everybody go see what I give you, and they go say, "Look, Ramlogan marrying off his second and best daughter to a boy with a college education, and this is all the man giving." Is that what eating me up, sahib. I know that for you, educated and reading books night and day, it wouldn't mean much, but for me, sahib, what about my cha'acter and sensa values?'

'You must stop crying and listen. When it come to eating the kedgeree, I go eat quick, not to shame you. Not too quick, because that would make people think you poor as a church-rat. But I wouldn't take much from you.'

Ramlogan smiled through his tears. 'Is just like you, sahib, just what I did expect from you. I wish Leela did see you and then she woulda know what sort of man I choose for she husband.'

'I wish I did see Leela too.'

'Smatterer fact, sahib, I know it have some modern people nowadays who don't even like waiting for money before they eat the kedgeree.'

'But is the custom, man.'

'Yes, sahib, the custom. But still I think is a disgrace in these modern times. Now, if it was *I* was getting married, I wouldn't want any dowry and I woulda say, "To hell with the kedgeree, man." '

*

As soon as the invitations were out Ganesh had to stop visiting Ramlogan altogether, but he wasn't alone in his house for long.

Dozens of women descended on him with their children. He had no idea who most of them were; sometimes he recognized a face and found it hard to believe that the woman with the children hanging about her was the same cousin who was only a child herself when he first went to Port of Spain.

The children treated Ganesh with contempt.

A small boy with a running nose said to him one day, 'They tell me is you who getting married.'

'Yes, is me.'

The boy said, 'Ahaha!' and ran away laughing and jeering.

The boy's mother said, 'Is something we have to face these days. The children getting modern.'

Then one day Ganesh discovered his aunt among the women, she who had been one of the principal mourners at his father's funeral. He learnt that she had not only arranged everything then, but had also paid for it all. When Ganesh offered to pay back the money she became annoyed and told him not to be stupid.

'This life is a funny thing, eh,' she said. 'One day somebody dead and you cry. Two days later somebody married, and then you laugh. Oh, Ganeshwa boy, at a time like this you want your own family around you, but what family you have? Your father, he dead; your mother, she dead too.'

She was so moved she couldn't cry; and for the first time Ganesh realized what a big thing his marriage was.

Ganesh thought it almost a miracle that so many people could live happily in one small house without any sort of organization. They had left him the bedroom, but they swarmed over the rest of the house and managed as best they could. First they had made it into an extended picnic site; then they had made it into a cramped camping site. But they looked happy enough and Ganesh presently discovered that the anarchy was only apparent. Of the dozens of women who wandered freely about the house there was one, tall and silent, whom he had learnt to call King George. It might have

been her real name for all he knew: he had never seen her before. King George ruled the house.

'King George got a hand,' his aunt said.

'A hand?'

'She got a hand for sharing things out. Give King George a little penny cake and give she twelve children to share it out to, and you could bet your bottom dollar that King George share it fair and square.'

'You know she, then?'

'Know she! Is I who take up King George. Mark you, I think I was very lucky coming across she. Now I take she everywhere with me.'

'She related to us?'

'You could say so. Phulbassia is a sort of cousin to King George and you is a sort of cousin to Phulbassia.'

The aunt belched, not the polite after-dinner belch, but a long, stuttering thing. 'Is the wind,' she explained without apology. 'It have a long time now – since your father dead, come to think of it – I suffering from this wind.'

'You see a doctor?'

'Doctor? They does only make up things. One of them tell me – you know what? – that I have a lazy liver. Is something I asking myself a long time now: how a liver could be lazy, eh?'

She belched again, said, 'You see?' and rubbed her hands over her breasts.

Ganesh thought of this aunt as Lady Belcher and then as The Great Belcher. In a few days she had a devastating effect on the other women in the house. They all began belching and rubbing their breasts and complaining about the wind. All except King George.

Ganesh was glad when the time came for him to be anointed with saffron. For those days he was confined to his room, where his father's body had lain that night, and where now The Great

Belcher, King George, and a few other anonymous women gathered to rub him down. When they left the room they sang Hindi wedding songs of a most pessimistic nature, and Ganesh wondered how Leela was putting up with her own seclusion and anointing.

All day long he remained in his room, consoling himself with *The Science of Thought Review.* He read through all the numbers Mr Stewart had given him, some of them many times over. All day he heard the children romping, squealing, and being beaten; the mothers beating, shouting, and thumping about on the floor.

On the day before the wedding, when the women had come in to rub him down for the last time, he asked The Great Belcher, 'I never think about it before, but what those people outside eating? Who paying for it?'

'You.'

He almost sat up in bed, but King George's strong arm kept him down.

'Ramlogan did say that we mustn't get you worried about that,' The Great Belcher said. 'He say your head hot with enough worries already. But King George looking after everything. She got a account with Ramlogan. He go settle with you after the wedding.'

'Oh God! I ain't even married the man daughter yet, and already he start!'

*

Fourways was nearly as excited at the wedding as it had been at the funeral. Hundreds of people, from Fourways and elsewhere, were fed at Ramlogan's. There were dancers, drummers, and singers, for those who were not interested in the details of the night-long ceremony. The yard behind Ramlogan's shop was beautifully illuminated with all sorts of lights, except electric ones; and the decorations – mainly fruit hanging from coconut-palm arches – were pleasing. All this for Ganesh, and Ganesh felt it and was pleased. The thought of marriage had at first embarrassed him,

then, when he spoke with his aunt, awed him; now he was simply thrilled.

All through the ceremony he had to pretend, with everyone else, that he had never seen Leela. She sat at his side veiled from head to toe, until the blanket was thrown over them and he unveiled her face. In the mellow light under the pink blanket she was as a stranger. She was no longer the giggling girl simpering behind the lace curtains. Already she looked chastened and impassive, a good Hindu wife.

Shortly afterwards it was over, and they were man and wife. Leela was taken away and Ganesh was left alone to face the kedgeree-eating ceremony the next morning.

Still in all his bridegroom's regalia, satin robes, and tasselled crown, he sat down on some blankets in the yard, before the plate of kedgeree. It looked white and unpalatable, and he knew it would be easy to resist any temptation to touch it.

Ramlogan was the first to offer money to induce Ganesh to eat. He was a little haggard after staying awake all night, but he looked pleased and happy enough when he placed five twenty-dollar bills in the brass plate next to the kedgeree. He stepped back, folded his arms, looked from the money to Ganesh to the small group standing by, and smiled.

He stood smiling for nearly two minutes; but Ganesh didn't even look at the kedgeree.

'Give the boy money, man,' Ramlogan cried to the people around. 'Give him money, man. Come on, don't act as if you is all poor poor as church-rat.' He moved among them, laughing, and rallying them. Some put down small amounts in the brass plate.

Still Ganesh sat, serene and aloof, like an over-dressed Buddha.

A little crowd began to gather.

'The boy have sense, man.' Anxiety broke into Ramlogan's voice. 'When you think a college education is these days?'

He put down another hundred dollars. 'Eat, boy, eat it up. I don't want you to starve. Not yet, anyway.' He laughed, but no one laughed with him.

Ganesh didn't eat.

He heard a man saying, 'Well, this thing was bound to happen some day.'

People said, 'Come on, Ramlogan. Give the boy money, man. What you think he sitting down there for? To take out his photo?'

Ramlogan gave a short, forced laugh, and lost his temper. 'If he think he going to get any more money from me he damn well mistaken. Let him don't eat. Think I care if he starve? Think I care?'

He walked away.

The crowd grew bigger; the laughter grew louder.

Ramlogan came back and the crowd cheered him.

He put down two hundred dollars on the brass plate and, before he rose, whispered to Ganesh, 'Remember your promise, sahib. Eat, boy; eat, son; eat, sahib; eat, pundit sahib. I beg you, eat.'

A man shouted, 'No! I not going to eat!'

Ramlogan stood up and turned around. 'You, haul your tail away from here quick, quick, before I break it up for you. Don't meddle in what don't concern you.'

The crowd roared.

Ramlogan bent down again to whisper. 'You see, sahib, how you making me shame.' This time his whisper promised tears. 'You see, sahib, what you doing to my cha'acter and sensa values.'

Ganesh didn't move.

The crowd was beginning to treat him like a hero.

In the end Ganesh got from Ramlogan: a cow and a heifer, fifteen hundred dollars in cash, and a house in Fuente Grove. Ramlogan also cancelled the bill for the food he had sent to Ganesh's house.

The ceremony ended at about nine in the morning; but Ramlogan was sweating long before then.

'The boy and I was only having a joke,' he said again and again at the end. 'He done know long time now what I was going to give him. We was only making joke, you know.'

*

Ganesh returned home after the wedding. It would be three days before Leela could come to live with him and in that time The Great Belcher tried to restore order to the house. Most of the guests had left as suddenly as they had arrived; though from time to time Ganesh still saw a straggler who wandered about the house and ate.

'King George gone to Arima yesterday,' The Great Belcher told him. 'Somebody dead there yesterday. I going tomorrow myself, but I send King George ahead to arrange everything.'

Then she decided to give Ganesh the facts of life.

'These modern girls is hell self,' she said. 'And from what I see and hear, this Leela is a modern girl. Anyway, you got to make the best of what is yours.'

She paused to belch. 'All she want to make she straight as a arrow is a little blows every now and then.'

Ganesh said, 'You know, I think Ramlogan really vex with me now after the kedgeree business.'

'Wasn't a nice thing to do, but it serve Ramlogan right. When a man start taking over woman job, match-making, he deserve all he get.'

'But I go have to leave here now. You know Fuente Grove? It have a house there Ramlogan give me.'

'But what you want in a small outa the way place like that? All the work it have doing there is work in the cane-field.'

'It ain't that I want to do.' Ganesh paused, and added hesitantly, 'I thinking of taking up massaging people.'

She laughed so much she belched. 'This wind, man, and then you – you want to kill me or what, boy? Massaging people! What you know about massaging people?'

'Pa was a good massager and I know all he did know.'

'But you must have a hand for that sort of thing. Think what go happen if any- and everybody start running round saying, "I thinking of taking up massaging people." It go have so much massagers in Trinidad they go have to start massaging one another.'

'I feel I have a hand for it. Just like King George.'

'She have her own sort of hand. She born that way.'

Ganesh told her about Leela's foot.

She twisted her mouth. 'It sound good. But a man like you should be doing something else. Bookwork, man.'

'I going to do that too.' And then it came out again. 'I thinking of writing some books.'

'Good thing. It have money in books, you know. I suppose the man who write the *Macdonald Farmer's Almanac* just peeling money. Why you don't try your hand at something like the *Napoleon Book of Fate*? I just *feel* you could do that sort of thing good.'

'People go want to buy that sort of book?'

'Is exactly what Trinidad want, boy. Take all the Indians in the towns. They ain't have any pundit or anything near them, you know. How they go know what to do and what not to do, when and not when? They just have to guess.'

Ganesh was thoughtful. 'Yes, is that self I go do. A little bit of massaging and a little bit of writing.'

'I know a boy who could make anything you write sell as hot cakes all over Trinidad. Let we say, you selling the book at two shillings, forty-eight cents. You give the boy six cents a book. Let we say now, you print four five thousand – '

'It make about two thousand dollars, but – wait, man! I ain't even write the book yet.'

'I know you, boy. Once you put your mind to it, you go write nice nice books.'

She belched.

*

As soon as Leela had come to live with Ganesh and the last guest had left the village, Ramlogan declared war on Ganesh and that very evening ran through Fourways crying out, chanting, his declaration. 'See how he rob me. Me with my wife dead, me now without children, me a poor widow. See how he forget everything I do for him. He forget all that I give him, he forget how I help burn his father, he forget all the help I give him. See how he rob me. See how he shame me. Watch me here now, so help me God, if I don't here and now do for the son of a bitch.'

Ganesh ordered Leela to bolt the doors and windows and put out the lights. He took one of his father's old walking-sticks and remained in the middle of the front room.

Leela began to cry. 'The man is my own father and here you is taking up big stick to beat him.'

Ganesh heard Ramlogan shouting from the road, 'Ganesh, you damn little piss-in-tail boy, you want property, eh? You know the only place you could take my property? You going to take it away on your chest, six foot of it.'

Ganesh said, 'Leela, in the bedroom it have a little copy-book. Go bring it. And it have a pencil in the table drawer. Bring that too.'

She brought the book and pencil and Ganesh wrote, *Carry away his property on my chest*. Below he wrote the date. He had no particular reason for doing this except that he was afraid and felt he had to do something.

Leela cried. 'You working magic on my own father!'

Ganesh said, 'Leela, why you getting 'fraid? We not staying in

this place long. In a few days we moving to Fuente Grove. Nothing to 'fraid.'

Leela continued to cry and Ganesh loosened his leather belt and beat her.

She cried out, 'Oh God! Oh God! He go kill me today self!'

It was their first beating, a formal affair done without anger on Ganesh's part or resentment on Leela's; and although it formed no part of the marriage ceremony itself, it meant much to both of them. It meant that they had grown up and become independent. Ganesh had become a man; Leela a wife as privileged as any other big woman. Now she too would have tales to tell of her husband's beatings; and when she went home she would be able to look sad and sullen as every woman should.

The moment was precious.

Leela cried for a bit and said, 'Man, I really getting worried about Pa.'

This was another first: she had called him 'man'. There could be no doubt about it now: they were adults. Three days before Ganesh was hardly better than a boy, anxious and diffident. Now he had suddenly lost these qualities and he thought, 'My father was right. I shoulda get married long before now.'

Leela said, 'Man, I getting really worried about Pa. Tonight he not going to do you anything. He just go shout a lot and go away, but he won't forget you. I see him horsewhip a man in Penal really bad one time.'

They heard Ramlogan shouting from the road, 'Ganesh, this is the last time I warning you.'

Leela said, 'Man, you must do something to make Pa feel nice. Otherwise I don't know.'

Ramlogan's shout sounded hoarse now. 'Ganesh, tonight self I sharpening up a cutlass for you. I make up my mind to send you to hospital and go to jail for you. Look out, I warning you.'

And then, as Leela had said, Ramlogan went away.

The next morning, after Ganesh had done his *puja* and eaten the first meal that Leela had cooked for him, he said, 'Leela, you got any pictures of your father?'

She was sitting at the kitchen table, cleaning rice for the midday meal. 'Why you want it for?' she asked with alarm.

'You forgetting yourself, girl. Somebody make you a policeman now to ask me question? Is a old picture?'

Leela wept over the rice. 'Not so old, man. Two three years now Pa did go to San Fernando and Chong take out a photo of Pa by hisself and another one with Pa and Soomintra and me. Just before Soomintra did get married. They was pretty photos. Paintings behind and plants in front.'

'I just want a picture of your father. What I don't want is your tears.'

He followed her to the bedroom, and while he put on his town clothes – khaki trousers, blue shirt, brown hat, brown shoes – Leela pulled out her suitcase, an Anchor Cigarettes coupons-gift, from under the bed and looked for the photograph.

'Gimme,' he said, when she had found it, and snatched it away. 'This go settle your father.'

She ran after him to the steps. 'Where you going, man?'

'Leela, you know, for a girl who ain't married three days yet you too damn fast.'

He had to pass Ramlogan's shop. He took care to swing his father's walking stick, and behaved as though the shop didn't exist.

And sure enough, he heard Ramlogan calling out, 'Ganesh, you playing man this morning, eh? Swinging walking-stick as if you is some master-stickman. But, boy, when I get after you, you not going to run fast enough.'

Ganesh walked past without a word.

*

Leela confessed later that she had gone to the shop that morning to warn Ramlogan. She found him mounted on his stool and miserable.

'Pa, I have something to tell you.'

'I have nothing to do with you or your husband. I only want you to take a message to him. Tell him for me that Ramlogan say the only way he going to get my property is to take it away on his chest.'

'He write that down last night in a copy-book. And then, Pa, this morning he ask me for a photo of you and he have it now.'

Ramlogan slid, practically fell, off his stool. 'Oh God! Oh God! I didn't know he was that sort of man. He look so quiet.' He stamped up and down behind the counter. 'Oh God! What I do to your husband to make him prosecute me in this way? What he going to do with the picture?'

Leela was sobbing.

Ramlogan looked at the glass case on the counter. 'All that I do for him. Leela, I didn't want any glass case in my shop.'

'No, Pa, you didn't want any glass case in the shop.'

'It for he I get the glass case. Oh God! Leela, is only one thing he going to do with the picture. Work magic and *obeah*, Leela.'

In his agitation Ramlogan was clutching at his hair, slapping his chest and belly, and beating on the counter. 'And then he go want more property.' Ramlogan's voice palpitated with true anguish.

Leela shrieked. 'What you going to do to my husband, Pa? Is only three days now I married him.'

'Soomintra, poor little Soomintra, she did tell me when we was going to take out the photos. "Pa, I don't think we should take out any photos." God, oh God! Leela, why I didn't listen to poor little Soomintra?'

Ramlogan passed a grubby hand over the brown-paper patch on the glass case, and shook away his tears.

'And last night, Pa, he beat me.'

'Come, Leela, come, daughter.' He leaned over the counter and put his hands on her shoulder. 'Is your fate, Leela. Is my fate too. We can't fight it, Leela.'

'Pa,' Leela wailed, 'what you going to do to him? He is my husband, you know.'

Ramlogan withdrew his hands and wiped his eyes. He beat on the counter until the glass case rattled. 'That is what they call education these days. They teaching a new subject. Pickpocketing.'

Leela gave another shriek. 'The man is my husband, Pa.'

*

When, later that afternoon, Ganesh came back to Fourways, he was surprised to hear Ramlogan shouting, 'Oh, sahib! Sahib! What happen that you passing without saying anything? People go think we vex.'

Ganesh saw Ramlogan smiling broadly behind the counter. 'What you want me to say when you have a sharpen cutlass underneath the counter, eh?'

'Cutlass? Sharpen cutlass? You making joke, sahib. Come in, man, sahib, and sit down. Yes, sit down, and let we have a chat. Eh, but is just like old times, eh, sahib?'

'Things change now.'

'Ah, sahib. Don't say you vex with me.'

'I ain't vex with you.'

'Is for stupid illiterate people like me to get vex. And when illiterate people get vex they does start thinking about working magic against people and all that sort of thing. Educated people don't do that sort of thing.'

'You go be surprised.'

Ramlogan tried to draw Ganesh's attention to the glass case. 'Is a nice modern thing, ain't so, sahib? Nice, pretty, little modern thing.' A drowsy fly was buzzing on the outside, anxious to join

its fellows inside. Ramlogan brought down his hand quickly on the glass and killed the fly. He threw it out of the side window and wiped his hands on his trousers. 'These flies *is* a botheration, sahib. What is a good way of getting rid of these botherations, sahib?'

'I ain't know anything about flies, man.'

Ramlogan smiled and tried again. 'How you like being a married man, sahib?'

'These modern girls is hell self. They does keep forgetting their place.'

'Sahib, I have to hand it to you. Only three days you married and you find that out already. Is the valua education. You want some salmon, sahib? Is just as good as any salmon in San Fernando.'

'Don't like San Fernando people.'

'How business there for you, sahib?'

'Tomorrow, please God, we go see what happen.'

'Oh God! Sahib, I didn't mean anything bad last night. Was only a little drunk I was, sahib. A old man like me can't hold his liquor, sahib. I don't mind how much you want from me. I is a good good Hindu, sahib. Take away everything from me and it don't make no difference, once you leave me with my cha'acter.'

'You is a damn funny sort of man, you know.'

Ramlogan slapped at another fly and missed. 'What go happen tomorrow, sahib?'

Ganesh rose from the bench and dusted the seat of his trousers. 'Oh, tomorrow is one big secret.'

Ramlogan rubbed his hands along the edge of the counter.

'Why you crying?'

'Oh, sahib, I is a poor man. You *must* feel sorry for me.'

'Leela go be all right with me. You mustn't cry for she.'

*

He found Leela in the kitchen, squatting before the low *chulha* fire, stirring boiling rice in a blue enamel pot.

'Leela, I have a good mind to take off my belt and give you a good dose of blows before I even wash my hand or do anything else.'

She adjusted the veil over her head before turning to him. 'What happen now, man?'

'Girl, how you let all your father bad blood run in your veins, eh? How you playing you don't know what happen, when you know that you run around telling Tom, Dick, and Harry my business?'

She faced the *chulha* again and stirred the pot. 'Man, if we start quarrelling now, the rice go boil too soft and you know you don't like it like that.'

'All right, but I go want you answer me later on.'

After the meal she confessed and he surprised her by not beating her.

So she was emboldened to ask, 'Man, what you do with Pa photo?'

'I think I settle your father. Tomorrow it wouldn't have one man in Trinidad who wouldn't know about him. Look, Leela, if you start this crying again, I go make you taste my hand again. Start packing. Tomorrow self we moving to Fuente Grove.'

*

And the next morning the *Trinidad Sentinel* carried this story on page five:

> BENEFACTOR ENDOWS CULTURAL INSTITUTE
>
> Shri Ramlogan, merchant, of Fourways, near Debe, has donated a considerable sum of money with the view of founding a Cultural Institute at Fuente Grove. The aim of the proposed Institute, which has yet to be named, will be

> the furthering of Hindu Cultural and Science of Thought in Trinidad.
>
> The President of the Institute, it is learnt, will be Ganesh Ramsumair, B.A.

And there was, in a prominent place, a photograph of a formally attired and slimmer Ramlogan, a potted plant at his side, standing against a background of Greek ruins.

The counter of Ramlogan's shop was covered with copies of the *Trinidad Sentinel* and the *Port of Spain Herald*. Ramlogan didn't look up when Ganesh came into the shop. He was gazing intently at the photograph and trying to frown.

'Don't bother with the *Herald*,' Ganesh said. 'I didn't give them the story.'

Ramlogan didn't look up. He frowned more severely and said, 'Hmmh!' He turned the page over and read a brief item about the danger of tubercular cows. 'They pay you anything?'

'The man wanted *me* to pay.'

'Son of a bitch.'

Ganesh made an approving noise.

'So, sahib.' Ramlogan looked up at last. 'Was really this you wanted the money for?'

'Really really.'

'And you really going to write books at Fuente Grove and everything?'

'Really going to write books.'

'Yes, man. Been reading it here, sahib. Is a great thing, and you is a great man, sahib.'

'Since when you start reading?'

'I learning all all the time, sahib. I does read only a little tiny little bit. Smatterer fact, it have a hundred and one words I just can't make head or tail outa. Tell you what, sahib. Why you don't

read it out to me? When you read I could just shut my eyes and listen.'

'You does behave funny afterwards. Why you just don't look at the photo, eh?'

'Is a nice photo, sahib.'

'You look at it. I got to go now.'

*

Ganesh and Leela moved to Fuente Grove that afternoon; but just before they left Fourways a letter arrived. It contained the oil royalties for the quarter; and the information that his oil had been exhausted and he was to receive no more royalties.

Ramlogan's dowry seemed providential. It was another remarkable coincidence that gave Ganesh fresh evidence that big things were ahead of him.

'Great things going to happen in Fuente Grove,' Ganesh told Leela. 'Really great things.'

5. Trials

FOR MORE THAN two years Ganesh and Leela lived in Fuente Grove and nothing big or encouraging happened.

Right from the start Fuente Grove looked unpromising. The Great Belcher had said it was a small, out of the way place. That was only half true. Fuente Grove was practically lost. It was so small, so remote, and so wretched, it was marked only on large maps in the office of the Government Surveyor; the Public Works Department treated it with contempt; and no other village even thought of feuding with it. You couldn't really like Fuente Grove. In the dry season the earth baked, cracked, and calcined; and in the rainy season melted into mud. Always it was hot. Trees would have made some difference, but Ganesh's mango tree was the only one.

The villagers went to work in the cane-fields in the dawn darkness to avoid the heat of day. When they returned in the middle of the morning the dew had dried on the grass; and they set to work in their vegetable gardens as if they didn't know that sugar-cane was the only thing that could grow in Fuente Grove. They had few thrills. The population was small and there were not many births, marriages, or deaths to excite them. Two or three times a year the men made a noisy excursion to a cinema in distant, wicked San Fernando. Little happened besides. Once a year, at the 'crop-over' harvest festival, when the sugar-cane had been reaped, Fuente Grove made a brave show of gaiety. The half-dozen bullock

carts in the village were decorated with pink and yellow and green streamers made from crêpe paper; the bullocks themselves, sad-eyed as ever, wore bright ribbons in their horns; and men, women, and children rattled the piquets on the carts and beat on pans, singing about the bounty of God. It was like the gaiety of a starving child.

Every Saturday evening the men gathered in Beharry's shop and drank a lot of bad rum. They became sufficiently enthusiastic about their wives to beat them that night. On Sunday they woke sick, cursing Beharry and his rum, continued sick all day, and rose fresh and strong early Monday morning, ready for the week's work.

It was only this Saturday drinking that kept Beharry's shop going. He himself never drank because he was a good Hindu and because, as he told Ganesh, 'it have nothing like a clear head, man'. Also, his wife didn't approve.

Beharry was the only person in Fuente Grove with whom Ganesh became friendly. He was a little man, scholarly in appearance, with a neat little belly and thin, greying hair. He alone in Fuente Grove read the newspapers. A day-old copy of the *Trinidad Sentinel* came to him every day by cyclist from Princes Town and Beharry read it from end to end, sitting on a high stool in front of his counter. He hated being behind the counter. 'It does make me feel I is in a pen, man.'

The day after he arrived in Fuente Grove Ganesh called on Beharry and found that he knew all about the Institute.

'Is just what Fuente Grove want,' Beharry said. 'You going to write books and thing, eh?'

Ganesh nodded and Beharry shouted, 'Suruj!'

A boy of about five ran into the shop.

'Suruj, go bring the books. They under the pillow.'

'*All* the books, Pa?'

'All.'

The boy brought the books and Beharry passed them one by one to Ganesh: *Napoleon's Book of Fate*, a school edition of *Eothen* which had lost its covers, three issues of the Booker's Drug Stores *Almanac*, the *Gita*, and the *Ramayana*.

'People can't fool me,' Beharry said. 'Tom is a country-bookie but Tom ain't a fool. Suruj!'

The boy ran up again.

'Cigarette and match, Suruj.'

'But they on the counter, Pa.'

'You think I can't see that? Hand them to me.'

The boy obeyed, then ran out of the shop.

'What you think of the books?' Beharry asked, pointing with an unlighted cigarette.

When Beharry spoke he became rather like a mouse. He looked anxious and worked his small mouth nervously up and down as though he were nibbling.

'Nice.'

A big woman with a tired face came into the shop. 'Suruj Poopa, you ain't hear me calling you to eat?'

Beharry nibbled. 'I was just showing the pundit the books I does read.'

'Read!' Her tired face quickened with scorn. 'Read! You want to know how he does read?'

Ganesh didn't know where to look.

'He does close up the shop if I don't keep a eye on him, and he does jump into bed with the books. I ain't know him read one book to the end yet, and still he ain't happy unless he reading four five book at the same time. It have some people it dangerous learning them how to read.'

Beharry replaced the cigarette in the box.

'This world go be a different and better place the day man start making baby,' the woman said, sweeping out of the shop. 'Life hard enough with you one, leave alone your three worthless children.'

There was a short silence after she had gone.

'Suruj Mooma,' Beharry explained.

'They is like that,' Ganesh agreed.

'But she right, you know, man. If everybody did start behaving like me and you it would be a crazy kinda world.'

Beharry nibbled, and winked at Ganesh. 'I telling you, man. This reading is a dangerous thing.'

Suruj ran into the shop again. 'She *calling* you, Pa.' His tone carried his mother's exasperation.

As Ganesh left he heard Beharry saying, '*She*? Is how you does call your mother? Who is *she*? The cat mother?'

Ganesh heard a slap.

He went often to Beharry's shop. He liked Beharry and he liked the shop. Beharry made it bright with coloured advertisements for things he didn't stock; and it was as dry and clean as Ramlogan's shop was greasy and dirty.

'It beat me what you does see in this Beharry,' Leela said. 'He think he could run shop, but he does only make me laugh. I must write and tell Pa about the sort of shop it have in Fuente Grove.'

'It have one thing you must write and tell your father to do. Tell him to go and open a stall in San Fernando market.'

Leela cried. 'You see the sort of thing Beharry putting in your head. The man is *my* father.' And she cried again.

But Ganesh still went to Beharry's.

When Beharry heard that Ganesh was going to set himself up as a masseur he nibbled anxiously and shook his head. 'Man, you choose a hard hard thing. These days nearly everybody you bouncing up is either massager or dentist. One of my own cousin – really Suruj Mooma cousin, but Suruj Mooma family is like my own family – a really nice boy he is, he too starting in this thing.'

'As *another* massager?'

'Wait, you go hear. Last Christmas Suruj Mooma take up the children by their grandmooma and this boy just come up to she

cool cool and say he taking up dentistry. You could imagine how Suruj Mooma was surprise. And the next thing we hear is that he borrow money to buy one of them dentist machine thing and he start pulling out people teeth, just like that. The boy killing people left and right, and still people going. Trinidad people is like that.'

'It ain't people *teeth* I want to pull out. But the boy doing all right, eh?'

'For the time, yes. He done pay back for the machine. But Tunapuna is a busy place, remember. Eh, I see the time coming when quack go find it hard getting two cent to buy a bread and some cheap red butter.'

Suruj Mooma came in hot and dusty from the yard with a *cocoye* broom. 'I was coming with a good good mind to sweep out the shop – eh! – and look at the first thing I hearing. Why for you must call the boy quack? It ain't as if he not trying.' She looked at Ganesh. 'You know what wrong with Suruj Poopa? He just jealous the boy. He can't even cut toenail, and a little boy pulling out big people teeth. Is just jealous he jealous the boy.'

Ganesh said, 'You have something there, *maharajin*. Is like me and my massaging. I ain't just rushing into it like that, you know. I learn and stop and study a lot about it, from my own father. It ain't quack work.'

Beharry, on the defensive, nibbled. 'Wasn't that I did mean at all. I was just telling the pundit here that if he set hisself up as a massager in Fuente Grove he go have it hard.'

*

It didn't take Ganesh long to find out that Beharry was right. There were too many masseurs in Trinidad, and it was useless to advertise. Leela told her friends, The Great Belcher told hers, Beharry promised to write to all the people he knew; but few cared

to bring their ailments to a place as far away as Fuente Grove. The villagers themselves were very healthy.

'Man,' Leela said. 'I don't think you really make for massage.'

And the time came when he himself began to doubt his own powers. He could cure a *nara*, a simple stomach dislocation, as well as any masseur, and he could cure stiff joints. But he could never bring himself to risk bigger operations.

One day a young girl with a twisted arm came to see him. She looked happy enough but her mother was weeping and miserable. 'We try everybody and everything, pundit. Nothing happen. And every day the girl getting older, but who go want to married she?'

She was a pretty girl, too, with lively eyes in an impassive face. She looked only at her mother, not once at Ganesh.

'Twenty time people break over the girl hand, if they break it over one time,' the mother continued. 'But still the hand can't set.'

He knew what his father would have done. He would have made the girl lie down, he would have placed his foot on her elbow, levered the arm upwards till it broke, then set it again. But all Ganesh said, after examining the hand, was, 'It have nothing wrong with the girl, *maharajin*. She only have a little bad blood, that is all. And too besides, God make she that way and is not for me to interfere in God work.'

The girl's mother stopped sobbing and pulled her pink veil over her head. 'Is my fate,' she said, without sadness.

The girl never spoke a word.

Afterwards Leela said, 'Man, you shoulda at least try to fix the hand first, and then you coulda start talking about God work. But you don't care what you doing to me. It look as though you only want to drive away people now.'

Ganesh continued to offend his patients by telling them that nothing was wrong with them; he spoke more and more about God's work; and, if he was pressed, he gave out a mixture he had

made from one of his father's prescriptions, a green fluid made mostly from shining-bush and leaves of the *neem* tree.

He said, 'Facts is facts, Leela. I ain't have a hand for massage.'

*

There was another disappointment in his life. After a year it was clear that Leela couldn't have children. He lost interest in her as a wife and stopped beating her. Leela took it well, but he expected no less of a good Hindu wife. She still looked after the house and in time became an efficient housekeeper. She cared for the garden at the back of the house and minded the cow. She never complained. Soon she was ruler in the house. She could order Ganesh about and he didn't object. She gave him advice and he listened. He began to consult her on nearly everything. In time, though they would never had admitted it, they had grown to love each other. Sometimes, when he thought about it, Ganesh found it strange that the tall hard woman with whom he lived was the saucy girl who had once asked, 'You could write too, sahib?'

*

And always there was Ramlogan to be mollified. The newspaper cutting with his photograph hung, mounted and framed, in his shop, above Leela's notice concerning the provision of chairs for female shop assistants. Already the paper was going brown at the edges. Whenever Ganesh went, for one reason or another to Fourways, Ramlogan was sure to ask, 'How the Institute going, man?'

'Thinking about it all the time,' Ganesh would say. Or, 'Is all in my head, you know. Don't rush me.'

*

Everything seemed to be going wrong and Ganesh feared that he had misread the signs of fate. It was only later that he saw the

providential pattern of these disappointing months. ‘We never are what we want to be,’ he wrote, ‘but what we must be.’

He had failed as a masseur. Leela couldn’t have children. These disappointments, which might have permanently broken another man, turned Ganesh seriously, dedicatedly, to books. He had always intended to read and write, of course, but one wonders whether he would have done so with the same assiduity if he had been a successful masseur or the father of a large family.

‘Going to write a book,’ he told Leela. ‘Big book.’

There is a firm of American publishers called Street and Smith, versatile, energetic people who had pushed their publications as far as South Trinidad. Ganesh was deeply impressed by Street and Smith, had been since he was a boy; and, without saying a word to Beharry or Leela, he sat down one evening at the little table in the drawing room, turned up the oil lamp, and wrote a letter to Street and Smith. He told them that he was thinking of writing books and wondered whether either of them was interested.

The reply came within a month. Street and Smith said they were very interested.

‘You must tell Pa,’ Leela said.

Beharry said, ‘The Americans is nice people. You must write this book for them.’

Ganesh framed the Street and Smith letter in passe-partout and hung it on the wall above the table where he had written his letter.

‘Is only the beginning,’ he told Leela.

Ramlogan came all the way from Fourways and when he gazed on the framed letter his eyes filled with tears. ‘Sahib, this is something else for the papers. Yes, man, sahib, write the books for them.’

‘Is just what Beharry, Fuente Grove so-call shopkeeper, tell him,’ Leela said.

‘Never mind.’ Ramlogan said. ‘I still think he should write the

books. But I bet it make you feel proud, eh, sahib, having the Americans begging you to write a book for them?'

'Nah,' Ganesh said quickly. 'You wrong there. It don't make me feel proud at all at all. You know how it make me feel? It make me feel humble, if I tell the truth. Humble humble.'

'Is the sign of a great man, sahib.'

The actual writing of the book worried Ganesh and he kept putting it off. When Leela asked, 'Man, why you ain't writing the book the American people begging you to write?' Ganesh replied, 'Leela, is talk like that that does break up a man science of thought. You mean you can't see that I thinking, thinking about it all all the time?'

*

He never wrote the book for Street and Smith.

'I didn't *promise* anything,' he said. 'And don't think I waste my time.'

Street and Smith had made him think about the art of writing. Like many Trinidadians Ganesh could write correct English but it embarrassed him to talk anything but dialect except on very formal occasions. So while, with the encouragement of Street and Smith, he perfected his prose to a Victorian weightiness he continued to talk Trinidadian, much against his will.

One day he said, 'Leela, is high time we realize that we living in a British country and I think we shouldn't be shame to talk the people language good.'

Leela was squatting at the kitchen *chulha*, coaxing a fire from dry mango twigs. Her eyes were red and watery from the smoke. 'All right, man.'

'We starting now self, girl.'

'As you say, man.'

'Good. Let me see now. Ah, yes. Leela, have you lighted the fire? No, just gimme a chance. Is "lighted" or "lit", girl?'

'Look, ease me up, man. The smoke going in my eye.'

'You ain't paying attention, girl. You mean the smoke *is* going in your eye.'

Leela coughed in the smoke. 'Look, man. I have a lot more to do than sit scratching, you hear. Go talk to Beharry.'

Beharry was enthusiastic. 'Man, is a master idea, man! Is one of the troubles with Fuente Grove that it have nobody to talk good to. When we starting?'

'Now.'

Beharry nibbled and smiled nervously. 'Nah, man, you got to give me time to think.'

Ganesh insisted.

'All right then,' Beharry said resignedly. 'Let we go.'

'It is hot today.'

'I see what you mean. It is *very* hot today.'

'Look, Beharry. This go do, but it won't pay, you hear. You got to give a man some help, man. All right now, we going off again. You ready? The sky is very blue and I cannot see any clouds in it. Eh, why you laughing now?'

'Ganesh, you know you look damn funny.'

'Well, you look damn funny yourself, come to that.'

'No, what I mean is that it funny seeing you so, and hearing you talk so.'

Rice was boiling on the *chulha* when Ganesh went home. 'Mr Ramsumair,' Leela asked, 'where have you been?'

'Beharry and me was having a little chat. You know, Beharry did look real funny trying to talk good.'

It was Leela's turn to laugh. 'I thought we was starting on this big thing of talking good English.'

'Girl, you just cook my food good, you hear, and talk good English only when I tell you.'

*

This was the time when Ganesh felt he had to respond to every advertiser's request to fill in coupons for free booklets. He came across the coupons in American magazines at Beharry's shop; and it was a great thrill for him to send off about a dozen coupons at once and await the arrival, a month later, of a dozen bulging packets. The Post Office people didn't like it and Ganesh had to bribe them before they sent a postman cycling down with the packets to Fuente Grove in the evenings, when it was cool.

Beharry had to give the postman a drink.

The postman said, 'The two of all you getting one set of big fame in Princes Town. Everywhere I turn it have people asking me, "Who is these two people? They come just like Americans, man." ' He looked down at his emptied glass and rocked it on the counter. 'And guess what I does do when they ask me?'

It was his manner of asking for a second drink.

'What I does do?' He downed his second glass of rum at a gulp, made a wry face, asked for water, got it, wiped his mouth with the back of his hand, and said, 'Man, I does tell them straight off who you is!'

Both Beharry and Ganesh were excited by the booklets and handled them with sensuous reverence. 'That America, boy, is the place to live in,' Beharry said. 'They does think nothing of giving away books like this.'

Ganesh shrugged a knowing shoulder. 'Is nothing at all for them, you know. Before you twist and turn three times – bam! – a book done print.'

'Ganesh, you is a man with a college education. How much book they does print every year in America, you think?'

'About four five hundred so.'

'You crazy, man. Is more about a million. So I read somewhere the other day.'

'Why you ask me then?'

Beharry nibbled. 'Just to make sure.'

Then they had a long discussion whether one man could ever get to know everything about the world.

Beharry annoyed Ganesh one day by showing a folder. He said casually, 'Look what these people in England send me.'

Ganesh frowned.

Beharry sensed trouble. 'Didn't *ask* for it, you know. You mustn't think I setting up in competition with you. They just send it, just like that.'

The folder was too beautiful for Ganesh's annoyance to last.

'I don't suppose they go just send it to *me* like that, though.'

'Take it, man,' Beharry said.

'Yes, take it before I burn it up.' The voice of Suruj Mooma, inside. 'I don't want any more rubbish in my house.'

It was a folder from the Everyman Library.

Ganesh said, 'Nine hundred and thirty book at two shilling a book. Altogether that make – '

'Four hundred and sixty dollars.'

'Is a lot of money.'

Beharry said, 'Is a lot of book.'

'If a man read all those book, it go have nobody at all to touch him in the line of education. Not even the Governor.'

'You know, is something I was talking about to Suruj Mooma about only the other day. I don't think Governor and them is really educated people.'

'How you mean, man?'

'If they was really educated they wouldn't want to leave England where they printing books night and day and come to a place like Trinidad.'

Ganesh said, 'Nine hundred and thirty book. Every book about one inch thick, I suppose.'

'Make about seventy-seven feet.'

'So with shelf on two walls you could find room for all.'

'I prefer big books myself.'

The walls of Ganesh's drawing-room were subject to a good deal of scrutiny that evening.

'Leela, you got a ruler?'

She brought it.

'You thinking of alterations, man?'

'Thinking of buying some book.'

'How much, man?'

'Nine hundred and thirty.'

'Nine hundred!' She began to cry.

'Nine hundred and thirty.'

'You see the sort of idea Beharry putting in your head. You just want to make me a pauper. It ain't enough for you to rob my own father. Why you don't send me straight off to the Poor House?'

So Ganesh didn't buy all the Everyman Library. He bought only three hundred volumes and the Post Office delivered them in a van late one afternoon. It was one of the biggest things that had happened to Fuente Grove, and even Leela was impressed, though reluctantly. Suruj Mooma alone remained indifferent. The books were still being taken into Ganesh's house when she told Beharry loudly, so that everybody could hear, 'Now, you don't start copying anybody and making a fool of yourself, you hear. Leela could go to the Poor House. Not me.'

But Ganesh's reputation, lowered by his incompetence as a masseur, rose in the village; and presently peasants, crumpling their grimy felt hats in their hands, came to ask him to write letters for them to the Governor, or to read letters which the Government, curiously, had sent them.

For Ganesh it was only the beginning. It took him about six months to read what he wanted of the Everyman books; after that he thought of buying more. He made regular trips to San Fernando and bought books, big ones, on philosophy and history.

'You know, Beharry, sometimes I does stop and think. What

those Everyman people did think when they was parcelling up those books for me? You think they did ever guess that it had a man like me in Trinidad?'

'I ain't know about that but, Ganesh, you beginning to get me vex now. You always forgetting nearly all what you read. You can't even end what you was beginning to remember sometimes.'

'What to do, then?'

'Look, I have a copy-book here. I can't sell it because the cover get oily – is that boy Suruj playing the fool with the candles – and I go give you this copy-book. When you reading a book, make notes here of the things you think is important.'

Ganesh had never liked copy-books, since his school days; but the idea of note-books interested him. So he made another trip to San Fernando and explored the stationery department of one of the big stores in the High Street. It was a revelation. He had never before realized that paper could be so beautiful, that there were so many kinds of paper, so many colours, so many glorious smells. He stood still, marvelling and reverent, until he heard a woman's voice.

'Mister.'

He turned to see a fat woman, traces of white powder on her black face, wearing a dress of a most splendidly floriferous design.

'Mister. How you selling the' – she fished out a piece of paper from her purse and read from it – 'Nelson *Introductory* reading-book?'

'Me?' Ganesh said in surprise. 'I ain't a seller here.'

She began to laugh all over the place. 'Kee! Kee! Kyah! I did take you for the clurkist!'

And she went in search of the clerk, laughing and shaking and bending forward to hide her laughter.

Left alone, Garesh began taking surreptitious sniffs at the paper, and, closing his eyes, passed his hands over many papers, the better to savour their texture.

'What you think you feeling?'

It was a boy, wearing a white shirt, a tie, unmistakable badge of authority, and blue serge shorts.

'What you think you feeling? Yam or cassava in the market?'

Ganesh in a panic bought a ream of light blue paper.

Now, with the desire to write on his paper strong within him, he decided to have another look at Basdeo's printing shop. He went to the narrow, sloping street and was surprised to find that the building he knew had been replaced by a new one, all glass and concrete. There was a new sign: ELITE ELECTRIC PRINTERY; and a slogan: *When Better Printing is Printed We Will Print It.* He heard the clatter of machinery and pressed his face against a glass window to look in. A man was sitting at a machine that looked like a huge typewriter. It was Basdeo, long-trousered, moustached, adult. There could be no doubt that he had risen in the world.

'Got to write my book,' Ganesh said aloud. '*Got* to.'

There were diversions, however. Presently he developed a passion for making note-books. When Leela complained he said, 'Just making them now and putting them away. You never know when they go be useful.' And he became a connoisseur of paper-smells. He told Beharry, 'You know, I could just smell a book and tell how old it is.' He always held that the book with the best smell was the Harrap's French and English dictionary, a book he had bought, as he told Beharry, simply for the sake of its smell. But paper-smelling was only part of his new passion; and when he bribed a policeman at Princes Town to steal a stapling-machine from the Court House, his joy was complete.

In the beginning, filling the note-books was frankly a problem. At this time Ganesh was reading four, sometimes five, books a week; and as he read he scored a line, a sentence, or even an entire paragraph, in preparation for his Sunday. This had become for him a day of ritual and perfect joy. He got up early, bathed, did his

puja, ate; then, while it was still cool, he went to Beharry's. He and Beharry read the newspaper and talked, until Suruj Mooma pushed an angry head through the shop door and said, 'Suruj Poopa, your mouth always open. If it ain't eating, is talking. Well, talk done now. Is time to eat.'

Ganesh would take the hint and leave.

The least pleasant part of Sunday was that walk back to his own house. The sun was wicked and the lumps of crude asphalt on the road were soft and hot underfoot. Ganesh played with the idea of covering all Trinidad with a huge canvas canopy to keep out the sun and to collect the water when it rained. This thought occupied him until he got home. Then he ate, bathed again, put on his good Hindu clothes, dhoti, vest, and *koortah*, and attended to his note-books.

He brought out the whole pile from a drawer in the bedroom bureau and copied out the passages he had marked during the week. He had evolved a system of note-taking. It had appeared simple enough in the beginning – white paper for notes on Hinduism, light blue for religion in general, grey for history, and so on – but as time went on the system became hard to maintain and he had allowed it to lapse.

He never used any note-book to the end. In each he began with the best of intentions, writing in a fine, sloping hand, but by the time he had reached the third or fifth page he lost interest in the note-book, the handwriting became a hasty, tired squiggle, and the note-book was abandoned.

Leela complained about the waste. 'You go make we all paupers. Just as Beharry making Suruj Mooma a pauper.'

'Girl, what you know about these things? Is not a shop-sign I copying out here, you know. Is copying right enough, but it have a lot of thinking I doing at the same time.'

'I getting too tired hearing you talking, talking. You say you come here to write your precious books. You say you come here

to massage people. How much people you massage? How much book you write? How much money you make?'

The questions were rhetorical and all Ganesh could say was: 'You see! You getting to be just like your father, talking like a lawyer.'

Then, in the course of a week's reading, he came upon the perfect reply. He made a note of it there and then, and the next time Leela complained he said, 'Look, shut up and listen.'

He hunted about among his books and note-books until he got a pea-green note-book marked *Literature*.

'Just let me sit down, man, before you start reading.'

'And when you listen don't fall asleep. Is one of your nasty habits, you know, Leela.'

'Can't help it man. The moment you start reading to me you does make me feel sleepy. I know some people does feel sleepy the moment they see a bed.'

'They is people with clean mind. But listen, girl. A *man may turn over half a library to make one book*. It ain't me who make that up, you know.'

'How I know you ain't fooling me, just as how you did fool Pa?'

'But why for I go want to fool you, girl?'

'I ain't the stupid little girl you did married, you know.'

And when he brought the book and revealed the quotation on the printed page, Leela fell silent in pure wonder. For however much she complained and however much she reviled him, she never ceased to marvel at this husband of hers who read pages of print, chapters of print, why, whole big books; this husband who, awake in bed at nights, spoke, as though it were nothing, of one day writing a book of his own and having it *printed*!

*

But it was hard for her when she went to her father's, as she did on most of the more important holidays. Ramlogan had long ago come to regard Ganesh as a total loss and a crook besides. And then there was Soomintra to be faced. Soomintra had married a hardware merchant in San Fernando and she was rich. More than that, she looked rich. She was having child after child, and growing plump, matronly, and important. She had a son whom she had called Jawaharlal, after the Indian leader; and her daughter was called Sarojini, after the Indian poetess.

'The third one, the one coming, if he is a boy, I go call him Motilal; if she is a girl I go call she Kamala.'

Admiration for the Nehru family couldn't go much farther.

More and more Soomintra and her children looked out of place in Fourways. Ramlogan himself grew dingier and the shop grew dingier with him. Left alone, he seemed to have lost interest in housekeeping. The oilcloth on the table in the back room was worn, crinkled, and cut about; the flour sack hammock had become brown, the Chinese calendars fly-blown. Soomintra's children wore clothes of increasing cost and fussiness, and they made more noise; but when they were about Ramlogan had time for no one else. He petted them and pampered them, but they soon made it clear that they considered his attempts at pampering elementary. They wanted more than a sugar-coated sweet from one of the jars in the shop. So Ramlogan gave them lollipops. Soomintra got plumper and looked richer, and it was a strain for Leela not to pay too much attention when Soomintra crooked her right arm and jangled her gold bracelets or when, with the licence of wealth, she complained she was tired and needed a holiday.

'The third one come,' Soomintra said at Christmas. 'I wanted to write and tell you, but you know how it hard.'

'Yes, I know how it hard.'

'Was a girl, and I call she Kamala, like I did say. Eh, girl, but

I forgetting. How your husband? I ain't see any of the books he writing. But then, you see, I isn't a big reader.'

'He ain't finish the book yet.'

'Oh.'

'Is a big big book.'

Soomintra jangled her gold bracelets and at the same time coughed, hawked, but didn't spit – another mannerism of wealth, Leela recognized. 'Jawaharlal father start reading the other day too. He always say that if he had the time he would do some writing, but with all the coming and going in the shop he ain't really have the time, poor man. I don't suppose Ganesh so busy, eh?'

'You go be surprise how much people does come for massage. If you hear anybody wanting a massage you must tell them about him. Fuente Grove not so hard to reach, you know.'

'Child, you know I go do anything at all to help you out. But you go be surprise the number of people it have these days who going around calling theyself massagers. Is people like that who taking the work from really good people like Ganesh. But the rest of these little boys who taking up massaging, I feel they is only a pack of good-for-nothing idlers.'

Kamala, in the bedroom, began to cry; and little Jawaharlal, wearing a brand-new sailor suit, came and lisped, 'Ma, Kamala wet sheself.'

'Children!' Soomintra exclaimed, thumping out of the room. 'Leela girl, you ain't know how lucky you is, not having any.'

Ramlogan came in from the shop with Sarojini on his hip. She was partly sucking a lemon lollipop, partly investigating its stickiness with her fingers.

'I been listening,' Ramlogan said. 'Soomintra don't mean anything bad. She just feeling a little rich and she got to show off a little.'

'But he *going* to write the book, Pa. He tell me so heself. He

reading and writing all the time. One day he go show all of all you.'

'Yes, I know he going to write the book.' Sarojini was dragging the lollipop over Leela's uncovered head, and Ramlogan was making unsuccessful efforts to stop her. 'But stop crying. Soomintra coming back.'

'Ah, Leela! Sarojini take a liking to you. First person she take a liking to, just like that. Ah, you mischeevyus little girl, why for you playing with your auntie hair like that?'

Ramlogan surrendered Sarojini.

'Looking prettish girlish,' Soomintra said, 'wif prettish namish. We having a famous family, you know, Leela. This little girl name after a woman who does write nice nice poetry and again it have your husband writing a big big book.'

Ramlogan said, 'No, when you think about it, I think we is a good family. Once we keep cha'acter and sensa values, is all right. Look at me. Supposing people stop liking me and stop coming to my shop. That harm me? That change my – '

'All right, Pa, but take it easy,' Soomintra interrupted. 'You go wake up Kamala again if you walk up and down like that and talk so loud.'

'But still, man, the truth is the truth. It does make a man feel good to have all his family around him, and seeing them happy. I say that every family must have a radical in it, and I proud that we have Ganesh.'

*

'So is that what Soomintra saying, eh?' Ganesh was trying to be calm. 'What else you expect? Money is all she and she father does think about. She don't care about books and things. Is people like that did laugh at Mr Stewart, you know. And they call theyself Hindus! Now, if I was in India, I woulda have people coming from

all over the place, some bringing me food, some bringing me clothes. But in Trinidad – bah!'

'But, man, we got to think about money now. The time coming when we won't have a cent remaining.'

'Look, Leela. Look at this thing in a practical way. You want food? You have a little garden in the back. You want milk? You have a cow. You want shelter? You have a house. What more you want? Chut! You making me talk like your father now.'

'Is all right for you. You ain't have no sisters to face and hear them laughing at you.'

'Leela, is the thing everybody who want to write have to face. Poverty and sickness is what every writer have to suffer.'

'But you ain't writing, man.'

Ganesh didn't reply.

*

He kept on reading. He kept on making notes. He kept on making note-books. And he began to acquire some sensitivity to type-faces. Although he owned nearly every Penguin that had been issued he disliked them as books because they were mostly printed in Times, and he told Beharry that it looked cheap, 'like a paper'. The works of Mr Aldous Huxley he could read only in Fournier; in fact, he had come to regard that type as the exclusive property of Mr Huxley.

'But is just the sort of type I want my book to be in,' he told Beharry one Sunday.

'You think they have that sort of type in Trinidad. All they have here is one sort of mash-up type, ugly as hell.'

'But this boy, this man I was telling you about, Basdeo, he have a new printing machine. It like a big typewriter.'

'Line of type.' Beharry passed his hand over his head and nibbled. 'It does just show you how backward this Trinidad is.

When you look at those American magazines, you don't wish people in Trinidad could print like that?'

Ganesh couldn't say anything because just then Suruj Mooma put her head through the door and gave Ganesh his hint to leave.

He found his food neatly laid out for him in the kitchen, as usual. There was a brass jar of water and a little plate of fresh coconut chutney. When he was finished he lifted up the brass plate to lick it and found a short note below it, written on one of his best sheets of light blue paper.

I, cannot; live: here. and, put; up: with. the, insult; of: my. Family!

6. The First Book

HE DIDN'T FEEL IT at all, at first.

Then he got up on a sudden and kicked the brass jar over, spilling water all over the floor. He watched the jar circling until it stopped on its side.

'Let she go!' he said aloud. 'Lesshego!'

He spent some time walking up and down. 'Going to show she. Not going to write at all. Not going to write a single line.'

He gave the jar another kick and was surprised to see a little more water spill. 'Let she feel sorry and shame. Let she go. Saying she coming here to live with me and then she can't even have a thing like a baby, a small tiny little thing like a baby! Let she shame! Lesshego!'

He went to the drawing-room and began pacing there, among his books. He stopped and gazed at the wall. Instantly he began working out whether he could really have fitted in seventy-seven feet of book-shelves on it. 'Just like she father. No respect for books. Only money, money, money.'

He went back to the kitchen, picked up the jar, and mopped up the floor. Then he bathed, singing devotional songs with a certain fierceness. From time to time he stopped singing and cursed and sometimes he shouted, 'Going to show she. Not going to write a single line.'

He dressed and went to see Beharry.

'The Governor say the truth, man,' Beharry said, when he had

heard. 'The trouble with we Indians is that we educate the boys and leave the girls to fend for theyself. So now it have you more educated than Leela and me more educated than Suruj Mooma. That is the real trouble.'

Suruj Mooma made a sudden irruption into the shop and as soon as she saw Ganesh she began crying, hiding her face in her veil. She tried to embrace him across the counter, failed; and, still crying, ducked under the counter and passed over to where Ganesh was standing. 'Don't tell me,' she sobbed, and flung an arm over his shoulder. 'Don't tell me a single word. I know it already. I myself didn't think she was serious or I woulda try to stop she. But we have to fight things like that. Ganesh, you must be brave. Is what life is.'

She edged Beharry off the shop-stool, sat on it, and cried by herself, wiping her eyes with the corner of her veil. Beharry and Ganesh watched her.

'I would never leave Suruj Poopa,' she said. 'Never. I ain't educated enough.'

Suruj appeared at the door. 'I hear you calling me, Ma?'

'No, son. I ain't calling you, but come.'

Suruj did as he was told and his mother pressed his head against her knees. 'You think I go ever want to leave Suruj and he Poopa?' She gave a short scream. 'Never!'

Suruj said, 'I could go now, Ma?'

'Yes, son, you could go now.'

When Suruj had gone she became a little calmer. 'That is the trouble, giving girls education these days. Leela spend too much of she time reading and writing and not looking after she husband properly. I did talk to she about it, mark you.'

Beharry, rubbing his belly and looking down thoughtfully at the floor, said, 'The way I look at it is this. These young girls not like we, you know, Ganesh. These young girls today think that getting married is some sort of game. Something like rounders.

Running away and running back. Is a lot of fun for them. They want you to go and beg them – '

'You never had to beg me once, Suruj Poopa.' Suruj Mooma burst into fresh tears. 'I never once leave you. Is the sort of woman I is. I go never leave my husband. I ain't educated enough.'

Beharry put his arm around his wife's waist and looked at Ganesh, a little ashamed of having to be so openly affectionate. 'You mustn't mind, man. Not to mind. You ain't educated, is true. But you full of sense.'

Crying and wiping her eyes and crying again, Suruj Mooma said, 'Nobody bother to educate me, you know. They take me out of school when I was in Third Standard. I always come first in my class. You know Purshottam, the barrister in Chaguanas?'

Ganesh shook his head.

'Me and Purshottam was in the Third Standard together. I always come first in my class but still they take me out of school to make me married. I ain't educated, man, but I would never leave you.'

Ganesh said, 'Don't cry, *maharajin*. You is a good woman.'

She cried a bit more; and then stopped abruptly. 'Don't mind, Ganesh. These girls these days does behave as if marrying is something like rounders. They run away but all the time they run away only to come back. But what you going to do now, Ganesh? Who go cook for you and keep your house clean?'

Ganesh gave a brave little laugh. 'Somehow I never get worried by these things. I always believe, and Suruj Poopa could tell you this, that everything happen for the best.'

Beharry, his right hand under his vest now, nodded and nibbled. 'Everything have a reason.'

'Is my philosophy,' Ganesh said, throwing up his arms in an expansive manner. 'I ain't worried.'

'Well,' Suruj Mooma said, 'eat philosophy at your house and come and eat food here.'

Beharry went on with his own thoughts. 'A wife does keep a man back – a man like Ganesh, I mean. Now that Leela gone he could really start writing the book. Eh, Ganesh?'

'Not writing no book. *Not* . . . *going* . . . to . . . write . . . any . . . book.' He began to stride up and down the short shop. 'Not even if she come back and beg me.'

Suruj Mooma looked incredulous. 'You not going to write the book?'

'No.' And he kicked at something on the floor.

Beharry said, 'You ain't serious, Ganesh.'

'I ain't laughing.'

Suruj Mooma said, 'You mustn't mind what he saying. He just want we to beg him a little bit.'

'Look, Ganesh,' Beharry said. 'What you want is a time-table. And look, eh, I ain't begging you. I ain't go have you playing the fool and throwing away your abilities. I making a time-table for you right now and if you don't follow it, it going to have big trouble between the two of we. Think, your own book.'

'With your picture in front and your name in big big letters,' Suruj Mooma added.

'And getting it print on that big typewriter machine you tell me about.'

Ganesh stopped pacing.

Suruj Mooma said, 'Is all right now. He go write the book.'

*

'You know my note-books,' Ganesh said to Beharry. 'Well, I was thinking if it wouldn't be a good idea to start off with that. You know, printing a set of things about religion, from different authors, and explaining what they say.'

'Antheology,' Beharry said, nibbling.

'Right. A antology. What you think?'

'I thinking.' Beharry passed his hand over his head.

'It go learn people a lot,' Ganesh encouraged.

'Is just what I was thinking. It go learn people a lot. But you think people *want* to learn?'

'They *ain't* want to learn?'

'Look, Ganesh. You must always remember the sort of people it have in Trinidad. Every- and anybody not educated up to your standard. Is your job and is my job to bring the people up, but we can't rush them. Start small and later on fling out your antology at them. Is a good idea, mark you. But leave it for now.'

'Something simple and easy first, eh?'

Beharry placed his hands on his thighs. 'Yes. The people here just like children, you know, and you got to teach them like children.'

'A primer like?'

Beharry slapped his thighs and nibbled furiously. 'Yes, man. That self.'

'Leave it to me, Beharry. I go give them this book, and I go make Trinidad hold it head and bawl.'

'That is the way Suruj Mooma and me like to hear you talk.'

*

And he did write the book. He worked hard at it for more than five weeks, sticking to the time-table Beharry had drawn up for him. He rose at five, milked the cow in the semi-darkness, and cleaned out the cow-pen; bathed, did his *puja*, cooked, and ate; took the cow and calf out to a rusty little field; then, at nine, he was ready to work on the book. From time to time during the day he had to take salted water to the cow and calf. He had never had to mind a cow before and it came as a surprise to him that an animal which looked so patient, trusting, and kindly required so much cleaning and attention. Beharry and Suruj Mooma helped with the cow, and Beharry helped with the book at every stage.

He said, 'Beharry, I going to dedicate this book to you.'

And he did that too. He worked on the dedication even before the book was completed. 'Is the hardest part of the whole book,' he said jocularly, but the result pleased even Suruj Mooma: *For Beharry, who asked why.*

'It sound like po'try,' she said.

'It sound like a *real* book,' Beharry said.

Finally the day came when Ganesh took his manuscript to San Fernando. He stood on the pavement outside the Elite Electric Printery and looked in at the machinery. He was a little shy at entering and at the same time anxious to prolong the thrill he felt that soon that magnificent and complicated machine and the grown man who operated it were to be dedicated to the words he had written.

When he went inside he saw a man he didn't know at the machine. Basdeo was at a desk in a wire-cage full of pink and yellow slips on spikes.

Basdeo came out of the cage. 'I remember the face.'

'You did print my wedding invitation long time now.'

'Ah, that is a thing for you. So much wedding invitation I printing and you know I never get one invite. What you have for me today? Magazine? Everybody in Trinidad bringing out magazine these days.'

'Book.'

Ganesh was alarmed at the casual way in which Basdeo, whistling through his teeth, flipped his grubby fingers through the manuscript.

'You does write on nice paper, you know. But is only a booklet you have here, man. Come to that, it more like a pamphlet than a booklet.'

'It don't take much to see that it ain't a big *book*. And it don't take much to know too that we all have to start small. Like you. Remember the old machine you did have. Now, look at all this here.'

Basdeo didn't reply. He went to his cage and came out again with a cinema handbill and a stumpy red pencil. He became serious, the businessman, and, bending over a blackened table, started to write down figures on the back of the handbill, pausing every now and then to blow away invisible dust from the sheet or to brush it with his right little finger. 'Look, how much you know about this thing?'

'Printing?'

Basdeo, still bending over the table, nodded, blew away some more dust, and scratched his head with the pencil.

Ganesh smiled. 'I study it a little bit.'

'What point you want it to be in?'

Ganesh didn't know what to say.

'Eight, ten, eleven, twelve, or what?' Basdeo sounded impatient.

Ganesh was thinking rapidly about the cost. He said firmly, 'Eight go do me.'

Basdeo shook his head and hummed. 'You want any leading?'

He was like a Port of Spain barber boosting a shampoo. Ganesh said, 'No. No leading.'

Basdeo looked dismayed. 'For a book this size and in this print? You sure you don't want leading?'

'Sure, sure. But, look, before we go any farther just show me the type you going to print the book in.'

It was Times. Ganesh groaned.

'Is the best we have.'

'Well, all right,' Ganesh said, without enthusiasm. 'Another thing. I want my picture, in the front.'

'We don't make blocks here, but I could fix that up. Extra twelve dollars.'

'For one little little picture?'

'A dollar a square inch.'

'Is expensive, man.'

'You expect other people to pay for your picture? Well, that settle. Altogether – but wait, how much copies you want?'

'A thousand in the beginning. But I don't want you to break up the type. You never know what could happen.'

Basdeo didn't look impressed. 'Thousand copies,' he mumbled abstractedly, working away at his calculations on the back of the handbill. 'Hundred and twenty-five dollars.' And he flung down his pencil on the table.

So the process began, the thrilling, tedious, discouraging, exhilarating process of making a book. Ganesh worked with Beharry on the proofs, and they both marvelled at the way the words looked so different in print.

'They look so *powerful*,' Beharry said.

Suruj Mooma could never get over it.

At last the book was completed and it was Ganesh's joy to bring home the thousand copies in a taxi. Before he left San Fernando he told Basdeo, 'Remember now, keep the type set up. You never know how fast the book go sell, and I don't want Trinidad bawling for the book when I ain't have any left.'

'Sure,' Basdeo said. 'Sure. They want 'em, you want 'em, I print 'em. Sure thing, man.'

Though Ganesh's joy was great there was one disappointment he couldn't quite stifle. His book looked so small. It had no more than thirty pages, thirty small pages; and it was so thin nothing could be printed on the spine.

'Is this boy Basdeo,' Ganesh explained to Beharry. 'All the big talk he give me about point and leading, and after all that he not only give me that ugly type he call Times, but he had to give me small small type.'

Suruj Mooma said, 'He make the book look like nothing, man.'

'Is the trouble with Indians in Trinidad,' Beharry said.

'All of them not like Suruj Poopa, you know,' Suruj Mooma interrupted. 'Suruj Poopa want to see you get on.'

Beharry went on, 'You know, Ganesh, it wouldn't surprise if somebody did pay this boy Basdeo to do what he do to your book. Now, another printer who didn't jealous you woulda make the book run to sixty pages and he woulda give you thick thick paper too.'

'Anyway, you mustn't mind,' Suruj Mooma said. 'Is *some*thing. Is a damn lot more than most people do in this place.'

Beharry pointed to the frontispiece and nibbled. 'Is a nice picture of you here, you know, Ganesh.'

'He look like a real professor,' Suruj Mooma said. 'So serious, and with his hand under his chin like if he thinking real deep.'

Ganesh took another copy and pointed to the dedication page. 'I think Suruj Poopa name look nice in print too,' he said to Suruj Mooma.

Beharry nibbled in embarrassment. 'Nah. You only making joke, man.'

'I think the whole thing look nice,' Suruj Mooma said.

*

Early one Sunday afternoon Leela was standing at the window of the kitchen at the back of Ramlogan's shop in Fourways. She was washing the midday dishes and was about to throw some dirty water out of the window when she saw a face appear below her. The face was familiar, but the impish smile on it was new.

'Leela!' the face whispered.

'Oh – is *you*. What you doing here?'

'I come back for you, girl.'

'Go away quick march from here, you hear, before I throw this tureen of dirty water all over your face and wash away the grin.'

'Leela, is not only come I come for you; but I have something to tell you, and I want to tell you first.'

'Say it quick. But I must say you was able to keep it to yourself a damn long time. Eh, eh, is nearly three months now you drive

me away from your house and in all that time you never bother to send a message to ask me, "Dog, how you is?" or "Cat, how you is?" So why for you come now, eh?'

'But, Leela, is you who leave me. I couldn't send you a message because I was writing.'

'Go and tell that to Beharry, you hear. Look, I go call Pa in a minute and what he have for you ain't nice, I could tell you.'

The smile on the face became more impish, and the whisper was more conspiratorial. 'Leela, I write a book.'

She trembled on the brink of belief. 'You lying.'

He produced it with a flourish. 'Look at the book. And look here at my name, and look here at my picture, and look here at all these words I write with my own hand. They print now, but you know I just sit down at the table in the front-room and write them on ordinary paper with a ordinary pencil.'

'Oh, man! Oh, man! Oh, man, you really write the book.'

'Careful! Don't touch it with your soapy hand.'

'Look, I go run and tell Pa.' She turned and went inside. Ganesh heard her saying, 'And we must let Soomintra know. She wouldn't like it at all at all.'

Left alone under the window in the shade of the tamarind tree, Ganesh began to hum and take a minute interest in Ramlogan's back yard, though he really saw nothing, neither the copper cask, rusted and empty, nor the barrels of water full of mosquito larvae.

'Sahib!' Ramlogan's voice rasping from within. 'Sahib! Come inside, man, sahib. Why you pretending that you is a stranger and standing up outside? Come in, sahib, come in, sit down in your old place in the hammock. Oh, sahib, is a real honour. I too too proud of you.'

Ganesh sat in the hammock which was now, once again, made from a sugar-sack. The Chinese calendars had disappeared from the walls which looked mildewed and dingy as before.

Ramlogan was passing his fat hairy hands over the cover, and

he smiled until his cheeks almost covered his eyes. 'The book smooth smooth,' he said. 'Look, Leela, feel how smooth it is. And the print on the cover, man. It look as if, sahib, is really part of the paper. Oh, sahib, you make me really proud today. Remember, Leela, was just last Christmas I was telling you and Soomintra that Ganesh was the radical in the family. Is my opinion that every family should have a radical in it.'

'Is just the beginning,' Ganesh said.

'Leela,' Ramlogan said, with mock severity. 'Girl, your husband come all the way from Fuente Grove and you ain't even ask him if he hungry or if he thirsty?'

'I ain't hungry and I ain't thirsty,' Ganesh said.

Leela looked miserable. 'All the rice finish, and the *dal* that remain over not much really.'

'Open a tin of salmon,' Ramlogan ordered. 'And get some bread and butter and peppersauce and some avocado pears.' And he went himself to look after the preparations, saying, 'We have a author in the family, man, girl. Girl, we have a author in the family, man.'

They seated him at the table which was again bare, without its oilcloth and vase and paper roses, and they fed him in enamel dishes. Ramlogan and Leela watched him eat, Ramlogan's gaze shifting from Ganesh's plate to Ganesh's book.

'Have some more salmon, sahib. I ain't a pauper yet that I can't afford to feed the radical in the family.'

'More water, man?' Leela asked.

Chewing and swallowing almost continually, Ganesh found it hard to acknowledge Ramlogan's compliments. All he could do was swallow quickly and nod.

Ramlogan at last turned the green cover of the book.

'I really wish I was a proper reader, sahib,' he said. But in his excitement he betrayed his literacy. 'A Hundred and one Questions and Answers on the Hindu Religion, by Ganesh Ramsumair, B.A.

It sound nice, man. Eh, Leela? Just hear it again.' And he repeated the title, shaking his head and smiling until tears came to his eyes.

Leela said, 'Man, I tell you a long time now that you must stop going around calling yourself a B.A.'

Ganesh chewed hard and swallowed with difficulty. He looked up from his plate and addressed Ramlogan. 'Is something me and Beharry was talking about only the other day. Is a thing I ain't approve of, you know: this modern method of education. Everybody start thinking is the little piece of paper that matter. It ain't that does make a man a B.A. Is how he does learn, how much he want to learn, and why he want to learn, is these things that does make a man a B.A. I really can't see how I isn't a B.A.'

'You is a B.A., man, sahib. I like to see the man who go come and tell me to my face that you ain't a B.A.'

Ramlogan turned a few more pages and read aloud: 'Question Number Forty-Six. Who is the greatest modern Hindu? Leela, just let me hear you answer that one.'

'Let me see now. Is – is Mahatma Gandhi, eh?'

'Right, girl. Fust class. Is the selfsame answer it have in the book. Is really a nice book, man, sahib. Full of nice little things to know.'

Ganesh, swallowing water from a brass jar that practically covered his face, gurgled.

'Let we see now,' Ramlogan continued. 'Listen to this one, Leela. Question Number Forty-Seven. Who is the second greatest modern Hindu?'

'I did know. But I forget now.'

Ramlogan was exultant. 'Is the same thing I was saying. *All* sort of nice things in the book. The answer here is Pandit Jawaharlal Nehru.'

'Was that self I was going to say.'

'Try this one. Question Number Forty-Eight. Who is the third greatest modern Hindu?'

'Leave the book alone now, Pa. I go read it by myself.'

'You is a sensible girl. Is the sort of book, sahib, they should give to children in school and make them learn it off by heart.'

Ganesh swallowed. 'And big people too.'

Ramlogan turned some more pages. Suddenly the smile went off his face.

'Who is this Beharry you give the book to?'

Ganesh saw trouble coming. 'You know him, man. A thin little man break-up like match-stick who does get good hell from his wife. You did meet him that day you come to Fuente Grove.'

'He ain't a educated man, not true? He does keep shop like me, not true?'

Ganesh laughed. 'But he ain't no sort of shopkeeper at all. Is Beharry who start asking me question and give me the idea for the book.'

Ramlogan put *101 Questions and Answers on the Hindu Religion* on the table, rose, and regarded Ganesh with sadness. 'And you mean, sahib, you mean you give that man the book rather than give it to your own father-in-law, the man who help you burn your father and everything? Was the least you could do for me, sahib. Who start you off? Who give you the house in Fuente Grove? Who give you the money for the Institute?'

'The next book go be yours. I done think of the dedication too.'

'Don't worry about dedication and edication. I did just hoping to see my name in your first book, that is all. I was right to hope for that, wasn't I, sahib? People now go look at the book and say, "I wonder who daughter the author married." And the book go tell them?'

'The next book is yours.' Ganesh hurriedly polished his plate with his fingers.

'Just answer me that, sahib. The book go tell them? You dragging my name in the mud, sahib.'

Ganesh went to gargle at the window.

'Who it is who always standing up for you, sahib? When everybody laughing at you, who did protect you? Ah, sahib, you disappoint me. I give you my daughter, I give you my money, and you don't even want to give me your book.'

'Take it easy, Pa,' Leela said.

Ramlogan was crying openly. 'How I go take it easy? Tell me, how I go do that? It isn't as if a *stranger* do me something. No, no, Ganesh, today you really hurt me. You take up a big knife, you sharpen it, you hold it with your two hands and you push it right inside my heart. Leela, go bring the cutlass in the kitchen.

'Pa!' Leela screamed.

'Bring the cutlass, Leela,' Ramlogan sobbed.

'What you doing, Ramlogan?' Ganesh shouted.

Leela, sobbing, brought the cutlass.

Ramlogan took it and looked at it. 'Take this cutlass, Ganesh. Come on, take it. Take it and finish off the job. Cut me up twenty-five times, and every time you chop me think is your own soul you chopping up.'

Leela screamed again, 'Pa, don't cry. Pa, don't talk so. Pa, don't behave so.'

'No, Ganesh, come, chop me up.'

'Pa!'

'Why I musn't cry, eh, girl? How? The man rob me and I ain't say nothing. He send you home and ain't write a line to ask, "Dog, how you is?" or "Cat, how you is?" And I ain't say nothing. Nothing, nothing, nothing! Is all I does get in this world. People go look at the book and say, "Who daughter the author married?" And the book ain't going to tell them.'

Ganesh put away the cutlass under the table. 'Ramlogan! Is only the beginning, Ramlogan. The next book – '

'Don't talk to me. Don't speak to me. Don't say another word

to me. You disappoint me. Take your wife. Take she and go home. Take she, go home, and never come back.'

'All right, if is how you want to behave. Leela, come, let we go. Go and pack your clothes. Ramlogan, I going from your house. Remember is you who drive me away. But still, look here. On the table. I leaving this book for you. I sign it. And the next one – '

'Go,' Ramlogan said. He sat down in the hammock, held his head in his hands, and sobbed silently.

Ganesh waited for Leela in the road. 'Trader!' he muttered. 'Damn low-caste trader!'

When Leela came out with her small Anchor Cigarettes coupons-suitcase, Ganesh said, 'How your father so much like a woman, eh?'

'Man, don't start again so soon.'

*

Beharry and Suruj Mooma called that evening and as soon as Leela and Suruj Mooma saw each other they began crying.

'He write the book,' Suruj Mooma wailed.

'I know, I know,' Leela agreed, with a sharper wail, and Suruj Mooma embraced her.

'Don't mind you educated. You must never leave him. I would never leave Suruj Poopa although I read up to Third Standard.'

'No! No!'

When that was over they went to Beharry's shop and ate. Later, while the women washed up, Beharry and Ganesh discussed how the book could best be distributed.

'Gimme some,' Beharry said. 'I go put them in the shop.'

'But Fuente Grove is a damn small place, man. Nobody does ever come here.'

'If it ain't do good it ain't go do harm.'

'We have to paint some signs and send them to Rio Claro and Princes Town and San Fernando and Port of Spain.'

'Handbills?'

'Nah. Is a book we talking about, not a theatre show.'

Beharry smiled weakly. 'Was just an idea. Really Suruj Mooma idea. But we must have a advertisement in the *Sentinel*. With a coupon to full up and cut out and send.'

'Like the American magazines. Is a good idea, that.'

'Eh, is something that was worrying Suruj Mooma. You ask the printer to keep the print?'

'Yes, man. I know about the business, you know.'

'Suruj Mooma was getting real worried.'

They grew so enthusiastic that Ganesh wondered whether he shouldn't have printed two thousand copies of the book. Beharry said he visualized Trinidad storming Fuente Grove to get copies, and Ganesh agreed that the idea wasn't far-fetched. They were so excited they fixed the price of the book at forty-eight cents, and not thirty-six, as they had planned in the beginning.

'Clear three hundred dollars profit,' Beharry said.

'Don't use that word,' Ganesh said, thinking of Ramlogan.

Beharry brought out a heavy ledger from a shelf under the counter. 'You go want this. Suruj Mooma make me buy it some years now, but I use only the first page. You go want it to show your expenses and your sale.'

*

Soon the *Trinidad Sentinel* carried a three-inch column advertisement for the book, with a coupon to fill in, and the coupon was full of dotted lines, as Ganesh had insisted. The *Sentinel* gave the booklet a three-inch review.

Ganesh and Beharry warned and bribed the Post Office people; and waited to deal with the rush.

After a week only one coupon was filled and sent. But the writer had attached a letter begging for a free copy.

'Throw it away,' Beharry said.

'So Trinidad does behave,' Ganesh said.

Bookshops and even ordinary shops refused to handle the book. Some of them wanted a fifteen-cent commission on every copy and Ganesh couldn't agree to that.

'All they thinking about is money, money,' he told Beharry bitterly.

A few hawkers in San Fernando agreed to display the book and Ganesh made many journeys to see how the sales were going. The news wasn't encouraging, and he walked a good deal about San Fernando with the book in his shirt pocket so that anyone could see the title; and whenever he was on a bus or in a café he took out the book and read it with absorption, shaking his head and stroking his chin when he came across a question and answer with which he was particularly pleased.

It made no difference.

Leela was as distressed as he was. 'Don't mind, man,' she said. 'You must remember that Trinidad just full of people like Soomintra.'

Then The Great Belcher came to Fuente Grove and she brought a long thin boy with her. The boy wore a three-piece suit and hat and stood in the yard in the shade of the mango tree while The Great Belcher explained. 'I hear about the book,' she said warmly, 'and I get Bissoon to come. He have a hand for selling.'

'Only printed matter,' Bissoon said, coming up the steps to the verandah.

Ganesh saw that Bissoon wasn't a boy, but an elderly man; and he saw too that, although Bissoon wore a three-piece suit, a hat, collar and tie, he wore no shoes.

'They does keep me back,' he said.

Bissoon was anxious to make it clear that although he had taken a lot of trouble to come to Fuente Grove, he had not come as a suppliant. When he came into the drawing-room he didn't take off his hat, and from time to time he rose from his chair and spat

through the open window in a clean strong arc. He flung his feet over one arm of the chair and Ganesh watched his toes playing with each other, dropping a fine powder of dust on to the floor.

The Great Belcher and Ganesh looked at Bissoon, full of respect for his selling hand.

Bissoon sucked his teeth loudly. 'Lemmesee the book.' He snapped his fingers. 'The book, man.'

Ganesh said, 'Yes, the book.' And shouted for Leela to bring the book from the bedroom where, for safety, all the copies were kept.

'Bissoon, what *you* doing here?'

For a moment Bissoon's composure broke up as he turned and saw Leela.

'Ah, is you. Leela. Ramlogan daughter. How your father, girl?'

'You do well to ask. Pa got you in mind, I could tell you. All those books you sell him he didn't want to buy.'

Bissoon was calm again. 'Oh, yes. American books. Pretty books. Nice books. Salesmanship. Fastest-selling books I ever handle. Reason I sell them to your father. Last set he get. Lucky man, Ramlogan.'

'I ain't know about that. But you go be an unlucky man if you ever go back to Fourways, I could tell you.'

'Leela,' Ganesh said, 'Bissoon come here to sell my book.'

The Great Belcher belched and Bissoon said, 'Yes, lemmesee the book. When you in the book business time don't wait for you, you know.'

Leela gave him the book, shrugged her shoulders, and left.

'Stupid man, Ramlogan,' Bissoon said.

'More a woman than a man,' The Great Belcher said.

'Materialist,' Ganesh said.

Bissoon sucked his teeth again. 'You got any water in this place. It making hot and I thirsty.'

'Yes, yes. We got water, Bissoon, man,' Ganesh said eagerly, rising, and shouted to Leela to bring the water.

Bissoon shouted, 'And, eh, Ramlogan daughter, don't bring me any mosquitoey water, you hear.'

'No mosquitoes here, man,' Ganesh said. 'Dryest place in Trinidad.'

Leela brought the water and Bissoon put down the book to take the brass jar. Ganesh and The Great Belcher looked at him intently. Bissoon drank the water in the orthodox Hindu way, not letting the jar touch his lips, just pouring the water into his mouth; and Ganesh, sympathetic Hindu though he was, resented the imputation that his jars were dirty. Bissoon drank slowly, and Ganesh watched him drink. Then Bissoon delicately put down the jar on the floor and burped. He pulled out a silk handkerchief from his coat-pocket, wiped his hands and his mouth, and dusted his coat. Then he took up the book again.

'Ques-tion Num-ber One. What is Hin-du-ism? Answer: Hin-du-ism is the re-li-gion of the Hin-dus. Question Number Two. Why am I a Hin-du? Answer: Be-cause my pa-rents and grand-pa-rents were Hin-dus. Ques-tion Num-ber Three – '

'Stop reading it so!' Ganesh cried. 'You breaking up the words and the sentences and you making the whole thing sound like hell.'

Bissoon gave a decisive rub to his toes, got up, dusted his coat and trousers, and started towards the door.

The Great Belcher rose hurriedly, belching, and stopped Bissoon. 'God, is this wind troubling me again. Bissoon, you mustn't go now. Is for a good cause we want you to sell the book.'

She took his arm and he allowed himself to be led back to his chair.

'Is a holy book, man,' Ganesh apologized.

'Sort of kyatechism,' Bissoon said.

'Just what it is.' Ganesh smiled appeasingly.

'Hard book to sell, kyatechisms.'

'Nah!' The Great Belcher blended a belch into the word.

'Look, is experience I have in this business, you know.' Bissoon's feet were draped again over the arm of his chair, and his toes were again playing with each other. 'All my life, ever since I leave the grass-cutting gang, I in the book business. Now I could just look at a book and tell you how hard or how easy it is to sell. I start off as a little boy, you know. Start off with theatre handbills. Had to give them away. I give away more theatre handbills than any other body in Trinidad. Then, I move up to San Fernando, *selling* kyalendars, then – '

'These books is different books,' Ganesh said.

Bissoon picked up the book from the floor and looked through it. 'You right. Handle poetry – it go surprise you how much people in Trinidad does write poetry – and I handle essays and thing, but I never handle a kyatechism before. Still, is experience. Gimme nine cents commission. Remember, if any sort of printed matter could sell in Trinidad, Bissoon is the man to sell it. Gimme thirty of your kyatechisms to start off with. Mark you, I warning you now that I don't think they go sell.'

When Bissoon had left, The Great Belcher said, 'He have a hand. He go sell the books.'

And even Leela was cheerful. 'Is a sign. Is the first sign I ever believe in. Is Bissoon who sell those books to Pa. Is those books that put the idea of authoring in your head. And is Bissoon who selling them for you. Is a sign.'

'Is more than a sign,' Ganesh said. 'Anybody who could sell a book to your father could sell milk to a cow.'

But secretly he too believed it was a good sign.

*

Beharry and Suruj Mooma could not hide their disappointment at the poor reception of the book.

'Don't let them worry you,' Suruj Mooma said. 'Is just jealous

they jealous in Trinidad. I still think is a good book. Already it have some question and answer Suruj know off by heart.'

'It have a lot in what Suruj Mooma say,' Beharry said judiciously. 'But I feel the real trouble is that Trinidad just ain't ready for that sort of book. They ain't educated enough.'

'Hah!' And Ganesh gave a short dry laugh. 'They want a book that *look* big. Once it look big they think it good.'

'Perhaps they want more than a booklet,' Beharry ventured.

'Look,' Ganesh said sharply. 'Is a damn good *book*, you hear.'

Beharry, growing bolder, nibbled energetically. 'I don't think you go really deep enough.'

'You think I should throw out another one at they head?'

'Companion volume,' Beharry said.

Ganesh was silent for a while. '*More Questions and Answers on the Hindu Religion*,' he dreamed aloud.

'*More Questions and Answers*,' Beharry said, '*Companion Volume to 101 Questions and Answers*.'

'You make it sound good, man, Beharry.'

'Well, write it, man. Write it.'

*

Before Ganesh even began thinking constructively about the companion volume Bissoon returned with bad news. He gave it with respect and sympathy. He took off his hat when he came into the house, didn't fling his feet over the arm of the chair, and when he wanted water he said, '*Tonnerre!* But it hot today. You think you could give me just a little sip of water?'

'I is not like some people who does go round boasting that they right,' he said, after he had drunk. 'Nah, I is not that sort of man. I know I did tell you, but I not going to even talk about it now. Wasn't your fault that you didn't know. You ain't have my experience in the business, that is all.'

'You ain't sell none at all?'

'Sell ten, and all the people I sell it to going to behave like your wife father when they get to find out. Had to sell it to them as sort of charm. Pappa, that cost me a lot of work.'

'Ninety cent commission you have to get, then.'

'Don't bother. You keep that for the next one you write. Anything in the way of printed matter, if it can sell, Bissoon is the man to sell it.'

'Can't understand it, Bissoon.'

'Is easy. You a little too early. You see, is the sort of book you go have hell even giving away because people go think you want to work some sign of magic on them. Still, you mustn't give up.'

'Damn funny sort of sign!'

Bissoon looked up bewildered.

*

In spite of everything Ganesh still felt that something might be made of the book. He sent signed copies to the heads of all the Governments he could think of, and when Beharry found that Ganesh was sending them free, he was annoyed.

'I is a independent man,' he said. 'And I don't hold with that sort of curry-favouring. If the King want to read the book, he got to pay for it.'

This didn't stop Ganesh sending a copy to Mahatma Gandhi, and doubtless it was only the outbreak of the war that prevented an acknowledgement.

7. The Mystic Masseur

MANY YEARS AFTER the event, Ganesh wrote in *The Years of Guilt*: 'Everything happens for the best. If, for instance, my first volume had been a success, it is likely that I would have become a mere theologian, writing endless glosses on the Hindu scriptures. As it was, I found my true path.'

In fact, when the war began, his path was none too clear.

'Is a hell of a thing,' he told Beharry. 'I feel I make for something big, yet I can't see what it is.'

'Is just why you going to do something big. I still believe in you, and Suruj Mooma still believes in you.'

They followed the war news with interest and discussed it every Sunday. Beharry got hold of a war map of Europe and stuck red pins on it. He talked a lot about strategy and ta'tics, and this gave Ganesh the idea of publishing monthly surveys of the progress of the war, 'as a sort of history book for later on'. The idea excited him for a little, then lingered and died at the back of his mind.

'I wish Hitler would come over and start bombing up Trinidad,' he exclaimed one Sunday.

Beharry nibbled, eager for argument. 'Why, man?'

'Bomb everything to hell. Then it going to have no more worries about massaging people and writing books and all that sort of nonsense.'

'But you forgetting that we is just a tiny little dot on some maps. If you ask me, I think Hitler ain't even know it have a place

called Trinidad and that it have people like you and me and Suruj Mooma living on it.'

'Nah,' Ganesh insisted. 'It have oil here and the Germans thirsty for oil. If you don't look out, Hitler come here first.'

'Don't let Suruj Mooma hear you. She cousin join the Volunteers. The dentist follow I did tell you about. Dentistry stop paying, so he join up. He tell Suruj Mooma is a nice, easy work.'

'Suruj Mooma cousin have a eye for that sort of thing.'

'But what if the Germans land here tomorrow?'

'The only thing I sure about is that Suruj Mooma cousin go start breaking all sort of world record for running.'

'No, man. If the Germans come, what we going to use for money? What about my shop? And the court-house? Is things like that does worry me.'

So, discussing the implications of the war, they began to discuss war in general. Beharry was full of quotations from the *Gita*, and Ganesh read again, with fuller appreciation, the dialogue between Arjuna and Krishna on the field of battle.

It gave a new direction to his reading. Forgetting the war, he became a great Indologist and bought all the books on Hindu philosophy he could get in San Fernando. He read them, marked them, and on Sunday afternoons made notes. At the same time he developed a taste for practical psychology and read many books on The Art of Getting On. But India was his great love. It became his habit, on examining a new book, to look first at the index to see whether there were any references to India or Hinduism. If the references were complimentary he bought the book. Soon he owned a curious selection.

'Is a lot of book you getting, you know, Ganesh,' Beharry said.

'I was thinking. Suppose you didn't know about me and you was just driving through Fuente Grove in your Lincoln Zephyr. You think you would guess that my house just full up with a hundred and one sort of book?'

'Wouldn't guess,' said Beharry.

Leela's pride in Ganesh's books was balanced by her worry about money. 'Man, all this book-buying go do,' she said, 'but it not going to pay. You got to start thinking of making some money now.'

'Look, girl. I have enough worries and I don't want you to make my head any hotter, you hear.'

*

Then two things happened almost at the same time, and his fortunes were changed for ever.

The Great Belcher, continually on circuit, called one day.

'Is a blow, Ganesh,' she began. 'A big big blow. You can't trust nobody these days.'

Ganesh respected his aunt's sense of the dramatic. '*What* happen now so, then?'

'King George do me a nasty trick.'

Ganesh showed his interest. She paused to belch and call for water. Leela brought it and she drank. 'A nasty nasty trick.'

'*What* she do so?'

She belched again. 'Wait, you go hear.' She rubbed her breasts. 'God, this wind! King George leave me. She pick up a married man near Arouca. Is a blow, Ganesh.'

'Oh God!' Ganesh sympathized. 'You telling me is a blow. But you mustn't worry. You go get somebody else.'

'She was nobody at all when I pick she up. All the clothes she had she had on she back. I buy she clothes. I take she round, show she to people. I get the Bombays to make she nice jewellery from my own gold.'

'Is like what I do for this husband that God give me,' Leela said.

The Great Belcher immediately laid her sorrow aside. 'Yes, Leela? I hearing right? Is how you does always talk about your

husband, girl?' She nodded slowly up and down and put her right palm to her jaw as though she had toothache.

'It *shock* me to hear about King George,' Ganesh said, trying to make peace.

Leela became shrill. 'Eh, eh, I have a husband who lose all sensa values and dragging my name in the mud, and still you don't want me to complain?'

Ganesh stood between the women, but The Great Belcher moved him aside. 'No, gimme a chance, boy. I want to hear this thing out to the end.' She sounded more hurt than annoyed. 'But, Leela, who you is to ask your husband what he doing or what he ain't doing? Oho! This is the thing they call ed-u-ca-tion?'

'What wrong with education? I educated, is true, but I don't see why that should make everybody think they could insult me as they well want.'

Ganesh laughed unhappily. 'Leela is a good girl. She don't mean anything, really.'

The Great Belcher turned on him sharply. 'What she say is the gospel truth, though. Everybody in Trinidad have the idea that you just sitting down here, scratching. Scratching not like hoeing, you know. It don't grow food.'

'I ain't scratching, man. I reading and I writing.'

'Is your story. I did come to let you know about King George, seeing as she did help you out so much at your wedding, but I really want to tell you, boy, that you have me worried. What you going to do about the future?'

Through her sobs Leela said, 'I does keep on telling him that he could become a pundit. He know a lot more than most of the other pundits in Trinidad.'

The Great Belcher belched. 'Is exactly what I come to tell him today. But Ganesh make to be a lot more than a ordinary pundit. If he is a Hindu he must realize by now that he have to use his learning to help out other people.'

'What else you think I doing?' Ganesh asked petulantly. 'I sit down and spend my good good time writing a whole big book. Wasn't for my benefit, you know.'

'Man,' Leela pleaded, 'don't start behaving so. Listen to what she have to tell you.'

The Great Belcher went on unperturbed. 'It have a long time now I studying you, Ganesh. You have the Power all right.'

It was the sort of statement he had grown to expect from The Great Belcher. 'What Power?'

'To cure people. Cure the mind, cure the soul – chut! Man, you making me confuse, and you well know what I mean.'

Ganesh said acidly, 'You want me to start curing people soul when you see me catching good hell to cure their toenail!'

Leela coaxed, 'Man, the least you could do for me is to give it a try.'

'She right, you know, Ganesh. Is the sort of Power you don't even know you have until you start using it.'

'All right, then. I have this great Power. How I go start using it? What I go tell people? "Your soul a little run down today: Here, take this prayer three times a day before meals." '

The Great Belcher clapped her hands. 'Is exactly what I mean.'

'You see, man. I did tell you you only had to listen a little bit.'

The Great Belcher went on, 'Is the sort of thing your uncle, poor man, used to do until he dead.' Leela's face grew sad again at the mention of the dead, but The Great Belcher snubbed her by refusing to cry. 'Ganesh, you have the Power. I could see it in your hands, your eyes, in the shape of your head. Just like your uncle, God bless him. He woulda be a great man today, if only he did live.'

Ganesh was interested now. 'But how and where I go start, man?'

'I go send you all your uncle old books. They have all the prayers and everything in it, and a lot more besides. Isn't really

the prayers that important, but the other things. Oh, Ganeshwa, boy, I too too glad now.' In her relief she began to cry. 'I carrying around these books like a weight on my chest, looking for the proper person to give them to, and you is the man.'

Ganesh smiled. 'How you know that?'

'Why else you think God make you live the sort of life you been living? Why else you think you been spending all these years doing nothing but reading and writing?'

'Yes, is true.' Ganesh said. 'I did always feel I had something big to do.'

Then all three of them cried a little, Leela prepared a meal, they ate, and The Great Belcher took up her sorrow where she had left it. As she made ready to leave she began belching and rubbing her breasts and moaning, 'Is a blow, Ganesh. King George do me a nasty trick. Ohh! Ohh! Ganesh, Ganesh, is a blow.' And wailing, she left.

A fortnight later she brought a parcel wrapped in red cotton spattered with sandalwood paste and handed it over to Ganesh with appropriate ceremony. When Ganesh untied the parcel he saw books of many sizes and many types. All were in manuscript, some in Sanskrit, some in Hindi; some were of paper, some of palm strips. The palm strips bound together looked like folded fans.

Ganesh warned Leela off. 'Don't touch these books, girl, or I don't know what going to happen to you.'

Leela understood and opened her eyes wide.

*

And at about the same time Ganesh discovered the Hollywood Hindus. The Hollywood Hindus are Hindus who live in or near Hollywood. They are holy, cultivated men who issue frequent bulletins about the state of their soul, the complexities and variations of which are endless and always worth description.

Ganesh was a little annoyed. 'You think I could do this sort of thing in Trinidad and get away with it?' he asked Beharry.

'I suppose, if you really know, you only jealous them.'

'Man, I could write a book like that every day if I put my mind to it.'

'Ganesh, you is a big man now. The time come when you must forget other people and think about yourself.'

So he tried to forget the Hollywood Hindus and set about 'preparing himself', as he said. The process, it soon became clear, was going to take time.

Leela began to complain again. 'Man, nobody seeing you go think that it have a war going on and that everywhere people making money. The Americans come to Trinidad now, and they giving away work, with all sort of big pay.'

'Don't approve of war,' Ganesh said.

*

It was during this period of preparation that my mother took me to see Ganesh. I never knew how she got to know about him; but my mother was a sociable woman and I believe that she must have met The Great Belcher at some wedding or funeral. And, as I said at the beginning, if I had been more acute I would have paid more attention to the Hindi phrases Ganesh muttered over me while he thumped my foot about.

Thinking now about that visit I made to Ganesh as a boy, I am struck only by my egotism. It never crossed my mind then that the people I saw casually all around me had their own very important lives; that, for instance, I was as unimportant to Ganesh as he was amusing – and puzzling – to me. Yet when Ganesh published his autobiography, *The Years of Guilt*, I read it half hoping to find some reference to myself. Of course, there was none.

Ganesh devotes quite a third of *The Years of Guilt* to the comparatively short period of his preparation, and it is perhaps

the most rewarding thing in the book. The anonymous critic of *Letras* (Nicaragua) wrote: 'The section contains little of what is popularly conceived of as autobiography. What we get instead is a sort of spiritual thriller, handled with a technique which would not have disgraced the creator of Sherlock Holmes. All the facts are stated, the most important spiritual clues are widely and obviously laid, but the reader keeps guessing the outcome till the last revelation when it is clear that the outcome could only have been what it in fact was.'

Ganesh was undoubtedly inspired by the Hollywood Hindus but what he says owes nothing to them. It was quite a new thing when Ganesh said it, but the path that he followed has been trodden so often since that it has become a rut; and there is little point in going over it here.

*

Presently The Great Belcher came again. She appeared to have recovered from the defection of King George and she told Ganesh almost as soon as she saw him, 'I want to talk to you in private now, to see how well you study your uncle books.'

After the examination she said she was satisfied. 'It just have one thing you must remember all the time. Is something your uncle use to say. If you want to cure people, you must believe them, and they must know that you believe them. But first, people must get to know about you.'

'Loudspeaker van in San Fernando and Princes Town?' Ganesh suggested.

'Nah, they might mistake it for the Borough Council elections. Why you don't get some leaflets print and get Bissoon to give them out for you? He have a lot of experience and he wouldn't go giving them away to any- and everybody.'

Leela said, 'I wouldn't let Bissoon touch a thing in this house. The man is a blight.'

'Is strange,' Ganesh said. 'Last time he was a sign. Today he is a blight. Don't worry with Leela. I go get Basdeo to print some leaflets and Bissoon to give them away.'

Basdeo was a little plumper when Ganesh went to see him about the folders – that was how, on Beharry's advice, he had begun to call the leaflets – and the first thing he said to Ganesh was, 'You still want me to keep the type for your first book?'

Ganesh didn't reply.

'You does give me a strange feeling,' Basdeo said, scratching his neck below the collar. 'Something tell me not to break up the type and I keeping it. Yes, you does give me a strange feeling.'

Still Ganesh didn't speak, and Basdeo became gayer. 'I have some news. You know so much wedding invitation I keep on printing and nobody at all invite me to a wedding. And, mark you, I does beat a damn good drum. So I think I would invite myself to a wedding. So I get married.'

Ganesh congratulated him and then coldly outlined his request for an illustrated folder – the illustration was his photograph – and when Basdeo read the copy, which was all about Ganesh's spiritual qualifications, he shook his head and said, 'Tell me, man, but tell me, how people does get so crazy in a small small place like Trinidad?'

And after all this, Bissoon refused to handle the folders, and made a long speech about it.

'Can't handle that sort of printed matter. I is a seller, not a give-awayer. Look, I go tell you. I start as a little boy in this business, giving away theatre handbills. Then I move up to San Fernando, *selling* kyalendars. Is not that I have anything against you or your wife. But is my reputation I got to be careful about. In the book business you got to be careful about your reputation.'

Leela was more displeased than Ganesh. 'You see what I say? The man blight. Giving we all that amount of big talk. Is the

trouble with Indians in Trinidad. They does get conceited too quickly, you hear.'

The Great Belcher looked on the bright side. 'Bissoon ain't what he used to be. He losing his hand, ever since his wife run away. She run away with Jhagru, the Siparia barber, some five six months, I think. And Jhagru is a married man, with six children! Bissoon shoot off a lot of big talk then about killing Jhagru, but he ain't do nothing. He just start drinking. Too besides, Ganesh, you is a modern educated man and I think you should do things in a modern way. Put a advertisement in the papers, man.'

'Coupon to full up?' Ganesh asked.

'If you want, but you *must* put a picture of yourself. Same picture you put in your book.'

'Is just like I say in the beginning,' Leela said. 'Advertisement in the papers is the best thing. You wouldn't waste any of the folders if you do that.'

Beharry and Ganesh worked on the copy and they produced that challenging advertisement which was to be so famous later on: WHO IS THIS GANESH? The 'this' was Beharry's idea.

There was one other thing. Ganesh was not happy to be called simply a pundit. He felt he was more than that and he felt that he was entitled to a weightier word. So, remembering the Hollywood Hindus, he nailed a signboard on the mango tree: GANESH, *Mystic*.

'Is nice,' Beharry said, looking at it closely and nibbling, while he rubbed his belly under his vest. 'Is very nice, but you think people go believe you is a mystic?'

'But the advertisement in the papers – '

'That was two weeks back. People forget that long time. If you want people to believe you, you must start a advertising campaign. Yes, advertising campaign.'

'So they won't believe, eh? All right, let we see how much they won't believe.'

He built a small shed in his front yard, thatched it with *carat*

palm which he had to get all the way from Debe, and put up some stands in it. On these stands he displayed about three hundred of his books, including the *Questions and Answers*. Leela put out the books in the mornings and brought them in at night.

'Won't believe!' Ganesh said.

Then he waited for clients, as he called them.

Suruj Mooma told Leela, 'I feel sorry for you, Leela, girl. Ganesh gone mad this time.'

'Well, is his books, and I don't see why he shouldn't let people see them. Other people does drive about in their big car to show it off.'

'I so glad Suruj Poopa is not a big reader. I so glad nobody bother to educate me after Third Standard.'

Beharry shook his head. 'Yes, man. This education and reading is a dangerous thing. Is one of the very first things I tell Ganesh.'

Ganesh waited for a month. No clients came.

'Is another twenty dollars you throw away on that advertisement,' Leela moaned. 'And that sign and those books. You make me the laughing-stock in Fuente Grove.'

'Well, girl, is only the country district here, and if plenty people ain't see, plenty people ain't here to laugh. Personally, I feel we want another advertisement in the papers. Proper advertising campaign.'

Leela began to sob. 'No, man. Why you don't give up and take a work? Look at Suruj Mooma cousin, look at Sookram. The boy give up dentistry and Sookram give up massaging and take a work like a brave man. Suruj Mooma tell me that Sookram getting more than thirty dollars a week from the Americans. Man, for my sake, why you don't make up a brave mind and take a work?'

'You looking at this thing from the wrong point of view. Your science of thought tell you that the war going to last for ever? And what go happen to Sookram and the other massagers when the Americans leave Trinidad?'

Leela still sobbed.

Ganesh forced a smile and became coaxing. 'Look, Leela girl, we go put another advertisement in the papers, and we go have my picture and we go have your picture. Side by side. Husband and wife. Who is this Ganesh? *Who* is this Leela?'

She stopped crying and her face brightened for a moment, but then she began to cry in earnest.

'God, woman! If man did listen to woman all the time, nothing at all woulda happen in this world. Beharry was right. A woman does keep a man back. All right, all right, leave me and run back to your father. Think I care?'

And he stuck his hands in his pockets and went to see Beharry.

'No luck?' Beharry queried, nibbling.

'Why you have this thing about asking damn fool questions, eh? But don't think I worried. What is for me I will get.'

Beharry put his hand under his vest. It was a warning, as Ganesh knew now, that Beharry was going to give advice. 'I think you make a big big mistake in not writing the companion volume. That's where you go wrong.'

'Look, Beharry. It have a damn long time now you judging me like some blasted magistrate, and telling me where I go wrong. I read a lot of psychology book about people like you, you know. And what those book have to say about you ain't nice, I can tell you.'

'Is only for you I worried.' Beharry pulled away his hand from his vest.

Suruj Mooma came into the shop. 'Ah, Ganesh. How?'

'How "how"?' Ganesh snapped. 'You can't see?

Beharry said, 'Is a suggestion I have to make to you.'

'All right, I listening. But I ain't responsible for what I do when I finish listening.'

'Is really Suruj Mooma idea.'

'Oh.'

'Yes, Ganesh. Me and Suruj Poopa been thinking a lot about you. We thinking that you must stop wearing trousers and a shirt.'

'It don't suit a mystic,' Beharry said.

'You must wear proper dhoti and *koortah*. I was talking only last night to Leela about it when she come here to buy cooking-oil. She think is a good idea too.'

Ganesh's annoyance began to melt. 'Yes, is a idea. You feel it go bring me luck?'

'Is what Suruj Mooma say.'

Next morning Ganesh involved his legs in a dhoti and called Leela to help him tie the turban.

'Is a nice one,' she said.

'One of my father old ones. Make me feel funny wearing it.'

'Something telling me it go bring you luck.'

'You really think so?' Ganesh cried, and almost kissed her.

She pulled away. 'Look what you doing, man.'

Then Ganesh, a strange and striking figure in white, went to the shop.

'You look like a real *maharaj*,' Suruj Mooma said.

'Yes, he look nice,' said Beharry. 'It make me wonder why more Indians don't keep on wearing their own dress.'

Suruj Mooma warned, 'You better not start, you hear. Your legs thin enough already and they look funny even in trousers.'

'It look good, eh?' Ganesh smiled.

Beharry said, 'Nobody would believe now that you did go to the Christian college in Port of Spain. Man, you look like a pukka brahmin.'

'Well, I have a feeling. I feel my luck change as from today.'

A child began crying inside. 'My luck don't change,' Suruj Mooma said. 'If it ain't Suruj Poopa, is the children. Look at my hands, Ganesh. You see how smooth they is. They can't even leave finger-prints now.'

Suruj came into the shop. 'The baby *crying*, Ma.'

Suruj Mooma left and Beharry and Ganesh began a discussion about dress through the ages. Beharry was putting forward a daring view that dress wasn't necessary at all in a hot place like Trinidad when he broke off suddenly and said, 'Listen.'

Above the rustle of the wind through the sugar-cane came the rattle of a motor car bumping along the lumpy road.

Ganesh was excited. 'Is somebody coming to see me.' Then he became very calm.

A light green 1937 Chevrolet stopped in front of the shop. There was a woman at the back and she was trying to shout above the beat of the engine.

Ganesh said, 'Go and talk to she, Beharry.'

The engine was turned off before Beharry could get down the shop steps. The woman said, 'Who is this Ganesh?'

'This is this Ganesh,' Beharry said.

And Ganesh stood, dignified and unsmiling, in the centre of the shop doorway.

The woman looked at him carefully. 'I driving all from Port of Spain to see you.'

Ganesh walked slowly towards the car. 'Good morning,' he said, but in his determination to be correct he was a little too curt and the woman was discomfited.

'Good morning.' She had to fumble for the words.

Speaking slowly, because he wanted to speak properly, Ganesh said, 'I do not live here and I cannot talk to you here. I live down the road.'

'Hop in the car,' the taxi-driver said.

'I prefer to walk.'

It was a strain for him to talk correctly and the woman noted, with obvious satisfaction, that he was moving his lips silently before every sentence, as though he were mumbling a prayer.

Her satisfaction turned to respect when the car stopped outside

Ganesh's house and she saw the GANESH, *Mystic* sign on the mango tree and the book-display in the shed.

'Is books you selling on the side, or what?' the taxi-driver asked.

The woman looked sideways at him and nodded towards the sign. She began to say something when the taxi-driver, for no apparent reason, blew his horn and drowned her words.

Leela came running out, but with a glance Ganesh told her to keep out of the way. To the woman he said, 'Come into the study.'

The word had the desired effect.

'But take off your shoes here in the verandah first.'

Respect turned to awe. And when the woman brushed through the Nottingham lace curtains into the study and saw all the books, she looked abject.

'My only vice,' Ganesh said.

The woman just stared.

'I don't smoke. I don't drink.'

She sat awkwardly on a blanket on the floor. 'Is a matter of life and death, mister, so whatever I say you mustn't laugh.'

Ganesh looked straight at her. 'I never laugh. I listen.'

'Is about my son. A cloud following him.'

Ganesh didn't laugh. 'What sort of cloud?'

'A black cloud. And every day is getting nearer. The cloud even talking to the boy now. The day the cloud reach him the boy go dead. I try everything. The real doctors and them want to put the boy in the mad-house in St Ann's, but you know that once they put anybody there they does get mad for true. So what I do? I take him to the priest. The priest say the boy possess, and paying for his sins. It have a long time now I see your advertisement, but I didn't know what you could do.'

As she spoke Ganesh scribbled in one of his note-books. He had written, *Black boy under a black cloud*; and he had drawn a

great black cloud. 'You mustn't worry. Lots of people see clouds. How long your son has been seeing the cloud?'

'Well, to tell you the truth, the whole bacchanal begin not long after his brother dead.'

Ganesh added to the black cloud in his note-book and said, 'Hmmh!' Then he chanted a short Hindi hymn, snapped his note-book shut, and threw his pencil down. 'Bring the boy tomorrow. And don't worry about priests. Tell me, *you* see the cloud?'

The woman looked distressed. 'No. That is the thing. None of we ain't see the cloud, apart from the boy.'

'Well, don't worry. Things would be bad if you really did see the cloud.'

He led her to the taxi. The taxi-driver was sleeping with the *Trinidad Sentinel* over his face. He was awakened, and Ganesh watched the car drive away.

'I did feel this coming, man,' Leela said. 'I did tell you that your luck change.'

'We don't know what going to happen yet, girl. Give me a chance to think this thing out.'

He remained a long time in the study consulting his uncle's books. His ideas were slowly beginning to form, when Beharry came in a temper.

'Ganesh, how you so ungrateful?'

'What happening now?'

Beharry looked helpless in his anger. He nibbled so furiously that for a while he couldn't speak. When he could, he stammered. 'Don't tell me you don't know. Why you couldn't walk up to the shop to tell me what happen, eh? For a hundred and one weeks you coming up all the time, but today you prefer to make me leave my shop, leave only little Suruj in charge, and come to see you.'

'But I was going to come later, man.'

'Tell me, what go happen if somebody come to the shop and beat up little Suruj and Suruj Mooma and thief everything?'

'Was going to come, Beharry. Only thing I was doing a little thinking first.'

'No, you wasn't. You just getting conceited now, that is all. Is the trouble with Indians all over the world.'

'But this new thing I handling is something really big.'

'You sure you could handle it? But look, you see how stupid I is, still letting myself be interested in your affairs! You could handle it?'

'God will give me a little help.'

'All right, all right. Give me all this flashy talk. But don't come round begging me for anything, you hear.'

And Beharry left.

Ganesh read and thought deeply all that day and most of the night.

'I don't know why for you wasting all this time on one little black boy,' Leela said. 'Anybody would think you was a schoolchild doing homework.'

*

When Ganesh saw the boy next morning he felt he had never seen anyone so tormented. It was torment heightened by a deep sense of helplessness. Though the boy was thin now and his arms looked bony and brittle, it was clear that he had once been strong and healthy. His eyes were dead, lack-lustre. In them you could see not the passing shock of momentary fear, but fear as a permanent state, fear so strong that it had ceased to thrill.

The first thing Ganesh said to the boy was, 'Look, son, you mustn't worry. I want you to know that I can help you. You believe I can help you?'

The boy didn't move but it seemed to Ganesh that he had recoiled a little. 'How I know that you not laughing at me, just as everybody else laughing at the back of their mind?'

'You see me laughing? I believe in you, but you must believe in me too.'

The boy looked down at Ganesh's feet. 'Something tell me you is a good man and I believe in you.'

Ganesh asked the boy's mother to leave the room and when she left he asked, 'You see the cloud now?'

The boy looked Ganesh in the face for the first time. 'Yes.' The voice was part whisper, part scream. 'It here now and the hands it reaching out getting longer and longer.'

'Oh, God!' Ganesh gave a sudden shriek. 'I see it now too. Oh, God!'

'You see it? You see it?' The boy put his arms around Ganesh. 'You see how it chasing me? You see the hands it have? You hear what it saying?'

'You and me is one,' Ganesh said, still a little breathlessly, breaking into pure dialect. 'God! Hear my heart beating. Only you and me see it because you and me is one. But, listen to something I going to tell you. You fraid the cloud, but the cloud fraid me. Man, I been beating clouds like he for years and years. And so long as you with me, it not going to harm you.'

The boy's eyes filled with tears and he tightened his embrace on Ganesh. 'I *know* you is a good man.'

'It just can't touch you with me around. I have powers over these things, you know. Look around at all these books in this room, and look at all those writings on the wall and all the pictures and everything. These things help me get the power I have and cloud fraid these things. So don't frighten. And now tell me how it happen.'

'Tomorrow is the day.'

'What day?'

'It coming to get me tomorrow.'

'Don't talk stupidness. It coming tomorrow all right, but how it could take you away if you with me?'

'It saying so for a year.'

'What, you seeing it for a whole year?'

'And it getting bigger all the time.'

'Now, look, man. We must stop talking about it as though we fraid it. These things know when you fraid them, you know, and then they does behave like real bad Johns. How you getting on at school?'

'I stop.'

'What about your brothers and sisters?'

'I ain't have no sisters.'

'And your brothers?'

The boy broke into a loud cry. 'My brother dead. Last year. I didn't want him to dead. I never want Adolphus to dead.'

'Eh, eh, but who saying you want him to dead?'

'Everybody. But it ain't true.'

'He dead last year?'

Tomorrow go make one year exact.'

'Tell me how he dead.'

'A truck knock him down. Ram him against a wall, break him up and mash him up. But he was trying to get away even then. He try to pull hisself away and all he could do was take his foot out of the shoe, the left foot. He didn't want to dead either. And the ice only melting in the hot sun and running down on the pavement next to the blood.'

'You see this?'

'I didn't see it happen. But it was really me that shoulda go to buy the ice, not he. Ma ask me to go and buy some ice for the grapefruit juice and I ask my brother to go instead and he go and this thing happen to him. The priest and everybody else say was my fault and I have to pay for my sins.'

'What sort of damn fool tell you that? Well, anyway, you mustn't talk about it now. Remember, you wasn't responsible. Wasn't your fault. Is clear as anything to me that you didn't want

your brother to dead. As for this cloud, we go fix him tomorrow self, when he get so close to you I could reach him and settle him.'

'You know, Mr Ganesh, I think he getting fraid of you now.'

'Tomorrow we go make him run, you watch and see. You want to sleep here tonight?'

The boy smiled and looked a little perplexed.

'All right. Go home. Tomorrow we go settle this Mister Cloud. What time you say he was coming to get you?'

'I didn't tell you. Two o'clock.'

'By five past two you go be the happiest boy in the world, believe me.'

On the verandah the boy's mother and the taxi-driver sat silently, the taxi-driver on the floor with his feet on the step.

'The boy go be all right,' Ganesh said.

The taxi-driver rose, dusting the seat of his trousers, and spat into the yard, just missing the display of Ganesh's books. The boy's mother also rose and put her arm around her son's shoulders. She looked without expression at Ganesh.

After they had gone away Leela said, 'Man, I hope you could help the lady out. I feel too sorry for she. She just sit down quiet all the time, not saying anything, she face small with sadness.'

'Girl, this is the most important case anybody ever handle in the world. I know that that boy going to dead tomorrow unless I do something for him. It give you a funny feeling, you know. Is like watching a theatre show and then finding out afterwards that they was really killing people on the stage.'

'I was thinking, man. I didn't like the taxi-driver. He come here, he see all the books, he never mention them once. He ask for water and for this and that and he ain't even say, "Thank you." And he making a pile of money bringing these poor people here every day.'

'Girl, but why you have to be like your father for? Why you

have to try to take my mind off what I doing? You want me to start driving taxi now?'

'I was just thinking.'

When he had washed his hands after eating, Ganesh said, 'Leela, take out my clothes – the English clothes.'

'Where you going?'

'It have a man I want to see in the Oilfields.'

'What for, man?'

'*Tonerre!* But you full of questions today. You and Beharry is one.'

She asked no more questions and did as she was told. Ganesh changed from dhoti and *koortah* to trousers and shirt. Before he left he said, 'You know, sometimes I glad I get a college education.'

He came back radiant later in the afternoon and immediately began clearing out the bedroom. He paid no attention to Leela's objections. He placed the bed in the drawing-room, the study; and took the table from the study into the bedroom. He turned the table over on its top and arranged a three-sided screen round the legs. He made Leela hang a heavy curtain over the window, and he went over the wooden walls systematically, blocking up every chink and cranny that let in light. He rearranged the pictures and quotations, giving the goddess Lakshmi pride of place just above the screened and upturned table. Below the goddess he placed a candle-bracket.

'It look frightening,' Leela said.

He walked about the darkened room, rubbing his hands, and humming a song from a Hindi film. 'It don't matter if we have to sleep in the study.'

Then they agreed on arrangements for the next day.

All that night camphor and incense burned in the bedroom and in the morning Ganesh, rising early, went to see how the room smelled.

Leela was still asleep. He shook her by the shoulder. 'It look

all right and it smell all right, girl. Get up and milk the cow. I hear the calf bawling.'

He bathed while Leela milked the cow and cleaned out the cow-pen; did his *puja* while Leela made tea and *roti*; and when Leela started to clean the house, he went for a walk. The sun was not yet hot, the leaves of razor-grass still looked frosted with the dew, and the two or three dusty hibiscus shrubs in the village carried fresh pink flowers that were to quail before midday. 'This is the big day,' Ganesh said aloud, and prayed again for success.

Shortly after twelve the boy, his mother and father arrived, in the same taxi as before. Ganesh, dressed once more in his Hindu garments, welcomed them in Hindi, and Leela interpreted, as arranged. They took off their shoes in the verandah and Ganesh led them all to the darkened bedroom, aromatic with camphor and incense, and lit only by the candle below the picture of Lakshmi on her lotus. Other pictures were barely visible in the semi-darkness: a stabbed and bleeding heart, a putative likeness of Christ, two or three crosses, and other designs of dubious significance.

Ganesh seated his clients before the screened table, then he himself sat down out of view behind the screen. Leela, her long black hair undone, sat in front of the table and faced the boy and his parents. In the dark room it was hard to see more than the white shirts of the boy and his father.

Ganesh began to chant in Hindi.

Leela asked the boy, 'He ask whether you believe in him.'

The boy nodded, without conviction.

Leela said to Ganesh in English, 'I don't think he really believe in you.' And she said it in Hindi afterwards.

Ganesh spoke in Hindi again.

Leela said to the boy, 'He say you must believe.'

Ganesh chanted.

'He say you must believe, if only for two minutes, because if you don't believe in him completely, he will dead too.'

The boy screamed in the darkness. The candle burned steadily. 'I believe in him, I believe in him.'

Ganesh was still chanting.

'I believe in him. I don't want him to dead too.'

'He say he go be strong enough to kill the cloud only if you believe in him. He want all the strength you could give him.'

The boy hung his head. 'I don't doubt him.'

Leela said, 'He change the cloud. It not following you now. It chasing him. If you don't believe, the cloud will kill him and then it will kill you and then me and then your mother and then your father.'

The boy's mother shouted, 'Hector go believe! Hector go believe!'

Leela said, 'You must believe, you must believe.'

Ganesh suddenly stopped chanting and the room was shocked by the silence. He rose from behind his screen and, chanting once more, went and passed his hands in curious ways over Hector's face, head, and chest.

Leela still said, 'You must believe. You beginning to believe. You giving him your strength now. He getting your strength. You beginning to believe, he getting your strength, and the cloud getting frighten. The cloud still coming, but it getting frighten. As it coming it getting frighten.'

Ganesh went back behind the screen.

Leela said, 'The cloud coming.'

Hector said, 'I believe in him now.'

'It coming closer. He drawing it now. It not in the room yet, but it coming. It can't resist him.'

Ganesh's chants were becoming more frenzied.

Leela said, 'The fight beginning between them. It starting now. Oh, God! He get the cloud. It not after you. It after him. God! The cloud dying,' Leela screamed, and as she screamed there

seemed to be a muffled explosion, and Hector said, 'Oh God, I see it leaving me. I can feel it leaving me.'

The mother said, 'Look at the ceiling. At the ceiling. I see the cloud. Oh, Hector, Hector. It ain't a cloud at all. Is the devil.'

Hector's father said, 'And I see forty little devils with him.'

'Oh God,' Hector said. 'See how they kill the cloud. Look how it breaking up, Ma. You see it now?'

'Yes, son. I see it. It getting finer and finer. It dead.'

'You see it, Pa.'

'Yes, Hector, I see it.'

And mother and son began to cry their relief, while Ganesh still chanted, and Leela collapsed on the floor.

Hector was crying, 'Ma, it gone now. It really gone.'

Ganesh stopped chanting. He got up and led them to the room outside. The air was fresher and the light seemed dazzling. It was like stepping into a new world.

'Mr Ganesh,' Hector's father said. 'I don't know what we could do to thank you.'

'Do just what you want. If you want to reward me, I don't mind, because I have to make a living. But I don't want you to strain yourself.'

Hector's mother said, 'But you save a whole life.'

'It is my duty. If you want to send me anything, send it. But don't go around telling all sorts of people about me. You can't take on too much of this sort of work. A case like this does tire me out for a whole week sometimes.'

'I know how it is,' she said. 'But don't worry. We go send you a hundred dollars as soon as we get home. Is what you deserve.'

Ganesh hurried them away.

When he came back to the little room the window was open and Leela was taking down the curtains.

'You ain't know what you doing, girl,' he shouted. 'You losing the smell. Stop it, man. Is only the beginning. In no time at all,

mark my words, this place go be full of people from all over Trinidad.'

'Man, I take back all the bad things I say and think about you. Today you make me feel really nice. Soomintra could keep she shopkeeper and she money. But, man, don't again ask me to let down my hair and go through all that rigmarole again.'

'We not going to do that again. I only wanted to make sure this time. It make them feel good, you know, hearing me talk a language they can't understand. But it not really necessary.'

'Manwa, I did see the cloud too, you know.'

'The mother see one devil, the father forty little devil, the boy see one cloud, and you see one cloud. Girl, whatever Suruj Mooma say about education, it have it uses sometimes.'

'Oh, man, don't tell me you use a trick on them.'

Ganesh didn't say.

*

There was no report of this incident in the newspapers, yet within two weeks all Trinidad knew about Ganesh and his Powers. The news went about on the local grapevine, the Niggergram, an efficient, almost clairvoyant, news service. As the Niggergram noised the news abroad, the number of Ganesh's successes were magnified, and his Powers became Olympian.

The Great Belcher came from Icacos, where she had been mourning at a funeral, and wept on Ganesh's shoulder.

'At long last you find your hand,' she said.

Leela wrote to Ramlogan and Soomintra.

Beharry came to Ganesh's house to offer his congratulations and make up his quarrel. He conceded that it was no longer fitting that Ganesh should go to the shop to talk.

'From the first Suruj Mooma believe that you had some sort of Powers.'

'So I did feel too. But ain't it strange though that for so long I did feel I had a hand for massaging people?'

'But you was dead right, man.'

'How you mean?'

Beharry nibbled. 'You is the mystic massager.'

8. More Trouble with Ramlogan

WITHIN A MONTH Ganesh was getting as many clients as he could handle.

He had never imagined there were so many people in Trinidad with spiritual problems. But what surprised him even more was the extent of his own powers. No one could lay evil spirits better, even in Trinidad, where there were so many that people had acquired especial skill in dealing with them. No one could tie a house better, bind it, that is, in spiritual bonds proof against the most resolute spirit. If he ran up against a particularly tough spirit there were always the books his aunt had given him. So, balls-of-fire, *soncouyants*, *loups-garoux*, all became as nothing.

In this way he made most of his money. But what he really liked was a problem which called for all his intellectual and spiritual strength. Like the Woman Who Couldn't Eat. This woman felt her food turn to needles in her mouth; and her mouth actually bled. He cured her. And there was Lover Boy. Lover Boy was a Trinidad character. Racehorses and racing-pigeons were named after him. But it was an embarrassment to his friends and relations that a successful racing-cyclist should fall in love with his cycle and make love to it openly in a curious way. He cured him too.

So, Ganesh's prestige had risen until people who came to him sick went away well. Sometimes even he didn't know why.

His prestige was secured by his learning. Without this he might easily have been lumped with the other thaumaturges who swarmed

over Trinidad. They were nearly all fakes. They knew an ineffectual charm or two but had neither the intelligence nor sympathy for anything else. Their method of tackling spirits remained primitive. A sudden kick in the back of a person possessed was supposed to take the spirit by surprise and drive it out. It was because of these ignorant people that the profession had a bad name. Ganesh elevated the profession by putting the charlatans out of business. Every *obeah*-man was quick enough to call himself a mystic, but the people of Trinidad knew that Ganesh was the only true mystic in the island.

You never felt that he was a fake and you couldn't deny his literacy or learning – not with all those books. And he hadn't only book-learning. He could talk on almost any subject. For instance, he had views about Hitler and knew how the war could be ended in two weeks. 'One way,' he used to say. 'Only one. And in fourteen days, even thirteen – bam! – no more war.' But he kept the way a secret. And he could discuss religion sensibly as well. He was no bigot. He took as much interest in Christianity and Islam as in Hinduism. In the shrine, the old bedroom, he had pictures of Mary and Jesus next to Krishna and Vishnu; a crescent and star represented iconoclastic Islam. 'All the same God,' he said. Christians liked him, Muslims liked him, and Hindus, willing as ever to risk prayers to new gods, didn't object.

But more than his powers, learning, or tolerance, people liked his charity. He had no fixed fee and accepted whatever was given him. When someone complained that he was poor and at the same time persecuted by an evil spirit, Ganesh took care of the spirit and waived the fee. People began to say, 'He not like the others. They only hot after your money. But Ganesh, he is a good man.'

He was a good listener. People poured out their souls to him and he didn't make them feel uncomfortable. His speech became flexible. With simple folk he spoke dialect. With people who looked pompous or sceptical or said, 'Is the first time in my life I come

to anybody like you,' he spoke as correctly as possible, and his deliberate delivery gave weight to what he said and won confidence.

So clients came to Fuente Grove from every corner of Trinidad. Soon he had to pull down the book-shed and put up a canvas-roofed bamboo tent to shelter them. They brought their sadnesses to Fuente Grove, but they made the place look gay. Despite the sorrow in their faces and attitudes they wore clothes as bright as any wedding crowd: veils, bodices, skirts all strident pink, yellow, blue, or green.

The Niggergram had it that even the Governor's wife had consulted Ganesh. When he was asked about this he grew stern and changed the subject.

*

On Saturdays and Sundays he rested. On Saturday he went to San Fernando and bought about twenty dollars' worth of books, almost six inches; and on Sunday, from habit, he took down Saturday's new books and underlined passages at random, although he no longer had the time to read the books as thoroughly as he would have liked.

On Sunday, too, Beharry came in the morning, to talk. But a change had come over him. He seemed shy of Ganesh and wasn't as ready with talk as before. He just sat on the verandah and nibbled and agreed with everything Ganesh said.

Now that Ganesh had stopped going to Beharry's, Leela began. She had taken to wearing a sari and it made her look thinner and frailer. She spoke to Suruj Mooma about Ganesh's work and her own fatigue.

As soon as Leela left, Suruj Mooma exploded. 'Suruj Poopa, you was listening to she? You see how Indian people does get conceited quick quick? Mind you, it ain't *he* I mind, but she. You hear all that big talk she giving we about wanting to break down the old house and build up a new one? And why all this damn

nonsense about wearing sari? All she life she knocking about in bodice and long skirt, and *now* she start with sari?'

'Man, was your idea Ganesh should wear dhoti and turban. It ain't have anything wrong if Leela wear sari.'

'Suruj Poopa, you ain't have no shame. They does treat you like dog and still you sticking up for them. And too besides, he wearing dhoti and Leela wearing sari is two different things. And what about the other set of nonsense she sit down on she thin tail here and giving we? All about feeling tired and wanting holiday. She ever had holiday before? Me ever had holiday? Ganesh ever had holiday? You ever had holiday? *Holiday!* She working hard all the time cleaning out cow-pen and doing a hundred and one things *I* wouldn't dirty myself doing, and we ain't hear not one single squeak about tiredness and holiday. Is only because she feeling a little money in she purse that she start with this nonsense, you hear.'

'Man, it ain't nice to talk like this. If people hear you they go think you just jealous.'

'*Me* jealous? Me jealous *she*? Eh, but what is this I hearing in my old age?'

Beharry looked away.

'Tell me, Suruj Poopa, what cause I have to jealous a thin little woman who can't even make a baby? I never leave my husband and run away from my responsibility, you hear. Is not me you got to complain about. Is them who is the ungrateful ones.' She paused, then continued, solemnly. 'I remember how we did take in Ganesh and help him and feed him and do a hundred and one other things for him.' She paused again, before snapping, 'And now what we get?'

'Man, we wasn't looking for anything in return. We was just doing we duty.'

'You see what we getting. Tiredness. Holiday.'

'Yes, man.'

'Suruj Poopa, you ain't listening to me. Every Sunday morning bright and early you jump out of your bed and running over to kiss the man foot as though he is some Lord Laloo.'

'Man, Ganesh is a great man and I must go and see him. If he treat me bad, is on his head, not mine.'

And when Beharry went to see Ganesh he said, 'Suruj Mooma not well this morning. Otherwise she woulda come. But she send to say how.'

*

For Ganesh the most satisfying thing about these early mystic months was the success of his *Questions and Answers*.

It was Basdeo, the printer, who pointed out the possibilities. He came to Fuente Grove one Sunday morning and found Ganesh and Beharry sitting on blankets in the verandah. Ganesh, in dhoti and vest, was reading the *Sentinel* – he had the paper sent to him every day now. Beharry just stared and nibbled.

'Like I tell you,' Basdeo said, after the salutations. He was a little more than plump now and when he sat down he could cross his legs only with difficulty. 'I still keeping the print of your book, pundit. Remember, I did tell you I did feel something special about you. Is a good good book, and is my opinion that more people should have a chance to read it.'

'It still have more than nine hundred copies remaining.'

'Sell those at a dollar a copy, pundit. People go snap them up, I tell you. It have nothing to shame about. After you sell off those I print another edition – '

'Revise edition,' Beharry said, but very softly, and Basdeo paid no attention.

'Another edition, pundit. Cloth cover, jacket, thicker paper, more pictures.'

'De luxe edition,' Beharry said.

'Exactly. Nice de luxe edition. What you say, sahib?'

Ganesh smiled and folded the *Sentinel* with great care. 'How much the Elite Electric Printery going to make out of this?'

Basdeo didn't smile. 'This is the idea, sahib. I print the book at my own expense. A nice big de luxe edition. We bring them here. You ain't pay a cent so far. You sell the book at two dollars a copy. Every copy you sell you keep a dollar. You ain't even have to lift your little finger. And is a good holy book, sahib.'

'What about other sellers?' Beharry asked.

Basdeo turned apprehensively. 'What other sellers? No body but the pundit sahib going to handle the books. Only me and Ganesh pundit sahib.'

Beharry nibbled. 'Is a good idea, and is a good book.'

So *101 Questions and Answers on the Hindu Religion* became the first best-seller in the history of Trinidad publishing. People were willing to pay the money for it. The simple-minded bought it as a charm; the poor because it was the least they could do for Pundit Ganesh; but most people were genuinely interested. The book was sold only at Fuente Grove and there was no need of Bissoon's selling hand.

He came, though, to ask for a few copies. He looked longer, thinner, and at a hundred yards couldn't be mistaken for a boy. He had grown very old. His suit was frayed and dusty, his shirt was dirty, and he wore no tie.

'People just ain't buying from me these days, sahib. Something gone wrong. I feel your kyatechism go bring back my hand and my luck.'

Ganesh explained that Basdeo was responsible for distribution. 'And he don't really want any sellers. It have nothing I could do, Bissoon. I sorry.'

'Is my luck, sahib.'

Ganesh turned up the edge of the blanket on which he was sitting and brought out some five-dollar notes. He counted four and offered them to Bissoon.

To his surprise Bissoon rose, very much like the old Bissoon, dusted his coat, and straightened his hat. 'You think I come to beg you for charity, Ganesh? I was a big big man when you was wetting your diaper, and you want now to give me *charity*?'

And he walked away.

It was the last Ganesh saw of him. For a long time no one, not even The Great Belcher, knew what became of him, until Beharry brought the news one Sunday morning that Suruj Mooma thought she had glimpsed him in a blue uniform in the ground of the Poor House on the Western Main Road in Port of Spain.

*

One Sunday Beharry said, 'Pundit, it have something I feel I must tell you, but I don't know how to tell you. But I must tell you because it does hurt me to hear people dirtying your name.'

'Oh.'

'People saying bad things, pundit.'

Leela came out to the verandah, tall, thin, and fragile in her sari. 'Oh, Beharry. But you looking *well* today. How you is? And how Suruj Mooma? And Suruj and the children, they well too?'

'Ah,' Beharry said apologetically. 'They well. But how *you* is, Leela? You looking *very* sick these days.'

'I don't know, Beharry. One foot in the grave, as they does say. I ain't know what happening, but I *so* tired these days. It have so much things to do these days. I feel I *have* to take a holiday.' She flopped down at the other end of the verandah and began to fan herself with the *Sunday Sentinel*.

Beharry said, 'Ahh, *maharajin*,' and turned to Ganesh, who was paying no attention to Leela. 'Yes, pundit. People complaining.'

Ganesh said nothing.

'It have some people even saying you is a robber.'

Ganesh smiled.

'Is not *you* they complaining about, pundit.' Beharry nibbled

anxiously. 'Is the taxi-drivers they don't like. You know how it hard to get up here, and the taxi-drivers charging anything up to five shillings.'

Ganesh stopped smiling. 'Is true?'

'Is true true, pundit, so help me God. And the thing, pundit, is that people saying that you own the taxis, and that if you don't charge people for the help you does give them, you does take it out of them in taxi fare.'

Leela got up. 'Man, I think I go go and lie down a little bit. Beharry, tell Suruj Mooma how for me.'

Ganesh didn't look at her.

'All right, *maharajin*,' Beharry said. 'You *must* take good care of yourself.'

'But, Beharry, it have a lot of taxis coming here, man.'

'Is where you wrong, pundit. Is only five. The same five. And all of them charging the same price.'

'But who taxis they is?'

Beharry nibbled and played with the edge of his blanket. 'Ah, pundit, that is the hard part. Wasn't me did notice it, you know, pundit. Was Suruj Mooma. These woman and them, pundit, they does notice thing we can't even see with magnifying glass. They sharp as razor-grass, man.' Beharry laughed and looked at Ganesh. Ganesh was serious. Beharry looked down at his blanket.

'Who taxis?'

'It make me shame to say, pundit. Your own father-in-law. Is what Suruj Mooma say. Ramlogan, from Fourways. It have a good three months now he running those taxis here.'

'Oho!' Ganesh rose quickly from his blanket and went inside.

Beharry heard him shouting. 'Look, girl, I ain't care how tired you is, you hear. You never too tired to count money. What I want is the facts. You and your father is proper traders. Buy, sell, make money, money.'

Beharry listened, pleased.

'Wasn't your father idea. He too stupid. Was your idea, not so? You and your father ain't care what sort of name I have in this place once you making your money. And, eh, eh, is *my* money. A year back, how much motor car coming to Fuente Grove in a whole month? One, two. Today? Fifty, sometimes a hundred. Who is the cause of that? Me or your father?'

Beharry heard Leela crying. Then he heard a slap. The crying stopped. He heard Ganesh walking heavily back to the verandah.

'You is a good good friend, Beharry. I go see about this right away.'

*

Before midday he had eaten, dressed – not in English clothes but in his normal Hindu attire – and was on his way to Fourways in a taxi. It was one of Ramlogan's. The driver, a fat little man bumping cheerfully up and down in his seat, handled the steering-wheel almost as if he loved it. When he wasn't talking to Ganesh he sang a Hindi song, which apparently had only four words. *Let us praise God.*

He explained, 'Is like this, pundit. We five taxi-boys does remain in Princes Town or San Fernando, and we does tell people that if they going to see you they must only use these taxis, because you say so. Is what Mr Ramlogan say. But even I say is better for them, seeing how you bless the taxi yourself.'

He sang *Let us praise God* a few times. 'What you think of your pictures, sahib?'

'Pictures?'

The driver sang the song again. 'Picture on the door, hanging by where other taxi does have the tariff.'

It was a framed picture, issued by the Gita Press of Gorakhpur in India, of the goddess Lakshmi standing, as usual, on her lotus. There was no tariff.

'Is a too nice idea, sahib. Mr Ramlogan say was your own idea,

and all five of we taxi-boys take we old hat off to you, sahib.' He became earnest. 'It does make a man feel good, sahib, driving a car with a holy picture inside it, especially when said picture bless by you. And the people like it too, man.'

'But what about the other taxi-drivers and them?'

'Ah, sahib. Is we biggest problem. How to keep the son-of-a-bitches away? You have to be very very careful with them. Pappa, they could lie too, you know. Eh, Sookhoo find one man the other day who did sticking up he own holy picture.'

'What Sookhoo do?'

The driver laughed and sang. 'Sookhoo smart, sahib. He drive the man car on the grass one day and take up the crank and he go over and tell him cool cool that if he don't stop playing the fool, you was going to make the car bewitch.'

Ganesh cleared his throat.

'Sookhoo is like that, sahib. But listen to the upshot. Two days good ain't pass before the man car get in an accident. A bad accident too.'

The driver began to sing again.

*

Ramlogan kept his shop open all week. The laws forbade him to sell groceries on Sunday; but there was no regulation against the selling of cakes, aerated water, or cigarettes on that day.

He was sitting on his stool behind the counter, doing nothing at all, just staring out into the road, when the taxi pulled up and Ganesh stepped out. Ramlogan held out his arms across the counter and began to cry. 'Ah, sahib, sahib, you forgive a old, old man. I didn't mean to drive you away that day, sahib. All the time since that day I only thinking and saying, "Ramlogan, what you do your cha'acter? Ramlogan, oh Ramlogan, what you go and do your sensa values?" Night and day, sahib, I praying for you to forgive me.'

Ganesh tossed the tasselled end of his green scarf over his shoulder. 'You looking well, Ramlogan. You getting fat, man.'

Ramlogan wiped his tears away. 'Is just wind, sahib.' He blew his nose. 'Just wind.' He had grown fatter and greyer, oilier and dingier. 'Ah, sit down, sahib. Don't bother about me. I is all right. You remember, sahib, how when you was a little boy you use to come in Ramlogan shop and sit down right there and talk to the old man? You was a fust-class talker, sahib. It use to flubbergast me, sitting down behind the counter here and hearing you giving off ideas. But now' – Ramlogan waved his hands around the shop and fresh tears came to his eyes – 'everybody gone and leave me. Me one. Soomintra don't even want to come by me now.'

'Is not about Soomintra I come to talk – '

'Ah, sahib. I *know* you just come to comfort a old man left to live by hisself. Soomintra say I too old-fashion. And Leela, she always by you. Why you don't sit down, sahib? It ain't dirty. Is just how it does look.'

Ganesh didn't sit down. 'Ramlogan, I come to buy over your taxis.'

Ramlogan stopped crying and got off his stool. 'Taxi, sahib? But what *you* want with taxi?' He laughed. 'A big, educated man like you.'

'Eight hundred dollars apiece.'

'Ah, sahib, I know is help you want to help me out. Especially these days when taxi ain't making any money at all. Is not the sort of job you, a famous mystic, want. I buy the taxi and them, sahib, only because when you getting old and lonely it must have something for you to do. You remember this glass case, sahib?'

It looked so much part of the shop now that Ganesh hadn't noticed it. The woodwork was grimy, the glass in many places patched and repatched with brown paper and, in one instance, with part of the cover of *The Illustrated London News*. The short legs stood in four salmon tins filled with water, to keep out ants.

It required memory rather than imagination to believe the glass case was once new and spotless.

'I glad I do my little piece to help modernize Fourways, but nobody ain't appreciate me, sahib. Nobody.'

Ganesh, for the moment forgetting his mission, looked at the newspaper-cutting and Leela's notice. The cutting was so brown it looked scorched. Leela's notice had faded and was almost unreadable.

'Is what life is, sahib.' Ramlogan followed Ganesh's gaze. 'Years does pass. People does born. People does married. People does dead. Is enough to make anybody a proper philosopher, sahib.'

'Philosophy is my job. Today is Sunday – '

Ramlogan shrugged. 'You ain't really *want* the taxis, sahib.'

'It go surprise you how much time I have on my hand these days. Let we say we make a bargain right now, eh?'

Ramlogan became very sad. 'Sahib, why for you want to make me a pauper? Why for you want to make me sad and miserable in my old, old age? Why for you prosecuting a old illiterate man who don't know A from B?'

Ganesh frowned.

'Sahib, wasn't a trick I was working back on you.'

'Working *back*? Trick? What trick you have to work back? Anybody passing in the road this hot Sunday afternoon and hearing you talk like this go swear I work some trick on you.'

Ramlogan placed the palms of his hands on the counter. 'Sahib, you know you getting me vex now. I ain't like other people, you know. I know you is a mystic, but don't provoke me, sahib. When I get vex, I don't know what I could do.'

Ganesh waited.

'If you wasn't my son-in-law, you know I take up your little tail and fling it through that door?'

'Ramlogan, ain't you does ever get a little tired of being smart smart all the time, even in your old age?'

Ramlogan thumped the counter. 'When at your wedding you rob me, we didn't get any of this damn mystical stupidness. Look, move out of here before I lose my temper. And too besides, is Government road and anybody can run taxi to Fuente Grove. Ganesh, you just try and do anything and I put you in the papers, you hear.'

'Put me in the papers?'

'One time you did put *me* in the papers. Remember? But it ain't going to be nice for you, I guarantee you. Oh, God! But I take enough from you in my lifetime! Just just because you married one daughter I did have. If you was a reasonable man, we coulda sit down, open a tin of salmon, and talk this thing over. But you too greedy. You want to rob the people yourself.'

'Is a favour I want to do you, Ramlogan. I giving you money for the taxis. If I buy my own, you think you could find people to drive your taxis from Princes Town and San Fernando to Fuente Grove? Tell me.'

Ramlogan became insulting. Ganesh only smiled. Then, when it was too late, Ramlogan appealed to Ganesh's good nature. Ganesh only smiled.

Ramlogan sold, in the end.

But when Ganesh was leaving, he burst out. 'All right, Ganesh, you making me a pauper. But watch. Watch and see if I don't put you in the papers and tell everybody everything about you.'

Ganesh got into his taxi.

'Ganesh!' Ramlogan shouted. 'Is war now!'

*

He might have run the taxis as part of his service to the public, and not charge for it; but Leela made difficulties and he had to give in. It was her idea, after all. He charged four shillings for the trip from Princes Town and San Fernando to Fuente Grove; and if this was a little more than it ought to have been, it was because

the roads were bad. At any rate the fare was cheaper than Ramlogan's, and the clients were grateful.

Leela tried to explain away Ramlogan's threats. 'He getting old now, man, and it ain't have much for him to live for. You mustn't mind all the things he say. He don't mean it.'

*

But Ramlogan was good as his word.

One Sunday, when The Great Belcher had called at Fuente Grove, Beharry came with a magazine, 'Pundit, you see what they write about you in the papers?'

He passed the magazine to Ganesh. It was a ragged thing called *The Hindu*, printed atrociously on the cheapest paper. Advertisements took up most of the space, but there were lots of quotations from the Hindu scriptures in odd corners, stale Information Office hand-outs about the British War Effort, repeated urgings to 'Read The Hindu'; and a column of original scandal headed *A Little Bird Tells Us*. It was to this that Beharry drew Ganesh's attention.

'Suruj Mooma bring it back from Tunapuna. She say you should hear the amount of scandal it causing.'

There was one item that began, 'A little bird tells us that the so-called mystic in South Trinidad has taken up driving taxis. The little bird also twittered into our ears that the said so-called mystic was party to a hoax played on the Trinidad public concerning a certain so-called Cultural Institute . . .'

Ganesh passed the paper to The Great Belcher. 'Leela father,' he said.

The Great Belcher said, 'Is why I come, boy. People talking about it. He call you the business Man of God. But you mustn't get worried, Ganesh. Everybody know that Narayan, the man who edit it, just jealous you. He think he is a mystic too.'

'Yes, pundit. Suruj Mooma say that Narayan went up to Tuna-

puna and start telling people that with just a little bit of practice he could be just as good as you in the mystic business.'

The Great Belcher said, 'Is the thing about Indians here. They hate to see another Indian get on.'

'I ain't worried,' Ganesh said.

And, really, he wasn't. But there were things in *The Hindu* that people remembered, such as the description of Ganesh as the business Man of God; and the accusation was parroted about by people who didn't know better.

He didn't have the business mind. In fact, he despised it. The taxi-service was Leela's idea. So was the restaurant, and that could hardly be called a business idea. Clients had to wait so long now when they came to see Ganesh that it seemed only considerate to give them food. So Leela had built a great bamboo tent at the side of the house where she fed people; and since Fuente Grove was so far from anywhere else, she had to charge a little extra.

And then people made a lot of fuss about Beharry's shop.

To understand the affair – some people made it the scandal – of Beharry's shop, you must remember that for years most of Ganesh's clients had been used to fake spirit-charmers who made them burn camphor and ghee and sugar and rice, and kill cocks and goats. Ganesh had little use for that sort of silly ritual. But he found that his clients, particularly the women, loved it; so he too ordered them to burn things two or three times a day. They brought the ingredients and begged him, and sometimes paid him, to offer them up on their behalf.

He wasn't really surprised when, one Sunday morning, Beharry said, 'Pundit, sometimes me and Suruj Mooma does stop and think and get worried about the things people bringing to you. They is poor people, they don't know whether the stuff they getting is good or not, whether it clean or not. And I know that it have a lot of shopkeepers who wouldn't mind giving them the wrong sort of stuff.'

Leela said, 'Yes, man. Is something Suruj Mooma been telling me she worried about for a long long time.'

Ganesh smiled. 'Suruj Mooma doing a lot of worrying these days.'

'Yes, pundit. I know you woulda see my point. The poor people ain't educated up to your standard and is up to you to see that they getting the right stuff from the proper shopkeeper.'

Leela said, 'I think it would make the poor people feel nicer if they could buy the stuff right here in Fuente Grove.'

'Why you don't keep it by you then, *maharajin*?'

'It wouldn't look *nice*, Beharry. People go start thinking we working a trick on them. Why not at your shop? Suruj Mooma done tell me that it wouldn't be any extra work. In fact, I think that you and Suruj Mooma is the correctest people to handle the stuff. And I *so* tired these days, besides.'

'You overworking yourself, *maharajin*. Why you don't take a rest?'

Ganesh said, 'Is nice for you to help me out this way, Beharry.'

So clients bought the ingredients for offerings only from Beharry's shop. 'Things not cheap there,' Ganesh told them. 'But is the only place in Trinidad where you sure of what you getting.'

Nearly everything Beharry sold came to Ganesh's house. A fair amount was used for ritual. 'And even that,' Ganesh said, 'is a waste of good good food.' Leela used the rest in her restaurant.

'I want to give the poor people only the best,' she said.

*

Fuente Grove prospered. The Public Works Department recognized its existence and resurfaced the road to a comparative evenness. They gave the village its first stand-pipe. Presently the stand-pipe, across the road from Beharry's shop, became the meeting-place of the village women; and children played naked under the running water.

Beharry prospered. Suruj was sent as a boarder to the Naparima College in San Fernando. Suruj Mooma started a fourth baby and told Leela about her plans for rebuilding the shop.

Ganesh prospered. He pulled down his old house, carried on business in the restaurant, and put up a mansion. Fuente Grove had never seen anything like it. It had two stories; its walls were of concrete blocks; the Niggergram said that it had more than a hundred windows and that if the Governor got to hear, there was going to be trouble because only Government House could have a hundred windows. An Indian architect came over from British Guiana and built a temple for Ganesh in proper Hindu style. To make up for the cost of all this building Ganesh was forced to charge an entrance fee to the temple. A professional sign-writer was summoned from San Fernando to rewrite the GANESH, *Mystic* sign. At the top he wrote, in Hindi, *Peace to you all*; and below, *Spiritual solace and comfort may be had here at any time on every day except Saturday and Sunday. It is regretted, however, that requests for monetary assistance cannot be entertained*. In English.

Every day Leela became more refined. She often went to San Fernando to visit Soomintra, and to shop. She came back with expensive saris and much heavy jewellery. But the most important change was in her English. She used a private accent which softened all harsh vowel sounds; her grammar owed nothing to anybody, and included a highly personal conjugation of the verb to be.

She told Suruj Mooma, 'This house I are building, I doesn't want it to come like any erther Indian house. I wants it to have good furnitures and I wants everything to remain prutty prutty. I are thinking about getting a refrigerator and a few erther things like that.'

'I are thinking too,' Suruj Mooma said. 'I are thinking about building up a brand-new modern shop, a real proper grocery like those in Suruj Poopa books, with lots of tins and cans on good good shelf –'

'– and all that people says about Indians not being able to keep their house properly is true true. But I are going to get ours painted prutty prutty – '

'– a long time now Suruj Poopa say that, and we going to paint up the shop, paint it up from top to bottom, and we going to keep it prutty prutty, with a nice marble-top counter. But, mark you, we not going to forget where we live. *That* going to be prutty prutty too – '

'– with good carpets like therse Soomintra and I see in Gopal's, and nice curtains – '

'– morris chairs and spring-cushions. But look, I hear the baby crying and I think he want his feed. I has to go now, Leela, my dear.'

With so much to say to each other now, Leela and Suruj Mooma remained good friends.

And Leela wasn't talking just for the sake of talk. Once the house was completed – and that, for a Trinidad Indian, is in itself an achievement – she had it painted and she expressed her Hindu soul in her choice of bright and clashing colours. She commissioned one house-painter to do a series of red, red roses on the blue drawing-room wall. She had the British Guianese temple-builder execute a number of statues and carvings which she scattered about in the most unlikely places. She had him build an ornate balustrade around the flat roof, and upon this he was later commissioned to erect two stone elephants, representing the Hindu elephant god Ganesh. Ganesh thoroughly approved of Leela's decorations and designed the elephants himself.

'I don't give a damn what Narayan want to say about me in *The Hindu*,' he said. 'Leela, I going to buy that refrigerator for you.'

And he did. He placed it in the drawing-room, where it hid part of the rose-design on the wall but could be seen from the road.

He didn't forget the smaller things. From an Indian dealer in San Fernando he bought two sepia reproductions of Indian drawings. One represented an amorous scene; in the other God had come down to earth to talk to a sage. Leela didn't like the first drawing. 'It are not going to hang in my drawing-room.'

'You have a bad mind, girl.' Under the amorous drawing he wrote, *Will you come to me like this?* And under the other, *or like this?*

The drawings went up.

And after they had settled that they really began hanging pictures. Leela started with photographs of her family.

'I ain't want Ramlogan picture in my house,' Ganesh said.

'I are not going to take it down.'

'All right, leave Ramlogan hanging up. But see what I going to put up.'

It was a photograph of a simpering Indian film-actress.

Leela wept a little.

Ganesh said blandly, 'It does make a change to have a happy face in the house.'

The one feature of the new house which thrilled them for a long time was the lavatory. It was so much better than the old cess-pit. And one Saturday, in San Fernando, Ganesh came upon an ingenious toy which he decided to use in the lavatory. It was a musical toilet-paper rack. Whenever you pulled at the paper, it played *Yankee Doodle Dandy*.

This, and the sepia drawings, were to inspire two of Ganesh's most successful writings.

*

Narayan's attacks increased, and varied. One month Ganesh was accused of being anti-Hindu; another month of being racialist; later he was a dangerous atheist; and so on. Soon the revelations of The Little Bird threatened to swamp *The Hindu*.

'And still he are calling it a little bird.'

'You right, girl. The little bird grow up and come a big black *corbeau.*'

'Dangerous man, pundit,' Beharry warned. When Beharry came now to see Ganesh he had to go to the fern-smothered verandah upstairs. Downstairs was one large room where clients waited. 'The time go come when people go start believing him. Is like a advertising campaign, you know.'

'If you ask me,' said Leela, in her fatigued, bored manner, 'the man is a disgrace to Hindus in this place.' She rested her head on her right shoulder and half-shut her eyes. 'I remember how my father did give a man a proper horse-whipping in Penal. It are just what Narayan want.'

Ganesh leaned back in his morris chair. 'The way I look at it is this.'

Beharry nibbled, all attention.

'What would Mahatma Gandhi do in a situation like this?'

'Don't know, pundit.'

'Write. That's what he would do. Write.'

So Ganesh took up pen again. He had considered his writing career almost over; and was only planning, in a vague way, a spiritual autobiography on the lines of the Hollywood Hindus. But this was going to be a big thing, to be attempted much later, when he was ready for it. Now he had to act immediately.

He wanted to do things properly. He went to Port of Spain – his courage failed him at the last moment and he wore English clothes – to the Registrar-General's Office in the Red House. There he registered Ganesh Publishing Company, Limited. The insignia of the firm was an open lotus.

Then he began to write again and found, to his delight, that the desire to write had not died, but was only submerged. He worked hard at his book, sitting up late at night after treating clients all day; and often Leela had to call him to bed.

Beharry rubbed his hands. 'Oh, this Narayan going to get it good.'

The book, when it came out two months later, was a surprise to Beharry. It looked like a real book. It had hard covers; the type was big and the paper thick; and the whole thing looked substantial and authoritative. But Beharry was dismayed at the subject. The book was called *The Guide to Trinidad.*

'Basdeo do a nice job this time,' Ganesh said.

Beharry agreed, but looked doubtful.

'It go knock hell out of Narayan. It go do you a lot of good and it go do Leela a lot of good.'

Beharry dutifully read *The Guide to Trinidad.* He found it good. The history, geography, and population of Trinidad were described in a masterly way. The book spoke about the romance of Trinidad's many races. In a chapter called *The East in the West*, readers were told that they would be shocked to find a mosque in Port of Spain; and even more shocked to find, in a village called Fuente Grove, a genuine Hindu temple which looked as if it had been bodily transported from India. The Fuente Grove Hindu temple was considered well worth a visit, for spiritual and artistic reasons.

The anonymous author of the *Guide* was enthusiastic about the island's modernity. The island, he stressed, had three up-to-date daily newspapers, and foreign advertisers could consider them good investments. But he deplored the absence of any influential weekly or monthly paper, and he warned foreign advertisers to be wary of the mushroom monthlies which claimed to be organs of certain sections of the community.

Ganesh sent free copies of the *Guide* to all the American Army camps in Trinidad, 'to welcome', as he wrote, 'our brave brothers-in-arms'. He also sent copies to export agencies and advertising agencies in America and Canada which dealt with Trinidad.

Beharry did his best to hide his bewilderment.

Leela said, 'It are beat me, if I see why for you doing all this.'

He left her to her worries; ordered her to get tablecloths, lots of knives, forks, and spoons; and warned her to look after the restaurant properly. He told Beharry it would be wise for him to lay in large stocks of rum and lager.

*

Presently the American soldiers began to pour into Fuente Grove and the village children had their first chew of gum. The soldiers came in jeeps and army lorries, some in taxis with girl-friends. They saw elephants in stone and were reassured, if not satisfied, but when Ganesh took them on a tour of his temple – he used the word 'tour' – they felt they had their money's worth.

Leela counted more than five thousand Americans.

Beharry had never been so busy in all his life.

'Is like what I did think,' Ganesh said. 'Trinidad is a small place and it ain't have much for the poor Americans to do.'

Many of them asked for spiritual advice and all who asked received it.

'Sometimes,' Ganesh said, 'I does feel that these Americans is the most religious people in the world. Even more than Hindus.'

'Hollywood Hindus,' muttered Beharry, but he nibbled so badly Ganesh didn't catch what he was saying.

*

After three months *The Hindu* announced that it had to cut the number of its pages because it wished to help the war effort. Not many people besides Ganesh noticed that there were fewer advertisements for patent medicines and other internationally known products. *The Hindu* lost the glamour of illustrated advertisements; and Narayan was making money only from plain statements about small shops here and there in Trinidad.

But The Little Bird still twittered.

9. Press Pundit

GANESH FOUND HIMSELF now a philosopher and arbiter. Indian villages in Trinidad still had *panchayats*, councils of elders, and he was often invited by them to give judgement in a case of minor theft or assault, or to settle a quarrel between husband and wife. Often, too, he was asked to address prayer-meetings.

His arrival at such a meeting was impressive. He came out of his taxi with dignity, tossed his green scarf over his shoulder, and shook hands with the officiating pundit. Then two more taxis came up with his books. Helpers fell upon these taxis, grabbed armfuls of books, and took them to the platform. The helpers were proud and busy people then, and looked almost as solemn as Ganesh. They ran from taxi to platform and back again, frowning, never saying a word.

Seated on the platform under a tasselled red canopy, and surrounded by his books, Ganesh looked the picture of authority and piety. His gaily-dressed audience rippled out from the platform in widening circles of diminishing splendour, from well-dressed businessmen and shopkeepers just below the platform to ragged labourers at the back, from extravagantly bedecked children sleeping on blankets and cushions to naked, spidery-limbed children sprawling on sugar-sacks.

People came to hear him not only because of his reputation but also because of the novelty of what he said. He spoke about the good life, about happiness and how to get it. He borrowed from

Buddhism and other religions and didn't hesitate to say so. Whenever he wished to strengthen a point he snapped his fingers and a helper held a book open towards the audience so that they could see that Ganesh wasn't making it all up. He spoke in Hindi but the books he showed in this way were in English, and people were awed by this display of learning.

His main point was that desire was a source of misery and therefore desire ought to be suppressed. Occasionally he went off at a tangent to discuss whether the desire to suppress desire wasn't itself a desire; but usually he tried to be as practical as possible. He spoke with fervour about the Buddha's Fire Sermon. Sometimes from that he moved on naturally to the war, and war in general, and to the quotation from Dickens's *Child's History of England* that 'war is a dreadful thing'. At other times he said that happiness was only possible if you cleared your mind of desire and looked upon yourself as part of Life, just a tiny link in the vast chain of Creation. 'Lie down on the dry grass and feel Life growing out from the rocks and earth beneath you, through you, and upwards. Look at the clouds and sky when it isn't hot and feel that you are part of all that. Feel that everything else is an extension of you. Therefore you, who are all this, can never die.'

People sometimes understood and when they got up they felt a little nobler.

*

And it was precisely for this that now, in 1944, The Little Bird began attacking Ganesh. It seemed to have reconciled itself to his 'so-called mysticism'.

The Little Bird said: 'I am just a little birdie but I think it is surely a retrograde step for any community these days to look up to a religious visionary . . .'

The Great Belcher told Ganesh, 'And, boy, Narayan start copying you. He start giving lectures now – in the towns. And he

showing his own books and thing too. Something about religion and the people.'

'Opium,' Beharry said.

Every new revelation of The Little Bird was carefully studied in Fuente Grove.

'It ain't your mystical powers he jealousing now, pundit. He working for the elections in two years' time. First election with universal adult franchise. Yes, universal adult franchise. Is what he have his eye on.'

Later issues of *The Hindu* seemed to show that Beharry was right. Spare inches of the magazine were no longer filled up with quotations from the *Gita* or the *Upanishads*. Now it was all: *Workers' Unite! Each One Teach One, Mens Sana in Corpore Sano, Per Ardua ad Astra*, The Hindu *is an Organ of Progress, I may not agree with what you say but I will fight to the death to defend your right to say it*. The Little Bird began to agitate for A Fair Day's Pay for a Fair Day's Work, and Homes for the Destitute; later it announced the opening of *The Hindu* 'Homes for Destitutes' fund.

*

One day Leela said to Suruj Mooma, 'I are thinking of taking up social welfare work.'

'My dear, is the said selfsame thing that Suruj Poopa *begging* me to do a long long time now. But, my dear, I ain't have the time.'

The Great Belcher was enthusiastic and practical. 'Leela, it have nine years I know you, and is the best idea you ever have. All this food I does come here and see you throwing away, you could give to poor people.'

'Ah, Aunt, it are not much that I does throw away. If something are not use today, well it are use tomorrow. But how I could start up with this social welfare work?'

'I go tell you how they does do it. You just get some children

together, bring them inside the restaurant, and feed them up. Or you go outside, look for children, and feed them outside. Christmas-time come round now, you pick up two three balloons and you go round giving them away.'

'Yes, Soomintra beginning to stock a lot of prutty prutty balloons.'

And every Sunday now Leela, with the help of The Great Belcher, did social work.

*

Ganesh worked on, unperturbed by Narayan and The Little Bird. It was as if Narayan's taunts had encouraged him to do just the thing for which he was attacked. In this he was far-sighted; for certainly it was the books he wrote at this time which helped to establish his reputation, not only in the country, but also in Port of Spain. He used the material of his talks for *The Road to Happiness*. After that came *Re-incarnation*, *The Soul as I See It*, *The Necessity for Faith*. These books sold regularly and well; but none of them had spectacular success.

And then, one after the other, appeared the two books that made his name a household word in Trinidad.

The first book began: 'On Thursday, May 2, at nine o'clock in the morning, just after I had had breakfast, I saw God. He looked at me and said . . .'

What God Told Me must surely rank as a classic in Trinidad literature. Its stark simplicity, almost ingenuousness, is shattering. The character of the narrator is beautifully revealed, especially in the chapters of dialogue, where his humility and spiritual bewilderment counter-point the unravelling of many knotty metaphysical points. There were also some chapters of spirited prophecy. The end of the war was predicted, and the fate of certain local people.

The book set a fashion. Many people in many parts of Trinidad began seeing God. The most celebrated was Man-man of Miguel

Street in Port of Spain. Man-man saw God, tried to crucify himself, and had to be put away.

And only two months after the publication of *What God Told Me* Ganesh scored a stupendous success of scandal. His inspiration was the musical toilet-roll rack. Because *Profitable Evacuation* was published during the war its title was misunderstood; fortunately, for it might not have been allowed if the authorities knew that it was concerned more or less with constipation. 'A vital subject,' Ganesh wrote in his Preface, 'one that has adversely dogged human relationships since the beginning of time.' The gist of the book was that evacuation could be made not only pleasurable but profitable, a means of strengthening the abdominal muscles. The system he recommended is roughly that which contortionists and weight-lifters call excavation.

This, printed on thick paper, with a cover of brightest yellow decorated with a lotus, established Ganesh finally, without question.

*

Left to himself Ganesh might not have taken any further action against Narayan. The Little Bird was only a twitter of protest amid whole-hearted and discerning applause. But people like The Great Belcher and Beharry didn't like it.

Beharry, in particular, was upset. Ganesh had opened up to him vaster vistas of reading and knowledge; and it was because of Ganesh that he prospered. He had put up his new shop, all concrete and plaster and glass. Land-values in Fuente Grove had risen and he had profited by that too. From time to time he was asked by various Literary-Debating-and-Social-Welfare Societies to talk on aspects of Ganesh's career: Ganesh the man, Ganesh the mystic, the contribution of Ganesh to Hindu thought. His fate was bound up with Ganesh's and he, more than anyone, resented Narayan's attacks.

He did what he could to encourage Ganesh to act.

'The man attack you again this month, pundit.'

'*Gaddaha!*'

'But it does look bad bad, pundit. Especially now that Ramlogan beginning to write against you in *The Hindu*. Is dangerous.'

But Ganesh wasn't worried that Narayan was preparing for the 1946 elections. 'I ain't burning to be one of those damn crooks who does go up for elections.'

'You hear the latest, pundit? Narayan form a party. The Hindu Association. Is a election stunt, pundit. He ain't have a chance to win in Port of Spain. He have to come to the country and that is where he frighten you beat him.'

'Beharry, you and me know what sort of thing Indian associations is in this place. Narayan and those people just like little girls playing dolly-house.'

Ganesh's judgement was sound. At the first general meeting of the Hindu Association Narayan was elected President. The following were also elected: four Assistant-Presidents, two Vice-Presidents, four Assistant Vice-Presidents; many Treasurers; one Secretary-in-Chief, six Secretaries, twelve Assistant-Secretaries.

'You see? They ain't leave nobody out. Look, Beharry, boy, going about talking to all these prayer-meetings, I get to know Trinidad Indians like the back of my own hand.'

But then Narayan began playing the fool. He began sending off cables to India, to Mahatma Gandhi, Pandit Nehru and the All-India Congress; in addition to anniversary cables of all sorts: he noted centenaries, bicentenaries tercentenaries. And every time he sent a cable the news was reported in the *Trinidad Sentinel*. There was nothing to prevent Ganesh sending his own cables; but in India, where they didn't know what was what in Trinidad, what chance would a cable signed GANESH PUNDIT MYSTIC have against one signed NARAYAN PRESIDENT HINDU ASSOCIATION TRINIDAD?

*

The deputation was the work of Beharry.

Two men and a boy came out one Sunday afternoon to Ganesh's residence. One man was tall, black, and fat. He looked a little like Ramlogan; only, he was dressed in spotless white: his belly was so big it hung over his black leather belt and hid it. In his shirt pocket he carried a letter and a whole row of pens and pencils. The other man was thin, fair, and good-looking. The boy wore short trousers and his shirt-sleeves were buttoned at his wrists. Ganesh had often met the men and knew them as organizers. The boy he didn't know.

The deputation sat down carefully on the morris chairs in the verandah and Ganesh shouted for Leela to bring put some Coca-Cola.

The deputation looked through the drawing-room doors and examined the pictures and the two big Coca-Cola calendars on the walls.

Then they saw Leela, thin and elegant in her sari, opening the refrigerator. The fat man nudged the boy sitting next to him on the couch; and the whole deputation stopped staring.

The fat man became businesslike. 'Sahib, we ain't come here to beat about the bush. Beharry and your aunt – a nice *nice* woman, sahib – they ask me to come because of the amount of experience I have organizing prayer-meetings and things like that – '

The Coca-Cola came. Four frosted bottles on a glass-bottomed tray. Leela sighed. 'Wait jirst one moment. I are going to get the glasses.'

The fat man looked at the bottles. The thin fair man fingered the strip of adhesive-plaster above his left eye. The boy looked at the tassels on Ganesh's scarf. Ganesh smiled at them all in turn and they all smiled back, except the boy.

On another glass-bottomed tray Leela brought expensive-looking glasses of great beauty, arabesqued in gold, red, and green and ringed with gold bands.

The deputation held their glasses in both hands.

There was an awkward silence until Ganesh asked the fat man, 'What you doing these days, Swami?'

Swami took a sip of Coca-Cola, a refined lilliputian sip. 'Jirst living, sahib.'

'Jirst living, eh?' Ganesh smiled.

Swami nodded and smiled back.

'And what happen to you, Partap? I see you cut yourself, man.'

'A little accident in Parcel Post,' Partap said, fingering the adhesive-plaster.

Ganesh had always thought of this man as Partap of Parcel Post. He managed to bring in the Parcel Post into almost any conversation, and Ganesh knew that to annoy him you only had to suggest that he worked in the Post Office. 'Parcel Post, please,' he would say coldly.

Silence, for three little sips of Coca-Cola.

Swami put down his glass with decision, but with unintentioned violence, and Leela came and stood at one of the drawing-room doors. Swami took up his glass again and smiled. 'Yes, sahib,' he said, with great cheerfulness. 'We ain't come here to beat about the bush. You is the only man with authority among all Trinidad Indians to stand up to Narayan. We don't approve of the way Narayan attacking you. We come here today, sahib' – Swami became solemn – 'to ask you to form up your own own association. We go make you President straightaway and – you ain't have to look very far – you have three Assistant-Presidents sitting down quiet quiet in front of you drinking Coca-Cola.'

'What Narayan do you so?'

'Don't ask me,' Partap said surlily. 'Nasty attack on me and my family, pundit. Accusing my own father of bribery *and* corruption in the local Road Board. And he always does call me a Post Office man, just for spite. I write letters, but he don't print them.'

'And me he accusing of robbing poor people.' Swami looked

pained. 'Sahib, it have more than eighteen months now you know me. I organize a hundred and one prayer-meetings for you. Sahib, a man of my standing go ever rob poor people?' Swami was a solicitor's tout in Couva.

'And what Narayan do the boy?'

Swami laughed and took a big gulp of Coca-Cola. The boy looked down into his glass. 'Narayan ain't do him anything *yet*, sahib. He only here for the experience.'

The boy's face grew darker with embarrassment.

'But he is a bright little boy, you know.' The boy frowned into his glass. 'My sister son. A genius, man, sahib. First shot, he get a first grade in the Cambridge School Certificate.'

Ganesh thought of his own second grade at the age of nineteen. He said, 'Ummh,' and took his first sip of Coca-Cola.

Partap went on, 'It not right, sahib. Every day you open the *Sentinel*, two to one you find something on page three about Narayan sending off greeting cables.'

Ganesh took a long draught of Coca-Cola.

Swami said, 'You must do something, sahib. Start up your own association. Or bring out a paper. Is another thing where I have a whole ton of experience. When I was young, man, sahib, in the nineteen-twenties, a year didn't pass off without Swami bringing out a new paper. I had to go up to Port of Spain – law business, you know – and I went to the Registrar office. Man, it surprise me self the number of paper I bring out. But I change now. I say you must bring out a paper only when you have a good good reason.'

Everybody drank some Coca-Cola.

'But I must stop talking about myself. This little boy here, sahib, he is a born writer. Man, if you does hear the English word he does use – word as long as my hand, man!' Swami held out his right arm until his shirt tautened at the arm-pit.

Ganesh looked at the boy.

'He shy today,' Swami said.

'But don't let that fool you,' Partap said. 'He thinking all the time.'

They drank a lot more Coca-Cola and talked a lot more, but Ganesh refused to be convinced, although there was in their arguments much that attracted him. That business of bringing out his own newspaper, for example, had repeatedly crossed his mind. In fact, sometimes on Sundays he had shouted to Leela to bring him paper and red pencils and he had made up dummy issues of newspapers. He had ruled columns, indicated which were for advertisements, which for edification. But this pleasure, like that of making note-books, was a private one.

*

Shortly afterwards, however, two things occurred that decided him to take action against Narayan.

You might say that the first began in the offices of the London *Messenger.* The war ended, throwing journalists more or less upon their own resources. The *Messenger* flew a correspondent to South America to cover a revolution that looked promising. Considering that the only human interest story he could get there was from a woman in a night-club who said, 'You are in bed. You hear bim-bam-bom. You say, "Revolution", and you go to sleep again,' the correspondent had done well. Having covered that revolution he flew back by way of Para, Georgetown, and Port of Spain, and uncovered crises in all three places. Apparently Trinidad natives were planning a revolt and British officials and their wives were taking revolvers to dances. The libel was publicity and pleased Trinidad. Ganesh was more concerned with the correspondent's analysis of the political situation, as reported back in the *Trinidad Sentinel.* Narayan was described as President of the extremist Hindu Association. Narayan, 'who received me at his party headquarters', was the leader of the Indian community. Ganesh didn't mind that.

He didn't mind the disparaging reference to the Hindu fanatics of South Trinidad. But he was needled when the correspondent lingered over romantic details when speaking of Narayan and described him as 'chain-smoking, balding C. S. Narayan, veteran journalist', and much more. He could take any amount of abuse from Narayan himself. England could, if it wished, think of Narayan as the leader of Trinidad Indians. But that England would read and remember that C. S. Narayan was chain-smoking, balding, and a veteran journalist was more than he could bear.

'I know is unreasonable, Beharry. But is how I feel.'

Beharry sympathized. 'A man could take big things. Is the little things like that what does cut up a man tail.'

'Something go have to happen, and then I go do for Narayan.'

Beharry nibbled. 'Is the way I like to hear you talk, pundit.'

And then, most opportunely, The Great Belcher brought great news.

'Oh, Ganesh, the shame! The shame to Indians that Narayan bringing!' She was so overcome she could only belch and ask for water. She got Coca-Cola. It made her burp between belches and she remained uncommunicative for some time. 'I done with Coca-Cola,' she said at last. 'I ain't modern enough for it. Next time is only water for me.'

'What shame?'

'Ah, boy. The Home for Destitutes Fund. You know Narayan start that?'

'The Little Bird talking about it for months now.'

'Home for Destitutes! As fast as the money collecting, the man buying estates. And was only by a chance I get to find out. I ain't know if you know how hard Gowrie having it these days. She is a sort of relation to Narayan. So, when I met Gowrie at Doolarie wedding and she start this big bawling and crying about money, I say, "Gowrie, why you don't go to Narayan and ask him? He having this fund for destitute." She say no, she can't go, because

she got she pride and the fund still open. But I talk she into going and so when I see she yesterday at Daulatram funeral, I ask she, "You ask Narayan?" She say yes, she ask Narayan. "And what he do?" I ask. She say Narayan just begin one crying and losing his temper when she ask him, saying that everybody think that because he open one little fund he is a rich man. He say, "Gowrie, I poorer than you. How you could look at me and think I is rich? Just last week I had to buy a whole estate for fourteen thousand dollars. Where I go find all that money?" So he say and so he begin one long crying and Gowrie say in the end she feel that *he* was going to ask she for money.'

Throughout the long speech The Great Belcher hadn't belched once. 'Is the Coca-Cola, you think?' Ganesh asked.

'No, so it does happen when I get carry away.'

'But how people ain't making a row about this fund, man?'

'Ah, boy, don't tell me you ain't know Trinidad. When people give money, you think they care who get it? Once they open they mouth and skin their teeth for a photo in the papers, they happy, you hear. And too besides, you believe they want this thing to come out for people to start laughing at them?'

'It ain't right. I ain't saying this because I is a mystic and all that, but I think that to any outsider it can't look right.'

'Is just how I feel,' The Great Belcher said.

*

So the deputation came again and sat, not in the verandah, but at the dining-table in the drawing-room. They looked at the pictures on the walls again. Once more Leela went through the ritual of taking out Coca-Cola from the refrigerator and pouring it into the beautiful glasses.

Swami was still dressed in white; there was the same array of pens and pencils in his shirt pocket, and the same letter. Partap had lost his adhesive plaster. The boy had discarded his short

trousers for a double-breasted brown suit a size or two bigger than he required. He had a copy of *Time* magazine and the *New Statesman and Nation.*

Partap said, 'Narayan so smart he stupid. He playing right in we hand now, pundit. He changing his name, man. With Indians he is Chandra Shekar Narayan.'

'And with everybody else,' Swami added, 'Cyrus Stephen Narayan.'

Leela brought large sheets of paper and many red pencils.

Ganesh said, 'I think over what you say, and we going to start up we own paper.'

Swami said, 'Is just what go knock hell out of Narayan.'

Ganesh ruled out columns on the sheet before him. 'Like in all things, we have to start small.'

The boy put *Time and the New Statesman* on the table. 'These is small papers. *Very* small papers.'

Swami laughed. It sounded like gargling in the next room. 'You see, sahib, the boy could talk good. And, man, he is a born writer. He know a lot more than plenty of big big man in this place.'

The boy repeated. 'Yes, these is very small papers.'

Ganesh smiled sympathetically. 'That go cost a lot, man. We have to start small and simple. Look at your uncle Swami. He start small when he did bringing out papers.'

Swami nodded solemnly.

'And Partap. And me. We did all have to start small. We starting up with four pages.'

'Only four pages?' the boy said petulantly. 'But that ain't no sort of paper at all, man.'

'Later we go build it up, man. Big big.'

'All right, all right.' The boy angrily pulled his chair away from the table. 'Go ahead and make up your so-call paper. But just leave me out of it.' He attended to his Coca-Cola.

'First page,' Ganesh announced. 'Bright page. No advertisements, except in the bottom right-hand corner.'

'I always did promise myself,' Partap said reverently, 'that if I did ever start up a paper, I woulda dedicate it to Mahatma Gandhi. I know a boy, if you treat him nice, could pick up a block with Gandhi picture from the *Sentinel* office. We could put this on the top of the front page and I could always find out some words or something to go with it.'

Ganesh marked out the space for the homage.

'That settle,' Swami said.

The front page going to be a page of attack, attack,' Ganesh said. 'Leave that to me. I working on this article exposing the Destitutes Fund and Leela busy writing a little report about the social welfare work she doing.'

Swami was so pleased he tried to cross his gargantuan legs. The chair creaked and Ganesh looked hard at him. Leela came out and swept through the room. 'Some people look as if they are never see furnitures before. Next time I are going to bring some benches.'

Partap sat bolt upright and Swami smiled.

The boy, sitting against the wall next to the refrigerator, said, 'Yes, the page settle. But I wonder what people go say when they see in one side the page dedication to Mahatma Gandhi and in the other side attack, attack.'

Swami said sharply, 'Shut up, boy. Otherwise, don't mind you big and wearing long pants, I haul you across my knee and I give you a sound sound cut-arse, right here, in front of the pundit self. And I leave you home next time and you never touch any paper I bring out. If you ain't have nothing but suckastic remarks, keep quiet.'

'All right, you is a big man and you go shut me up. But I want to see how all you going to full up the three other pages.'

Ganesh ignored the exchange and went on ruling columns on the inside pages. 'Page two.'

Partap sipped some Coca-Cola. 'Page two.'

'Yes,' Swami said, 'page two.'

Partap snapped his fingers. 'Advertisements!'

'A whole page advertisements on page two? You see the way inexperience people does talk?'

'*Some* advertisements,' Ganesh pleaded.

'Is what I did mean,' Partap said.

'Four columns on page two. Two for advertisement?'

Partap nodded.

Swami said, 'Is how *I* use to do it.'

'What you going to put in the two columns?' The boy.

Swami turned around quickly in his chair and again it creaked dangerously. The boy was holding up *Time* before his face.

'How about a little thing by you, pundit?' Partap asked.

'Man, already I writing up a whole front page. And I ain't want my name to appear in the paper. I ain't want to bring myself down to Narayan level.'

Swami said, 'Culture, sahib. Page two is the culture page.'

Partap said, 'Yes, culture.'

There was a long silence, broken only by the boy turning over the pages of *Time* with unnecessary rustle.

Ganesh tapped his pencil on the table. Swami propped his hands against his chin and leaned forward on the table, pushing it towards Ganesh. Partap crossed his arms and furrowed his brow.

'Coca-Cola?' Ganesh said.

Swami and Partap nodded absent-mindedly and Leela came out to do the honours. 'I have some enamel cups, you know, if that are going to make you people any happier.'

'Oh, we is all right,' Partap smiled.

'Cinema,' the boy said, behind *Time*.

'What you mean?' Swami asked eagerly.

'Film reviews,' Ganesh said.

Partap said, 'Film reviews is a first-class idea.'

Swami was enthusiastic. 'And on that selfsame page, advertisements for films. From the Indian companies. One review for one advertisement.'

Ganesh slapped the table. 'That self.'

The boy was humming.

The three men sipped Coca-Cola with abandon. Swami laughed and chuckled till his chair creaked.

The boy said coldly, 'Page three.'

'Two more columns of advertisement there,' Ganesh said briskly.

'And a nice big advertisement on the whole of page four,' Swami added.

'True enough,' Ganesh said, 'but why for you jumping ahead so?'

Partap said, 'Only two more columns to full up.'

'Yes,' Swami said sadly, 'two more.'

The boy walked to the table and said, 'Feecher.'

They looked at him inquiringly.

'Feecher article.'

'The paper finish!' Swami cried.

Partap said, 'Who go write the feecher?'

Ganesh said, 'People know my style. Is something for you people to write. Just gimme page one.'

'Serious, religious feecher on page three,' the boy said, 'to make up for page one which, if I ain't getting deaf, going to be a page of attack, attack.'

Swami said, 'I outa practice. In the old days, man, I coulda turn out a feecher in half a hour.'

Partap said hesitantly, 'A bright little thing about Parcel Post?'

The boy said, 'Serious *and* religious feecher.' To Swami he said, 'But what about that one you show me the other day?'

'Which one?' Swami asked casually.

'The flying one.'

'Oh. *That* little thing. The boy talking, sahib, about a few words I scribble off the other day.'

Partap said, 'I remember the one. The *New Statesman* send it back. Was nice, though. It prove, pundit, that in ancient India they did know all about aeroplanes.'

Ganesh said, 'Hmmh.' Then, 'All right, we go put it in.'

Swami said, 'I go have to polish it up a little bit.'

Partap said, 'Well, I glad that settle.'

The boy said, 'All you forgetting one thing. The name.'

The men became thoughtful once more.

Swami tinkled the ice in his glass. 'I better say it right away, sahib. I is like that, sahib. No beating about the bush. If you can't get a good name, blame me. I use up everything when I was a proper editor. *Mirror*, *Herald*, *Sentinel*, *Tribune*, *Mail*. Everything, man. Use them up, Hindu this and Hindu that.'

Ganesh said, 'Something simple.'

Partap toyed with his glass and mumbled, 'Something really simple.' And before he had time to take it back Partap had said, '*The Hindu?*'

'Damn fool!' Swami shouted. 'How you forgetting that that is the name of Narayan paper? Is so stupid you does get working in the Post Office?'

The chair scraped loudly on the floor and Leela rushed out in a panic. She saw Partap standing, pale and trembling, with a glass in his hand.

'Say that again,' Partap cried. 'Say that again and see if I don't break this glass on your head. Who does work in the Post Office? You could ever see a man like me licking stamps? You, a damn tout, running around licking – but I ain't going to dirty my mouth talking to you here today.'

Ganesh had put his arm around Partap's shoulders while Leela

swiftly retrieved the glass from his hand and cleared the table of the other glasses.

Swami said, 'I was only making joke, man. Who could look at you and say that you working in the Post Office? I could just look at you and see that you is a Parcel Post man. Parcel Post print all over you, man. Not so, boy?'

The boy said, 'He look to me like a Parcel Post man.'

Ganesh said, 'You see, they all say you does look like a Parcel Post man. Come on, sit down and behave like one. Sit down and take it easy and have some Coca-Cola. Eh, eh, where the glasses gone?'

Leela stamped her foot. 'I are not going to give any of these illiterate people any Coca-Cola in my prutty prutty glasses.'

Swami said, 'We sorry, *maharajin*.'

But she was out of the room.

Partap, sitting down, said, 'I sorry, mistakes are reliable. I did just forget the name of Narayan paper for the moment, that is all.'

'What about *The Sanatanist*?' Swami asked.

The boy said, 'No.'

Ganesh looked at the boy. 'No?'

'Is a easy name to twist around,' the boy said. 'It easy to make *The Sanatanist The Satanist*. And too besides, my father ain't a Sanatanist. We is Aryans.'

So the men thought again.

Swami asked the boy, 'You think anything yet?'

'What you think I is? A professional thinker?'

Partap said, 'Don't behave so. If you think anything, don't keep it secret.'

Ganesh said, 'We is big men. Let we forget the boy.'

The boy said, 'All right, stop worrying. I go ease you up. The name you looking for is *The Dharma*, the faith.'

Ganesh blocked out the name at the top of the front page.

The boy said, 'It surprise me that big big men sitting down

drinking Coca-Cola and talking about their experience ain't bother to worry about the advertisements.'

Partap, still excited, grew garrulous. 'I was talking to the Head of Parcel Post only last week and he tell me that in America and England – he was there on leave before the war – they does have big big men sitting down all day just writing off advertisements.'

Swami said, 'I ain't have the contacts I use to have for getting advertisements.'

Ganesh asked the boy, 'Think we need them?'

Swami said, 'Why for you asking the boy? If you ask me *my* advice, I go tell you flat that unless a paper have advertisements it does look like nothing and it go make people think nobody does read the paper.'

Partap said, 'If you ain't having advertisements, it mean having more columns to full up. Two and two is four, and four columns on the back page make eight columns, and one on the front – '

Ganesh said, 'We having advertisements; and I know one man bound to want to advertise. Beharry. Beharry's Emporium. Front Page.'

'Who else you know?' the boy asked.

Partap furrowed his brow. 'The best thing would be to appoint a business manager.'

Swami smiled at Partap. 'Very *nice* idea. And I think the best man for business manager is Ganesh Pundit.'

The vote was unanimous.

The boy nudged Swami and Swami said, 'And I think we have to appoint a sub-editor. The best man for that job is this boy here.'

That was agreed. It was further agreed that, on the first page of *The Dharma*, Swami should appear as Editor-in-Chief, and Partap as Editor.

*

There were times during the next two or three weeks when Ganesh regretted his plunge into journalism. The film companies were rude. They said they had enough advertisements as it was and they doubted whether any reviews in *The Dharma*, however favourable, would stabilize the film industry in India. That was Ganesh's contention. 'The Indian film industry,' he said, 'isn't as healthy as it looks. Let the effects of the war wear off and – bam! – things are going to get bad.' The executives advised him to stick to religion and leave the film industry alone. 'All right,' Ganesh threatened. 'No reviews for you. Not a single little word. *The Dharma* will ignore the very existence of the Indian cinema. Not a single word.' Quick thinking had, however, shown the two culture columns on page two as a blank and he had relented. 'I am sorry I lost my temper,' he wrote. 'Your treatment of me shall not influence my treatment of you.' Still the film companies refused to issue free tickets to *The Dharma* and Ganesh had to pay for the boy to go and see the two films for review.

Being a business manager was embarrassing. It meant going to see a man he knew and talking about the situation in India before springing the request for an advertisement. It wasn't very wise either, because Ganesh didn't want it known that he was too closely associated with *The Dharma*.

In the end he threw up the idea of getting advertisements. He got two or three inches from those of his clients who were shopkeepers; but he decided thereafter to print unsolicited advertisements. He thought of all the shops he knew and wrote copy for them. A difficult business, since the shops were nearly all alike and it wasn't satisfying to keep on writing 'Best Quality Goods at City Prices' or 'High-Class Commodities at Competitive Prices'. Finally he became inventive. He described superlative bargains in fictitious shops in unknown villages.

Swami was pleased. 'A master job, sahib.'

Partap said, 'This place you mention, Los Rosales, where it is?'

'Keskidee Bargain Shop? Brand-new place. Open only last week.'

The boy handed in libellous reviews of the films.

'We can't print this, man,' Ganesh said.

'Is all right for you to talk. You just go around getting advertisements. Me, I had to spend six whole hours watching those two pictures.'

The reviews were rewritten.

The boy said, 'Is your paper, pundit. If you make me lie, is on your head.'

'How about your article on the Destitutes Fund, sahib?'

'I have it right here. It go make Narayan a laughing-stock. And printing this report by Leela next to it, Narayan go have good hell knock out of him.'

He showed the report.

'What is all these dots over the paper?' the boy asked.

'Crossing out punctuation marks.'

'Is a nice little report, man, sahib.' Swami's voice was mellow.

It read:

REPORT OF MY SOCIAL WELFARE WORK
by Leela Ramsumair

1. In November last year I in my very small and humble way treated 225 destitutes by way of cash and refreshments. The expenses for this treat were met by donations willingly and cheerfully given by private individual Trinidadians.

2. In December I treated 213 poor children. Expenses were met by me and my husband, Pundit Ganesh Ramsumair, B.A., Mystic.

3. In January I was approached by Dr C. V. R. Swami, the Hindu journalist and religious organizer, with a request for immediately monetary assistance. He had been organizing a seven-day prayer-meeting, feeding on an average anything up

> to 200 brahmins per diem, in addition to about 325 others (Dr Swami's figures). He had run short of food. I gave him monetary assistance. Therefore he was able, on the 7th and last day of the prayer-meeting, to feed more than 500 brahmins in addition to 344 destitutes.
>
> 4. In February I visited Sweet Pastures Estate where I was met by approximately 425 children. They were all destitute. I fed them and gave 135 of the very poorest toys.
>
> 5. In March, at my residence in Fuente Grove, I treated more than 42 children of the very poorest. I think it advisable to state that while I was able to feed them all I was able to give clothes only to 12 of the very poorest.
>
> 6. In presenting this incomplete report for the inspection of the Trinidadian public, I wish to make it publicly known that I owe very much to the very many private individual Trinidadians who willingly and cheerfully donated money to bring comfort and solace to children of the very poorest without distinction of race, caste, colour, or creed.

The *Dharma* went to press.

*

The boy handled the layout of the paper with relish. He had a banner headline on page one and another on page three. At the top of page three he had, in twenty-four point italic:

> Today the aeroplane is a common or garden sight and it is commonly believed that progress in this field has only been made in the past forty years. But diligent research is proving otherwise and in this learned dispatch Dr C. V. R. Swami shows that 2,000 years ago there was –

And in huge black letters:

FLYING IN ANCIENT INDIA

He knew all about cross-headings and used them every paragraph. He put the last paragraph of every article in italic, with the last line in black letter.

Basdeo, the printer, told Ganesh afterwards, 'Sahib, if you ever send that boy again to have anything print, I think I go wring his neck.'

10. The Defeat of Narayan

'IF I NEEDED any further proof of the hand of Providence in my career,' Ganesh wrote in *The Years of Guilt*, 'I had only to look at the incidents which led to the decline of Shri Narayan.'

In Trinidad it isn't polite to look down on a man because you know he handles public funds unwisely. As soon as he is exposed the poor man becomes ridiculous enough, a subject for calypso. After *The Dharma* came out Narayan didn't have a chance.

'Now is your chance to finish him off, pundit,' Beharry said. 'Give him two three months to recover and – bam! – people stop laughing and begin to listen to him again.'

But no one could think of a plan.

Leela said, 'I would do like my father and give him a good horse-whipping.'

Beharry suggested more lectures.

The boy said, 'Kidnap the son of a bitch, pundit.'

Swami and Partap thought a lot but came up with nothing.

It was the Hindu wedding season and The Great Belcher was very busy.

Suruj Mooma was still thinking when Fate, unfortunately for Narayan, took a hand.

Two days after the publication of Volume One, Number One of *The Dharma* it was announced in the *Trinidad Sentinel* that a Hindu industrialist in India had offered thirty thousand dollars for the cultural uplift of Trinidad Hindus. The money was being kept

in trust by the Trinidad Government until it could be handed over to a competent Hindu body.

Narayan promptly claimed that the Hindu Association, of which he had the honour to be President, was competent enough to handle the thirty thousand dollars.

Leela said, 'They could handle a lot more, if you let them.'

'Is God Self send this chance, pundit,' Beharry urged. 'But you have to act fast. Narayan Association having their second General Meeting in four weeks. You couldn't do something there?'

'I thinking about it all all the time,' Ganesh said and for a moment Beharry recognized the old, pre-mystic Ganesh.

*

Four days later the San Fernando correspondent of the *Sentinel* reported that Pundit Ganesh Ramsumair of Fuente Grove was planning the formation of a representative assembly of Trinidad Hindus to be known as the Hindu League.

That day, in an interview, Narayan claimed that the Hindu Association was the only representative Hindu body in Trinidad. It had a fine record of social work, it was founded long before the League was even thought of, and it was clear to all right-thinking people that the League was being formed only with thirty thousand dollars in view.

Letters flew from both sides to the *Sentinel*.

Finally, it was announced that the Inaugural Meeting of the Hindu League was to be held at the residence of Pundit Ganesh Ramsumair in Fuente Grove. The meeting was to be private.

*

That Saturday afternoon about fifty men, most of them former clients, gathered in the ground floor of Ganesh's house. There were solicitors and barristers among them, solicitor's touts, taxi-

drivers, clerks and labourers. Leela, taking no chances, gave them diluted Coca-Cola in enamel cups.

Ganesh sat on orange cushions on a low platform below a carving of Hanuman, the monkey god. He recited a long Hindi prayer, then used a mango-leaf to sprinkle water from a brass jar over the meeting.

Partap, sitting cross-legged on a *charpoy* next to the boy, said in Hindi, 'Ganges water.'

The boy said, 'Go to France!'

Ganesh made them all swear a terrible oath of secrecy.

Then he stood up and tossed his green scarf over his shoulder. 'What I want to say today is very simple. We want to use the money given us well, and at the same time we want to stop Narayan making more trouble. He says he is competent to handle the money. We know that.'

There was laughter. Ganesh took a sip of Coca-Cola from a prutty prutty glass. 'To get the money, we mustn't only remove Narayan, we must form one united Hindu body.'

There were cries of approval.

'The Hindu Association isn't a very large body. There are more of us here than in the Hindu Association. The Association wants to get new members and I have called you here today to beg you to form your own branches of the Hindu Association.'

Murmurings.

The boy said, 'But I thought we was going to form the Hindu *League* today.'

Ganesh raised his hand. 'I am doing this only for the sake of Hindu unity in Trinidad.'

Some people cried in Hindi, 'Long live Ganesh!'

'But what about the League?' the boy said.

'We are not going to form the League. In less than three weeks the Hindu Association is going to hold its second General Meeting.

Many officers will be elected and I hope to see all of you among them.'

The meeting clapped.

Swami stood up with difficulty. 'Mr President Ganesh, sir, may I ask how you is going to see that happen?'

The meeting clapped again and Swami sat down.

'This is the problem: how can we win the elections at the General Meeting of the Association? The solution: by having more delegates than anybody else. How do we get delegates? By forming more branches. I expect the fifty of you here to form fifty branches. Every branch will send three delegates to the Meeting.'

Swami rose again. 'Mr President Ganesh, sir, may I ask how you is going to give each and every one of we here three delegates, sahib?'

'It have – there are hundreds of people who are willing to do me a favour.'

The boy got up amid applause for Swami and Ganesh. 'All right, it sound all right. But what make you feel that Narayan not going to do the same thing as we?'

Murmurs of, 'The boy little but he smart, man,' and, 'Who son he is?'

Swami got up almost as soon as he had sat down. There was more applause for him. He smiled, fingered the letter in his shirt pocket, and held up his hand for the ovation to cease. 'Mr President Ganesh, sahib, with your permission, sahib, I is going to answer the boy question. After all, he is my own nephew, my own sister son.'

Thunderous applause. Cries of, 'Shh! Shh! Let we hear what the man saying, man.'

'It seem to me, Mr President Ganesh, that the boy question sort of answer itself, sahib. First, who go take Narayan serious now? Who go listen to him? Mr President Ganesh, I is the editor-in-chief of *The Dharma*. That paper make Narayan a laughing-

stock. Second point, sahib. Narayan ain't have the brains to do anything like this.'

Laughter.

Swami held up his hand again. 'Third and last point, sahib. The element of surprise. That is the element that go beat Narayan.'

Shouts of, 'Long live Swami! Long live Swami's nephew!'

Partap asked, 'What about transport, pundit? I was thinking. I could get some vans from Parcel Post – '

'I have five taxis,' Ganesh said. 'And I have many taxi-drivers who are friends.'

The taxi-drivers in the gathering laughed.

Ganesh made the closing speech. 'Remember, is only Narayan we fighting. Remember, is Hindu unity we fighting for.' And before the gathering broke up he rallied them with a cry, 'Don't forget you have a paper behind you!'

*

The next day, Sunday, the *Sentinel* reported the formation of the Hindu League. According to the President, Pundit Ganesh Ramsumair, the League already had twenty branches.

On Tuesday – the *Sentinel* isn't published on Monday – Narayan said that the Hindu Association had thirty branches. On Wednesday the League said it had doubled its membership and had forty branches. On Thursday the Association had doubled *its* membership and had sixty. The League was silent on Friday. On Saturday the Association claimed eighty branches. Nobody said anything on Sunday.

On Tuesday Narayan stated at a press conference that the Hindu Association was clearly the competent Hindu body and was going to press for the grant of thirty thousand dollars immediately after the election of officers at its second General Meeting that Sunday.

*

The Hindu Association was to meet in Carapichaima at the hall of a Friendly Society, a large Mission-school-type building with pillars ten feet high and a pyramidal roof of galvanized iron. Concrete upstairs, downstairs lattice-work around the pillars. A large black and silver sign-board eloquent about the Society's benefits, including 'free burial of members'.

The second General Meeting of the Hindu Association was to begin at one in the afternoon but when Ganesh and his supporters arrived in taxis at about half-past one all they saw were three men dressed in white, among them a tall Negro with a long beard who looked holy.

Ganesh had warned that blows might pass and as soon as the taxi came to Carapichaima, Swami, armed with a stout *poui* stick, sat on the edge of his seat and began shouting, 'Where Narayan? Narayan, where you is? I want to meet you today!'

Now he calmed down.

Ganesh's men quickly overran the place. Partap, showing an initiative that surprised Ganesh, went with the advance party.

'Narayan ain't here,' the boy said with relief.

Swami beat his stick on the dusty ground. 'Is a trick, sahib. And *today* was the day I did want to meet Narayan.'

Then Partap came back with the news that the delegates of the Hindu Association were eating in a room upstairs.

Ganesh, with Swami, Partap, and the boy, walked across the dirt-and-asphalt yard to the wooden steps at the side of the building.

The boy said, 'All you better protect me good, you hear. If I get beat up here today it go have hell to pay.'

Half-way up the steps Swami shouted, 'Narayan!'

He was on the top landing, an old man, very small, very thin, in a soiled and clumsy white-drill suit. His face was screwed up into an expression of great pain. He looked dyspeptic. He turned away and went to lean on the half-wall of the top verandah, staring

intently at the mango trees and small wooden houses across the road.

Ganesh and his men walked noisily up the steps, the boy making more noise than any.

Swami said, 'Take my *poui* and hit him on he bald head while he looking over, sahib. Is the chance of a life-time.'

Ganesh said, 'You ain't know how right you is.'

The boy said, 'You have three witnesses here that he just overbalance and fall down.'

Ganesh didn't respond.

The boy said, 'Gimme the stick. *I* go settle Narayan.'

Swami smiled. 'You too small.'

Ganesh's supporters were distributing *The Dharma* right and left, to people passing in the road, to the eating delegates, to the delegates walking about the yard. At first they tried to get four cents a copy but now they were just giving the paper away.

Partap said calmly, 'You want me go and abuse Narayan now, pundit? Is the sort of thing I mad enough to do, you know.' He suddenly became frenzied. 'Look, all you people better hold me back before I send that thin little man to hospital, you hear. Hold me back!'

They held him back.

Narayan stopped staring across the road and walked slowly towards the landing.

Swami said, 'You want me kick him down the steps, sahib?'

They held him back too.

Narayan glanced at them. He looked sick.

'Leave him alone,' Ganesh said. 'He finish, poor man.'

The boy said, 'He look like a wet fowl.'

They heard him going down the steps, clop by clop.

The delegates who had been eating came out to the verandah in small groups, tumbler in hand. They were remaining as calm as possible and behaved as though Ganesh and his men were not

there. They washed their hands over the wall and gargled. They talked and laughed, loudly.

Ganesh's attention was caught by a short, stout gargler at the far end of the verandah. He thought he recognized the energy with which this man was gargling and spitting into the yard; and that over-all jauntiness was definitely familiar. From time to time the gargler gave a curious little hop, and that too Ganesh recognized.

The man stopped gargling and looked around. 'Ganesh! Ganesh Ramsumair!'

'Indarsingh!'

He was plumper and moustached, but the weaving and bobbing, the effervescence that made him a star pupil at the Queen's Royal College, remained. 'Hello there, old boy.'

'Man, you talking with a Oxford accent now, man. What happening, man?'

'Easy, old boy. Nasty trick you're playing against us. But you're looking well. Demn well.' He fingered his St Catherine's Society tie and gave another hop.

Ganesh would have been too embarrassed to talk correctly with Indarsingh. 'Man, I never did expecting to see you here. A big scholarship-winner like you, man.'

'Catching hell with law, old boy. Thinking of politics. Starting small. Talking.'

'Yes, man. Indarsingh was the champion debater at college.'

Swami and the others stood by, gaping. Ganesh said, 'I ask the pack of all of you to stand guard over me? Where Narayan?'

'He sitting down quiet quiet downstairs wiping he face with a dirty handkerchief.'

'Well, go and watch him. Don't let him start up anything funny.'

The men and the boy left.

Indarsingh took no notice of the interruption. 'Talking to

peasants now. Different thing altogether, old boy. Not like talking to the Lit. Soc. or the Oxford Union.'

'*Oxford* Union.'

'For years, old boy. Term in. Term out. Indarsingh. Three times nominated for Library Committee. Didn't get in. Prejudice. Disgusted.' Indarsingh's face saddened for a moment.

'What make you give up law so easy, man?'

'Talking to peasants,' Indarsingh repeated. 'An art, old boy.'

'Oh, it ain't so hard.'

Indarsingh paid no attention. 'Past few months been talking to all sorts of people. Getting practice. Bicycle clubs, football clubs, cricket clubs. No ten-minute things, old boy. Give them something different. One day, at cricket elections, talked for so long gas-lamp went out.' He looked earnestly at Ganesh. 'Know what happened?'

'You light back the lamp?'

'Wrong, old boy. Went on talking. *In the dark*.'

The boy ran up the steps. 'The meeting starting to start, sahib.'

Ganesh hadn't noticed that the garglers had left the verandah.

'Ganesh, going to fight you, old boy. Don't like tricks. Going to break you by talk, old boy.' He gave a little hop.

They started down the steps. 'Story to tell, old boy. About talking practice. Man called Ganga supported some fool for County Council elections. I supported other man. My man won. A close thing. Ganga starts row. Big row. Clamouring for recount. Talked *fifteen* minutes against recount. Ah, meeting starting. Lots of delegates here today, what?'

'What happen?'

'Oh, recount. My man lost.'

The room was crowded. There were not enough benches and many delegates had to stand up against the lattice-work. The confusion was increased by the number of wooden pillars sprouting up in odd places.

'No room, old boy. Didn't bargain for so many of us, what?

Not going to sit with you, though. Going to squeeze in somewhere in front. No tricks, remember.'

The delegates fanned themselves with *The Dharma*.

*

Perhaps, if *The Dharma* had not made him so ludicrous and the thirty-thousand-dollar grant so vulnerable, Narayan would have fought back. But he was taken so completely by surprise and knew the weakness of his own position so well, everything went smoothly for Ganesh.

But there were moments when Ganesh was worried.

When Narayan, for example, sitting as President at the table draped with the saffron, white, and green Indian tricolour, asked how Mr Partap, who, he knew, worked in Port of Spain and lived in San Fernando, could represent Cunaripo, which was miles away from either place.

Ganesh at once jumped to his feet and said that Mr Partap, it was true, was an esteemed member of the Parcel Post Service in Port of Spain and belonged to an honourable family in San Fernando; but he also, no doubt for merit in some past life, owned land in Cunaripo.

Narayan looked sick. He said drily, 'Oh, well. I suppose I represent Port of Spain although I work in Sangre Grande, only fifty miles away.'

There was general laughter. Everyone knew that Narayan lived and worked in Port of Spain.

Then Indarsingh began to make trouble. In a speech lasting almost ten minutes he wondered, in impeccable English, whether all the branches present had paid their subscriptions.

The Chief Treasurer, sitting next to Narayan, opened a blue exercise-book with a picture of King George VI on the cover. He said that many branches, particularly the new ones, hadn't paid; but he was sure they soon would.

Indarsingh shouted, 'Unconstitutional!'

There was silence.

He seemed to have expected a howl of protest, and the silence caught him unprepared. He said, 'Oh, I say, what?' and sat down.

Narayan twisted his thin lips. 'It is a little curious, however. Let me consult the constitution!'

Swami bellowed from the back, 'Narayan, you ain't going to consult no constitution!'

Narayan looked miserable and pushed the booklet aside.

'A man like you, robbing money that people scratch and scrape and save. Wanting to consult constitution!'

Ganesh stood up. 'Mr President, sir, I call on Dr Swami to withdraw those unkind remarks.'

The meeting took up the cry. 'Withdraw! Withdraw!'

'All right, I withdraw. Eh, who saying, "Shut up"? He want to taste my hand.' Swami looked menacingly around. 'Look, I want to make we position plain. We ain't here to fight anybody. We just want to see Hindus unite and we want to get the grant for *every*body, not for one man.'

Narayan looked sicker than ever.

There was laughter, not only from Ganesh's supporters.

Ganesh whispered to the boy, 'How you didn't remind me about the subscriptions, man?'

The boy said, 'It ain't for you, a big man, to talk to me so.'

Indarsingh was up again. 'Mr President, this is a democratic body, and in no other body – and I have travelled – have I heard of members who haven't paid subscriptions being allowed to vote. In fact, it is my considered opinion that, by and large – '

Narayan said, 'Is this a motion?'

Indarsingh looked hurt. 'It is, Mr President. A motion, certainly.'

Swami bellowed, 'Mr President, enough of this damn nonsense

motion and commotion, and listen to something sensible for a change. It is my motion that the constitution should be – be –'

'Suspended,' the boy prompted.

'– be suspended, or anyway that part which say that members have to pay before they vote. Suspended for this meeting, and this meeting only.'

Indarsingh lost his temper, bared an arm, quoted Gandhi, talked about the Oxford Union, and said he was ashamed of the corruption in the Hindu Association.

Narayan looked wretched.

At a signal from Ganesh, four men rushed to Indarsingh and lifted him outside. 'Undemocratic!' Indarsingh shouted, 'Unconstitutional!' He became quiet all of a sudden.

Narayan said, 'Who will second that motion?'

Every hand went up.

Narayan saw defeat. He took out a handkerchief and held it over his mouth.

Then the mood of the meeting changed.

The bearded Negro stood up and made a long speech. He said that he had been attracted to Hinduism because he liked Indians; but the corruption he had seen that day was entirely repugnant to him. It had, as a matter of fact, decided him to join the Muslims, and the Hindus had better look out when he was a Muslim.

The Chief Treasurer, the guardian of the blue exercise-book, a splendid figure in orange turban and silk *koortah*, said that Indians were bad people, and Hindus particularly bad. He had lost faith in his people and no longer thought it an honour to be Chief Treasurer of the Hindu Association. He was going to resign then and there and not offer himself for re-election.

Personal loyalties were forgotten. 'Stay, punditji,' the Hindu Association shouted, 'stay.'

The Chief Treasurer wept and stayed.

Narayan looked crumpled and more miserable than ever when

he rose to speak. He said – and his speech was fully reported in *The Hindu* – 'Dissension and dissatisfaction prevail among the rank and file of Hindus in Trinidad today. My friends, I have caused some of that dissension and dissatisfaction. I confess it.' He was weeping. 'My friends, will you forgive an old man?'

'Yes, ji,' the audience wept back. 'We forgive you.'

'My friends, we are not united. And now, with your permission, I am going to tell the story of an old man, his three sons, and a bundle of sticks.' He didn't tell it very well. 'United we stand, then, and divided we fall. My friends, let us fall united rather than stand united. My friends, Pandit Jawaharlal Nehru never wrangled with Shri Chakravarti Rajagopalacharya or with Shri Vallabhai Patel for the Presidency of the All-India National Congress. And so too, my friends, I have no desire to be the cause of dissatisfaction and dissension among the rank and file of Hindus in Trinidad today. My friends, I only want back my self-respect and I want your respect. My friends, I withdraw from public life. I do not want to be re-elected President of the Hindu Association of Trinidad, of which I am a founder member and President.'

Narayan was cheered loud and long. Some people wept. Some shouted, 'Long live Narayan!'

He wept too. 'Thank you, thank you, my friends.' And sat down to wipe his eyes and blow his nose.

'A diplomatic son of a bitch, pundit,' the boy said.

But Ganesh was wiping away a tear.

Ganesh was the only candidate for the Presidency and was elected without any fuss at all.

Swami and Partap were among the new Assistant-Presidents. The boy was a simple Secretary. Indarsingh was offered the post of Fourth Assistant to the Chief Secretary, but declined.

Ganesh's first act as President was to send a cable to the All-India Congress. Awkwardly, it wasn't the occasion of any important anniversary. He cabled:

KEEP MAHATMAJI IDEALS ALIVE STOP HINDU ASSOCIATION TRINIDAD WITH YOU INDEPENDENCE STRUGGLE STOP BEST WISHES

GANESH PRESIDENT HINDU ASSOCIATION
TRINIDAD AND TOBAGO

11. M.L.C.

VOLUME ONE Number Two of *The Dharma* never came out.

Swami and Partap could not hide their relief. But the boy told Ganesh, 'I ain't want to meddle in any more of this child-play, you hear.' And he told Swami, 'Next time you start up a paper leave me out.'

But *The Dharma* had served its purpose. Narayan kept his word and retired from public life. The election campaigns for Trinidad's first General Elections raged around him while he remained at his house in Mucurapo in Port of Spain a useless invalid. *The Hindu* dropped the *Each One Teach One* and *Per Ardua ad Astra* slogans and consoled itself once more with quotations from the Hindu scriptures. The Little Bird disappeared and its place was taken by *Sparks from a Brahmin's Log-fire*.

Ganesh didn't have time for the affairs of the Hindu Association. The island elections were two months off and he found himself embroiled. Indarsingh had decided to go up in Ganesh's ward and it was this rather than the promptings of the Association or Beharry or Swami that made Ganesh stand for the elections.

'Narayan did have a little point there, pundit,' Beharry said. 'About religious visionaries. And Suruj Mooma too, she say curing soul go do but it wouldn't put food in people mouth.'

Ganesh asked Leela's advice.

She said, 'But you have to go up. You not going to sit down and let that boy fool the people?'

'Indarsingh ain't a boy, man.'

'It are hard not to believe that. Suruj Mooma right, you know. Too much of this education is a bad bad thing. You remain here, educate yourself, and yet you is a bigger man than Indarsingh for all the Ox-ford he say he go to.'

The Great Belcher cried. 'Oh, Ganeshwa, is the word I was waiting for from your mouth. Is your *duty* to go up and help the poor people.'

So Ganesh went up for the elections.

'But,' Leela warned, 'it are not going to make me happy to see my husband getting into all sort of low argument with all sort of low people. I don't want you to drag your name in the mud.'

He didn't. He fought the cleanest election campaign in Trinidad history. He had no platform. And his posters were the simplest things: GANESH WILL DO WHAT HE CAN, A VOTE FOR GANESH IS A VOTE FOR GOD; sometimes even plainer statements, GANESH WILL WIN and GANESH IS A MAN OF GOOD AND GOD.

He held no election meetings, but Swami and Partap arranged many prayer-meetings for him. He worked hard to expand his *Road to Happiness* lectures; three or even four taxis had to take the books he required. Quite casually, in the middle of a lecture, he would say in Hindi, 'It may interest one or two of you in this gathering tonight to hear that I am a candidate for the elections next month. I can promise nothing. In everything I shall consult God and my conscience, even at the risk of displeasing you. But that is by the way. We were talking, you remember, about the transmigration of souls. Now, this theory was also put forward by a philosopher of Ancient Greece, but I have brought along some books tonight to show you that it is more than likely that the Greek got the idea from India . . .'

Beharry said one day, 'Suruj Mooma don't think the sign in front the house look nice, pundit. She say it so mildew it spoil the whole house.'

So Ganesh took down the sign which threatened that requests for monetary assistance would not be entertained, and put up a new and simpler one which said: *Spiritual solace may be had here at any time.*

At a prayer-meeting one evening Ganesh noticed the boy among the helpers taking away the books from the taxis to the platform. Swami said, 'I bring the boy to apologize for what he say, sahib. He say he want to make up by helping with the poster and them. He crying all the time, sahib. And don't mind he look little, he have a master hand for painting signs.'

The boy's lettering was elaborate. He was never content with a plain letter; he shadowed everything and sometimes it was hard to read what he had written. But he was keen and everybody liked him. Beharry, who was also working on the posters, said, 'I wish sometimes that God did give me a son like this. Suruj, he all right, but Suruj, pundit, he ain't have brains, man. He always in some Remove class. It does beat me. I is a intelligent man and Suruj Mooma ain't a fool.'

Beharry's praise spurred the boy on and he designed the most famous poster of the elections:

GANESH is
Able
Nice
Energetic
Sincere
HOLY

Against all this it was clear from the start that Indarsingh didn't have a chance. But he fought gamely. He got the support of the Party for Progress and Unity, the PPU, an organization hastily slung together two months before the elections. The PPU's aims, like its organization, were vague; and Indarsingh had to fend for himself. His speeches were long, carefully thought-out things –

later published by the author in book form with the title *Colonialism: Four Essays* – about The Economics of Colonialism, Colonialism in Perspective, The Anatomy of Oppression, The Approach to Freedom. Indarsingh travelled about with his own blackboard and a box of coloured chalks, illustrating his arguments with diagrams. Children liked him. They surrounded him at the beginning and end of a meeting and begged for 'a little tiny little piece of chalk you did thinking of throwing away'. The older people called him the 'Walking Dictionary'.

Once or twice Indarsingh attempted an attack on Ganesh but he soon learned better. Ganesh never mentioned Indarsingh at all.

Leela liked Indarsingh less and less as polling day came nearer. 'All this fancy talk in all this fancy accent he are giving the people here, it are beat me why they don't fling something big at his head.'

'It ain't nice to talk so, Leela,' Ganesh said. 'He is a good boy. He fighting a clean clean election and it ain't so clean in the rest of Trinidad, I can tell you.'

Leela turned to Beharry. 'You bear what he are saying? It are just this sort of goodness and big mind that is dangerous in Trinidad. He ain't have enough, it look like, from people like Narayan.'

Beharry said, 'Well, it have a lot in what the pundit say. Indarsingh is a good boy, but he still a boy. He does talk too big. Mark you, that all right for we here. I could understand and Ganesh pundit could understand, but is different for the ordinary people.'

*

One night Ganesh came back late to Fuente Grove from a prayer-meeting at Bamboo Walk, a village at the boundary of his ward. Upstairs in the drawing-room Leela, Beharry, and the boy were, as usual, working on the posters. They were at the dining-table.

But Ganesh saw somebody else kneeling next to the refrigerator, filling in the outlines of a GANESH IS A MAN OF GOOD AND GOD poster spread on the floor. He was a big fat man; but it wasn't Swami.

'Hello, sahib,' the man said casually, and went on filling in the letters.

It was Ramlogan.

'Hello, Ramlogan. It have a long time I ain't see you.'

Ramlogan didn't look up. 'Busy, sahib. Very busy with the shop.'

Ganesh said, 'Leela, I hope you have a lot of food for me tonight. Anything that leave over, I could eat all of it. I hungry like a horse. Eh, but Leela, you ain't give your father anything?'

She moved with alacrity to the refrigerator.

Ramlogan kept on filling in letters.

'What you think of it?'

'Is very nice wordings, sahib.' Still Ramlogan didn't look up.

'Leela think them up.'

'She is like that, sahib.'

Leela handed round the Coca-Cola.

Ramlogan, who was resting forward on his hands, knelt upright and laughed. 'It have years now I selling this Coca-Cola but you know, sahib, I never touch it before. Is so it does happen. You ever notice that carpenters always living in some sort of breakdown old shack?'

Leela said, 'Man, your food waiting for you in the kitchen.'

Ganesh went through the drawing-room to the large room next to the back verandah.

Leela had tears in her eyes. 'Man, is the second time in my life you make me feel proud of you.' She leaned on him.

He didn't push her away.

'The first time was with the boy and the cloud. Now is with Pa.'

She wiped her eyes and seated Ganesh at the kitchen table.

*

In the week before polling day Ganesh decided to suspend mystic activity and hold a *Bhagwat*, a seven-day prayer-meeting.

He said, 'Ever since I small I promising myself to hold my own *Bhagwat*, but I could never find the time.'

The boy said, 'But now is the time to move around, pundit, talking to the people and them.'

'I know,' Ganesh said sadly. 'But something telling me that if I don't have a *Bhagwat* now, I would never have one again.'

Leela didn't approve. 'Is easy for you, just sitting down and reciting prayers and thing to the people. But they don't come to *Bhagwat* just for prayers, I can tell you. They come for the free food.'

However, The Great Belcher and Suruj Mooma and Ramlogan rallied round and helped Leela with the great week-long task of cooking. The *Bhagwat* was held in the ground floor of the house; people were fed in the bamboo restaurant at the side; and there was a special kitchen at the back. Logs burned in huge holes in the ground and in great black iron pots over the holes simmered rice, *dal*, potatoes, pumpkins, spinach of many sorts, *karhee*, and many other Hindu vegetarian things. People came to the *Bhagwat* from many miles around and even Swami, who had organized so many *Bhagwats*, said, 'Is the biggest and best thing I ever organize.'

Leela complained more than ever of being tired; The Great Belcher had unusual trouble with the wind; Suruj Mooma moaned all the time about her hands.

But Ramlogan told Ganesh, 'Is like that with women and them, sahib. They complaining, but it have nothing they like better than a big fête like this. Was the same with Leela mother. Always going

off to sing at somebody wedding, coming back hoarse hoarse next morning and complaining. But the next time a wedding come round and you turn to look for Leela mother – she ain't there.'

As a supreme gesture Ganesh invited Indarsingh to the last night of the *Bhagwat*, on the eve of polling day.

Leela told Suruj Mooma and The Great Belcher, 'Is just what I are expecting from that husband of mine. Sometimes these man and them does behave as if they lose their senses.'

Suruj Mooma stirred the cauldron of *dal* with a ladle a yard long. 'Ah, my dear. But *what* we go do without them?'

Indarsingh came in an Oxford blazer and Swami, as organizer of the *Bhagwat*, introduced him to the audience. 'I got to talk English to introduce this man to you, because I don't think he could talk any Hindi. But I think all of all you go agree with me that he does talk English like a pukka Englishman. That is because he have a foreign education and he only *just* come back to try and help out the poor Trinidad people. Ladies and gentlemen – Mr Indarsingh, Bachelor of Arts of Oxford University, London, England.'

Indarsingh gave a little hop, fingered his tie, and, stupidly, talked about politics.

*

Indarsingh lost his deposit and had a big argument with the secretary of the PPU who had also lost his. Indarsingh said that the PPU had promised to compensate members who lost their deposits. He found he was talking to nobody; for after the election results the Party for Progress and Unity just disappeared.

It was Beharry's idea that the people of Fuente Grove should refer to Ganesh as the Hon'ble Ganesh Ramsumair, M.L.C.

'Who you want?' he asked visitors. 'The Onble Ganesh Ramsumair, Member of the Legislative Council?'

*

Here it might be well to pause awhile and consider the circumstances of Ganesh's rise, from teacher to masseur, from masseur to mystic, from mystic to M.L.C. In his autobiography, *The Years of Guilt*, which he began writing at this time, Ganesh attributes his success (he asks to be pardoned for using the word) to God. The autobiography shows that he believed strongly in predestination; and the circumstances which conspired to elevate him seem indeed to be providential. If he had been born ten years earlier it is unlikely, if you take into account the Trinidad Indian's attitude to education at that time, that his father would have sent him to the Queen's Royal College. He might have become a pundit, and a mediocre pundit. If he had been born ten years later his father would have sent him to America or Canada or England to get a profession – the Indian attitude to education had changed so completely – and Ganesh might have become an unsuccessful lawyer or a dangerous doctor. If, when the Americans descended on Trinidad in 1941, Ganesh had taken Leela's advice and got a job with the Americans or become a taxi-driver, like so many masseurs, the mystic path would have been closed to him for ever and he would have been ruined. Today these masseurs, despite their glorious American interlude, are finding it hard to make a living. Nobody wants the quack dentist or the unqualified masseur in Trinidad now; and Ganesh's former colleagues of the world of massage have had to keep on driving taxis, but at three cents a mile now, so great is the competition.

'It is clear,' Ganesh wrote, 'that my Maker meant me to be a mystic.'

He was served even by his enemies. Without Narayan's attacks Ganesh would never have taken up politics and he might have remained a mystic. With unfortunate results. Ganesh found himself a mystic when Trinidad was crying out for one. That time is now past. But some people haven't realized it and today in odd corners of Trinidad there is still a backwash of penurious mystics.

Providence indeed seemed to have guided Ganesh. Just as it told him when to take up mysticism, so it told him when to give it up.

*

His first experience as an M.L.C. was a mortifying one. The members of the new Legislative Council and their wives were invited to dinner at Government House and although a newly-founded scurrilous weekly saw the invitation as an imperialist trick all the members turned up. But not all the wives.

Leela was shy but she made out that she couldn't bear the thought of eating off other people's plates. 'It are like going to a restaurant. You don't know what the food are and you don't know who cook it.'

Ganesh was secretly relieved. 'I have to go. But none of this nonsense about knife and fork for me, you hear. Going to eat with my fingers, as always, and I don't care what the Governor or anybody else say.'

But the morning before the dinner he consulted Swami.

'The first idea to knock out of your head, sahib, is that you going to like what you eat. This eating with a knife and fork and spoon is like a drill, man.' And he outlined the technique.

Ganesh said, 'Nah, nah. Fish knife, soup spoon, fruit spoon, tea spoon – who sit down and make up all that?'

Swami laughed. 'Do what I use to do, sahib. Just watch everybody else. And eat a lot of good rice and *dal* before you go.'

The dinner was a treat for the photographers. Ganesh came in dhoti and *koortah* and turban; the member for one of the Port of Spain wards wore a khaki suit and a sun helmet; a third came in jodhpurs; a fourth, adhering for the moment to his pre-election principles, came in short trousers and an open shirt; the blackest M.L.C. wore a three-piece blue suit, yellow woollen gloves, and a monocle. Everybody else, among the men, looked like penguins, sometimes even down to the black faces.

An elderly Christian Indian member didn't bring a wife because he said he never had one; instead he brought along a daughter, a bright little thing of about four.

The Governor's lady moved with assurance and determination among the members and their wives. The more disconcerting the man or woman, the more she was interested, the more she was charming.

'Why, Mrs Primrose,' she said brightly to the wife of the blackest M.L.C. 'You look so *different* today.'

Mrs Primrose, all of her squeezed into floriferous print frock, adjusted her hat with the floral design. 'Ah, ma'am. It ain't the *same* me. The other one, the one you did see at the Mothers' Union in Granadina, she at home. Making baby.'

Sherry, opportunely, passed.

Mrs Primrose gave a little giggle and asked the waiter, 'Is a strong drink?'

The waiter nodded and looked down his nose.

'Well, thanks. But I doesn't uses it.'

'Something else, perhaps?' the Governor's lady urged.

'A little coffee tea, *if* you has it.'

'Coffee. I am afraid coffee wouldn't be ready for some time yet.'

'Well, thanks. I doesn't really want it. I was only being social.' Mrs Primrose giggled again.

Presently they sat down to dinner. The Governor's lady sat on the left of Mr Primrose. Ganesh found himself between the man in jodhpurs and the Christian Indian and his daughter; and he saw with alarm that the people from whom he had hoped to learn the eating drill were too far away.

The members looked at the waiters who looked away quickly. Then the members looked at each other.

The man in jodhpurs muttered, 'Is why black people can't get

on. You see how these waiters behaving? And they black like hell too, you know.'

Nobody took up the remark.

Soup came.

'Meat?' Ganesh asked.

The waiter nodded.

'Take it away,' Ganesh said with quick disgust.

The man in jodhpurs said, 'You was wrong there. You shoulda toy with the soup.'

'Toy with it?'

'Is what the book say.'

No one near Ganesh seemed willing to taste the soup.

The man in jodhpurs looked about him. 'Is a nice room here.'

'Nice pictures,' said the man with the open shirt who sat opposite.

The man in jodhpurs sighed wearily. 'Is a funny thing, but I ain't so hungry today.'

'Is the heat,' the man with the open shirt said.

The Christian Indian placed his daughter on his left knee, and, ignoring the others, dipped a spoon in his soup. He tested it with his tongue for warmth and said, 'Aah.' The girl opened her mouth to receive the soup. 'One for you,' the Christian said. He took a spoonful himself. 'And one for me.'

The other members saw. They became reckless and ate.

Unoriginal disaster befell Mr Primrose. His monocle fell into his soup.

The Governor's lady quickly looked away.

But Mr Primrose drew her attention to the monocle. 'Eh, eh,' he chuckled, 'but see how it fall down!'

The M.L.C.s looked on with sympathy.

Mr Primrose turned on them. 'What all you staring at? All you ain't see nigger before?'

The man in jodhpurs whispered to Ganesh, 'But we wasn't saying anything.'

'Eh!' Mr Primrose snapped. 'Black people don't wear monocle?'

He fished out the monocle, wiped it, and put it in his coat pocket.

The man with the open shirt tried to change the subject. 'I wonder how much car expenses they go pay we for coming here. I ain't ask to dine with the Governor, you know.' He jerked his head in the Governor's direction and quickly jerked it back.

The man with jodhpurs said, 'But they got to pay we, man.'

The meal was torture to Ganesh. He felt alien and uncomfortable. He grew sulkier and sulkier and refused all the courses. He felt as if he were a boy again, going to the Queen's Royal College for the first time.

*

He was in a temper when he returned late that night to Fuente Grove. 'Just wanted to make a fool of me,' he muttered, 'fool of me.'

'Leela!' he shouted. 'Come, girl, and give me something to eat.'

She came out, smiling sardonically. 'But, man, I thought you was *dining* with the Governor.'

'Don't make joke, girl. Done dine. Want to eat now. Going to show them,' he mumbled, as his fingers ploughed through the rice and *dal* and curry, 'going to show them.'

12. M.L.C. to M.B.E.

SOON GANESH decided to move to Port of Spain. He found it fatiguing to travel nearly every day between Port of Spain and Fuente Grove. The Government paid expenses that made it worth while but he knew that even if he lived in Port of Spain he could still claim travelling expenses, like the other country members.

Swami and the boy came to say good-bye. Ganesh had grown to like the boy: he saw so much of himself in him.

'But don't worry, sahib,' Swami said. 'The Hindu Association fixing up a little something for him. A little cultural scholarship to travel about, learning.'

Beharry, Suruj Mooma, and their second son Dipraj helped with the packing. Later, Ramlogan and The Great Belcher came.

Suruj Mooma and Leela embraced and cried; and Leela gave Suruj Mooma the ferns from the top verandah.

'I go always always keep them, my dear.'

The Great Belcher said, 'The two of you girls behaving as though somebody getting married.'

Beharry put his hand under his vest and nibbled. 'Is go Ganesh have to go. He do his duty here and God call him somewhere else.'

'I wish the whole thing did never happen,' Ganesh said with sudden bitterness. 'I wish I did never become a mystic!'

Beharry put his hand on Ganesh's shoulder. 'Is only talk you talking, Ganesh. Is hard, I know, to leave a place after eleven

years, but look at Fuente Grove now. New road. My new shop. Stand-pipe. We getting electricity next year. All through you.'

They took bags and cases into the yard.

Ganesh went to the mango tree. 'Is something we did forget.' He wrenched out the GANESH, *Mystic* sign.

'Don't throw it away,' Beharry said. 'We go keep it in the shop.'

Ganesh and Leela got into the taxi.

Ramlogan said. 'I always did say, sahib, you was the radical in the family.'

'Ah, Leela, my dear, look after yourself,' Suruj Mooma sobbed. 'You looking *so* tired.'

The taxi started and the waving began.

The Great Belcher belched.

'Dipraj, carry this signboard home and come back and help your mother with the ferns.'

Leela waved and looked back. The verandah was naked; the doors and windows open; on the balustrade the two stone elephants stared in opposite directions.

*

It would be hard to say just when Ganesh stopped being a mystic. Even before he moved to Port of Spain he had become more and more absorbed in politics. He still dispelled one or two spirits; but he had already given up his practice when he sold the house in Fuente Grove to a jeweller from Bombay and bought a new one in the fashionable Port of Spain district of St Clair. By that time he had stopped wearing dhoti and turban altogether.

Leela didn't take to Port of Spain. She travelled about a good deal with The Great Belcher. She visited Soomintra often and regularly went to Ramlogan's.

But Ganesh found that for an M.L.C. Port of Spain was a pleasant place. He got used to it and even liked it. There were two good

libraries, and so many bookshops! He dropped Indology, religion, and psychology and bought large books on political theory. He had long discussions with Indarsingh.

At first Indarsingh was bitter. 'Funny people in Trinidad, old boy. No respect for ideas, only personalities.'

But he softened as time went on and he and Ganesh worked on a new political theory.

'Came to me in a flash, old boy. Reading Louis Fischer's book about Gandhi. Socialinduism. Socialism-cum-Hinduism. Hot stuff, old boy. Outlines settled. Details demn tricky, though.'

*

So far the autobiography, and the private man.

But by this time Ganesh was a public figure of great importance. He was always in the papers. His speeeches inside and outside the Legislative Council were reported in detail; he was constantly photographed leading delegations of aggrieved taxi-drivers or scavengers or fish-vendors to the Red House; and he was always ready with a press conference or a letter to the editor. Everything he did or said was News.

*

He was a terror in the Legislative Council.

It was he who introduced the walk-out to Trinidad and made it popular as a method of protest. The walk-out was no sudden inspiration. It had crude beginnings. At first he simply lay flat on his back on the Council table and refused to move. Policemen had to lift him up. Acts like this caught the public imagination and in no time at all Ganesh became popular throughout the South Caribbean. His photograph appeared constantly in the newspapers. Then he discovered the walk-out. In the beginning he just walked out; later, he walked out and gave interviews to reporters on the steps of the Red House; finally, he walked out, gave interviews, and

addressed the crowd of beggars and idlers from the bandstand in Woodford Square. Often the Governor passed a weary hand over his forehead and said, 'Mr Ramsumair, what have we done to offend you this time? Please don't stage another walk-out.' And the invariable concomitant of a headline announcing the passing of a bill was GANESH STAGES A WALK-OUT. Later this was shortened and a typical newspaper headline was:

LAND RESETTLEMENT BILL PASSED
Ganesh Walks Out

They made a calypso about him which was the second road-march at the Carnival in 1947:

There is a gentleman of the opposition
Suffering a sort of legislative constipation.
Everybody moving – bills for so,
But with this gentleman nothing can go.

The reference to *Profitable Evacuation* was clear. But even before the calypso, Ganesh had begun to find his mystic career an embarrassment. Certain paragraphs of *What God Told Me* had often been read out in the Council Chamber; and in November 1946, just four months after he had published it, he suppressed *The Years of Guilt*, as well as his other books, and wound up Ganesh Publishing Company Limited.

There was no doubt that at this time Ganesh was the most popular man in Trinidad. He never went to a cocktail party at Government House. He never went to dinner there. He was always ready to present a petition to the Governor. He exposed scandal after scandal. And he was always ready to do a favour for any member of the public, rich or poor. For such favours his fees were never high. He always said, 'You must give only what you can afford.' People like Primrose and the Christian had high fixed rates, went to every cocktail party at Government House, and wore

dinner-jackets. You couldn't say that either of them really represented his constituency. The Christian, as a matter of fact, now owned most of his; and Primrose became so wealthy he had to be knighted.

In Colonial Office reports Ganesh was dismissed as an irresponsible agitator with no following.

*

He had no idea that he was on the road to the M.B.E.

This is how it happened.

In September, 1949, a wild strike ripped through some sugar estates in South Trinidad. It was the most exciting thing since the oilfield riots of 1937. Strikers burnt cane-fields and policemen beat up strikers and spat in the mouths of those they arrested. The press thundered with threats and counter-threats. Sympathy for the strikers was high and people who had never thought of striking themselves cycled past the pickets and whispered, 'Keep it up, boys!'

Ganesh was in Tobago at the time, investigating the scandal of the Help the Children Fund. He made a vague speech about it but the Niggergram at once spread a story that he was going to mediate. The sugar estates said they knew nothing about it. Ganesh told a *Sentinel* reporter that he was going to do all he could to bring about an amicable settlement. The estates denied that they had ever consented to having a mediator at all. Ganesh wrote to the *Sentinel* that whether the estates liked it or not he was going to mediate.

In the few days that followed, Ganesh was at the peak of his popularity.

He knew nothing about the strike except for what he had read in the newspapers; and it was the first time since he had been elected that he had to deal with a crisis in South Trinidad. Hitherto he had been mainly involved in exposing ministerial scandals in

Port of Spain. His whole approach to the strike was so thoughtless that we can perhaps – as he himself said later – see the hand of Providence once more in his career.

In the first place he went South in a lounge suit. He took books, but they were not religious books, only the writings of Tom Paine and John Stuart Mill and a large volume on Greek Political Theory.

The moment he got to Lorimer's Park, a few miles out of San Fernando, where the strikers waited for him, he sensed that something was wrong. So he said later. Perhaps it was the rain the night before. The banners were still damp and their denunciations looked half-hearted. The grass had disappeared beneath the mud churned up by the strikers' bare feet.

The strike-leader, a short fat man in a striped brown suit, led Ganesh to the platform. This was nothing more than two Morris car crates; smaller boxes served as steps. The top of the platform was wet and muddy. Ganesh was introduced to the half dozen or so members of the strike committee and the man in the brown suit immediately set to work.

He shouted, 'Brothers and sisters, you know why the Red Flag red?'

The police reporters scribbled conscientiously in longhand in their noteboooks.

'Let them write it down,' the leader said. 'Let them write down in their dirty little black books that we ain't fraid them. Tell me, we fraid them?'

A short stout man came out from the crowd and walked to the platform. 'Shut your tail up,' he said.

The leader insisted, 'Tell me, we fraid them?'

There was no response.

The man below the platform said, 'Cut out the talk and say something quick.' He was rolling up his shirt-sleeves almost up to his armpits. He had powerful arms.

The leader shouted, 'Let we pray.'

The heckler laughed. 'Pray for what?' he shouted. 'For you to get fatter and burst your suit?'

Ganesh began to feel uneasy.

The leader unclasped his hands after his prayer. 'The Red Flag dye with we blood, and is high time for we to hold up we head high high in the market-place like free and independent men and command big big armies in heaven.'

More men came out from the crowd. The whole crowd seemed to have moved nearer the platform.

The heckler shouted, 'Cut out the talk. Go back to the estates and beg them to take back the bribe they give you.'

The leader talked on, unheard.

The strike committee fidgeted in their folding chairs.

The leader slapped his forehead and said, 'But what happening? I forgetting that all you here to hear the great fighter for freedom, Ganesh Ramsumair.'

At last there was some applause.

'All of you know that Ganesh write some major book about God and thing.'

The heckler took off his hat and waved it up and down. 'Oh God!' he screamed. 'But it making stink!'

Ganesh could see his gums.

'Brothers and sisters, I now ask the man of good and God to address a few words to you.'

And Ganesh missed his cue. Stupidly, completely missed his cue. He forgot that he was talking to a crowd of impatient strikers as a man of good and God. He talked instead as though they were the easy-going crowd in Woodford Square and he the fighting M.L.C. and nothing more.

'My friends,' he said (he had got that from Narayan), 'my friends, I know about your great sufferings, but I have yet to give

the matter further study, and until then I must ask you to be patient.'

He didn't know that their leader had been telling them the same thing every day for nearly five weeks.

And his speech didn't get better. He talked about the political situation in Trinidad, and the economic situation; about constitutions and tariffs; the fight against colonialism; and he described Socialinduism in detail.

Just when he was going to show how the strike could be the first step in establishing Socialinduism in Trinidad, the storm broke.

The heckler took off his hat and stamped it into the mud. 'No!' he shouted. 'No! Noooh!'

Others took up the cry.

The leader waved his hands about for silence.

'My friends, I – '

The heckler stamped on his hat again and shouted, 'Noooooh!'

The leader stamped on the platform and turned to his committee. 'Why the hell black people so ungrateful?'

The heckler left his hat alone for a while and ran to the platform and tried to seize the leader by the ankles. Failing, he shouted, 'Nooooh!' and ran back to stamp on his hat.

Ganesh tried again. 'My friends, I have – '

'Ganesh, how much bribe they bribe you? Noooh! Noooh!'

The leader said to his committee, 'If I live for a million years I ain't going to lift up my little finger to do a thing for black people again. Talk about ungrateful!'

The heckler was still stamping on his hat. 'We don't want to hear nothing! Nothing! Nooooh!' He was so enraged he was in tears.

The crowd stepped nearer the platform.

The heckler turned to them. 'What we want, man? We want talk?'

The whole crowd answered. 'No! No! We want work! Work!'

The heckler was right below the platform.

The leader panicked and shouted, 'Keep your dirty black hand off the white people box! Look, move away quick sharp now – '

'My friends. I cannot – '

'Keep your tail quiet, Ganesh!'

'If you ain't move away quick, I calling the police and them over there. Look, haul all your tail away, you hear.'

The heckler tore at his hair and beat his fists on his chest. 'All you hearing that fat-arse man? You hearing what he want to do?'

And somebody shrieked, 'Come, man, let we done with this damn nonsense.'

The crowd flowed thickly forward and surrounded the platform.

*

Ganesh escaped. The policemen took care of him. But the strike committee were badly beaten up. The leader in the brown suit and one member of the committee had to spend some weeks in hospital.

Later Ganesh learned the whole story. The leader had of course been bribed; and what he had started as a strike was nothing more than a lock-out during the slack season.

Ganesh called a Press conference at the end of the week. He said Providence had opened his eyes to the errors of his ways. He warned that the labour movement in Trinidad was dominated by communists and he had often unwittingly been made their tool. 'From now on,' he said, 'I pledge my life to the fight against communism in Trinidad and the rest of the free world.'

He expanded his views in a last book, *Out of the Red* (Government Printer, Trinidad. Free on application). It was left to Indarsingh to note the 'capitalist mentality inherent in the title'; and he wrote an article for a weekly paper blaming the violence at Lorimer's Park on Ganesh, since he had cruelly raised the workers' hopes without having anything to offer them.

Ganesh never walked out again. He went to cocktail parties at

Government House and drank lemonade. He wore a dinner-jacket to official dinners.

In the Colonial Office report on Trinidad for 1949 Ganesh was described as an important political leader.

In 1950 he was sent by the British Government to Lake Success and his defence of British colonial rule is memorable. The Government of Trinidad, realizing that after that Ganesh stood little chance of being elected at the 1950 General Elections, nominated him to the Legislative Council and arranged for him to be a member of the Executive Council.

Indarsingh was elected in Ganesh's old ward, on a platform of modified Socialinduism.

In 1953 Trinidad learned that Ganesh Ramsumair had been made an M.B.E.

EPILOGUE

A Statesman on the 12.57

IN THE SUMMER of 1954 I was at an English university, waiting for the results of an examination. One morning I got a letter from the Colonial Office. A party of Colonial Statesmen were in Britain for a conference, and would I be willing to entertain a statesman from my own territorry? It was the vacation and I had much time on my hands. I agreed. It was arranged that I should be host for a day to G. R. Muir, Esq., M.B.E.

The day of the visit came and I was at the railway station to meet the 12.57 from London. As the passengers got off I looked among them for someone with a nigrescent face. It was easy to spot him, impeccably dressed, coming out of a first-class carriage. I gave a shout of joy.

'Pundit Ganesh!' I cried, running towards him. 'Pundit Ganesh Ramsumair!'

'G. Ramsay Muir,' he said coldly.

'Above all else, I am a writer. I make books and want to please the reader, to stimulate, to create very rich books that will develop in the reader's mind and echo as he reads along'

V. S. NAIPAUL

*

Picador is proud to be reissuing over the next few years seventeen of V. S. Naipaul's works beginning with his first comic masterpiece. *The Mystic Masseur.*

*

'Britain's greatest living writer. A prose stylist and thinker of unrivalled ambition and achievement'

Daily Telegraph